The Girl in the Picture

by
Charles E. Merkel II

PublishAmerica
Baltimore

First printing

All characters appearing in this work are fictitious. Any resemblance to real persons, living or dead, is purely coincidental.

ISBN: 1-4241-3047-6
PUBLISHED BY PUBLISHAMERICA, LLLP
www.publishamerica.com
Baltimore

Printed in the United States of America

Dedicated to

Lee Casper Merkel
My mother,
A former teacher and the most encouraging mom anyone ever had.

Acknowledgments

My special thanks to Laurie Rosin, my editor; Lori Yoder, my special literary assistant; Lisa Mathews, my technical advisor; Terry Rogers, a writer who challenged and supported me greatly; as well as Heidi Masano, Kelly Gallagher, Paul Rizzo, Peter Stacy, Cheryl Wolgamood, Fran McCollester, Jeff Myers and Verlo Miller.

Chapter 1

I felt pretty good that afternoon. I had just read a letter from Jeanine and was thinking that maybe she finally loved me. As I leaned against the low railing inside our orderly room, I fondled and studied the scented envelope, realizing for the first time the simple beauty of my name in her handwriting: *Specialist 4 Andy McClain.* I almost forgot where I was till I took a breath and the humid air reminded me.

I glanced around the makeshift frame, one-story structure. Screens instead of Sheetrock lined the interior, and the building's metal roof intensified the heat, which seemed to shimmer on the concrete floor. The only ventilation was two door less entry ways on adjacent walls.

The unmistakable rumbling of a two-and-a-half-ton truck sounded from outside. I looked through the entrance facing the service road, which ran parallel to and was no more than one hundred feet from the legendary Highway One. The vehicle, full of 'cruits, pulled in with a roar, and out piled replacement soldiers brand new in-country.

I slid to the doorway to see how many we were getting, and that was when I first saw him: Brian Kitzmiller, a kid who looked as if he should've been showing up for a high school geometry class, not reporting to an army unit in Vietnam. Standing near the back of the truck, he seemed forlorn and was inordinately thin, neither tall nor short, with blue eyes, brown hair, and a smattering of pimples. He wasn't blessed with movie-star features, but I suppose most women would call his gaunt puppy face cute. Like all new guys, he looked scared as hell.

I strained to hear the truck driver. "All right, two hundred and ninth Engineer Company, Long Binh. Kitzmiller, Cunningham, McKinney! Wait! Only Kitzmiller. Who the piss typed this manifest?"

A soldier tossed Brian his duffel bag from the truck bed—it couldn't have weighed more than thirty pounds—and nearly toppled him. He straightened, grinned sheepishly, and edged past me to the railing.

I settled in the doorway, eager to watch the hazing. Not everyone suffered through it—only the guys who looked more like boys than men. Two weeks before, it had been my ass they'd grilled, and I don't mind admitting that I'd never felt more alone or humiliated.

Our first sergeant, Clell Olmstead, also known as Top, conducted the ritual. The company's clerks and whoever else happened to be visiting the orderly room at the time (a total of ten in poor Brian's case) would witness the ordeal. A towering, significantly paunched man from Georgia, Top seemed to read my expression and put on his trademark "new 'cruit frown."

The company clerk, Frankie Huffer, an especially cocky ex-bulldozer operator, eyed the new guy cynically. "You Kitzmiller?"

"Yeah," Brian replied, panting as he dropped the duffel with a thud.

"'Yeah?'" said First Sergeant Olmstead. "Son, can you see okay?"

Brian's head swivelled to the right, where Top dominated his large, battered desk. "Oh, yes, First Sergeant. Yes, Specialist, I meant to say."

"Now, a specialist ain't no big shit," Olmstead said. "Especially Huffer here, but, damn, I hate to see a boy come in, first day and all, and start throwin' his weight around."

I was biting my lip, but like the others, I maintained a poker face.

"Sign in here and fill all the blocks out," Huffer demanded, pointing to the sign-in/sign-out book.

"Sure, Specialist. You need a copy of my orders?"

"Won't hurt. We got one, but maybe you got an amended—well, get signed in. I'm sure Top's got some questions for ya, but I ain't sure he's got your job figured out yet, do ya, Top?" Huffer's mouth twitched as he tried to hide his mirth.

"Oh, shit." Top leaned back, propped his legs on his desk, and crossed them at the ankles. He scrutinized Brian's orders. "This kid's got a clerk's MOS."

Brian corrected him. "Personnel Specialist."

"Personnel Specialist," echoed Top as he abruptly swung his feet to the floor and straightened in his chair. "*Personnel Specialist?* Son, this is fucking South Vietnam—a war zone. We don't need no personnel specialists. If anything we need *anti*personnel specialists. What are you gonna do for us? Formal personnelin'? Like, okay, whores with nice behinds over here. Ones with substantial tits over there. Ugly ones outside. Fellers lookin' to get laid, get your wallets out. What the heck do we need somebody like that for, kid?"

"Well," Brian said with a tone of complete respect, "at least, First Sergeant, you know what you're talking about."

At this, everyone in the room burst into laughter. Even Top couldn't hold back. "How old are you, son?" Top asked.

"Eighteen, almost ni—eighteen." Brian could see that Top was reading his 201 file.

"You finish high school?"

"Yes, First Sergeant."

"Where at?"

"Indianapolis—in Indiana."

"Hmm. Knew a homo from there once. What school?"

"Saint Sebastian."

"Saint Sebastian?" Top tossed Brian's file on his desk. "Some kind of Catholic school or somethin'? Shirts and ties? No girls?"

"Yes, First Sergeant."

"Son, why the hell would somebody go to a school like that for? Don't you like girls?" Now it was Top who had everyone snickering.

"Yes, First Sergeant, I like 'em a lot."

"You have a bunch of asshole buddies there or somethin'?"

"No, First Sergeant. Well, at least *I* didn't." Brian's attempt at humor didn't take.

"Hmm," Top murmured. "I got enough Catholics now to make my Georgia-Baptist ass feel unwelcome. Martinez, Flaherty, Wisnewski, Fuentes, Richio, shit, ain't one of them worth a fuck. But in the name of bein' a good administrator, I'd like you to tell me a little 'bout your religion, maybe enough to get some output from the Catholic riffraff I already got." I watched Top put on a serious face.

"Ah, what do you want to know, First Sergeant?" Brian asked, grimacing slightly.

"You can call me Top." He stood, circled his desk, and folded his arms. "First off, what the hell is a saint exactly?"

Brian took a deep breath. "Well, First Sergeant, uh, Top, it's when you die and go to heaven. Then you're a saint, not before."

Top smiled cynically. "I seen some Catholic book one time that had all the saints listed. And I got to tell you, that was a pretty short damn list."

"There's plenty more, Top. Those are only the ones they're sure went to heaven. You know, kinda like knowin' Ted Williams was going in the Hall of Fame the day he retired, even though it would take five years before he became eligible, where others, like maybe Zack Wheat, they really didn't know till later."

9

"Well, fuck a duck." Top raised his eyebrows approvingly. "If that don't make it clearer. Maybe you fish-eaters ain't so evil." Quickly frowning, he added, "But how do them popes really know who made it? Ted Williams had a bitchin' battin' average and a shitload of homers. Isn't decidin' who's in heaven and who ain't a little out of a man's jurisdiction? Like who was that French broad they burned for bein' a witch or a whore back a coupla hundred years ago?"

Brian looked perplexed. Then his eyes brightened. "Joan of Arc?"

"Yeah. Now bear with me." Top glanced around at us, then grinned. "Y'all say fuckin's a sin that could send your ass to hell, right? I mean, if you ain't married."

"Yeah, a sin, but it could be forgiven."

"Wait a minute, boy, don't get ahead of me." He wagged a finger at Brian. "How do y'all know that ol' Joanie didn't get it on at least once with some slick-talkin' frog or wop back then?"

"Now that's a good question." Chief Warrant Officer Milo Donaldson, an extraordinarily lazy thirty-year man, cut in.

Top nodded at the praise.

Brian wrinkled his brow. "Well, I guess they don't know for sure, even though the pope is supposed to be infallible. I don't know if I agree with that. But they sort of assume she didn't commit too many sins, and any she did, she got 'em confessed or at least was sorry for them when she died."

Top squinted and put his hands on his hips. "The pope's supposed to be infallible? Shit. Just because a sumbitch knows to take his four-foot hat off and put a beanie on when it's windy, that don't mean he's infallible! Damn bright for a wop, maybe, but not infallible."

Laughter rippled around the room.

Suddenly, Top reeled almost as if he'd been shot. "Whoa. By Jesus, Kitzmiller, you ever go confessin' sins yourself?"

"Well, sure," Brian said, looking as though he realized that this was not about to get any easier. "When I was younger, we had to go all the time."

"Oh, my," Top said, his eyes bulging. "I hear them priests get all them purty little darlin's tellin' about all that steamy stuff, and I mean down to the last detail, that was done to them by their boyfriends. Lordy, by the time they're through, they got a chubby so bad they could use it for a forklift."

A wild burst of laughter erupted.

Top put his hands up in an apparent gesture of order. "Hold on, fellas. We don't want to get disrespectful about a man's religion."

At this Brian looked relieved. "Thank you, First Sergeant. You think we could change—"

"You ever tell a priest about your lustin', son? Like lookin' at a fine morsel of a woman and wantin' to get to rootin' so bad you can taste it?"

Brian frowned as if concentrating. He brought his hand to his chin, then said, "Well, not exactly in those words." He was still getting as many laughs as Top, who raised an eyebrow.

"Son, is it a sin to go to the grand fireworks by yourself?"

"What?" Brian asked.

"Is it a sin to jack off?" Everyone roared. "Answer the question, son," Top demanded.

Brian looked embarrassed. "In our church, well, yeah, it would be, but—"

Top cut in, squinting. "What? In church? Hell, I'm not talkin' 'bout in church! I can't believe you'd do it there. Damn, boy. Even Fuentes's mother'd be shocked."

Frankie Huffer pounded his desk as the rest of us hooted.

Above the noise, Brian yelled, "No! That's not what I meant when I said 'in our church,' Top. I meant in the rules of our faith it would be a sin, technically."

"Oh, hell," Top said, feigning surprise. "I see what you were tryin' to say. I jumped a bit. You keep correctin' me if I'm wrong."

"Yeah, okay." Brian shifted his weight from foot to foot.

Top looked knowingly at his audience. He had a child's grin on his face. "So, Kitzmiller, how many times you figure you told them priests you jacked off?"

Brian glanced around the room. He looked at Top and smiled weakly.

"You might as well come clean with me, son. I know you've done it. There isn't a boy alive who don't do it. And of course a young feller like you, you must've done it hundreds of times, bein' a virgin and all. Ain't that right?"

Brian blushed deeply. "No. I mean, I'm no virgin."

"Well, dammit! You lyin' little fart." He tapped the tan folder on his desk. "I got your 201 file open right in front of me, and it don't say nothin' about no fuckin' in here. Come on, now, it isn't nothing to be ashamed of. Hell, kid, everybody's never done it till some point. And I don't see how you could've. You're too young, too shy, and didn't even go to school with no girls." Top nodded firmly. "I been doin' this a long-assed time, and I can spot a kid with a green wiener from a mile and a half off."

"Well, you're wrong this time," Brian said lightly. "And you could pretty much ask any girl in Indianapolis if you don't believe me."

This brought catcalls. Chief Donaldson spit on the floor as if truly offended.

Top spoke sympathetically. "Kitzmiller, I'm not tryin' to be an asshole or nothin', but I ain't sure you've ever had a date. Or ever even been kissed."

"Ah, come on, Top," Brian pleaded, his head down.

"Come on, my ass!" Top said. "I bet you ain't even had a real date, never even made out with one girl, let alone every girl in Indianapolis."

All eyes were on Brian. He looked straight at Top. "Well, I was jackin' around about that, obviously. What the deal is, though, I pretty much only dated—seriously—one girl. I went to some dances with some others, but…there was only the one. Girl."

Top glanced at his black wristwatch. "Get to the point, son. I've got a company to run."

"Well, this is her," Brian stammered, fumbling as he unbuttoned his left rear pocket. Then he nervously presented his wallet to Top.

"Jesus Keerist!" Top said as his jaw dropped. "You ain't shittin' me now?"

"Nope. That's Elaine, Top." He smiled shyly. "And when I get back home, we'll probably get married."

"My, oh, my, what shiny blond hair. Fellas, look at them dimples and baby skin."

Each of us was affected the same way when we saw the photograph, which appeared to be a graduation picture. The girl's looks were so wholesome and cheerful that she'd have made a great cover girl, but there seemed to be something more in that face. Her eyes were bright, seemingly full of happiness, and true or not, I felt that she possessed a certain brilliance of personality.

The wallet had come back to Top, who again ogled the photo. "Son," he finally said, "I'm your first sergeant. You may need me more than anyone you've ever known in these upcomin' long months, so don't ruin no rapport with me by tellin' no lie." He looked at Brian squarely and without the slightest trace of humor. "You ever nail this girl?"

Stillness pervaded as everyone watched Brian.

"Ah, come on, I…I don't wanna talk about that."

Top cocked his head. "Come on now, son. You got to."

"I really don't think it's right to talk about her that way. I mean, I'm gonna marry her."

"Oh, get off that shit. You'll damn sure drill her then, and everybody'll know it. Hell, your grandmother'll be tellin' her sister, 'Mabel, I just bet sweet little Kitzmiller got his socks fucked off last night judgin' by that beautiful ceremony.' Now I'm gonna ask you again, man to man. You ever put the joystick to this girl?"

"First Sergeant—" Brian swallowed and started again. "Top, I don't wanna answer that." He sounded almost desperate. "She means too much to me to talk about her that way. I love her. God, I don't even know you guys."

"Come on, tell me, and I'll leave it alone."

"Nah, I'm not sayin' nothin'. I can't."

"You ever get her skirt up?"

"Ah, come on."

"Ever get her little panties pulled down?"

Brian could see no way out. Nobly, he displayed as much aversion as I thought he could. "Hey, look, I'm not a virgin, okay? Elaine's my fiancée, and, yes, we have done it! Now I'm not going to say anything else!"

Silence settled. Everyone waited for Top to continue because seemingly no one, including him, even remotely remembered his promise to "leave it alone." Top eyed Brian like a frustrated father, then let out a troubled sigh.

"You mean to stand there and tell me that—shit, look at this." Top waved the 201 file. "R. A. one-six-nine-four-seven-three-three-one. R. A. You're regular army! You join the fuckin' army in September, when you're seventeen damn years old? And you're layin' pipe with somethin' like this? It don't add up at all! Son, fill my ass in 'cause I'm as lost as I have ever been!"

Brian flushed beet red. "Well, we knew, Elaine and me," he began slowly, with eyes as big as saucers, "that eventually I'd have to go in, with the draft and all."

"Oh, hell, son, but in wartime? Where's this girl now?"

"She's in college."

"Well, why the hell ain't you in college? You go to one of those preppie-type schools, and you got a girl like this? And instead of going on to school with her, where you can put it to her for four years, you join the army? In wartime? Oh, man, I'da dug my fingers into that girl's ass and held on for dear life."

"Well, the situation was this," Brian said, trying to show some semblance of composure. "She went to St. Mary's of the Woods College in Terre Haute, Indiana. It's an all-girls school. Anyway, Indiana State is there too, which is where I would've wanted to go because of her.

"I guess I didn't get along very well with my parents, especially my ol' man. To make a long story short, I couldn't go away to school. I'da had to stay and go to Indiana U extension in Indianapolis, and still live at home." He shook his head. "I didn't want to do it. No way.

"I thought about workin' a year and savin' money, but Elaine and me knew too many people like that. You think you're eventually goin' to school, but once you start workin', you never do. Then with the draft, I figured I'd be in sooner or later. I told my ol' man if he tried to stop me, I'd join up anyway the day I turned eighteen so he might as well sign my papers. I figured I'd get it over with, stay outta Nam, and pick my job, too, by signin' up for that extra year. Plus I'll have the GI Bill when I get out."

"'Cept you're over here anyways. And you damn sure ain't gonna get the job you thought."

Brian's expression saddened. "Well, I don't wanna say the recruiting sergeant lied to me, but he said it would be damn unlikely for me to be sent here, and it would be even more unlikely for me not to work in my MOS. Then a little over a month ago, my entire class in AIT came down on orders for Nam."

Top smiled weakly. "Ain't that the shits."

"Well, it doesn't matter now. I got a year to put in here, then another year and seven months when I get back to the States. I'll just do it. Then I'll probably go to school. Elaine will be a senior when I'll be a freshman. No big deal."

"'Cept," Top said, putting his finger up without a second's pause, "when somebody starts slippin' it to her while you're away. Happens exactly ninety-nine percent of the time, and, hell, that includes ugly girls. That young beaver gets hot and cravin' real bad. Hell, I ain't even sure it's their fault." Top shook his head magnanimously.

Brian looked at Top wistfully. "I really don't think it will. I mean, you don't know Elaine."

"Son, I hope you're right. Jesus Cheese, I do," Top said solemnly, as he again stared at Brian's records. "Shit, kid, some days it's truly one bad event after another. I haven't a clue why they sent you here. We need exactly one company clerk and one clerk-typist out of two hundred twenty-five men, and I ain't even sure about the clerk-typist. I got a company clerk." Top pointed at Huffer. "And I got two supply guys I can borrow anytime if I need extra typin' done. 'Course they couldn't spell *shit* if you spotted them the *s* and the *h*. But, son, dammit, I got to assign you to a job, one that you may not necessarily like." He looked around with a hopeless expression, as if to garner support in his contrived plight. "Well, one favorable state of affairs, you look pretty rugged and tough to me. That a right assumption?"

Again we all erupted.

"Well, I'm in pretty good shape, I guess. I ran some cross-country in high school. I'm not saying I'm the strongest guy in the world."

"Kid, what I need here is de-drummers, and hell, that's all I need right now. I'm sorry to tell you that. You ever de-drummed?"

Brian clearly had no idea what de-drumming was, and he sensed that Top might be pulling his leg. Gauging his audience perfectly, Brian looked around with a naughty little grin then said, "You mean with Elaine?"

We all doubled over in stitches.

"Now, jeemanie!" Top snorted, trying hard to check himself. "This is serious. I got to assign you to a job." Then Top guffawed, bent over laughing. "I ought to kick your ass, son. You're gonna have to learn that this place is not a damn joke."

"I'm sorry, First Sergeant...Top."

"Okay, if I put you in the asphalt platoon as a de-drummer, which is what I got to do, you start work at o-seven-hundred with the rest of the company, except for the cooks, who start at o-five-hundred. What de-drummin' amounts to, since Elaine ain't here, is you and two other men take axes and bust open the lids on fifty-five-gallon drums of tar, which weigh right around four hundred pounds, I'd guess. Then you and one of your crewmates dump it into a bin to be fired with cut-up gravel. You'll do that fifty to a hundred times a day to make asphalt."

The audience beamed with pleasure during this description. "That's one of our functions here, Kitzmiller," Top continued. "This company's unique; there ain't five others quite like it in Nam. In the 209th Engineer Company Construction Support, we not only make asphalt, we do everything to build roads. We got a quarry platoon sixty miles from here that blasts rock out of the earth and crushes it into gravel. Then we got an equipment platoon, which bulldozes jungle and grades out roads. Huffer can tell you about some of that. Then comes your asphalt platoon's better half, the men who don't actually work at the plant. Some of them guys truck fresh-ass asphalt to the site. Then you got the fuckers on spreaders and rollers. Kitzmiller, we do roads from the ground up."

Brian nodded and looked around nervously. Top waved the 201 file. "We got other platoons, too. The maintenance platoon maintains and repairs ever'thin'—trucks, heavy equipment, dozers, two-nineties, even jeeps. Ever'thin'! If they can't fix it, the fucker ain't busted."

Top's face took on a grave expression, causing some of the guys to snicker. "And then there's headquarters platoon, which is where I woulda liked to have you. It's made up of cooks, clerks, and pansy officers' drivers. Since neither platoon is big—like asphalt or maintenance—equipment and headquarters guys share the same barracks.

"Now, Kitzmiller, you should know we're buildin' enough road to make Charlie shit his pants. Even Ho Chi Minh knows about us. We're a prime target. Once North Vietnam gets them Russian bombers and them surface-to-surface missiles, we're really gonna see the shit—not that we ain't seen our share already."

Brian's eyes grew wide.

"Oh, Top." Donaldson's voice almost sang.

Two men had entered through the wrong doorway, the official entrance reserved for officers, sergeants, and those who worked there. The men were covered from head to toe with white dust, almost as if they had been plunged into a flour bin. I noticed Brian staring at them with his mouth open.

"Hey, boys, other door, *behind* the railing, *always,*" Top called. The two stopped, and looking woeful, turned and started to walk out. "All right, all right, dammit. Because you're workin' men and because you're new, I'll allow it this once. What can we do for you?"

They eyed each other, looking confused, and then the shorter man spoke. "Ah, First Sergeant, this is our afternoon off, and we was gonna sign out and head into town."

Top looked at him incredulously. "You're goin' to town fuckin' lookin' like that?"

"Well, First Sergeant, neither one of us got issued our jungle fatigues yet. An', well, we put all our other regular fatigues, the ones we got in basic, in the laundry on Monday, and they ain't due back from the gooks until tonight. Sergeant Bliss tol' us last week this would be our day—I mean our afternoon—off, permanent, so if we're gonna go, we gotta go this way."

"Well, hell's bells, you coulda dusted them damn fatigues off and then taken a shower. You look like a couple of ghosts. You're still soldiers, even if you do work in the asphalt platoon, and I ain't gonna let none of my men out of this company area lookin' like shit. You got that? Now you go back to work and tell Sergeant Bliss that your afternoon off may be Wednesdays from now on, but this week it's Thursday. Got it? You take a shower tomorrah and put on a clean uniform. The damn MPs would probably pick your asses up anyway for lookin' like a couple of retarded Yankee assholes."

Murmuring mild protests, the two privates retreated.

"And stay the hell away from those whorehouses, boys!" Top yelled. "They got VD over here worse on a man's dick than the Black Plague." Top winked at Donaldson. "Well, Private Kitzmiller, why don't you grab that damn bag and catch up to those boys? Have them show you the asphalt platoon where you can drop your shit. Then you can have them take you to meet Sergeant Bliss down at the plant and get yourself some de-drummin' observin' in so you'll know what you're doin' tomorrah. Okay, boy?"

Brian appeared in shock. Then he picked up his duffel bag and scurried after the men. As soon as he was out of earshot, everyone cracked up, but it wasn't the usual laughter.

"All right, McClain," Top said. "When he's been gone about twenty minutes, take your jeep down to the asphalt plant, pick him up, and bring him back. He's our boy, I think, if Captain Karch don't squash him. Damn, though, I don't see that happenin'. Look at this, Chief," he said to Donaldson, indicating Kitzmiller's file. "This kid's GT score is a hundred thirty-four. That's gotta be near the top of the whole company." Top continued to read as he lit a cigar. "Besides, I just got a feelin' he's perfect for a damn mail clerk. I mean, think about it, what else could he do?"

When I drove onto the bleached and tarred earth of the asphalt plant, my eyes began to burn and I had trouble breathing the dusty air. I spotted Brian and Sergeant Navin Bliss talking. Bliss didn't look happy. With the arrogance I'd already acquired—which was almost expected of an officer's driver, particularly the one who oversaw the asphalt platoon's operation—I drove right up to the sergeant and stopped. Bliss was a twenty-two-year-old overachiever with a tenth grade education. Determined not to say anything first, I put the jeep in neutral and started acting like I was looking for something on the seat next to me.

"What's up, McClain?" Bliss asked.

I turned my head. "Well, Sarge, it looks like there's been a mistake. I don't think you're going to get this guy for a de-drummer."

"Big fuckin' deal," Bliss retorted.

"Top says he's sorry." I still wanted to laugh, but I knew I should continue and possibly generate something of substance that Top might be able to use on Bliss later. "He says he knows you need a couple of guys, especially strong ones, but that Kitzmiller came on requisition, and Top doesn't want to piss off the guys at brigade."

"I don't give a fuck," Bliss said caustically. "My fuckin' sister could do the job better than this kid."

"Well, I'm not here to judge that, and neither is Top. Kitzmiller here is gonna take Dopplemeyer's place, and Top wants him to spend Dopplemeyer's last three weeks with him, learning the job."

Suddenly Bliss's face took on an air of astonishment, even intimidation. "Mail clerk?"

"That's right. Kitzmiller's got a personnel MOS and a high IQ and was hand-picked by brigade for us, I guess," I lied.

"Hey, that's great," said Bliss, turning to Brian. "Listen, that job sounds perfect for you. Sorry if I was pissed off just now. Prather and Karch been on my ass lately, and I really thought you might have a rough go of it until you got in shape. No offense."

I had to smile. Even though they'd hang a clerk who messed with someone's mail, the feeling prevailed that the mail clerk—even more than the cooks, company clerk, or first sergeant—was somebody you never wanted to cross.

"That's okay, Sergeant Bliss," Brian said humbly, obviously relieved. "You were probably right about me and the liftin' part."

As we drove back the quarter-mile to the core of the company area, I decided I wanted to get on the kid's good side, too. "I'm Andy McClain. I'm Lieutenant Prather's driver. I been here goin' on eight weeks now."

"Glad to meet you, Andy," Brian answered, sounding confused. "This place is a little strange, huh?"

"Yeah, you could say that. But honestly, it's not terrible, considerin' what we might have got. Of course, I've only been here around three weeks."

"I really don't know what to expect," Brian said slowly. "I guess I just wanna get to doin' a job and then get out of here. I don't know about you, but I sure didn't volunteer to come here."

"Shit, I bet there aren't ten of us in the whole company who did. Even the officers. Even Top."

"I got screwed, kinda, and I did it to myself," Brian said dolefully. "But I know I gotta make the best of it. What were you saying about…mail clerk?"

"Well, basically you've got to pick up, sort, and hand out mail every day, and act like you're from the USO or something. At least that's how Dopplemeyer does it. Plus you gotta do some typing and filing, run some errands. Shit, I'd say you pretty much got it made."

"Really?" Brian said happily. "But why didn't Top just tell me?"

I chuckled. "That's part of the game. He likes to see how bad he can jack the new guys around. He claims he's made 'cruit s cry before, though I've never seen that."

"The company's mailman." Brian smiled. "Man, I never ever thought I'd get to be something like that."

"Yeah, only don't tell Top I filled you in any. He's gonna want to do that himself, and you'll still have to get through an interview with Captain Karch, who's sort of from left field. If you get the job, nobody'll mess with you. And God knows you'll have a bird's-eye view of everything that happens around here, and I can tell you some of it's pretty bizarre." I paused for a moment, then added, "You'll sure be able to keep Elaine interested." Immediately I felt a funny kind of yearning, as if saying "Elaine" somehow lifted me into the realm of men who at least had a vague association with the beautiful girl in the picture.

Chapter 2

Brian reported to the orderly room on his second day to meet with the eccentric Captain Roger S. Karch. I was again waiting there for Lieutenant Prather and happened to be in a conversation with Dopplemeyer, the short-timer mail clerk. For some reason, we had really hit it off.

Top deposited his bulk in his creaking chair and began pulling papers from his In-box. Frankie Huffer was at his desk and struggled with the morning report.

None of us ever knew what to expect from Captain Karch. Top was the only one who seemed to have a fairly good handle on him, probably because a company commander needs to rely on his first sergeant more than anyone else. Except for Top and maybe Lieutenant Prather, Karch intimidated and controlled everyone. Even Colonel Gallagher, Karch's boss, referred to him as Captain Berserk.

As Karch entered our headquarters that morning, I casually slipped out of sight behind a board sporting some acetate-covered maps.

"Mornin', sir," Top said.

"Well, a good morning to you, First Sergeant. I've got business in Bien Hoa all day. What have you got for me before I go? Huffer, got the morning report ready for me to sign?"

"No, sir." Huffer answered. "Sorry, sir. Didn't know you'd need it this early. I'll have it in about fifteen minutes, though. Not much happened yesterday."

"Top, I thought I mentioned that I'd be going at around o-seven-hundred. Did you forget?"

Top scratched his head. "Sorry. It must've slipped my mind."

One of Karch's favorite ploys, practiced daily on his subordinates, was to make them feel as if they'd screwed up so they would owe Karch something when he forgave them.

Well, I got fifteen, twenty minutes maybe," he said magnanimously. "What's been going on around here, Top? I've hardly had time to talk to you for the last week."

"Well, sir, we're losin' men faster than we're gettin' them in. Bad enough we're now averagin' twenty a month back to the States, but I lost four men last month to accidents, one to a transfer, and, of course, poor Ramey." A sniper had killed Craig Ramey just after he arrived at a site with a truckload of asphalt.

I think I got a replacement for Dopplemeyer, though." Top nodded toward Brian, who sat nervously in a folding chair next to Huffer's desk.

Karch glanced at Brian, then motioned for Top to come into his office. "Let's discuss this, Top."

Dopplemeyer signaled to me, and I followed him into the tiny mail room, directly behind Karch's office. Several imperfections in the wall boards allowed one to see and hear nearly everything. Dopplemeyer and I found this wildly entertaining when Karch gave someone an ass-chewing or discussed something really important.

Once we hooked the door we were safe, though we suspected Karch knew about us all along and put on a show for any such flies that might be on the wall. Dopplemeyer and I were convinced that Karch was a sophisticated lunatic who loved power. I genuinely enjoyed the captain's offbeat reasoning, his self-importance, and the lectures he gave when disciplining a soldier. We were sure Karch believed himself to be equal to Patton, Lee, or MacArthur and that his own presence in Nam was a strategic move by those in high command, perhaps even orchestrated by army intelligence.

"Top," he said now, "am I to understand that you're talking about that boy out there?" He sounded put out.

"Sir, I know he's young."

"Does he have any college at all?"

"No, sir, but in this whole damn company, only Dopplemeyer and four others have any, and they're all under one-hundred-twenty days. Hell, sir, I've known a shitload of mail clerks in my time, and I could count on one hand the ones that had any college."

"That isn't the point," Karch said. "I've asked you to keep an eye out for someone who did, mainly to prove the son-of-a-bitch could read and at least had some hint of responsibility."

"Sir, this is a damn army construction company. Hell, two-thirds of these boys ain't even graduated high school. With the kind of jobs we got, our chances of them comin' in educated ain't likely. Now don't forget, we got this college guy Shifrin s'posed to come in, and I plan to make him company clerk. Huffer's gone in a month, you know."

"I know. Everyone keeps reminding me of that as if we're losing something. The morning report—far and away the most important responsibility a company clerk has—is never done till noon because fucking Huffer's got to run to battalion three times to check how to do the entries and bullshit with everybody. And then his numbers never balance. 'Specialist Huffer, you brickhead,' I say, 'if you've got two-hundred-twenty-six men and one goes in the hospital and one goes on leave, you've still got two-hundred-twenty-six men total, not two-hundred-twenty-eight or two-hundred-twenty-four.' I won't have another idiot as company clerk." I could see Karch's broad fingers pick up a pencil and tap the eraser impatiently on his desk. "Or as a mail clerk, either. Now, tell me about this kid."

"Well, look here, sir. The little peckerhead's got a GT score that's second in the whole company. And there's somethin' about this kid, sir. He's got a mail clerk's personality."

I watched the back of Karch's head bob. "Is that it?"

"Talk to him, sir. You'll like him. Remember, he's got three weeks to train with Dopplemeyer. He'll be ready by then," Top said calmly. "And, sir, you want to see one special gal, get him to show you the picture of his fiancée." Top grinned broadly. "If he snagged her, he can handle anything, including mail clerkin'."

A moment later Brian stood before Captain Karch and saluted. "Private Kitzmiller reports, sir."

I strained to look through a knothole while Dopplemeyer watched through a particularly large opening next to a warped board. Karch appeared to be looking down, perhaps studying Brian's file. He waved his hand in a short, jerky motion. "Yes, yes, have a seat, Kitzmiller."

"Thank you, sir."

After a few moments, Karch's head shot up. "Well, Kitzmiller, welcome to Vietnam. Nice to have you here. Being the intelligent young man that you are, you surely know by now that I'm the commander of one of the most crucial road-building entities in the war effort. Usually I let Top decide all assignments, and he does a fine job. But the position we're going to talk about this morning represents a major responsibility. I'm dealing with the single most important morale factor in the unit when I assign this position, and I damn sure better be right. Do you see where I'm coming from?"

"Oh, yes, sir."

"So Kitzmiller, let's cut to the chase. What makes you feel that you're qualified to be my mail clerk?"

"Sir, ah, first of all, I was trained as a personnel specialist. That's a tough school even to get into—"

"Cut the shit, Kitzmiller. Anybody can sign up for anything if they're R. A. Some of the dumbest fools I've seen in the military were clerks, personnel, and payroll people. Like Huffer out there."

At this, Dopplemeyer gave me a playful jab, and we grinned at each other. Karch suddenly turned around, and like lightning we moved our heads away from our peepholes. When Karch continued his sermon, we resumed spying.

"I've supposedly got a godsend coming, thanks to Top, a draftee who graduated from Columbia University, and he's going to take over as company clerk." Karch's voice hardened. "Huffer's here only because he got his ass shot off his bulldozer. Twice. After that he started whining about wanting to finish his tour of duty, begging to continue in a clerical position. Then he gets a visit from some fag reporter from the *Stars and Stripes*, and I'll be damned if there wasn't a story in that damn paper the next week about a hero who turned in his bulldozer and rifle for a typewriter. Before I can strangle the bastard, Colonel Gallagher calls me and congratulates me on my decision. Mother fuck!" Karch slammed his fist onto his desk. "I'm stuck with a company clerk who takes five tries to type a two-paragraph letter, and the damn thing never ends up with the same words it had when I drafted it."

Brian twisted around to look back into the orderly room as though he were checking to see if Huffer could hear any of this.

"Am I boring you, son?" Karch asked sarcastically.

Brian quickly faced the captain. "No, sir, you certainly are not."

"I will never suffer through anything like that again, I promise you. Now while the position of mail clerk wouldn't seem to affect me personally as much as company clerk, I see it as one damn serious job."

A pause ensued, and from the way Brian was fidgeting, I was pretty sure Karch was reaming him with one of his patented stares.

"Do you know what I hear day in and day out from the troops?" Karch asked.

"What, sir?"

"Every time I stop to talk to the guys, someone goes, 'Sir, are you sure somebody's not fuckin' with our mail?' And I know that's not happening. The process to and from the States is cumbersome and takes four or five days. I got a real twinkletoes in there now; you know, a glee clubber, a band member—sissy sort. But every time I ask why the good Lord would put a man like that in my unit, I smile and say, 'mail clerk.' That guy was born to be a fucking mail clerk."

23

I glanced at Dopplemeyer, who was reddening.

Have you ever had a job, Kitzmiller?"

"Yes, sir. I washed cars for a summer at a Texaco station, then I worked at a Burger Chef, and after I graduated, I worked for a janitorial service."

"Can you read, Kitzmiller?"

"Yes, sir, of course."

Karch opened a drawer and pulled out a paperback book that had a white-trimmed pink cover with absolutely nothing printed on it. "I recently took this off a man at the asphalt plant who was reading when he should have been watching the gauges on his boiler. Let me see here, top of page seventy-two. Read through the last paragraph on page seventy-three and tell me when you're done."

Brian took the book. In no time his eyes popped wide open as if he weren't sure that what he was reading could actually have been printed. "Sir, are you sure this is the right book?"

"Read it, Kitzmiller," Karch said impatiently.

In another minute Brian informed Karch he had finished.

"All right. Now let's see about your retention." Karch leaned forward. "What was the young lady's name in the story?"

"Edwina, sir."

"Can you describe her?"

"Well, I didn't get much in the way of a character description, but she has slim legs and eyes filled with despair."

"Go on."

"It said she was a true redhead and had, ah, a splendid behind."

"Okay, not bad. What was her boyfriend's name?"

"Prince, sir, but I don't think he was her boyfriend."

"What was Edwina wearing?"

"A green-and-white-checked dress, sir, a pair of green high heels, and"— Brian hesitated and looked embarrassed—" a pair of handcuffs."

"Anything strike you as unusual about the dress?"

"Not the dress itself, sir, as much as the way she was wearing it."

"Which was?"

Brian blushed. "Well, the skirt was pinned up to the back of it."

"You don't say, Kitzmiller? Now we finally seem to be going someplace. Why would she be wearing her dress that way? And did I hear handcuffs? And did you mention something about the gentleman not being her boyfriend? What makes you say that? Give me some facts."

Brian took a deep breath and exhaled loudly. "Sir, it has to do with a sexual situation. I think the guy is punishing her. That's the gist of it."

The back of Karch's neck was reddening. "Never mind the gist, Kitzmiller. I'm trying to determine if you retain what you fucking read. I think that's fairly important in a mail clerk, don't you?"

"Yes, sir."

"Then I'll conduct the test *and* the interview, and I'll decide whether you absorbed the content. Now, do you wish to continue?"

I don't think Brian knew if Karch was completely serious or not, but he was taking nothing for granted. "I'll continue, sir. I just wanted you to understand, in case you hadn't read it, that it's kind of dirty."

"I'm over twenty-one, Kitzmiller. Now why was she wearing her dress that way?"

Brian blushed again. "Sir, she's bent over the bedpost, and her hands are cuffed to the frame of the bed."

"And?"

"Well, Prince has a birch switch that he's using on her."

"What color panties does she have on?"

"Lime green, and they say Friday on them." He cleared his throat. "But they're not on, exactly."

"No?"

"They're pulled down to about her knees."

"You mentioned discipline of some sort?"

"Well, maybe torture, I think now."

"Why, Kitzmiller? Couldn't Prince be her father? Couldn't she have earned this situation by being late or having a messy room or shooting her mouth off?"

"Well, it doesn't say, but I'd bet Prince is not her father." Brian sniggered as if he expected Karch to find his comment funny.

"What did Prince do after he whipped her?"

Brian squirmed. "Sir, he had sex with her."

Dopplemeyer whispered "I'll bet Karch read that part a hundred times."

Pretty normal stuff, Private Kitzmiller. Men have sex with women all the time, must happen a billion times a day." Karch grabbed the book and opened it. "Are you sure there's not something you might want to add?"

"Sir," Brian began with determination. "She was tied up and crying and begging, and he did it anyway. I believe it said he gave her every inch of it, and she screamed as though she was still being flogged."

"Prince must've been pretty well endowed, huh?"

"Yes, sir. It mentioned that."

"You're not leaving anything out, are you?"

Brian looked down, then began slowly. "Prince, he…"

"Spit it out, Kitzmiller!"

"He did it up her butt."

At this Karch burst out laughing, harder and for a longer time than seemed even remotely appropriate. Finally he quieted. "Very well, Kitzmiller, I suppose you passed. Thanks for clearing that up for me. Now, tell me a little more about yourself. I hear you have a pretty interesting picture I should have a look at."

Brian hesitated, then he anxiously dug into his back pocket and handed over the photo.

"Someone you went out with a couple times?" Karch asked.

"No, sir, lot of times. We're sort of engaged."

Karch leaned back in his chair. I could not see his face, but I sensed he was skeptical. "How old is this girl?"

"Nineteen, sir. We were both born in the same year—forty-eight—but she was born in January, and I was born in December. We met at a dance after a football game, but we didn't actually start going out until that summer."

"I wouldn't get my hopes up too high, Kitzmiller. You're going to be gone a long time." Karch took a deep breath. "All right, you read well enough, and your scores are sufficient. But you're a youngster, and I'm not totally comfortable. I'll put you on the job on a probationary basis. If Dopplemeyer says you're good enough at the end of his tour, the job's yours. Otherwise, who knows where you'll end up."

Chapter 3

"The issue here," Lieutenant Prather said, completely changing the subject, "is to find some way to motivate the problem guys without pissing Bliss off. Bliss is a can-do son of a bitch, but he has his limitations." He grew pensive.

I was driving my boss back from the site of a road we were building across the southern section of Long Bien. We were headed to the asphalt plant where some trouble was brewing among the de-drummers. I fully expected Prather to be nervous, yet he remained remarkably calm.

Prather was a producer. During the three months he'd been in-country, the plant turned out nearly twice as much asphalt as it had at any time since our unit's arrival in mid-1965. Though he was usually quiet—except with me—most everyone in our platoon perceived him as a winner and seemed proud to be on his team.

He was a good officer, too—the best—and I was damn glad to be around him. He was probably the coolest guy I had ever met. He had little use for the army and wasn't afraid who knew it.

"Well, Andrew," he said suddenly, over the wind and traffic noise, "you've been here, what? Nearly three weeks? Is your sense of time starting to speed up for you?"

"Yessir," I yelled across to him. "I seem to have gotten used to doing time already, and I seem to be progressing with Jeanine, which is great for me. Plus, even after only three weeks, I feel like I've made some friends here. That helps. I couldn't imagine doing this year without friends."

"I know what you mean," he said. "But that's not only over here. I don't think a guy can survive anywhere without friends. I'm glad that's coming along relatively easily for you."

He gestured toward my feet. "By the way, I noticed a couple of *Playboy* magazines under your seat a couple of days ago. We come into contact with so much damn brass, I'm not sure you should have those in the jeep." He chuckled. "Certainly nothing in your MOS or job description calls for them."

I laughed. "Yes, sir," I said. "I wouldn't want them to end up in some colonel's latrine."

Prather folded his arms and said nothing, but he wore a huge smile.

At twenty-three, Prather wasn't real young for a first lieutenant. He was a graduate of the University of Missouri with a degree in civil engineering. Although he stood only five feet ten inches and weighed no more than 160 pounds, he had played varsity baseball, and his gait was athletic. His posture was West Point perfect, though he had become an officer the hard way, through OCS after he'd been drafted. Karch, OCS himself, thought a lot of Prather.

"So, tell me, Andrew, what team do you follow?" Prather always seemed to want to talk baseball when we were alone.

"I used to like the Braves. Our Louisville Colonels were their farm team. Then they moved to Atlanta. I guess I like the Cubs and White Sox and Cardinals about the same now." I shrugged.

"Do yourself a favor. Forget the Cubs and Sox," he ordered. "They're nothing but perpetual heartaches. The St. Louis Cardinals are the only team for a sharp guy like you."

"Yes, sir. I kind of miss Musial, though." The jeep bounced us around enough to break up my shouted words.

"Musial was a god." He smiled. "But the team is better now than it ever was."

"Sir, the night before your last driver rotated back home, he told me that you had eight girlfriends." I glanced at him and caught another quick smile. "How much truth is there to that?"

He put on a stern face. "Specialist McClain, how can you dare ask me such a personal question?"

"Because I want to know, dammit."

"Well," he said, stretching out his legs, "I'm a little backward when it comes to the ladies. I—"

"Yeah, right." I cut him off.

"Let's put it this way. I was engaged, and then I wasn't. I still might marry Katie, but in the interim, who knows? I'm somehow writing to eight different girls—seven from college, one from high school—and the problem is that I'm pretty damn excited about each one."

"Shit, sir, you're the god, not Stan Musial!"

As I pulled onto the plant's bleached apron, my eyes burned like they had two days before, and once more Sergeant Bliss was all riled up. He walked briskly to meet our jeep.

"Well, sir, it's happenin' again," he said angrily.

I looked at Prather, who, to my amazement, was picking his teeth with a pocketknife.

"What is, Sergeant?"

"Those big, dumb fuckers Adcock, Cassidy, and Lauck are giving me fits. If they were goin' any slower, they'd be goin' backwards."

Prather did not respond.

Bliss continued nervously. "They were the best damn rookie crew I ever saw. Came in all together and busted ass for ten weeks. Then somethin' happened." He shook his head mournfully. "The last few days they ain't worth a shit. They gotta realize we all got it rough. Guess we'll have to bust one of 'em. Then maybe the other two'll get the message. Besides, if we don't, Karch'll bust all three of them and be on our asses for not being tough enough."

"The hell with Karch," Prather said, and used another blade of his knife to attend to his nails.

Sergeant Bliss seemed surprised and put out. "So what am I supposed to do?"

Prather shrugged carelessly. "I'll talk to them."

"Shit, sir," Bliss said. "I suppose that's not my job anymore—to reward and discipline the men?"

"Let me talk to them first," Prather said. "If that doesn't work, they're all yours. I don't like to lead off with my cleanup hitter. And I especially don't like the idea of demoting these guys and cutting their pay when they're working harder than any other bastards in the whole support effort. Karch is smart enough to see that. He isn't going to bust our guys. We're the only ones who are ever going to do that, and I hope we'll never have to."

Bliss nodded, apparently appeased. Prather made small talk for another few minutes. Then, in his own good time, he took his clipboard and strolled over to the three malcontents, trailed by Sergeant Bliss. I followed ever so slowly with the jeep.

For what seemed like the longest time, Prather didn't say anything. He seemed interested solely in the production numbers on his clipboard. Finally he looked up, and his tone took on a congenial twist.

"Lauck," Prather said to the surliest of the three. "I understand you're from Southern Illinois."

I sensed Lauck was expecting an ass-chewing and Prather caught him off guard. "Ah, yessir, we got a place not far from Carbondale."

29

"That make you a Cub or a Cardinal fan?"

"Well, sir, me—my whole family—we're Cardinal fans. Big ones."

Prather smiled, then said firmly, "Lauck, I'm damn glad to hear that. I'm from Hannibal, and I was looking through the whole company roster to see if I could turn up any Cardinal fans. I'm convinced we're going to repeat 1964, only this time we're not going to put off taking the pennant race seriously until September."

The look in Lauck's eyes lost all hostility. "Yes, sir, I agree with that. And Adcock here's from Arkansas. He's a redbird fan, too."

The baseball conversation continued with Adcock involved. Cassidy jumped in, and they chatted for a good ten minutes. Then, abruptly, Prather was looking at his clipboard again. "Well, guys, I got to get rollin'."

"Good to talk to you, sir," Lauck said.

Prather nodded. He began to climb into the jeep, then paused and turned back to them.

"You know, guys, something else had me wondering. Don't hold me to this because we're always getting bogus input for these reports, but it seems that you men are down a few barrels from where you were when you were newer. Could that be possible?"

The three exchanged glances. "Well, sir," Lauck began, sounding as if he were talking to an old friend. "It's a bad job with the heat and all. Cassidy's back was botherin' him some a few days ago, but he's better. We kinda been pacin' ourselves."

"I see." He paused, then asked with concern, "Is there something Sergeant Bliss or I could do for you guys to get you back where you were, or is it actually too impossible a job?"

"Sir, we only get two breaks in the mornin' and two in the afternoon," Adcock said earnestly. "Now, we realize there's a fair amount of time when we're standin' around, not bustin' ass, but still, if we got, say, ten minutes each hour to cool down and have a smoke…well, we thought—I thought—we could do somewhat better."

Prather appeared to ponder this for a time, then suddenly announced, "Okay, from now on, every hour on the hour, you guys got ten minutes off."

Cassidy, Lauck, and Adcock all gazed at Prather, apparently too shocked to talk. After they had gone back to their labor, Sergeant Bliss was beside himself.

"Sir, what about the TO and E and the SOPs?" he blurted. "We can't do that!"

"Does it really throw the timing off much?" Prather asked innocently.

"Not exactly, Lieutenant, but that's not my point."

"Then fuck the SOPs and TO and E," Prather said with force. "Do you honestly believe that the asshole who wrote the Standard Operational Procedures ever de-drummed? Was he ever in Nam?" He put his hand on Bliss's shoulder, and his tone changed. "Let's give these guys the benefit of the doubt. Anybody can bust them. First let's see if this helps the situation."

We drove off, and I felt happy. As we headed for a work site some eight miles away, I realized how much confidence just being around a maverick like Prather was giving me. He cared about me and understood me, and I needed that. He seemed to shrug off rules to fit what a situation required and to hell with the consequences.

I wasn't much like that, but I wanted to be. I craved being around people I truly respected who made their own way. In my whole life the only real risk I'd taken was in basic training, but God, I was still happy about that! In many ways, that event broke me out of my shell, and my time with Prather was continuing to develop me.

What happened back in boot camp occurred out of despair over Jeanine, who was in college and seemingly slipping away from me forever.

After five weeks of pining and feeling sorry for myself, on top of the torture and degradation of the early weeks of basic training at Fort Leonard Wood, Missouri, I decided to gamble on the wildest plan of my life.

My platoon had a good chance at a weekend pass at the close of week five. All we needed to do was avoid finishing dead last among the company's five platoons in the Saturday morning inspection. In our first four weeks, we had ranked second four times, but guarantees do not exist in basic.

Nonetheless, I figured I had to do something about Jeanine. I had, after all, fired off twelve letters to her and gotten only three replies. So I became a soldier on a most terrifying mission and decided to do what only a few had done before me: I would leave the company area. One of my predecessors had been caught and punished severely. No matter. I would find a phone and call my beloved Jeanine and arrange the greatest weekend of all time.

At twenty-two-hundred hours, sixty minutes after "lights out," I took off. Officially I was AWOL, but because of being in the midst of those eight weeks of terrorism, my distorted perception had me mustering courage on a level worthy of the Silver Star.

I could not get the image of my platoon sergeant out of my mind. I could feel him screaming, spewing spit in my face. "You fucking yellow-ass deserter! You're goin' to the stockade, you maggot piece of shit. And in two years, when you're done with jail and you start back at week one, I just hope you end up back in my company. I'll squeeze your pussy balls off. We can't have shit like you out there screwin' this country's women!"

Floundering around the infinite maze of similar-looking company areas, I finally found a phone next to a Post Exchange. I was scared shitless, partly because of my absence and the mounting problems associated with reentry and partly because of my insecurity with Jeanine. As I dialed her number, everything grew hazy and I felt sort of rubbery. Then, for the first time in weeks, I was talking to my girl.

Feeling vulnerable I got right to the point and asked her to meet me in St. Louis on Friday night. We'd get a hotel room and stay until Sunday around noon. As I went through my proposal, the idea that I might as well be talking to Ann-Margaret or Mia Farrow hit me, but to my total amazement Jeanine was in an unusually joyous mood.

"Why don't you just sing it?" she said, laughing.

I didn't get it. She reminded me condescendingly of the old show tune, "Meet Me in St. Louie."

"Oh, sure," I replied. "From a Judy Garland movie. I can't remember how the damn thing goes. Shame, too, 'cause all the guys say I sound like Perry Como when we sing our cadence songs." I was trying damn hard to be funny, but was way too nervous to do the quick thinking I needed to pull it off.

A long pause ensued. "You're lucky I miss you, Andrew McClain. I'll have to cancel some groovy plans and break a promise to my father not to take the car more than fifty miles away without his knowing about it. Plus I know darn well that I'll have to do the research and make the reservations and probably come up with most of the money!"

She's goin' to do it! I thought, elated. "Well, yeah, I was getting to that."

She was joking. She even sounded excited. As I hung up I was as happy as I'd ever been. My bliss was short-lived because I faced the serious challenge of getting back to my unit, Charlie-5-3, unnoticed.

I slipped from the lighted phone booth and glanced around. I was lost. As I crept from one bend in the road to the next, I was overwhelmed by the enormity of the base and the uniformity of its hundreds of white-framed, green-roofed buildings, all arranged in identical clusters that served as the individual company areas for the largest basic-training facility in America.

I sat on a steep knoll and mentally tried to pick my way back, but I had no idea from which direction I had come. I got up and instinctively began to run. Soon, I found myself in a hurried nightmare.

The impending losses loomed large: I would forfeit the pass and perhaps the most exciting weekend I'd ever dreamt of. I'd lose the hellish weeks I'd already accrued, along with any control over my own life as a military prisoner. Losing Jeanine would be possible because I would have no way to call off the rendezvous except by mail, and there wasn't time. I ran faster, the white barracks beginning to blur in all directions.

All I could do was dart into the guarded areas of each company and read the sign posted in front of the their orderly rooms. A-2-4. I ran and ran. D-1-2. D-2-2. I tried a different direction: F-2-3, E-1-5. I saw a jeep—MPs—and I actually dove under the mess hall of E-2-4. They stopped as if they'd seen something, then drove on.

I ran away from there and crossed a PT field, then took a curved road until more barracks loomed again, just ahead. H-4-3. In an all-out sprint I had skipped ten companies. I was nearly in tears.

God, how could you allow this? I thought, trapped in a city of torture, a sea of perfect white buildings with perfectly kept lawns and large graveled areas, a world of thousands and thousands of young men preparing for war under the tutelage of the fiercest pit bulls ever to take human form.

Headlights loomed ahead. I ran through a ditch and threw myself onto the ground next to a huge tree, camouflaging my olive-green form on the green lawn in the black of night, a little like they had been teaching us. My heart pounded. I realized that I'd never known pressure before, *real* pressure—to realize that every action I took, every thought I allowed, was part of a dreadful puzzle of survival. Fear replaced my bravado of only minutes before. I began to think how incredibly dumb I was, to sacrifice what I had earned. I realized that I was reasoning just the way they wanted me to.

I watched the approaching headlights. The car had something on the roof. More cops, had to be. But no. No! Jesus, I was hiding from a damn base cab! The cab rolled along easily, slowly. I hesitated, wondering what might happen if the cab was part of some secret police system, but I had no other option. I rushed the cab with all I had.

Taxi! Taxi!" I called.

He stopped, his window down all the way.

"Hop in," the driver said.

"I'm lost. I need to go to C-five-three," I said as I climbed into the cab.

"Shit, boy!" he bellowed, laughing. "That's a basic company. You're AWOL, aren't ya?"

"I had to call my girl," I said, reaching for my wallet. "Her sister got hit by a car."

"Get off that shit, man. Your orderly room'd probably let you call then. You're out cattin' around. Where you been? Waynesville?"

The guy was dressed in civilian clothes. He seemed like someone who wasn't going to screw me over.

"Hell," I said, still out of breath. "What I really did was make a call. We're supposed to a have a pass this weekend. I called my chick in Kentucky, hoping she'd meet me somewhere."

He laughed and pounded the steering wheel. "I knew it! I see it at least once a week. I could tell by your eyes. Some guys got instinct and couldn't ever get lost, but some of you couldn't go piss without losing your ass."

I pulled six bucks from my wallet—all I had—and handed it forward.

"You keep your money," he told me. "Costs a quarter for a ride anywheres on base. If you want, you can give me a buck. C-five-three's not that far, if you know what you're doin'. But you ain't gotta go back right now unless you want to."

"Thanks," I said. "I appreciate that, and I'll give you two bucks. But, damn, I gotta get back right now."

He smiled, reached down below the right front seat, and handed me an ice-cold beer.

"Jesus!" I managed to say. I loved beer, and I hadn't had one in nearly six weeks. I stared with all my heart at the red, white, and blue can of Budweiser and stroked away some condensation, the way I might've touched Jeanine's face. I took the church key he passed me, punched two holes in the can, then chugged half of it, my eyes closed. "Oh, God," I said with a sigh once the ice-cold carbonation had cleared my tongue and throat.

"Tough to beat when you ain't had one in a while. A little like ass," he said philosophically.

"You're not kiddin'."

He whirled around a corner, sped up for about a quarter of a mile, made a sharp left at a stand of trees, then slowed to a crawl. "This is a good place to get out. See through this company, over to the one between those two barracks facing us?"

I nodded.

"That's C-five-three. If we rounded the corner ahead, we'd be right in front of it. You're better off to run through this company, then kinda float into your barracks. Go into the shitter. Stay in a few minutes, wash your face, take your shirt off. If by some miracle, your CQ or fireguard questions you about being outside, deny you left the company. Say you needed some air to keep from crackin' up. Or that you were pukin'. They're not gonna do anything. Everybody's dreamin' of doin' what you did."

Trembling, I gave him two bucks. He opened another can and told me to chug all I could. I managed to down most of it. "Geez, man," I said. "I don't know how to thank you."

"Forget it. I went through it, too. It's mostly bluff and bullshit. But be careful about this kinda thing, or you could really lose your ass."

I followed his instructions and in ten minutes was in my bunk. I stayed awake a long time, savoring my great adventure.

On Friday we squeaked out a fourth place finish that set us free for two days.

Jeanine picked me up at the bus station at nine Friday night.

"Andrew! This is a terrible place for a girl. The Saint Louis bus station! I got here an hour ago and I've been propositioned about fifty times. Plus two soldiers got in a fight and there's bums everywhere." She softened. "Let's go, can we? I've got pink champagne in our hotel room, and pink something else on, too."

I spent the greatest two days of my life in that hotel room.

Chapter 4

Dopplemeyer taught Brian a lot in a short time, including how to buy himself extra personal time by staying out of Top's and Karch's sight. "I've written the better part of a novel," Dopplemeyer said, "working an hour or two a day locked in the mail room. Andy here can vouch for that."

I nodded. We were on our way over to the mess hall for mail call. Brian looked proud to be carrying the mail sack slung over his shoulder.

"Having you show me the ropes like this is great!" The kid sounded amazed. "I still can't believe my luck."

"Brian, you're going to love being mail clerk. I honestly feel that I'm going to miss it."

"The entire company will associate you with the best times of the day—mail calls," I put in. "That's why Dopplemeyer is so well-liked."

"Of course," Dopplemeyer continued, "I can't wait to get back home and finish my education and get on with my banking career. And then there's the little matter of making the petite Thelma Wilson, Mrs. Dopplemeyer."

"That's pretty cool, Marvin," Brian said. "I wish I could come to your wedding."

"You're not going to be in time for that one, Briney boy. Maybe I'll come to yours, though. Thelma's a little doll, but boy, would I ever like to meet Elaine! Those eyes…" Dopplemeyer mused.

"Well, we'd be honored if you came." With a grunt Brian shifted the olive canvas sack to his other shoulder. "In fact, I'll take your forwarding address, and by God, I'll send you an invitation. You, too, Andy."

A vision of Elaine beatific in a white gown formed in my mind.

"We'll be there!" Dopplemeyer said with enthusiasm.

Dopplemeyer was different, for sure. He was six feet two, but plump, even after a year of army chow in Nam. He didn't appear to have an athletic bone in his body. His black, tonic-laden hair was thinning, and in contrast to everyone else's, his face was pale. He played bridge, canasta, and euchre, read the classics, and was exceptionally bright. He'd gone to the University of Virginia for two years, studying the unlikely combination of psychology and finance. He was drafted after he had made the mistake of taking a sabbatical to manage his father's paint store.

Marvin Q. Dopplemeyer was easily the most extroverted and optimistic man in our unit. A born comedian and psychologist, he had an opinion on everything, was full of advice, and was difficult to shut up and pry yourself away from.

Watching him work was one of my favorite pastimes. Even his preparations in front of the mail room's sorting boxes were a show in themselves. Rehearsing, Dopplemeyer commented on each piece of mail as if he were a sportscaster. He'd start out in a low drone.

"All right, Prather gets that long-awaited missive from Jill, and—uh-oh!—one from Margaret, too. This should be good." His voice would get a little louder. "Richio, with another one from the missus. Chapman, a pink one from Kathleen—smell this, guys. I think she really means it. Kensinger, another letter demanding payment. What's he do with all his money?"

Soon his rapid-paced dialogue would become quite audible. "Dillard, ah, look guys, his six-year-old, Amy, wrote this. Private Morgan, another one from your brother. Oh, boy! Hey, more indecent items for Wisnewski from American Dildo. Seriously, this guy's got a footlocker full of sexual paraphernalia, claims it's an ongoing joke from an old high school buddy. Yeah, sure, Wisnewski. Raymond Brody, from Beth. Dopplemeyer—hey, *me*, guys—from the incomparable and now short-skirted—you got to see the picture from yesterday—Thelma. Randall, Burks, Lee, all pastel, perfumed ones." As he sorted, his hands flew to the appropriate boxes, and like an accomplished pianist or typist, he never had to look.

The real performance came at lunch. Dopplemeyer had a spot outside the mess hall. The men usually lined up by platoon at 1230, 1240, and 1250 hours for mail. Dopplemeyer would carry his sack as if he were Santa Claus.

I rarely ate lunch because I didn't want to have diarrhea in the afternoon. Everyone had problems with the shits in Nam. The malaria pill they gave you on Mondays left a guy's system in shambles for at least a day, and the food itself was challenging. But for me lunch was always the worst. I couldn't stand to be taking Prather somewhere and have to crap in the boonies or in town. So for the past few weeks, I had ambled down to the mess hall with Dopplemeyer—and now Brian—helped with any packages, then stood under the small aluminum awning and watched the show.

Today and every day, the men mobbed Dopplemeyer, not unlike a pack of dogs expecting food. "Ladies and gentlemen, may I have your attention?" he began. "Well, I knew there'd be no ladies, but darn, I don't see any gentlemen, either."

From forty or so guys came some muffled laughs.

"Come on, Dopplemeyer, quit fuckin' with us."

"Oh, Private Kelleher can't keep it clean. Now I don't feel so bad about that letter from Rose Marie that I thought I saw this morning but couldn't seem to locate when I put the bundles together."

"Dopplemeyer! I been waiting three weeks—"

"Oh, here we go. Uh-oh, don't get your hopes up. It's even addressed, Mickey 'Dear John' Kelleher. Here, read, assimilate, and then go sell your envelopes and stationery."

"Rosie!" Kelleher yelled gleefully, kissing his letter.

"Okay, anyone else interested in what I have, or do we just want to watch Kelleher and help him with the big words?"

"Come on!"

"Reynolds! Brown, Tommy Brown, this could be it! Your subpoena to appear before the Judge Advocate General. Miller! Bessemer! DeSanto! Oh, Paulie, who's Phyllis? Man, smell this Chanel!"

"Give it, Dopplemeyer! Never mind who she is."

"DeSanto, am I going to have to drop Beverly a line and maybe find out who Phyllis is?"

"Ah, eat it, Dopplemeyer. She's just a friend."

"Hey, guys, DeSanto here says Phyllis is just a friend. A rich friend, I guess, who has the money to dump seven ounces of Chanel perfume on her letter."

I glanced at Brian, who was grinning broadly as he watched Dopplemeyer take a group of tired, surly men and get them giggling like children.

"Post! Graber! Putz! Putz, do me a favor, please? Promise me you're going to change your name when you get back to Ohio. Borman! Starr! Starr, I thought Rita broke it off with you. This must be her telling you she's suing your ass for all those nights back at the drive-in. Martin, from your mother. Sacowitz. Forgan. Forgan, what the hell kinda name is 'Tonda' anyway? Amish?"

"Don't know, Dopplemeyer. Never asked. She's got a sister named Teila, though."

"That's charming, Forgan." Before the platoon could disperse, Dopplemeyer raised his voice. "All right, you guys, I've got a little surprise for you today. As you know I am quite short—"

"Not as short as me, Dopplemeyer," Specialist McVee of the maintenance platoon yelled. "I'm so short my dick lies on the ground like a garden hose. Shoorrt! Short, you motherfuckers! Nine days and a wake-up!"

"No, not as short as you, McVee, but I won't be going home on a navy ship like you, either."

"You dream on, Dopplemeyer! Shooorrt! I got time to jet my ass over there and marry your ol' Thelma, divorce her, too, before your ass even gets there!" He threw back his head and drummed on his chest with balled fists. "Shhhooooooorrrrrrrrt!"

"Good one, McVee, 'cept she's not your style. She likes to be taken out to dinner. You never ate anything you didn't have to unwrap first. Now shut up and stop your sorority girl sniggering. I guarantee you're going to want to know about this gentleman standing next to me. He happens to be my replacement and your new mail clerk. I doubt he has the patience I do, so for all those reasons you had better be nice to him. This is Brian Kitzmiller from Indianapolis."

"Hi," Brian said meekly. But the men, reading their mail, paid no attention.

"Well, Briney, what do you think?" Dopplemeyer asked as we turned to leave. "You could do that, couldn't you?"

"Not like that. I mean, you're a real entertainer. Maybe after a while, I could do it some."

"You'll develop your own routine. Listen, when I started I was scared stiff," he said, and winked at me. "At first you simply read the names and try to learn faces. But in no time, you're a hero to them and, before you know it, a friend."

Chapter 5

The following day, Brian returned with his first sack of letters around midmorning, and I wondered what was taking Prather so long. I was nervous about using the orderly room as my permanent hangout. I wasn't sure Top appreciated it, and I was damn sure Karch resented drivers, period.

As I thumbed through a *Saturday Evening Post* that Huffer had left in his desk, Top said, "Hey, McClain, you and Prather goin' to that site near Bien Hoa today or not?"

"Yeah, Top. As soon as he's ready."

"I got some medical records I think should be back at the 93rd Evac hospital. I got a feelin' if I keep 'em in my desk any longer I'm gonna lose the motherfuckers entirely."

"Sure, Top. We can—"

A violent explosion shook the room. A couple of confused, silent seconds followed, then we heard a secondary explosion and screams. The sound of men shouting and rushing past the orderly room came next. Top stormed out of the room with Brian and me on his heels. Jet-black smoke billowed up from the road, and the horrific screams persisted.

We raced to the crest overlooking the highway, along with fifty or so unarmed men from our own and neighboring companies. A five-ton army truck had run over a land mine on Highway One. Orange flames consumed the vehicle just down the incline from us.

This was a shocking rarity. Because of our own immense army presence and our proximity to Bien Hoa Air Force Base with all the potential hell it could unleash, the endless Highway One traffic streamed past our area unimpeded, day after day.

In front of the many soldiers now assembled lay row after row of concertina wire. Unless we ran or drove around to the main outside gate, we couldn't get down to the fiery wreck. Suddenly Top, an infantryman in two wars, recognized our risk. "This is a duck shoot! Get out of the line of fire!"

he yelled. "Goddammit, move it, boys! This is how Charlie works! Get a weapon and stay back!"

Men scurried in all directions. Top grabbed me by the arm and pointed at my jeep while he continued to shout instructions, then reentered the orderly room and emerged immediately with two loaded M-14s.

Top tossed one to me as he climbed into the jeep. "A man's hurt bad down there!" he shouted. "The MPs ain't gonna leave their guard bunker, and he'll be dead by the time help arrives." Brian jumped in the jeep uninvited, and I drove the three of us down to the scene.

The truck lay on its right side with both of its fuel tanks now exploded and feeding the inferno. The soldier riding shotgun had been trapped and undoubtedly burned to death. The driver's left foot and lower leg had been blown off, but he had managed to pull himself through the cab window and get to the ground before the fuel tanks ignited. He had slithered a few yards away to avoid being incinerated.

Top dragged the screaming man another fifty feet from the roaring fire, then knelt at his side. We rushed to help but stopped at the sight. Brian turned a pasty white, and I felt the blood drain from my face, too.

"Tourniquet!" Top yelled. He pointed at the blood pumping from the soldier's stump. "Get me a stick or a tire iron or bayonet. It's his only chance."

Top took off the man's belt and wrapped it around the top of his thigh. "Calm down, boy. You're gonna make it." He patted the guy's shoulder. "Femoral artery. I'm gonna shut you off like a faucet."

Frantically, Brian and I searched for something Top could use, but we came up empty. Two soldiers in a jeep bound for Saigon pulled over and, magically it seemed, answered Top's request for a tire iron. Top immediately slid it under the taut belt, then grunted through an excruciating 360-degree turn. The wounded man screamed again, then passed out. When the blood slowed to an ooze, Top took my belt, looped it around the iron and wrapped the soldier's leg once. With my help, he tied another knot, fastening the bottom of the tourniquet. He took Brian's belt and did the middle. The bloody contrivance looked cruel and grotesque, but it worked. "He may lose more of that leg," Top said, standing up, "but he ain't gonna bleed to death."

Within four minutes a medevac chopper arrived and took off with the victim. MPs, followed by explosives experts and a mine-sweep team, came well after the chopper's departure.

I was thoroughly shaken. A couple of times during the ordeal, I thought I would faint. After the Huey roared off, I noticed Brian over by the concertina wire, throwing up. He did it in plain view of the men still in the company area, but I doubted anyone would razz him about it. The charred body was eventually extricated from the cab, and many hours later a crane from the 96th Engineers lifted the blackened shell of the truck onto a lowboy and hauled it away.

I looked at Top with new eyes. He was, I realized, a hell of a lot more than bullshit and worn-out stories about the brown-shoe army.

Never again would I take our safe area for granted. Even though Highway One was the largest, most traveled road in the country, this was still Vietnam.

Chapter 6

Six weeks after my encounter with the exploded truck, the monsoon season set in as Prather and I returned to the 209th after long hours of driving between the plant and road-building sites. As 6 P.M. approached, the sky turned to a gray so deep that charcoal would've seemed light by comparison. I pulled over and put up the top on the jeep.

"Let's see if we can grab a beer somewhere and wait out the rain," Prather suggested, eyeing the lowering sky.

The rules for hitting bars in Vietnam during duty hours were explicit: Don't do it. Compounding matters, we were in an off-limits part of town. Such indiscretions were common, but getting killed or captured or being arrested by our own MPs loomed as a possibility. I was always happy, though, whenever Prather wanted to do something like this.

Suddenly the rain came down in sheets, soaking us as it streamed through the vehicle's open sides. I stopped in front of the first place I could see, a bar with the contrived name "El Paso Girls." We sprinted through the doorway into the dim candlelight.

All six stools were occupied, so we seated ourselves at the only open table along the wall. A plump Vietnamese lady approached us.

Prather did the talking. "Hello, mamason," Prather said cordially, ignoring her unfriendly countenance, "You have beer here?"

The woman gave a surly grunt, then cackled, "Have Carring Brack Rable." The black market ensured that American beer, cigarettes, and soft drinks were available everywhere. In fact, anyone could obtain nearly anything on the black market, from popular consumer items to pornography to worse, actual military supplies, including weapons and ammunition.

"Two Black Labels then, please."

She shuffled off, and I took in the shabby room. At one table, two young Vietnamese men, one wearing black, speared us with their eyes. *My God,* I thought, my mouth for an instant going dry, *this is a Viet Cong hangout.* Then thankfully, I discovered a Green Beret sergeant with his feet resting on a nearby table. He was drawing on a cigar and drinking with a major who slouched and slurred his words and watched us warily. As my eyes adjusted to the poor lighting, I realized that the major had a huge reddish spot on his cheek and around his eye, as if he'd just been punched hard in the face.

"Fuckin' I Corps, man," the major complained. "Fuckin' MPs. You understand what I'm sayin', Hal?"

"Fuck it, man," the beret said, "and fuck you."

Not far from the major and the beret sat four Australian soldiers. After we'd settled in, they apparently resumed a boisterous conversation. All large men and heavily armed, they seemed to have nothing to do with the Americans. When one of them winked at the beret, I felt as if I had entered the *Twilight Zone.*

The sound of vehicles momentarily droned in despite the downpour, and the door banged open. A couple of American soldiers, moving as if the wooden crates they carried were heavy, hoisted their burdens onto the bar.

"Got more," one of them barked to the beret, who nodded. A third man entered but immediately whipped around and rushed outside into the pounding rain.

Prather and I looked at each other. "Sergeant Tibble!" I whispered.

Our company supply sergeant had quite a reputation as a hard-ass, a drunk, and a conniver. Most black market operations involved corrupt people who were somehow associated with supplies or goods, and Tibble fit the bill.

Prather's eyes went to his beer, and he spoke in an undertone. "He must've seen us. I'd give anything to know what's in those crates." Prather stared at them again.

"Yeah," I said uneasily, and looked around the room. All eyes were on us.

Prather lifted his glass. "I got a feeling that if we moseyed up and started checking them…" His voice was low and serious, and his face betrayed nothing.

"Jesus, sir!" I expelled a breath I didn't know I was holding.

To my relief, he grinned. "Only kidding. I don't think we'd leave here alive." He took a swallow of his brew. "Watch yourself. We'll finish these, and if it's still raining too hard, we'll have one more. Forget the cartons…for now." He added, chuckling, "I guess we know why this part of town is off-limits."

As I considered how best to investigate Tibble's wrongdoing, one of the Aussies, a huge albino with a bad complexion, headed toward our table and stared hard at me.

"So who's gonna win the National League this year, Lieutenant?" I tried to keep my voice from betraying my taut nerves. Prather, on the other hand, sounded and looked completely relaxed.

"I'm gonna tell you something, McClain. The Cardinals, along the mighty Mississippi, have got it in the bag."

"I think the Dodgers may have something to say about that, sir." I watched the Aussie pass us, stroll to the rear of the joint, and begin pissing out the back door.

The lieutenant refilled his glass and mine. "You're doin' okay," he said, barely moving his lips. His remark did nothing to stop the churning in my stomach. I wanted out.

One of the other Aussies loudly ordered three shots of Wild Turkey and stepped over to the beret and the major.

"I don't want any more shit, you got me?" the major said, putting his hand to his face.

"And what's that supposed to mean?" the Aussie demanded. He looked at the major but subtly motioned toward us. "Come on. Have a drink, mate."

The major could not be cajoled. "You fuckin' ask Hal, you asshole," he said drunkenly as he shook his head.

The beret looked up and shrugged. "You can cut his dick off as far as I'm concerned."

"Hal!" said the major, almost in tears. "You sonofabitch, you bastard fuck."

The Aussie laughed. "Much ado, my good man, about nothing." He then turned and sauntered over to us. Because he was so trim and fit at six foot three and maybe 190 pounds, I hadn't noticed that he was older than the rest. He must have been in his late thirties or early forties.

"Normally, mates, this place is hoppin', but tonight the regulars and the Gold-Coast girls don't seem to be here yet. But that's no reason to be unsociable. I'm Colonel John Wathan." He leaned over and extended his hand, which Prather and I both shook. "Mamason," he called over his broad shoulder, "two more beers for these gents and three shots of old blood eye for the table."

I was extremely uncomfortable, but we downed the shots, drinking to Old Glory. Prather spoke only in short phrases when spoken to and appeared so preoccupied, I feared he was offending our host.

To my surprise the colonel then became almost fatherly, asking me a lot of questions about my life back home.

45

Prather must have decided a little acknowledgment might be prudent, because he bought the next round. After a time I was convinced our new friend was full of shit and was trying to win us over to cover up the crates' delivery.

Then the colonel put his hand on my shoulder. "You mark my words, mates. Just as World War One vets yearn for their youth and the war that shaped them, someday you'll crave these days when you were young and serving your country. You'll remember your first real year away from your homeland with other young men like yourselves." He cuffed the back of my head with a force just beyond gentle.

Prather drove because we both figured he was less drunk. When we turned onto Highway One, with only four miles to go and driving at last on a paved road, we started laughing like two little kids.

"A fine couple of investigators we are," Prather hooted. "We didn't get outsmarted, just out-drank, out-manned, and out-bullshitted."

Relief finally washed over me, and I allowed myself a good guffaw. "What about Tibble?" I asked.

"That bastard could be making a fortune selling stuff meant for us and sabotaging our mission in the process. I'll talk to Karch, and we'll watch him. Tibble'd beat any investigation now, especially having the advantage of knowing we're on to him." He paused. "I know you can keep this to yourself." Prather looked at me and smiled. "You did great back there, McClain."

His assessment and his trust upped my confidence level to previously unattained heights. That feeling had me floating, but I kept thinking about what the Aussie colonel had said. His words fascinated and disturbed me. I could see no reason to long for these days ever again. I only wanted to get home.

Chapter 7

When we arrived at the 209th, too late for supper, I just wanted to think. For no reason, except possibly my state of inebriation, I climbed to the top of our ten-foot command bunker, unrolled my poncho, then lay back on the soaked sandbags and stared at the moon.

The Aussie colonel's lumping us all into one group started me thinking about the two hundred men who gave our company a distinct personality. I smiled as I reviewed all our unique characters: Karch, Top, Prather, Dopplemeyer, Huffer, and even Tibble. I thought of Hobson and cracked up.

Private Donald H. Hobson established his individuality from minute one of his arrival a month before. When he first bounced off the truck, Hobson appeared unremarkable, except for light-complexioned skin, which accentuated vividly the swollen pimples he must've squeezed that morning. He stood about six feet two, weighed 180.

Then he smiled and started to talk. His buck teeth had huge gaps between them. He also had a considerable speech impediment; all of his *l*'s were *w*'s, as were his *r*'s, and his *s*'s were lucky to be *z*'s and not *th*'s. His babble never ended, though his talk was not necessarily unintelligent. He knew sports as well as anyone, and he liked to talk about cars and girls. But he never seemed to shut up.

Top had gone after Hobson as if he were a village idiot. "All right, Hobson, you say you been laid? It's my job to tell whether you're a lyin' sack of shit or a real soldier. Real soldiers don't lie, unless they're West Point. See, they're protected under the honor code, which says they can't lie, so that makes it easy for them to get away with it. Now, tell me, boy. What does a pussy look like?"

But Hobson just didn't get the intimidation. "Oh, awhite, awhite, Firt Thahgeant. Leth tee, a putty…"

We laughed convulsively.

Brian cut in loudly, "You're from Indiana? Then you gotta play basketball!"

"Boy, I wuv backetbaw," Hobson stated reverently, his eyes alight. "I din't know we'd hab backetbaw."

Frankie Huffer fancied himself a star in the four-team league as well as its commissioner, and at Hobson's announcement, his face reddened with surging anger. He faced Kitzmiller as if he'd blasphemed, then reeled toward Hobson. "But you gotta be able to play, motherfucker." He smiled meanly. "No shithook is gonna get past the first game."

"If dairth a way you can wuk me in…"

"Ah, fuck me." Huffer shook his head in disgust. "I tell you what. You come with us at chow time. You don't need any supper if you're really interested. You watch us, and if you think you can play, then after one game, we'll let you try. But I'll flat fuckin' tell you this: We ain't havin' our game ruined by no charity cases."

"Oh, come on," Brian said. "I'm not that good, and neither is McClain, but we play every night. Besides, whatta you care? You got less than three weeks left."

"Hey, piss on you, Kitzmiller," Huffer said nastily. "That's my point. I was in Bien Hoa the days both you guys started. This league's gone downhill since me and Donatelli founded the fucker. Fuck, my team was sixteen and two the first month, and that's the worst we ever were up until Donatelli left. You and McClain are damn lucky to be even playin'," he added. "I hate to see all that work go to hell, is all."

"Shit," Brian said. "Gimme a break. I say let Hobson play, no matter what. How's he gonna get to know the guys? What's the main idea behind—"

"Hey, fuck, Kitzmiller! Us guys who founded this league wanted it pure— just ballplayers, no pussies, no…doinkos!"

"Damn, Huffer," I said, feeling embarrassed for Hobson. "Who gives a shit? This is Nam, not the NBA."

"Hey, I'm just tryin' to leave you with some fuckin' pride, something you know shit about," Huffer retorted. "When I leave Nam, I'll be wearin' a Purple Heart with a damn oak-leaf cluster, and I shoulda got a Bronze Star, too, and in a fuckin', goddamn engineer company. Shit! Remember, you fuckers, that better men went before you."

Top broke out laughing. "You tell 'em, Huffer. 'Course the only fightin' I ever saw you do was for your tenth beer on any given night."

Huffer's face twisted with indignation. "Hey, fuck, Top, thanks a hell of a lot. Damn, I figured you'd be with me on this. I ain't no World War Two or Korea vet, but goddamn, I done a job over here. I figured *you'd* know what the fuck I meant." Huffer had argued himself into a corner of incoherence. "We stood for being Americans, bein' men, even if that meant gettin' your fuckin' ass shot by Charlie. Damn. When we did anything, we did it fuckin' right! Can't you see that, Top?"

"Huffer, I suggest you calm your ass down." The first sergeant moved closer to Huffer and punctuated his words with a finger jabbing the loudmouth's chest. "As far as I'm concerned, anybody who wants to play basketball or do any other fuckin' recreation we got here, can. Period. I respect that you got wounded an' all, but in the brown-shoe army, we didn't go braggin' about gettin' shot. We tried to put the hole in the other guy, you understand? I got a Purple Heart myself, but it ain't my favorite medal."

Top turned to Hobson and spoke as if he suddenly felt sorry for the newcomer. "You're goin' to the maintenance platoon, son, and Sergeant Kulp will be glad to have you. We need another mech. You make yourself at home and do whatever you want on your own time."

Huffer rolled his eyes, then squinted at Hobson. "Just show up," he muttered.

Again Hobson's eyes became wide and brilliant. "Thankth, Hufforr. Thankth a wot faw wettin' me."

Top sent me to help Hobson get squared away in the maintenance platoon. I found myself fascinated with him. There he was, strongly extroverted despite his speech impediment and goofy appearance. I thought of how hard it had been for me to develop any confidence at all and how shy I'd been with the opposite sex. Jeanine was my first and only girlfriend. I was no great prize, either, but at least I didn't have to cope with Hobson's problems. It made no sense.

He told me that he had a "faborite" girlfriend back in Kokomo, and her name was Juwie Foust, but he also "wiked" Betina Doowittle and Evewyn Adams. He especially enjoyed what Evelyn had to offer at the drive-in. He talked about home as if he'd be there on Saturday night.

I felt sorry for him. He had a long year ahead, and those girls might all be history by then. The guys would pick on him endlessly—this countrified small-towner who somehow had such a high opinion of himself.

And what a way for him to start, too. No doubt Huffer would alert the other guys, and they'd make it really tough on Hobson on the court. I had never liked Frankie Huffer, and I told myself that even if it meant forfeiting my own reputation, I would offer to buy Hobson a beer later—not that I really wanted to. What if he singled me out as his only friend? How would I ever get rid of him? Shit!

Hobson had waited eagerly outside the orderly room for twenty minutes in the still-hot sun for Huffer, Kitzmiller, and me. Soon other players surrounded him, those cruelly silent forewarned soldiers, none of whom he'd met.

Eleven of us proceeded down the interior road to the large paved clearing that had been intended as a formation area for troops and a possible truck convoy staging ground. Plus it presented an area where several Hueys could land at once. I don't remember its serving any purpose other than as a basketball court. Along with a lone signal corps company, the bleached asphalt rectangle separated us physically from the rest of the battalion.

Brian led the procession with Hobson on his heels like a puppy. For the men who had just met him, all of them intent on humiliating him, Hobson's stream of excited chatter provided continuous entertainment.

Frankie Huffer broodingly muttered that legendary or not, a lifer was a lifer, especially a lifer first sergeant. Top had the power not only to fuck over the game and the league, but them, too, as individuals. Especially, he continued in a louder tone, if he thought he'd "get his fat ass patted by Karch, or even better, some homo reporter for the *Stars and Stripes,* or some nigger congressman that just might wander into the company area one fine day with thirty fuckin' photographers following his ass."

We had only four black soldiers in the 209th at that time, and George Champion was one of them. He played on Brian's and my team. He looked around ruefully as Huffer ranted.

Huffer noticed Champion's reaction. "Hey, sorry, George. Fuck, I'm just making a point. Nothin' against you. You seem to do your job as good as anybody, and you're a *player."*

George half nodded, accepting the perfunctory apology and recognition. I wondered what else he could do.

Huffer's tirade kept getting louder. Suddenly, his face aglow with the cruelest of smiles, he punted the basketball toward the back of Hobson's head and yelled his name. Both Hobson and Brian wheeled. Hobson's hand shot up at the last second and diverted the ball, which skittered through the first few coils of concertina wire separating the compound from Highway One.

"Can't catch a pass, Hobson?" Huffer asked before anyone had really grasped what happened.

Hobson was all grins. "Din't tee it in time," he said, jogging to the wire to retrieve the ball.

Brian and I followed. As Hobson knelt, long arm extended, his face pressed against the barbed wire, and he strained, determined at his task. Huffer and his crew smirked and exchanged glances.

We could see a thickening trickle of blood on Hobson's nose where a barb must have pierced the skin, and he had a ragged scratch across a third of his forehead.

"Damn you, Huffer," I said. "What an asshole thing to do."

"Eat me," he responded, grinding his hips as he and his teammates laughed.

I could feel myself reddening, but Hobson was oblivious to anything but the basketball. His fingers groped for and lightly tickled it. Ever so gently, he pressed harder, and the barbs cut a little deeper.

I glanced at Brian and was startled. His gaze was riveted on Hobson's bleeding face, and he grimaced as if he could feel the cuts.

Hobson pressed harder, a barb near his eye. Then to our relief, he made a whimpering sound of joy, and like a bomb defuser, he carefully brought the ball safely through the wire.

"Dot it!" he announced with the elation of one who had just saved a life or won a hundred thousand dollars.

"Didn't ya, though," Huffer said sarcastically, and elbowed Chud.

On the court, Huffer took charge. "Okay, there's eleven of us. Diggs, you sit out first. You guys got Hobson." He smiled, then a glint of alarm crossed his face. "Fuck! The fuckin' scum from the 96th are comin'. We gotta play now! No warmin' up. Let's go. This is our court! We built it, even though it ain't in our company area. Nobody ever did anything but shoot around 'til we founded the league. Let's go!" Then he glanced toward the other end of the court.

Hobson was kneeling next to the broken pole that once supported the other goal. "Wha' happened?" he asked sadly.

Huffer was beside himself. "Hey, Hobson, it got broke! Okay? Some stupid shit from the 96th hit it with a deuce-and-a-half fuckin' green truck. Jeezus, you fuckin' clown. Let's play!"

Huffer assigned his players their defensive positions, and Bobby Glasscock, our court leader, along with Champion, our only ex-high school player, did the same. Brian looked at me and nodded toward Hobson. "Indiana, basketball capital of the world," he said.

"Count on it," I replied. "Now I see why Elaine calls you Briney. You're such a gullible little shit." But I noticed, since our team was shirtless, just how muscular Hobson was.

Frankie Huffer was ready to play. He pressed his tongue hard against his cheek and seemed to suppress a grin. No one had to guess who he'd guard. "Hobson, take it out. Let the games begin!"

He fired the ball as hard as he could to Hobson, who didn't move other than to open his hands. The ball should have made a resounding *smack*, but instead it nestled like a baby in Hobson's grip. Huffer was in Hobson's face, waving his arms like a madman. "Hey! Hey! Come on!"

Hobson raised the ball above his head, his ever-present grin still plastered on his face. Huffer's teammates, who were by now very much into humiliating Hobson, seemed greatly amused.

Suddenly Hobson flicked the ball over Huffer's head to me. The move was effortless, and the ball arrived so fast, it shot through my hands. I caught it against my chest using my arms, like a fourth grader. I reeled toward the basket and stopped short when I saw Wilcott waiting for me.

Wilcott had my number. He'd stolen the ball from me countless times and had blocked at least ten of my shots. I was greatly intimidated by him, and my already suspect dribbling dropped several notches. Everything seemed badly clogged inside the lane; passing the ball to Champion was out.

I looked back, and there stood Hobson in the same place! He was grinning, openmouthed, watching the frantic movements of the others, almost as if he were watching a cartoon. Huffer had abandoned him momentarily, but now rushed back to cover him.

I threw poor Hobson the ball a little late, realizing instantly that it was a stupid pass and knowing full well that Huffer would snatch it from him. But that didn't happen, and Hobson again raised the ball above his head with that gap-toothed grin on his face.

Huffer had always enhanced his defense by yelling at his opponent. "Hey! Come on! Shoot it, you fuck!" he shrieked, and swung madly at the ball.

Hobson scooted around him as if Huffer were paralyzed and blasted into the lane a full second before Huffer realized Hobson was gone. As the lane closed, Hobson came across the free-throw line and seemingly whipped the ball to Champion on his left.

But instead of leaving his hand, the ball completed a beautiful arc in front of Hobson's body. Then, having somehow slipped between the remaining two defenders, he launched himself—combat boots, fatigue pants, and all—to the basket. His hand ever so lightly brushed the front rim, allowing the ball to roll off his fingertips and in.

Before anyone could quite absorb what had happened, a cussing Huffer stormed underneath the basket and grabbed the ball to fire it back inbounds.

Hobson had retreated, prancing like a prize stallion, but suddenly he reeled, sprinted toward Huffer, then leapt high in the air, snaring the pass with one hand.

Hobson flipped the ball to Brian, who missed a lay up but managed to push the ball back to Hobson. In one motion behind his back, Hobson passed to Champion for an easy shot.

Huffer had no sanctuary. As he tried to get away from a smothering Hobson, he picked up his dribble in desperation. Hobson bumped the ball and powered it off Huffer's forehead, controlling it easily.

He passed to Glasscock, who dished to me, and I flung it back to Hobson. My pass was long; but like a gazelle, Hobson raced to grab it. He waited for the last possible moment as Chud and Kendrick both charged toward him, then effortlessly shot from thirty-five feet.

We watched a ball that could only be alive. Its backward spin must've had five times the rpms of a normal shooter's, and it arched to a theretofore-unimagined height. As it descended, a wondrous work of kinetic art, this brown rubber moon passed through the chain net with no more than a whisper...*chhh.*

Hobson was everywhere, a laughing panther blocking shots, stealing passes, rebounding, giggling, having the time of his life.

He played basketball as physically as I'd ever seen, he never seemed to look when he passed, and his dribbling ventured behind his back, through his legs, and through his defender's legs. His moves were quick and fluid, almost godlike. Those who had laughed were now intimidated by his toughness and sheer force.

"Jesus Christ, Huffer, what'd you piss him off for?" Wilcott whined.

Hobson's performance fired us, and we played the best game defensively of our lives. When the rout was over we had won 21-4. Hobson had scored 14 while Champion, Glasscock, and I accounted for the rest. Hobson's generous attempts to have Brian score the final basket resulted in their only four goals.

Our opponents were psychologically crushed, but they had to play again. Grinning, Hobson strolled up to Huffer with the ball.

"Hey, Huffer! You guyth det it out firt dit time," he announced, giving the ball a ferocious two-handed twist and catching it on his finger. With the ball spinning madly, Hobson gently flipped it off his finger to Huffer. When Huffer attempted to catch it, it shot off his hand and skittered away, rolling just a little faster than he could walk comfortably.

Huffer refused to run. He walked after the runaway ball, pursuing it for a good fifty yards and cursing at every step. "Fuck! Motherfuck! Cock-loving asshole!"

At this, Brian and I looked at each other and completely lost it. I felt as if I wouldn't be able to recover enough from laughing to play again.

Two more games ensued, with some of the guys from the 96th getting in when Huffer and his strongest followers stormed off the court during the second game. The results were the same. Hobson could not be touched. Some skill was required just to watch him.

Afterwards, we had a free-throw contest for money. The recognized champion was Donatelli, who was back in Philly with his record intact of twenty-three straight. Hobson took the pot hitting ninety-seven in a row.

"Aww, thit," he exclaimed, laughing and slapping himself on the forehead. "I wanted a hunnerd tho bad! I done it befaw, at weast a thouthand timeth."

We were ecstatic and childlike as we made our way to the EM club to celebrate. Our exuberance at the bar prompted a guy from the signal company to ask the bartender if the war had just ended. We learned that Hobson had been a starter on a very fine Kokomo East team that had made it to the Indiana High School final four, two years in a row.

"All-State honorable mention in Indiana," Brian said, "is like first-string on any college—hell, any pro team except maybe the Celtics or Lakers."

Hobson had averaged eighteen points a game and received several scholarship offers, but he'd gotten his original girlfriend, Becky Kay Knoop, pregnant. He decided to get married and go to work at the Chrysler plant. Becky miscarried a week before the wedding and then, prompted by her parents, called off the whole affair.

Hobson was too late for school that year, and in the interim he was drafted. Because he'd worked in a car plant, he reasoned, he was assigned to mechanics school, even though he'd requested to be a bus driver.

"Hey, Brian, show Hobson here, Elaine," I demanded, well into our fourth beer of the celebration. "Brian's got a chick you ain't gonna believe."

"Ah, not now," Brian objected.

Hobson's eyebrows rose. "Bwine, tome on, leth thee her. Tome on!"

"It's not anything like McClain's making it out to be. Just my girlfriend."

"Bwine, I reawy want to thee her. Tome on, pleath." At this Hobson reached into his own wallet and whipped out a slew of pictures including Becky Kay, Evelyn, Julie, Betina, and three others he hadn't told me about.

We studied the photographs closely amid mild obscenities and primal noises. I produced a picture of Jeanine, which Hobson praised. I told them about our rendezvous in St. Louis and how Jeanine had pink champagne waiting in our hotel room and how those two days were the best of my life.

Eventually Brian got out Elaine's photo. Hobson made such a fuss over her that several guys we didn't even know got in on the admiration. Brian seemed both proud and embarrassed.

"Wow, Bwine, theth bootiful," Hobson said, grinning broadly. "You know, I figured you'd hab a reawy tough gufwiend."

Brian smiled, turning beet red. "Well, I'm just lucky."

We drank and talked longer than usual. We learned that Hobson also had played football as a halfback and defensive back.

"Boy, I wuved pwayin' defent. Thereth nuffin' like when the reteever and the ball and you, all arribe at the tame time. I'b hit thum guyth toe hard, I tought I bwoke ebry bone in teir body." He grinned.

The jokes and accolades continued to fly, and the laughter was crazy. Brian suddenly burst out laughing, spraying everyone with beer.

"I keep seeing Huffer playing against the Lakers." Everyone doubled over. "Think of it. Frankie Huffer takes the pass, picked up by Elgin Baylor." We roared.

When we finally headed for the barracks, Brian had me laughing so hard I thought I was going to puke. "Jerry West all over Specialist Huffer!"

Hobson came from behind and put his arms around both of us. "You guyth are reawy gweat. We're goin' to hab a good time dit year."

I thought then that I was pretty damn lucky that he'd picked me for a friend.

Chapter 8

A crack of thunder sent me scrambling down the bunker and through pitch blackness in a deluge to the barracks. I must have fallen asleep, daydreaming about Hobson. I was happy that I'd found the bunker roof—a place where I could enjoy some peace and solace. It was never used unless we were under attack, so I knew I'd go up there again.

Moments later I was relaxing on my bunk in dry underwear. The luminous dial on my watch read three. I closed my eyes and listened to the rain on the metal roof. If a storm like that kept up for five days, the whole world would be under water.

At four-thirty Billy Squires got up, along with Frank McCollough, who was Captain Karch's driver, to go on the KP run. The "run" was an early morning work detail where one of us drivers got a deuce-and-a-half truck and, along with a person riding shotgun, took off down Highway One, through Bien Hoa and to a waiting site in the boonies, where we picked up a group of Vietnamese women. We brought them back to work all day in our company's mess hall. We rotated the morning job and never really thought of it as an official work detail because it was voluntary.

"Hey, McClain, Kitzmiller, you guys got any extra M-fourteen magazines?" Billy asked. "I only got one. I lost my other one, and that fuckin' Tibble won't give me another. Says I'll probably have to pay for the one I lost. He thinks I fired it off somewheres, the asshole."

"I got one you can borrow," I said. The magazine he referred to was a box-shaped clip of twenty 7.62 mm rounds, the type of bullet fired by either an M-14 rifle or an M-60 machine gun. I reached in my locker and handed him the ammo. A chilling thought suddenly came over me: Why the hell was Tibble making it hard for us to check out ammunition, which we had to sign for, to go on a legitimate and potentially dangerous detail? Dammit to hell! I vowed to take the issue up with Prather.

A new regime began that morning at seven, with Frankie Huffer's departure. In the three weeks since the game he'd pretty much stopped talking to everyone other than his closest cronies. He kept up his purposely loud conversations during chow, of course, to piss us off.

"I swear there's not a motherfucker in that orderly room that's got any brains at all," he'd say. "Shit, I shouldn't give a fuck, but I just hate to see it all go to hell. Top is just too damn dumb to have a bunch of stupid, candy-assed, cheese-eatin' suckasses to baby-sit. It ain't gonna work. But that's the fuckin' army. I feel sorry for the guys, is all."

What a guy.

We all shook hands with him and said good-bye, though he scarcely nodded. Then he plopped into the front seat of his last jeep. He was wearing shades and gazing straight ahead.

"Ah, hell," the driver said. "I was supposed to leave this baby down at the motor pool and pick up another one while they serviced her. Shit."

Brian covered his face with his hands. "Oh, my God," he whispered. "What if Huffer misses his plane?"

As usual, when I was attempting to mind my manners around Brian, I found myself trying to suppress laughter. Huffer probably sensed that because he noisily drew up some phlegm, then blew it more or less in our direction. Then came a burst from the engine and the subsequent crunching of gears, and that was the last we saw of Specialist Huffer.

About twenty minutes later, Shifrin handed Top the morning report to review, and the old first sergeant's eyes almost bugged out.

"Shifrin? You work on this last night?"

"No, Top."

"Well it's three pages long. How the hell did you get it done so fast? This would've took Huffer all mornin'."

Shifrin merely shrugged. Everything he did was perfect. He comprehended operational functions almost too easily. He was the master of spelling and typing, little crafts you rarely thought about as polished in a soldier.

"Karch's gonna love this," he said joyously.

That afternoon I happened to be there when Karch called both Shifrin and Kitzmiller into his office, with Top beaming off to the side.

"Shifrin and Kitzmiller—a couple of relatively new men to the 209th of sunny South Vietnam. Shifrin, you have three days in over here, and Kitzmiller has nine weeks. Neither one of you has enough time in grade as a

PFC or time in service for this, but Top's spent the last hour getting that restriction waived. This is a new team, with Huffer gone, and I want you both to feel like you definitely represent the executive branch of this company. You two have done the army an excellent job so far. I want you to know that when that happens, we intend to take care of you."

Karch reached into the same drawer he'd pulled the book out of a couple of months before. "As of today you're both promoted to Spec Four." He handed them their orders announcing the same, and Top gave them their appropriate patch.

Specialist 4, or E-4, was equivalent to corporal in grade and pay. I had been promoted to E-4 back at Fort Leonard Wood (I continued to be stationed there for three months after AIT, also with a waiver for time in grade) because the major I was driving took pity on me when I came down on orders for Nam. E-4 represented a critical promotion because it was not automatic. It separated those who could do a job and stay out of trouble and those who couldn't. It also signaled that you'd been there awhile; an E-4 could easily have been in country a whole year. Most went home as E-4s, so strangers didn't look at them as a recruit.

"Good job, men." Then Karch was out the door.

Top leaned back in his chair, lit a cigar, and contentedly blew the smoke at the ceiling. With two clerks like them, he'd endure fewer ass-chewings.

Joseph Shifrin proved quiet and extremely likable, and in no time I felt very close to him. Because he lived in headquarters platoon and worked with Brian, he quickly fell into our circle of friends. His six-foot-two height looked even taller because he didn't even weigh 150 pounds. He had graduated less than a year before from Columbia University in New York City, where he'd studied economics and physics. He was logical, philosophical, and quick-witted. A master at organization, he turned the drawers and files of confusion, mystery, and trash into functional points of reference in his first month. Despite his education and near genius IQ, he wasn't in the least bit snobbish.

Shifrin was engaged to a girl named Jill Daugherty. Above his bunk he had a five-by-seven framed picture taken on a skiing trip in Killington, Vermont, of them hugging each other and laughing, half covered with snow. She was lovely, and they looked like the happiest couple in the world. Sometimes I would stare curiously at that picture and feel certain that they had transcended all the petty games and moods that Jeanine and I had not gotten past yet. Shifrin had his own struggles, though—the war, of course, and the uproar over the engagement in the Jewish Shifrin and Catholic Daugherty families.

Early in the afternoon the day after the promotions, Specialist Reese Fillmore returned from Oregon. Fillmore, like an idiot, had added six months to his tour of duty in exchange for a thirty-day leave anywhere in the world. Like most, he went home. While he was there, someone notified the governor along with the mayor of Fillmore's hometown about his extension, and they honored him as a hero and a patriot. (Such happenings were not unheard of *then.*) He was all over the newspapers and had been treated, along with his parents, to a day on the town. Many of the stores presented him with a gift certificate, and the mayor presented him with a full-sized Oregon state flag. He'd brought it back to Nam and, with the permission of Sergeant Helton, the mess sergeant, hung it from a rafter in the mess hall.

"You know," Brian mused out loud after he and I came back to the office from lunch, "I think every state should send us a flag."

The idea interrupted a conversation between Top and Chief Donaldson, who came over to listen.

Brian gestured at Joe, picking through the mess in the bottom drawer of a file cabinet. "This is kind of a coincidence, but Shifrin and me went through the company roster two days ago and counted up forty-two states that the guys are from. I think the least each state can do is send us a flag for our mess hall. Then Hobson and I could sit under the Indiana flag while we ate and of course we could, if we wanted to, put the Kentucky flag right next to it, and the New Jersey flag, so you two guys could sit at the hallowed Hoosier table."

Shifrin and I exchanged smiles.

"How you gonna get 'em?" Top asked. "Hell, you'd have to write to each state individually. There ain't no department of flags."

"Well, Top, I suppose I could write to the governors. Yeah, I'll do seven letters a day," he proclaimed. "In a week they'll be out and—you know, Joseph, if you did a couple a day, we could have it done in five days."

"That's precisely what we need, more work," Shifrin said, laughing. "But I guess the mess hall could stand a little decorating." He turned serious. "But you know, it just might work and wouldn't it be something if it did. Maybe we could put in a stipulation, that if they don't send us a flag, we'll report them to *Life* and *Time* and the *New York Times*." He looked at Brian. "I'll help, under one condition. You thought of it, Specialist Kitzmiller, so you compose the letter."

Brian immediately began to draft the request while Donaldson scowled over his shoulder. The letter was strong and to the point. Shifrin took out a comma or two, but it remained Brian's letter.

The two got serious about their mission. Kitzmiller and Shifrin typed forty-nine letters to the governors of every state but Oregon, allowing for future soldiers from one of the eight states not currently represented. They got more and more excited by the hour, and in three days all the letters were out.

Almost everyone who knew about the project was excited. "Stupid fuckin' idea," Chief Donaldson jeered. "Probably won't get one inside a year, and they'll want to charge Uncle Sam for that one."

"Hell, you shoulda went away with Huffer," Top said, shutting the chief up.

Maryland's was first to arrive and in less than a week. Then flags from Minnesota, Connecticut, and happily for Brian, Indiana—beating Kentucky by one day. Within a month we had them all hanging from the walls and rafters of the mess hall. The place looked downright festive, and many a meal conversation included a gentle tug or even an ostentatious kiss from a resident. Top marveled how such a simple gesture improved morale. Because the idea had been Brian's, his popularity continued to grow throughout the company. Top and Karch were happy, too, and that was good for us all.

Our good fortune couldn't continue forever. Not long after we decorated the mess hall, one of Top's old buddies from brigade personnel came to ask a favor. The two had served together in World War II and were a part of the old-brown-shoe army that Top was so proud of. Their paths had crossed several times part of the "below the surface" network that looked out for one another—*good old boys*. The man, who looked infinitely more sophisticated than most lifer sergeants, was a sergeant major and more or less in charge of personnel—determining needs, requisitioning, reassignment, the whole works—for the entire brigade.

After the visit, Top sat glumly at his desk. "Damn, why us?" he groaned, his shoulders slumped. "I got enough bad eggs to look after."

Chapter 9

We were getting a bad egg. In fact an egg so bad that he would dwarf the many rough characters we already had, along with those in the 96th. Top was always quick to point out that you got all kinds in the construction-related engineer units anyway, and in his words, "We don't need no special transplants."

Now, because Sergeant Major Rollins evidently had some favors to repay and some more due him from Top, we were to get Private Douglas Cheedah, who was about to be released from the stockade, where he'd done time for being AWOL. Word was that several aggravated-assault and battery charges leveled at him had been plea bargained away. Cheedah had been in the stockade—*military prison*—twice in Nam, once for thirty days and his just completed sixty-day stay. All in all he had nearly eight months in Vietnam, but only half of it counted because time in the stockade—so-called bad time—and because time spent absent without leave wasn't deducted.

He arrived in a jeep that afternoon with two MPs. When they parked in front of our company sign, he just sat there, sullen and scary, and I didn't think he was going to move.

"Okay, this is it, bad man," the driver barked as Top stayed in the background. "Two-oh-ninth Engineers. Report to your new unit!"

Cheedah sat staring straight ahead and remaining motionless for a long time. Eventually the MPs looked at each other quizzically. Obviously they wanted no part of Private Cheedah. The sit-in went on and on with Top doing nothing—probably hoping against hope that they'd just leave. Finally the tall, grotesquely muscled prisoner stood up slowly, then deliberately stepped down from the back of the vehicle. He left his duffel bag, ignoring the driver, who announced, "Forgot something."

He was around six-feet-four and weighed at least 220 pounds, which seemed chiseled on his frame. He was blond and balding, and his skin was brown from filling sandbags and smashing gravel. His eyes were blue and so piercing that I couldn't look at him for more that a couple of seconds.

His record was disgraceful. He'd been expelled from three different high schools. Then, he was given a choice: join the service or go to jail for, among other misdeeds, three counts of burglary and beating the shit out of his girlfriend. He joined the army and signed up to drive trucks. He was nearly tossed in basic when he got into one fight after another, but eventually, after sixty days in the stockade, he completed his training. Upon graduation, he was quickly judged unqualified to drive after leaving the scene of a multi-fatality accident, which he had caused. Unable to perform his MOS, he was put on continuous work details. He'd been given other chances as a cook and as a mechanic, but he couldn't stay out of trouble.

Next Cheedah had volunteered for the infantry—usually an easy job to land, no matter what—but was judged too incorrigible to be trusted as a member of a combat team.

To us, the most amazing fact about this guy was that he'd gone Absent Without Leave in Vietnam. This was unheard of then. Yet Cheedah had disappeared for twenty days, and because of his vivid but varied tales, no one could figure out what he'd done. How in the hell could a man survive on his own, wandering from town to town, village to village, through jungles and rice paddies, in a war-ravaged country, as an itinerant, criminal tourist?

Top talked quietly to the MPs. He didn't want this man any more than he wanted Ho Chi Minh in his unit, but a promise was a promise, and Cheedah would get his last shot. Then they could dishonorably discharge him and get him back stateside, perhaps in jail.

The MPs drove off after tossing Cheedah's bag into the dirt. Top stood squinting in the horrible heat at his new man. But Cheedah ignored Top. Surprisingly he turned to Shifrin.

"What's your name, boy?" he asked.

Shifrin hesitated. "Joe," he answered quietly, showing no trace of intimidation.

"You got a cigarette, Joe?" Cheedah asked, cocking his head, his eyebrows arched, as if he were used to getting what he asked for.

"Nope," Shifrin answered.

"How 'bout you, kid?" he asked Brian.

Brian also answered negatively. Top, fearing he was losing ground, then ordered Cheedah into the office.

"Let's go, Private. We're gonna talk. Inside."

"Well, well, you must be the first sergeant. I'll be a sumbitch. I didn't see you standing there."

Top gave Cheedah an icy stare. "Now, goddammit!"

Brian nudged me, then Shifrin. "I bet this guy doesn't have to prove he's not a virgin."

Shifrin bit his lip and stayed in control, but I couldn't. I let out a short burst of laughter, which was a mistake. Both Top and Cheedah glared at me.

"Something funny?" Cheedah asked, as if he not only had authority but real power, even though I outranked him by three grades.

I looked away and then, realizing that was no good, responded, "Wasn't talkin' about you."

"Like hell," he answered. "You ain't too fuckin' smart, are you? Fuckin' with me. I don't appreciate it, and I ain't takin' fuckin' shit off anybody. You starched fatigues suck shit."

Top turned irate. "Cheedah, who in the fuck do you think you are? I haven't even decided where I'm gonna put you or even if I'm gonna keep you here, and you're tryin' to start a goddamn fight. You don't quite understand where the hell you are, do—"

"Hey, Top, I don't give a shit where I'm at. Understand? Go ahead, do what you want. I don't give a shit. I'd go back to Long Binh Jail, but they don't want me, either, and that's a goddamn fact. I'll get a DD, and then I'll be stateside. You send me back to LBJ, and I'll be on the streets of Oklahoma and Texas that much sooner. So let's don't kid each other. I don't give a fuck who you are."

Top had his hands on his hips. His eyes were fierce. He wasn't used to being stood up to, especially in front of other men. "How old are you, Cheedah?"

"Twenty-two."

"Twenty-two. Why do you want to fuck your whole life up? You know you coulda come in here and showed me you'd work, and you coulda salvaged your whole army experience. Then, when you got out, you may have even got a general discharge and given yourself a start in life. Why would you wanna blow a damn decent chance like that?"

Cheedah smiled. "Because I'm a little bit different, First Sergeant. I don't think that way. I don't give a fuck, period. About anything." He waited, giving the silence an opportunity to accentuate that last point. "Now," he said raising his hands in a peaceful gesture and becoming almost friendly. "Supposin' I was to give this a shot, just to see. I'm sure it's got some advantages—beer, pay, better work hours than the stockade, a better job than bustin' rocks. All right, fine. But I tell you right now, I ain't afraid of the other shit that keeps everybody else shittin' their pants. My ol' man's doin' life in Leavenworth. I got a brother doin' ten years for robbery, and he killed two men. State couldn't prove it. Understand? Doin' what *I* want, it's how I'm made." He grinned broadly as if he were speaking to a child. "See, Top, you ain't gonna reform me."

"If that's the way you feel, let's forget it then. I'll get them MPs back. I don't give a fuck, either. I got a company to run, and no bad-assed misfit's gonna give me another headache."

We went inside the orderly room. Cheedah leaned back, maintaining his grin and helping himself to a cigarette from an abandoned pack of Chief Donaldson's. Something horrible emanated from that smile, and coupled with his eyes, which flared with a taunting but relaxed hatred, he was intimidating beyond words.

I could tell, however, that Top felt an obligation to Rollins to give this a shot beyond fifteen minutes. I was sure he was looking for a way. "Man wants to throw his whole young life away, it's a damn shame, but it ain't my problem."

Cheedah laughed. "Some pitch, First Sergeant, some fuckin' pitch. I really wanna throw myself at your goddamn boots and beg to work my ass off because you got so much fucking aura around you that I can't resist it." He laughed again.

A long silence then passed, and I was sure Top wasn't going to break it first.

Then from out of the blue, as if he'd made a momentous decision that would please everyone, Cheedah announced, "Okay, First Sergeant, give me a fuckin' job. I'm gonna take your job. I may not like it, but fuck it, you're a man. I respect that and that alone. This military kiss-ass major-colonel-general-sergeant shit don't mean fuckin' beans to me. But you're a man. I'll give you that. You want to see what happens, then we'll see."

Still angry at being pushed around verbally, Top took a deep breath. I'm sure he knew it couldn't work. Yet he scrutinized Cheedah. Top wasn't about to give Cheedah a regular job now—not after his disrespect and aggressiveness. Top would make Cheedah earn it.

"I ain't got a regular job yet. Maybe I did a while ago, and maybe I will again in a week. That'll be up to you. What I do need in the next ten days is a shitload of sandbags filled, and I understand you're good at that. We got a man who seemin'ly can't do nothin', and I got two new men for the equipment platoon that they can do without for a few days. You're with them.

I expect a good goddamn day's work out of you, too. In a few days we'll talk again about what you might do for us beyond that."

"Fillin' fuckin' sandbags, huh?" Cheedah laughed. "Shit. I shoulda known that was comin'. Ah, what the fuck."

Three days went by. Cheedah worked, and he was also at the EM club each night, drinking hard. He had borrowed twenty bucks from Top, of all people. At fifteen cents a beer, he was knocking down about twenty a night. On his fourth evening we were down at the club ourselves after playing basketball. At least two hundred men were there, drinking that night. I sat at a round table with Brian, Hobson, Champion, Shifrin, and Glasscock. Cheedah saw us and, to our dismay, decided to join us. We tried to come off as if we knew lots of guys like him, but we had difficulty pulling it off. As he dragged up a chair without asking, we were all uneasy. Word was he'd already cold-cocked a guy from the 96th the night before, and rumors flew that there might be trouble if that guy came back with his friends.

"Hey, McClain, Laughing Boy, you gonna buy me a beer?"

"Sure." I couldn't have said no. I didn't want him for an enemy.

He was wearing a sleeveless T-shirt. He had huge, unusually hard shoulders and arms. His triceps seemed bigger than most people's biceps. Emblazoned on his right shoulder was a tattoo—a German Iron Cross, embedded with a devil's skull. Above were the words Born To Raise Hell. On his left shoulder was a naked lady standing in a flaming roadster, holding an unfurled banner: If You Can Beat Me You Can Eat Me! Across his back, in the region of his right shoulder, was a springing spotted cat. He noticed our curiosity and told us quickly that he had one more tattoo that he was particularly proud of and volunteered right then and there to show us. "Yep, right above the ole lavender monster," he said with a laugh, "I got a triangular roof with a hanging sign that says The Tool Shed."

Caught off guard, we laughed, with Cheedah bellowing the loudest. Then he cuffed Shifrin on the back of the head and added, "Little fact like that wouldn't keep you from giving me a blow job, would it?"

Shifrin looked away, then shook his head. I headed for the bar. When I came back with a tray of seven ice-cold Carling Black Labels, I gave Cheedah the first one. By the time I'd placed a beer in front of each guy, Cheedah had tossed his empty, crushed can on the table, wiped his mouth, and said, "Thought you were gonna buy me a beer, McClain."

I felt awkward. I wanted to do a favor or two for this guy to keep him off my back, but I didn't want to appear to be kissing his ass. Fortunately for me,

Hobson had also chugged his beer and announced, "Yep, 'bout time for annuter wound." He got up and came back with another $1.05 round of seven.

"So how's it going so far, Cheedah?" Brian asked.

Cheedah flashed that horrible smile, then squinted cocking his head. "Kitzmiller, do yourself a favor. Don't ever go to prison. There's some big boys in there that might be very interested in you. You understand what I'm sayin?"

Brian blushed. "Ah, eat it."

"Did the firt thardent tay anytang about where you're gonna wouk yet, Teeda?" Hobson asked.

Cheedah watched Hobson carefully as he talked, then said, "Wow! What a mouthful!" Then, "No, nobody's said shit. I just might go see that grumpy fuckin' bear tomorrah mornin' and tell him I'm a little sick of fillin' sandbags. Must've done five hundred already here, and counting what I manufactured back at LBJ, I believe I've filled half the bags in Nam. I'm gonna start initialin' them, so I can prove that. Then the troops'll know they got an official Doug Cheedah Sandbag."

The atmosphere loosened up in the hour that followed. We were surprised to see a personable side to Cheedah. He definitely liked to tell stories, and every one of us found him riveting in a freakish way. He was more eloquent than I'd have guessed, too. We laughed at his rude jokes and murmured exclamations at his stories of mangling men in fights or spitting in an officer's face or backing his father down with a crowbar when he was fourteen.

"Hey," Glasscock said, "I don't mean any disrespect, but that's an unusual name, Cheedah. What kind of name is it?"

"It's an animal's name. Big fuckin' cat like a leopard, only faster than anything on earth. Surprised you never heard of it."

"That's *cheetah*," Brian pointed out. "Happens to be spelled different."

Cheedah was grinning. "Far as I know our family name was once Cheatham. But then it changed for two reasons. First off, my granddaddy was about the fastest motherfucker you ever saw in a fight. He'd smoke a man's head, I mean smoke it—fourteen, fifteen punches before the opposin' dude ever knew he was in a fight. Then of course it's a little late. Well, Granddaddy liked his cards, too, and from time to time a few unwise men accused him of cheatin' and said he had the right name. So, after a few barroom discussions, Granddaddy changed it. And it made sense. Hell, he never cheated a soul, but he was as fast as a damn cheetah, so he set that little matter straight. Only poor Grandpa couldn't read, so he damn sure couldn't spell." He roared. "But what the fuck?"

Brian was the first to call him by his first name. "Hey, Doug, what's this about you going AWOL over here for three weeks?"

Cheedah's eagerness to share this bizarre story radiated in his eyes. "Yeah, fuck, yeah, I did it."

"How'd you survive? I mean, where'd you go? Weren't you a little afraid?" Brian continued.

Again we got the smile. Something evil oozed from him. Though I'm a little ashamed to admit it, I actually wanted to hear what he had to say.

"I knew exactly what I was goin' to do, and despite what you might think, it wasn't that big an accomplishment. I just walked off the compound during the night. In the mornin' I came down Highway One, hitchhikin', like a guy would on his day off. Got picked up four times by our guys, once by the MPs themselves. I made it to Saigon and fucked around, stayed in a hotel three days next to the best whorehouse I know of in the world. Walked the streets a lot. Even saw Westmoreland riding around like some fuckin' king three separate times."

"I had two hundred bucks on me. I'd waited until the day after payday to book, plus I cleaned a little ass playin' poker half the night. I'm gonna give you boys a little advice, if you ever want to try it. If you got money, a lot more's possible than if you don't. I left Saigon after three days and nights in that whorehouse. I thought I might make my way up to Hanoi. What the fuck, I mean I'm over here. It's an anus of a country, I didn't figure on comin' back, so I thought I might take it all in."

He shocked the whole beer barn with a piercing scream followed by a maniacal laugh. Then in a deep mocking voice, he said, "When I left Bravo Company, Third Battalion of the Four-Hundred-Seventy-Second Transportation Asswipe Brigade, I stole our CO's forty-five and a couple of clips. Took my own bayonet, after I sharpened it for an afternoon."

He poured half a beer down his throat, then went on. "Anyway, I caught a ride to about thirty miles north of here. I had two canteens of water and a pint of Early Times and some beef jerky that my uncle sent me. I also took a fairly good map, compass, cigarettes, Zippo. Fuck, I figured I was ready for anything."

"I remember I went through some rice paddies and hit a village, just some old ladies talking up that gook gobbly-cackle. I went on the edge of some jungle, then I come on a fuckin' tiny path, kinda wandered on and on. What was funny as fuck, I hear this stompin' around, so I freeze and wait it out. I'm thinkin' 'fuckin' Cong.' Then I see a whole fuckin' squad of ground pounders. Yep, our infantry boys. I yell out, 'Hey, looks like fuckin' Fort Polk's finest!' Man, you shoulda seen 'em. They shit! They hadn't seen me. Hell, I coulda bushed half of 'em with my fuckin' pistol. They're freakin' out, half froze, and I'm standing there wavin'. I get the feelin' their squad leader wants to talk to me or shoot me, but he doesn't have the balls to do anything. So they go on by, lookin' for Charlie, I guess. Good fuckin' luck, you clumsy bastards. And I go the other direction on vacation." At this he burst into laughter again.

We didn't know whether to believe him or not, but we were all ears.

"I kept headin' north, day and night. I was conscious of Charlie. I mean I knew he was out there, and I took this into consideration. But to be honest, I was a lot more worried about steppin' into a fuckin' booby trap or landmine than gettin' shot. I got up near Pleiku, then I wandered west. I'd been through a few villages. Those people were mostly very nervous, and I can tell you they didn't want any trouble. One fuckin' mornin' about ten or so I squatted down to take a shit just inside a tree line. About the time I was pickin' out some nice broad leaves, I got a fuckin' burst, had to be an AK-forty-seven. I hit the ground hard and pulled my pistol. I put it in my mouth while I pulled my pants up. I waited damn near twenty minutes, and then I decided to move. I started crawlin' slow, and I mean on my fuckin' chest, for prob'ly fifteen minutes. Then I got up and went tree to tree, deeper into the jungle.

"It wasn't until afternoon that I figured I might've lost him. I mean I ain't got a lot of patience, but I figured I been as patient as any man might've been. But that was it, fuck it, no more, I was done. 'Okay Charlie boy,' I thought, 'you leave me alone, and I'll leave you alone, or let's do it right now.' Then, after a while I almost felt free. I did feel fuckin' free. Then I felt him. I mean I didn't see him, smell him, or hear him. I just felt the little dink's presence. You with me?"

He squashed another can in his hand then helped himself to Glasscock's beer. "I like to mix it up you know, always have. So I was a little mad at this teeny bastard, but I wasn't about to lose my cool. I was just gonna lay back and take his ass out. I slowed down and crouched like I saw something ahead, but I'm focusing on what's behind me, which ain't that hard to do. I heard him then, so I go a little slower and pull my pistol like I'm gonna shoot something ahead. I'm lookin' down now with my head cocked so I can sorta see around my shoulder." He demonstrated this.

"Then I manage to turn around in this thick clump of vegetation, and I saw him, finally. He was assumin' I wasn't doin' what I was doin', so he sped up, just enough. He must've been a little impatient by that time, too. He came into my little den, and I swear to God, right after he passed me, the little dog knew he'd made a mistake. His shoulders slumped like he was sorry, so fuckin' sorry. I mean, *bang,* that quick, after three hours.

"I thought about noise. I didn't want to use my pistol if I didn't have to. Very carefully, but quick, I reached over his left shoulder and grabbed the barrel of his rifle. Then, I guess by reflex he pulled back and down. I had my knife completely through his neck before he knew it was in. The blade went in so easy, at first I wadn't sure it was inside him. I mean I cut him so hard and clean, I damn near decapitated him. Hmmp…What a nice feelin'.

"I took his ears for souvenirs, I got 'em in an envelope in my footlocker. They're shriveled, damn near black now, I shoulda put 'em in a bottle of whiskey. A buddy of mine in the stockade tol' me." He shook his head at this obvious mistake. "Ah, well, live and learn. Anyway, I had an AK-forty-seven now, but only one partial clip of ammo. I felt damn good about havin' that rifle, though. I felt like I could protect myself from a longer range, and I could hunt better."

Cheedah demanded that someone go and buy another round. Champion shook his head, smiling, but he obeyed, and Cheedah continued. "I got near a village that night. Gooks were workin' in a small rice paddy. They had a water buffalo. I decided to shoot it and have a feast for dinner. I was also enjoyin' the fact, in my mind, that here I was alone and all and I was about to go in and kill their fuckin' animal and see if any of them had balls enough to do anything. Then I changed my mind when I saw this sweet-lookin' gook, about seventeen or so. I gotta say she really made an impression, and I decided I'd rather have her than the water buffalo. Man, she was somethin', and I got to thinkin' what the fuck was I gonna do with a water buffalo anyways? I might have had one big fuckin' steak. So I sorta start lickin' my lips thinkin' about that gook. She was better than any whore I saw in Saigon. I decided to wait until dark."

I remember thinking that Cheedah was from another world, one I knew was there but had not experienced. He went on, his eyes wide, seemingly searching us for approval or possible betrayal.

"She—well, *they*—lived in this little hut not far from that paddy. Anyway, long after dark I went into that hooch. Walked in like I owned it. They were sleepin' on these mats and had little piles of leaves and torn up garments, like for bedding. A stinky candle burned on the floor. Their whole gig made me think of Indians livin' in teepees. The mamason woke up first, and she screamed somethin' in gook. The papason, realized he was in a jam and stared hard at me, too scared to move. Myself, I wasn't too alarmed. I had my AK-forty-seven around my shoulder, and I had the bayonet in one hand and my forty-five in the other. I thought about takin' 'em all out but the girl. But I didn't. I'll be fucked if I know why. I mean I wadn't afraid, but I just didn't feel quite right about it. So I go, 'Sorry, wrong house,' and turned around and left. Said piss on the cow, too." Cheedah turned his new beer upside down and chugged the whole can.

"Goddamn, you guys, give me some fuckin' beer, all right? You bring me six beers, and I'll show you somethin' about drinkin'. Go on, get six beers and tell that fat-ass bartender not to open 'em, either."

"Hey, look, Cheedah," Shifrin said suddenly, "you want to start chuggin' beers, that's up to you. But if you get drunk and rowdy, we're not gonna be any part of it. I guess what I'm sayin' is if you're gonna do it, buy your own six beers."

Cheedah squinted. "Shifrin, you talk like you're somebody's boss or somethin'. Spec Four, that ain't exactly a general. You know somethin', Jewboy? I got an expression concernin' a man's rank: 'Stripes don't cover ass.' That make sense?"

Shifrin took a breath, then a swig from his can, and I wondered how Cheedah even knew he was Jewish. I was concerned Cheedah was going to press this, but he backed off.

"As I was sayin', I decided to leave the dink family alone. Cost myself a good ride but, hell, I still had a damn good time traipsin' around all them days.

"Anyway, my trip got boring. I fucked around another couple of days, and then I caught a ride from a Huey pilot I met in Pleiku, a crazy bastard who didn't give a fuck. Took my ass to Da Nang. That's where it ended up, my vacation. I got in this big fight in a bar in Da Nang with a bunch of wing nuts. You talk about pussies, the air force is full of them. I'm beatin' the fuck outta everybody that wants to join in, havin' a ball, when all of a sudden the MPs come in and start swingin' their fuckin' clubs. I clipped a dude, too. I hit an MP about as hard as you can hit a man. He'd swung at another guy and missed. I saw this movement outta the corner of my eye and started movin' to where I thought he'd end up, and sure enough—man, I took a half step and jacked that ol' boy like you couldn't believe. He never knew what hit him. I split his face wide open, and it felt good. Trouble was, then the MPs came solely after me. And since the fight was basically me against a bunch of chickenshits to start with, those same individuals joined in with the damn cops.

"Look at this." He pointed to a scar on his forehead. "Fuckin' MP got me with a stick. I never went down till about twelve bodies were on me, though. Next I knew I'm in handcuffs on a Huey, headed for LBJ and yellin' my ass off for that damn MP. I didn't see him again, but I'll never forget him. His name is indullable in my brain, and I'll get the fucker someday."

"What was his name?" Brian asked.

"Smith."

At this we all burst out laughing, Cheedah the loudest. "So I'm about due for another vacation. Gonna cross the DMZ someday and march up to Hanoi. Check out some of that commie pussy. Glasscock, go get me six beers—and now."

Glasscock grimaced, but did it. "There you go, Chief," Bobby announced, pushing six beers in front of Cheedah.

"Glassdick, you're a damn good sumbitch. Your wife ever needs an extra eight inches, just to see what it's like, I'm available, free, for you."

"That's good to know, Cheedah." He stretched, throwing his chest out. "'Cept I bottom out myself with her."

"That's good, Glassdick, but I'd keep goin'. Don't let that screamin' stop you. Hey, that reminds me, boys," Cheedah was now taking the tops off his beers with a P-thirty-eight. He was amazingly adroit with the tiny can opener, and he stacked the metal circles in a little pile. "You know how I can make my dick eleven inches long? Eleven, that's no shit! You wanna know how I do it?"

"How?" Hobson asked, grinning.

"Fold it in half!" Cheedah screeched.

When we stopped laughing I noticed Shifrin just sitting with his arms folded, and Cheedah had six open cans of beer standing in front of him.

"Who says I can't drink all these fuckers in thirty seconds?"

"I have some doubt," Brian said.

"When do you get paid, Kitzmiller?"

"Same day as you."

"All right. I bet twenty bucks I can kill all these in no more than thirty seconds."

Brian looked around. I could see he really didn't want to bet. In fact I had a feeling that we had all gone too far with this guy. "Nah," he said. "I can't afford it. I got a hundred a month automatically goin' into savings, and that only leaves me around thirty bucks for the whole month."

"Come on, Kitzmiller, what the fuck? Either you're gonna have fifty bucks total to fuck around on the next few days, or you're gonna see a feat so stah-pendous you'll be tellin' your grandkids that was the best twenty bucks you ever spent."

"Nah, I don't wanna."

"Okay, Wonderboy, ten bucks."

"I might be interested," Glasscock said. "But you can't spill any."

"All right. Glassdick's in for ten. McClain? You in?"

"I suppose," I heard myself saying, hating myself for it, half knowing that these kinds of bets might now come up daily if not hourly.

"All right. McClain takes his head out of the officer's asses long enough to place a little wager." Cheedah grinned and moved on. "Shifrin, I never knew a New York Jew that didn't get a hard-on at the chance to make some money. You—"

"Nope. I'm not in."

"Hobson? You like money? Half a dozen rides at the whorehouse just for the taking. You a player?"

"Otay. But I don't tee how you can do it wittout 'pilling tum. And tatz againt the ruleth. Wight?"

"Hobson, now I might have a little run down my fuckin' chin. That's okay, though. I'm a gentleman, and my word's good, you're not gonna be taken. By the way, the last guy that questioned me talks like you, too—now."

Cheedah let that sink in for only an instant. "George Champion, you seem like a fella who knows the score. You in?"

"I guess, man."

"Good, man. Champion is used to making wise wagers with honest men."

"Wait a minute, Cheedah," Champion said. "Now it's true we rarely have a man of your caliber amongst our asses. But suppose you lose? That's forty bucks. When you gonna pay us?"

"Forty?" he asked indignantly. Several other tables had stopped what they were doing and were listening. "Hey, I'm not done with Kitzmiller and Shifrin yet. And don't worry, Champion, I'm good for it. Kitzmiller, you in now? All your buddies are. Ten bucks, no biggie."

"Yeah, I guess."

"Shifrin, you don't wanna be the odd man out?"

"Yeah, I do, Cheedah."

"Okay, Shifrin sits on the sidelines goin' over his fuckin' duty roster. Hey, I tell you what. If I do it, your bet will be that I stay off the duty roster for six weeks against my ten."

"Nope."

Cheedah winked and shook his head. "All right, boys, let's not lose sleep over the Jewboy. Whose gotta watch with a second hand?"

"I do," Hobson answered.

"Okay, you're the timer. Start whenever you're ready. Man, am I thirsty!"

Much of the background conversation had dwindled so that the jukebox was now the primary source of sound. I remember thinking that we usually avoided many of our own comrades from the 209th at the club because we were leery about how they behaved when they were drunk. Now all eyes were on us as we hosted what had to be one of the major-league rabble-rousers and brawlers in the entire armed forces.

Hobson began the countdown. "On your mawk, get tet, *doe!*"

I'd never seen anything like it. Cheedah opened his throat somehow and poured the beers down as fast as if he were emptying them on the floor. After each one he extended his arm, crushed the can and dropped it on the floor. Then, after a quick breath, he quaffed another one. The extended-arm ritual of crushing the cans between chugs took roughly twice as long as the actual drinking. The crowd began yelling various forms of encouragement, with some chanting. In a mere twenty-six seconds, Cheedah finished. He had consumed a six-pack in under half a minute. He stood and put his arms up, and Hobson announced the time, causing those around us who understood what had happened to cheer.

Cheedah began walking in small circles, making strange guttural noises not unlike wheezing, and then he began punching himself in the solar plexus. About the time Champion noted that we should've stipulated that we won if he puked, Cheedah began to do what he was trying to do—make himself burp. His first couple of burps were somewhat muffled and of normal duration, but as he got going they grew louder, and one belch took nearly ten seconds to get out.

"*Aaaaaaaaaahhhhhhhh*, now that's the way God intended a man to drink a beer! Pay me, boys. And whose turn is it to buy a round?"

"Yours, you crazy man," Champion answered, grinning. "We got our asses hustled."

Most of the guys were sending eighty percent of their monthly pay home for savings. That left about thirty bucks for the remainder of the month. You could live on a compound like ours fairly comfortably for a dollar a day. You might drink four or five cans of Coke for ten cents each. Beers were fifteen cents, a pack of cigarettes twenty cents, and miscellaneous toiletries from the PX sold for a fraction of their stateside prices. That left some money for going in to town on our afternoon off. If you played cards or gambled in any way, you were asking for trouble. While everyone was in pretty good shape before Cheedah's feat, they were down to three or four bucks afterwards.

"Hey, Cheedah that was something," Brian said, full of admiration. "We pay you on payday, right?"

"No, Kitzmiller, you pay me right now. I won't be here in two weeks."

"But you said before, 'When do you get paid?' That implies payday."

Cheedah stabbed the air with his finger. "That's just an expression, Kitzmiller, and you know it. If anybody wanted a special stipulation, they shoulda said somethin' before the fact, not after. I mean, they'd kill you in Texas for that shit." He squinted and tilted his head. "Now you know damn well I was prepared to pay you guys. I'll take it now."

We looked at one another, knowing full well that Cheedah probably had little cash left from the original twenty bucks Top had lent him three days before. There was no point in arguing about money with a person like this. We had been dumb enough to bet him. Live and learn, as he had said. Grudgingly we tossed military payment certificates onto the center of our table until they equaled fifty bucks.

"Well, boys, you've seen a man do what he said he was going to do. I guess I will buy the next round." He looked around the room. His smile had a sloppiness about it and his voice now had a less-sane edge. "I think we're going to have a little fun tonight."

The comment did not make me happy. I could sense what he meant. Plus, as midnight approached every one of us except Shifrin had drunk too much. Getting completely soused was not part of our agenda.

Cheedah returned with ten beers. "Help yourselves, boys."

Hobson and Glasscock each grabbed one. Champion and I were still nursing ours. Brian and Shifrin had quit several rounds before but stayed because of their buddies.

"I'll see you guys in the morning," Shifrin announced, and pushed away from the table.

Not counting Brian, Shifrin looked younger than any of us, yet he was easily the most mature man in the company. I wondered why they didn't just take a guy like that and make him an officer.

"Yeah, I'm goin', too," Brian added, and stood. "I still gotta write Elaine tonight."

Cheedah frowned angrily. "Hey, dipshits. It ain't even last call. What the fuck's wrong with you pussies? 'I still gotta write Elaine,'" he mimicked in a falsetto. "What's she gonna do, send you a piece of ass? They don't close this place 'til midnight. You dumb fucks realize what the guys in the stockade would do for this set-up? Let's drink up and raise a little hell."

"Not me," Shifrin reiterated. "Have a good time, guys." He got up and made for the door.

At this we took our cue. Cheedah objected, saying that no one could leave with any beer he'd bought. Hobson and Glasscock chugged the one they had, and we left Cheedah with several fresh beers.

"Tee you tomorrah, Teedah," Hobson said.

Chapter 10

"McClain! McClain!" Top whispered urgently, shaking me awake. "I need you to drive Cheedah down to the field hospital. He done got the shit kicked out of him."

I checked my watch; only an hour had passed since we had left Cheedah at the EM club. I threw on some pants and a T-shirt. The hospital was three miles away. I brought the jeep around and hurried into the orderly room. Cheedah slumped in Brian's chair. His face had been gashed badly from being kicked several times.

When my eyes met his, he smiled cynically. "You officer-driving-pussy, McClain." he said. "Thanks a lot for the help. Fuckers ganged up on me."

"Get your face stitched up," Top said, "and I'll send someone for you in a coupla hours. Then I want you to report to Captain Karch at 0700. We ain't gonna tolerate you startin' a damn brawl. You'll get that beer barn closed down, and fuck over everybody!"

The doctors were busy with casualties from a firefight some ten miles away, and I wanted to turn Cheedah over officially into someone's care other than the half-asleep clerk who pointed us to metal chairs against the wall.

"When you're in a unit, you stick together," Cheedah berated me. "Unless you're some kinda yella pussy."

"If you want to get in a fight, that's your business," I told him again and again. "You're not my responsibility, and I think the other guys feel the same way. We're not gonna get busted, lose money, and get the hell beat out of us because you want to get drunk and start fights." Finally I shut up and let him bitch.

I stayed with Cheedah for two hours, then came back to the barracks and fell asleep instantly. When I awoke the next morning, an idea occurred to me: *Captain Karch versus Cheedah. Man, that would be great!* Looking forward to the show, I dressed quickly and headed for the orderly room, skipping breakfast.

I was disappointed. When Top had sent Frank McCollough, Captain Karch's driver, back to the hospital for him, Cheedah was gone. The bad boy had disappeared.

News of Cheedah's departure sent a shock wave from the orderly room through the rest of the company. Karch stayed in the orderly room, hoping to be on top of any developments, but none surfaced. No one—nurse, doctor, medic, or clerk—had noticed Cheedah's departure.

By ten o'clock the captain lost his composure. "Goddammit, Top. Why didn't you send two fuckin' men down to guard him? We can't have a man go AWOL in Vietnam, particularly a son of a bitch who's done it before. We gotta look like the dumbest fuckers ever. Christ! He could be executed for deserting in wartime. I'd have shot the fucker before I'd have let him out of my sight. You don't reform scum like that, Top. You eliminate them. That's the only chance you got!" Karch had been a cop in New York City; he had a different way of doing things.

Shifrin, Brian, and I exchanged glances with McCollough. Top glared angrily at Karch but said nothing.

"How the fuck does somebody get off the compound at night?" Karch continued to rant. "Pain-in-the-ass MPs are rampant. A hundred thousand men are stationed here, and not one of them gets out without going through a gate. There must be a half a million miles of concertina wire around us, too. I'm not sure he *could* get off the compound."

"Sir," Brian interjected. "*He* could get off. And on and back off again."

Karch was not about to have an eighteen-year-old kid butt into his conversation, particularly with an opinion different from his own. "Yeah, Kitzmiller? How the fuck do you know? You think you could do it? You think it's that goddamn easy?"

"Sir, I'm sorry. No I don't think I could—but *he* could." Brian went on to tell Karch much of what Cheedah had told us at the club. "Maybe I'm wrong, sir, but I suspect that nothing about this guy is normal or average."

Karch seemed to regret the tension he'd created with his first sergeant. "Forget it, Top. Hellfire, everything's not our fault. I hope Charlie puts the son of a bitch out of his misery. I never want to hear about him again."

"Sir," Top said. "I gotta say I'm sorry about this. But those same people sent us Shifrin. I can't turn my back on 'em when it's our turn to take a shit bushel."

Karch rubbed his face. "I know. The disappointment to me is that we got a damn good record going here. Hell, Westmoreland knows about us, and it's because we conduct our business right. Shit, what a way to start the day. What the hell, we knew we were in for it when we took these damn jobs, didn't we, Top?" At this he strolled out, with McCollough on his heels.

A hard silence followed Karch's departure. Top was not to be so easily placated. "You know, I do everything I can to get that man the people we need, then I train 'em, and keep 'em in line, and see they get promoted and all. I got fuckin' Charlie takin' potshots and sometimes killin' my people. All that pompous bastard cares about is his fuckin' image and how fast he's gonna make major and how his career is going to be a huge fuckin' success because of his one fuckin' year at war. The hell! I got three wars under my belt, and I gotta tell ya, what he thinks matters ain't what fuckin' matters."

"Hey, Top, I really don't see how any of this can even remotely be pinned on you," Brian stated.

"I don't, either," I added quietly, and Shifrin nodded.

"Let me tell you somethin', boys. You're all good kids, and you're smart, and you ain't afraid to put in a day's work. You ain't gonna make a career out of the army, but I tell you it ain't a bad way to go. You'll get assholes around you in any walk of life. When you get stuck with one in the military, though, you're really stuck. I don't care for servin' under Captain Karch. Hell, he ain't gonna hurt me. But he will ruin people's careers and make people's lives miserable because he's got the fuckin' moxie to lead but ain't fit to be a leader. In this man's army, that kind is goddamn hard to derail. In fact they thrive."

I caught sight of Prather as he came to the doorway. I nodded to Top and walked out. As I started the jeep, Prather stopped to say something to Lieutenant Thornberry.

Shifrin wandered out and approached me. "Well, that was quite a revealing moment," he said quietly.

Even though the sergeant had lost his cool, my respect for him grew. If Top hadn't been so pissed off and humiliated, we might have gone the whole year without knowing how he really felt about Karch.

Time passed. When my weekly half day off came at the beginning of July, Brian and I shared free time together for the first time. He had just changed his day to coincide with mine. Shifrin and Brian could not take off the same day, because that would leave Top by himself, so Hobson, Glasscock, Brian, and I headed into Bien Hoa.

We had to be back by eighteen hundred, so we didn't have much time, even though the ride took only ten minutes. For some that caused too much stress, and indeed many guys stayed around the company area, reading or playing basketball or going to the PX. Others would take the morning off instead of the afternoon and sleep until eleven. I liked going to town. Walking around fascinated me and some of the bars were interesting. Sometimes we would go to our air-force base there, to the swimming pool where we could catch some rays and actually cool off.

We rode on a Lambretta, a combination motorcycle/small bus with a roof but open sides, which could accommodate eight to ten passengers. The fare into town was ten piasters, about ten cents. With the temperature in the high nineties, the breeze was welcome.

"Man, I wonder what the Red Sox did last night," Brian said suddenly. He sat beside me.

"Who gives a shit about the Red Sox?" I asked.

"I never told you about this because you got such a big mouth about the Cardinals and the National League, but I happen to dig the Red Sox. I loved Ted Williams when I was a kid. Plus, there's something about those beautiful uniforms and Fenway Park. Of course they've never been a contender since Ted's been gone, but I never forgot 'em, and I always watched 'em in the standings. And I tell you, this year I'm a pretty excited about the old Red Sox."

I was embarrassed. I wanted to launch into a tirade about the Bosox, but I had to admit, I didn't know where they were in the standings. "Didn't the old Red Sox finish in the basement last year?"

"Yeah, dumb ass, but they start out at zero and zero each April."

At this I broke out laughing as Brian turned his head to hide his ear-to-ear grin.

"It figures a guy like you would have a team like the Boston Red Sox," I said. "Jeez, do they even have anybody besides Yastremzski? I guess I always think of them with a bunch of guys like Jerry Lumpe and Clint Courtney. You know, guys who can sort of disappear, and it takes four years to notice they're gone."

"I guess you aren't the expert some of the guys think you are. Courtney and Lumpe were never on the Red Sox. You don't know Jerry Lumpe from Lumpie Rutherford on Leave It To Beaver."

I was smiling. "I didn't say Lumpe and Courtney were ever on the Red Sox. I said guys like Lumpe and Courtney. Let's see, guys who can actually play on the Red Sox…well, there's Yaz, oh, and that number-eight guy. What's Yaz's number?"

"Eight, dipshit."

"Oh. Hey, let's not forget Rico Petricelli," I said. "They still got Frank Malzone, and Bill Monbouquette, or are those guys on the Senators or A's now?"

"Oh, you stupid shit! You honestly haven't heard of Tony Conigliaro? Reggie Smith? Jim Lonborg, who happens to be having one hell of a year?" Brian tried to lecture sternly but was having a hard time not laughing.

"Oh sure, sure," I said. "Which one of those guys was on *Bowling for Dollars* all those times?"

We pulled into town. "I'll tell you this, funny man," Brian said as we stood to exit. "The Red Sox will be around till the end this year. They got a shitload more talent than people realize."

"I'll write to Dean Chance and Harmon Killebrew and Al Kaline and Frank Robinson then and tell them not to spend their World Series checks too soon."

We walked the streets for nearly an hour, checking out the near-primitive shops. For the most part the people ignored us, with the exception of the children looking for handouts or wanting to take us to a whorehouse. As we walked by the bars a Vietnamese girl might smile and invite us in. After a while in the sun, Glasscock suggested we grab a beer.

We walked in to a place called the Kitten's Lounge, and as we were getting accustomed to the darkness we heard our names being called.

"There they are! Top's and Prather's boys—and ole Donny Hobson. Get over here and have a drink on our ass." The fanfare and invitations came from Paul Ghent and Mitch Woodson from the maintenance platoon. Except for Hobson who lived with them, we didn't know them well, but they had always seemed like decent enough guys. Woodson, a loose-limbed, lanky cowboy from Montana, had a joyous fit when his flag arrived. He was so moved that he struck up a conversation with Brian after mail call, and the two developed a rapport. Ghent was on the quiet side, seemingly willing to share a laugh or drink a beer, but not particularly easy to get to know. From Arkansas, he was small and wiry with pale gray eyes the color of dirty ice.

We sat down with them. An attractive Vietnamese girl named Li San came over for our orders and tried to hustle us for Saigon Teas. When we wouldn't go for that, she ran her fingers through Brian's hair. "You very young. You cherry boy?"

We all burst out laughing. Brian, a little taken aback, countered, "Li San, you're not related to our first sergeant, are you?"

"I no know your first sahgent, but I pretty sure you cherry boy," she said, and went off to get our beers.

Over the laughter, Woodson asked, "How about it, Kitzmiller?"

"I think we ought to head down to a whorehouse," Bobby said solemnly. "Man, I can show you guys a place that's got some really out-of-sight broads. French-Vietnamese, and they are beautiful."

I knew I wasn't going to go. I didn't want to pass judgment on anyone else, but I was happy that Jeanine's letters came often, and I didn't want to tempt bad luck by violating our relationship. I didn't pray as much as I should have, but when I did, I prayed that I would come home safe to Jeanine. Asking God for such important assistance, then turning around and going to a whorehouse seemed hypocritical. I felt bad enough because I read *Playboy,* cussed, told dirty jokes, and drank all the time.

I was also afraid of diseases. Word filtered through both official and grapevine sources that a strain of clap was incurable. As the story went, if you got it, they'd send you to Korea, in quarantine, until they found a cure. Some guys said this was bullshit military folklore, but we never really knew for sure. Finally, the idea of visiting a prostitute, even if I'd been in the States, or someplace like Amsterdam, was haunting—I felt weird about paying for sex.

"Come on, McClain," Glasscock said as our beer arrived. "Get off this Jeanine shit. Man, I'm even married. Do you think you love Jeanine any more than I love Audrey?"

"Do what you want," I answered. "Right now going to a whorehouse just doesn't fit into the way I got my life sorted out."

I don't think Bobby gave a shit one way or the other about my decision. He was determined to go and didn't want to go by himself—we had been strongly advised not to wander around town alone.

"What do you think, Brian?" he asked.

"I guess I feel the same way Andy does. And I'm not sure what to believe about the clap and all. I mean, suppose you couldn't go home for five years or something?"

Glasscock's neck turned blotchy, and the redness spread up to his face. "Look, dipshit, you wear a rubber. You can wear two rubbers. You aren't gonna get VD if you do that. Do you think I'd risk giving it to Audrey? Fuck, I'm goin' home in two months. It's just that when you've been gettin' it and then you're not, you just need it. I guess I'm oversexed, but I'm not ashamed of it. You guys can keep jackin' off, but for me, shit, these are the best three bucks I ever spend. Hobson, how about you?"

Hobson, who had had a longing look on his face, was suddenly all smiles. "Dat tounds interetting, Bobby. It damn ture do. I tink I might go wid ya."

"Good man, Donny. You're gonna fuckin' love it. Ghent, Woodson, what d'ya think?"

They broke out laughing. "Man, we just came from there," Woodson said. "That's the first place we go every week. That way if we want to get our nut again, we can go at four or five, before we go back. Man, we got this shit figured. We been goin' damn near every week. I ain't sure about this idiot, but I been usin' a rubber, and nothin's happened."

"You guys goin' again later?" Glasscock asked. "You might as well come with us."

Woodson laughed. "*Come* with us! Get it?" Then he shook his head. "Nah, me and Ghent got some drinkin' to do. Some talkin', too."

"What the hell could be so important that you wouldn't get laid for a second time in one day for only three bucks?" Glasscock asked, pushing back his chair.

Woodson then laid a bombshell on us. "Ghent here is going to the infantry."

Silence followed, and Glasscock sat back down.

"What?" I asked.

"Tell 'em," Woodson said in disgust. "Tell 'em what the hell you're gonna do to yourself."

"Aw, eat it," Ghent mumbled, then looked at Brian. "I'm gonna go see your buddy Shifrin tomorrow about typin' me up a 1049 and gettin' the hell out of the 209th and into the jungle." He began to sound enthused, and his eyes came to life. "I done talked it over with Sergeant Martineau and Sergeant Kulp. Kulp says it's stupid, but what the hell did I expect him to say? Martineau's a lifer, and he said he wouldn't stand agin me. I still gotta talk mah way past Top and maybe Captain Karch, but I don't give a shit. I got a right to request anything I want, and I want into the infantry."

"Man, Ghent." Brian's face looked like he had swallowed something disgusting. "That'll get approved instantly. They need ground-pounders bad 'cause they're gettin' killed so fast. Jeez, why would you want to do that?"

"I got mah reasons," answered Ghent. When no one spoke, he went on. "I come over here to a fuckin' war expectin' to be in the fuckin' war. Instead I'm turnin' wrenches in the motor pool. Hell, I got mah whole life to do that. I guess I kinda dreamt about bein' a real soldier, since I was a boy. Mah ole man was in the infantry, mah granddad was in the artillery, and mah uncle was a marine. It ain't right, them havin' one up on me when everything is so close. I wanna see some action."

Ghent seemed one of the least likely guys to be considering such a move. He was no more than five-feet-eight and couldn't have weighed a hundred and forty-five pounds. In my dealings with him, which admittedly were brief, he never seemed to be the least aggressive.

"I don't know, man," I said. "I got a buddy in the 173rd Airborne, and he'd do anything to get out of it."

"But that's just it. I know it'll get bad. That's what war's all about, man. But I wanna know. I wanna do it. Hell, they won't be a one of us again ever this close to combat. If you got the desire and the balls, sign up and go to it, is the way I see it."

"He wants to go back to Little Rock in front of every girl he knows wearin' that combat infantry badge. Don't ya, Ghent?" Woodson asked, half laughing.

"What the hell, that's part of it—and any other ribbons I might pick up over and above the full row everyone gets for just comin' over here. See, I always figured I had balls. I'm a little fucker, though, and, I'm kinda easygoin', so I ain't been in many fights. But I ain't afraid of it. In high school I played one year of JV baseball and football both, then I quit. I needed to work, so I was never able to get a varsity letter. Sounds kinda stupid, but here's where I could make up for that. But, hell, that's only part of it. Man, I want the adventure. I want to go out in the boonies and look for Charlie with mah life on the line. The way I got it figured, we're soldiers first. They always told us that, right? So I'm just doin' my job."

"I can't believe you, Ghent," Glasscock said. "Man, I got two months to go. Sixty-three days. I am gettin' short. In my whole year, though, I never thought about any of that shit. I just wanna get back and get my hands down Audrey's pants. Get back to work at the shit paper mill. Go fishing whenever I want. Play golf on Saturdays and watch the Packers on Sundays. Come home to real food for dinner and settle back to a few beers. I always figured we were pretty damn lucky to be in the 209th. I don't think we lost over four guys in the past two years and two of them were by accidents. Jesus, man, I don't think you know what you're doing."

"Dent?" Hobson asked. "What dut your mom and dat tay about it? And what about tum of toze girlth you know?"

"Well, mah mother is about to have a shit fit, but I can't let that stop me. And I ain't got a girlfriend. But even if I was lucky, like Brian here, and had a chick like Elaine, I'd want her to be proud of me and what I did over here. Not that you guys ain't got the right to be proud," Ghent said.

"Little fucker's got me thinkin' too," Woodson chimed in. "But I ain't anywhere near being convinced yet. What he says, though, about the adventure, the one chance not everybody gets, is true. And what the piss, I'd like to have a little more say about winnin' the war than we do. Hell, it'll probably be over in a year or so, and we'll all be heroes anyway."

"It ain't right for everyone," Ghent said. "But if I'm gonna do it, I gotta do it right now. Sergeant Martineau thought that if I had more than six months done, they wouldn't take me unless I extend, and I don't exactly wanna spend one more day over here than I have to. I just wanna be doin' somethin' different for the next half a year."

"I heard there were three guys from D Company of the 96th that volunteered for combat last month," Brian said. "Top laughed about it. Said they put the 1049s in, and they were gone in less than ten days. Said that their first time under fire they'll hate themselves for it. What if you get all shot up and you're crippled for the rest of your life?"

"Yeah, Ghent," Glasscock said. "Suppose you get shot right in the balls or dick and you can't ever do it again? Or your face gets burned so bad no chick ever wants to look at you? Or you get paralyzed? What are you going to think about this move that you're about to do now, at age what? Twenty? How about five years from now, and you meet this great chick? Or when you're sixty, and the last piece of ass you got was today?"

"Glasscock, it's mah life. Everybody out in the boonies is takin' that chance. I ain't afraid to take mine. Suppose all them years come up, and I ain't done it? And I'm pissed because I let the opportunity go? Sure, I thought about all those possibilities, and it scares me a little, but I got balls enough to go anyways. Thirty days from now you guys are gonna be sayin,' 'I wonder what ol' Ghent is doin' tonight?' You guys'll be sleepin' in your ol' stick-and-tin barracks with ceilin' fans, and I'll be sleepin' under the stars, in the mud, keepin' one eye open and listenin' for Charlie. And you know somethin'? It wouldn't surprise me if you all weren't, maybe a little bit envious of your ol' buddy Ghent."

"Oh, man, Ghent," Brian said. "I wish you all the luck ever. I'll even pray for you. But envy? Man, you and me don't think alike."

Glasscock and Hobson left for their paid romance, and, shortly thereafter, Brian and I left, too. We wandered around a bit in silence, not feeling all that great. There hung a dead fish-human waste odor that seemed magnified during the broiling day. Occasionally a young boy would try to line us up with a girl. "GI, three-hundred pi. You come with me, okay? You come, fuck my sister for three hundred pi. You love it. She tight."

Eventually we came back around to the bar where Li San worked. It had gotten crowded with GIs. "Let's check if Glasscock and Hobson came back," I suggested. "We can all go back together."

Brian nodded halfheartedly, and I could tell he only wanted to hail a Lambretta and go. Squinting through the smoke-filled barroom, we saw no sign of our guys, and as we squeezed through the soldiers I felt unsettled in a place so packed. A couple of grenades would wipe out sixty of us.

We were on the way out when we passed a soldier seated by himself at a table. I thought it a little odd that anyone would be sitting alone. As I headed for the door, with Brian right behind me, the soldier grabbed me by the arm.

"Hey, Murph," he said, "sit your ass down here, and let's have a beer."

Startled, I managed a short laugh. "Wrong guy," I said.

"Fuck you, Murph. Sit down!"

His grip was strong, and I could sense that this could lead to a fight. "I'm not Murphy, man," I said firmly. "I've never seen you."

"Hey, you fucker, you owe me a beer." At this he grabbed me by the shirt and half dragged me to the chair.

"Hey," I said. "Where do you think you know me from?"

"From right here. Last month you were in here with that Sergeant Sorenson or somethin', remember? Then a coupla months ago you were in here by yourself. Both times we got blasted. Remember?"

"Not me, man, I'm sorry."

He looked at Brian. "This guy's name ain't Murphy?"

Brian smiled. "No, he's not a Murphy, he's a McClain, but what the hell, one Irishman's as bad as another."

"Well, fuck me," the drunk soldier said. "I'll be damned. Well, I guess I'll buy you fuckers a beer anyway."

Neither of us wanted another beer. We were starting to run late, but for some reason we sat down with him. He informed us his name was Augie Cerrelli. He was nineteen years old and from Jersey. I hoped we hadn't run into a smaller version of Cheedah. He wasn't a big guy—not quite six feet— and he was neither muscular or fat, just wiry and worn looking. I could tell by his patch that he was in the infantry. "So you're in the Big Red One?"

"Fuckin'-A right, I am. First Infantry Division, baddest of the bad, coolest of the cool, biggest and goddamn best." He added humbly, "I'm a goddamn grunt. A nobody U.S.-issue, GI-fuckin' grunt. Been here damn near seven months. Five to go. Fuck, man. I'm half done here, but I'll be damned if I know if I'll make it or not." He ran his hands over his head and frowned. "At least, I like it more than I did." His eyes drifted as if he were thinking about this for a few moments. He laughed suddenly, then got eerily quiet. "You fuckers get into it much with Charlie?"

I looked at Brian and could tell he didn't have any good ideas. "Nah," I replied. "We got it pretty good. Got shot at a couple of times. That's about it."

"Rear-echelon motherfucks," he stated. "Yeah, I'd say you got it pretty good if you only got shot at a coupla times." His face contorted. "In what? A day?"

I sensed where this conversation was leading, and I was uncomfortable. Our beers arrived, and I made sure I beat Augie with the money. "We been in some interesting spots, but as far as actual fire, only a few times in half a year."

"Jesus," he said, contemplating that. "I bet it's more dangerous in my old neighborhood in Camden."

"Yeah, well, I'm not lookin' to volunteer for it," I said, hoping to sound reasonable. Then, in an effort to change directions, I said, "I bet you've seen your share of shit."

He looked down wistfully. "Yeah, man, I have indeed." Then he was all smiles. "Fuck it, you're looking at a man who don't give a shit. I mean, you're either gonna get zapped or not, right? I know that, and I got pretty good at it out there."

"Where are you out of?" Brian asked.

"Our base camp's between here and Saigon," he said. I ain't 'sposed to be up here. We been in from the boonies now for five days. Goin' out again for ten days or so tomorrow. I'm getting used to the routine, man. But I'm gonna go where I want when I'm off, I tell you that. You guys get fucked today?"

I looked at Brian. I felt no urgency in justifying not getting laid. "Yeah." I murmured.

"Me, too, guys. I nailed a little-assed gook that couldn't have been more than sixteen. Nice. Course she knew more than your average thirty-year-old back stateside." He laughed. "But what the hell. We're here to kill these people some days and fuck 'em on others. I wonder if they got it written down which days we do which one." He bent over laughing again, and then the smile vanished. Slowly he wiped his brow with his arm. "Yes, I have killed many, many men."

I glanced at Brian again, and I could tell he was getting freaked out. I wanted to go. But we remained silent, not asking him what he intended us to.

"I've killed eight men—that I'm sure of because I shot 'em until they didn't move anymore. I've *hit* fucking more. It ain't no big occurrence, you know. Hell, I got a Bronze Star, and I been put in for a Silver. It's weird, man. I mean you get in it, then you're out of it. It's either-or. It doesn't last forever if you don't get hit. Either you're gone, or it's them, and so far, man, I done okay. I've lost some real fucking buddies, though."

At this he shocked us by bursting into tears. "Fuck, this man. This is some fucked-up shit. I mean you've heard of 'kill or be killed'? 'Search and fucking destroy'? You think Charlie wants to be found and destroyed? Fuck. Every day is a goddamm gamble, and that's the best you can say. You fuckers don't have any idea."

He sobbed, and I felt embarrassed. I'd have bet a good many of those in the bar were aware of his state, which would explain why he was sitting alone. He sat with tears running down both cheeks, oblivious to shame. After a minute or so he chugged half of his beer. He stared at some other soldiers and laughed suddenly. Then he looked straight ahead, and again the tears poured down his face. I suspected he was crazy.

"Hey, man," I heard myself saying though I felt I was on unknown, possibly perilous ground. "It's okay. You're...you're hanging in there. You'll make it." I felt utterly stupid.

He sniffled, then coughed, choking on some phlegm. "Shit, man, you ain't said the half of it. I mean, a lot of dudes talk about it being their time and all, but fuck, I don't believe it. See, guys get killed for different reasons. In the beginning, it's because of panic. You know, a guy just in-country is likely to lose his head. Maybe he runs when he needs to be on the ground. Or maybe he freezes and ain't worth a fuck to nobody. Or he might do something completely dumb like firing too much, drawing attention, then running out of ammo too quick. Or maybe not know what the hell to look out for, like mines.

"Then there's guys that been around and don't panic hardly ever. They get too relaxed, mostly because they're so fucking bored and tired. I mean, you don't know what bored is until you been traipsing around in the hot fucking jungle day after day, hour after hour, and not even seeing a trace of Charlie. After weeks of that, you just can't keep up with it, being an alert, alive, can-do soldier. That haze, it gets in your blood, and you find yourself being stupid. You're too bored and tired to care."

"I never thought about that," Brian said.

"When the shit hits, though—and Jesus forgive me—there's nothing like it. In a fucking second you can go from dead-ass bored to the most excited you've ever been. You don't know what a wild time is until you've been in an all-out fire fight. Guys firing all over the place, people getting hit on both sides. All fucking hell roaring, zinging over your head. Then sometimes it can get really great, like when we get air support—Hueys, even F-4s, and then that momentum turns ass around. There isn't anything like it, man, and like all you do is try to zap as many gooks as you can while they're running the fuck away. That ain't as easy as it sounds. But good God almighty!"

He lit a cigarette, and though his hands shook, no one would have thought of him as cowardly, not for an instant. "Then you realize, man, that you lived through another bad one. You're alive, and you really feel it. There's dead gooks that you killed, and you see their zapped fucking bodies in those ridiculous black pajamas all shot to hell, and you don't only see the blood— and, man, there is a lot of fucking blood to see—but you smell it. It's like you're an animal, man, a wolf or a lion—something that hunts and kills."

His eyes were wild with a dangerous ferocity. He chugged his beer, then continued. "You start sortin' matters out and go looking for your own buddies. Always after a bad one somebody, man, you never thought could've fucking bought it, ever—they're gone." He shuddered, and his jaw quivered. "A guy can be the baddest fucker you ever saw, but when he's dead, he looks so fucking—I don't want to say it, man—so fucking weak and all used up and worthless. Somebody that you were counting on to keep you alive and lean on for fucking strength all these months, man, and you realize that he ain't gonna do all that fucking and drinking and all that hell-raising he'd been bragging about. He isn't anything anymore."

At this he broke into tears again and buried his head in his arms. "I don't want to kill anybody, man, I don't want to kill these people. I just wanna go home, bad. I don't wanna leave any more of my friends over here. It's bad, man. It's bad. And I can do it as good as anybody. I fucking swear to God I can."

Brian put his hand on the guy's shoulder. "It's okay, Augie."

I felt as if we didn't belong there, as if he was, in some realistic nuts-and-bolts way, what a hero was: not pretty but real. I sensed that everyone present felt embarrassed and wary. Others who had watched this scene said nothing. Some had laughed amongst themselves but kept their distance and were quick to turn away. No one wanted to live what Augie was living. And no one wanted to mess with a guy who was in the throes of drunkenness and combat fatigue.

I wondered then about Top a generation ago in the Pacific. Had he been like this once? I had no idea, but I thought what an endless trap this was, this serving your country for a career. Poor Top was back for his third war.

We stayed for two beers with Augie, longer than we wanted, mainly because we didn't know what else to do. I knew I'd never forget him—a person exactly my age, a true twentieth-century warrior.

Chapter 11

The next day, I had time to spend in the orderly room because Lieutenant Prather was meeting with Captain Karch in the officer's mess with Ralph Snyder, a civilian advisor from a civil-engineering firm back in the States. Snyder was an expert on road construction and soil and frequently came up from Saigon to confer with the engineering officers.

Ghent came in and put in his 1049 for the infantry, listing the 4th Infantry Division as his first choice followed by the 1st Cavalry.

Shifrin—having been tipped off, along with Top, by Brian—accepted his part of the chore with a grunt. "Ghent, you need to understand that you don't automatically get a Combat Infantry Badge because you've spent thirty days with an infantry unit in a combat zone under combat conditions. You actually have to have your MOS changed to eleven bravo from your mechanic's MOS. Plus I'll have to put these transfer requests for specific divisions in one at a time."

"I don't care—" Ghent began.

Top came over to Shifrin's desk. "In the damn army twenty-four years, and I never realized that. But nobody oughta get a CIB unless they're actual infantrymen. Well, Ghent, since you ain't gonna get the damn badge without changing to a grunt MOS, you ought to forget this idea of yours."

Ghent's chin jutted out. "First Sergeant, I don't care about the infantry badge. I wanna go into the boonies. I got a right to put in for anythin' I want, and that's what I wanna do."

"Yeah, you gotta right to put in for anything," Top said angrily, "but you're putting in to be a dead fuckin' kid! Plus, goddammit, you're puttin' those boys already out there in danger. They gotta worry about stayin' alive and dependin' on their teammates. You ain't never trained for the infantry, so you got no fuckin' business out there. You're a crackerjack mechanic. Your contribution here is important. Every reliable man is important. Out there you're only another body."

"I ain't gonna let them guys down," Ghent replied angrily. "I fired expert in basic. I can shoot with anybody, and I believe I can take it out there. You ain't got no right to say—"

Top's eyes were bulging. "Shut up, Ghent! Don't tell me what I can and can't tell you. I'm your first sergeant, boy! I'll say what the fuck I want. I also served in the damn infantry—not just once, either. In heat so bad you couldn't breathe. Bugs, snakes, mosquitoes, everythin' they got over here but worse out in them Pacific islands, boy. Had the shits so bad for so long, I'd take a drink and it came right out my asshole. Then they send us to fuckin' twenty-five-below-zero Korea-winter weather with the fuckin' wind blowin' right through us."

As Top yelled, I felt glad that Ghent and not me was the target of his wrath. "You think you even know one fuckin' aspect of real soldierin'? I'm tellin' you that you won't even be able to handle the goddamn discomfort, let alone fuckin' Charlie, who's been fightin' since he was four! Damn you, Ghent, don't you ever tell me what the fuck not to tell you!"

Top had worked himself into a frenzy and was sweating profusely. He raged on. "You tell me you fired expert with a rifle? You qualified with an M-14, and half your shots was off a pillowy sandbag. You ain't never even fired one round from an M-sixteen. Those boys spent eight weeks alone in AIT, eatin', sleepin', and shittin' with the damn thing, not just qualifying, and you ain't never even held one. The goddamn Colt Industries piece of shit fails ever other day, jams worse than a Jap toaster, and you're gonna know how to break her down and fix her under fire? Get the hell out of my orderly room, boy!" With that he returned to his desk.

But Ghent held his ground. "You got the right to say anythin' you want, Top. You was one of them. But you can't stop me from requestin' what I want, and I don't mean no disrespect, First Sergeant, but you know it's so. I'm goin' unless the Fourth don't want me or the cav."

Shifrin stepped in. "Ghent, what Top says makes a lot of sense. I don't think there's anybody in this company who doesn't admire your courage, but it's the wrong move. Your life is too precious."

"Look, Shifrin, mah mind's made up. Just type up mah 1049, and while you're at it, let 'em know I want to change my MOS, too."

Top looked furious but said nothing. He nodded briefly at Shifrin and began shuffling papers on his desk.

"Okay, Ghent," Shifrin said. "It'll be ready in twenty minutes. Why don't you stop in at lunch to sign it?"

Ghent nodded, muttered his thanks, and left the orderly room, which was stone silent for a while.

"Well," Top said. "You just watched a boy argue his way to the worst mistake of his life."

Brian left for the mail and upon his return flipped me a letter. This was another advantage of being a driver: If I was around, I didn't have to wait until mail call. Jeanine's letter was short, but I was thrilled to get it:

> *Dear Andy,*
>
> *The days go by quicker now, and in only a few weeks I'll start up at U of L again. I cannot believe I'm starting my junior year or that I've known you for over two years. I hope my whole life doesn't go by this fast.*
>
> *Summer seems unusually hot this year though maybe it's because you're always writing about hot weather. I never thought I'd see the day when you were complaining about missing winter. See, how many times have I told you that you never appreciate anything until you have to do without it?*
>
> *Get this, Amelia has the grooviest boyfriend. His name is John Teeter, and he's a graduate assistant in philosophy. He is so bright. We stayed up the other night until four talking about life and among other topics, the war. God, why are we there? Why are you there? Anyway, she's really got herself something, if she doesn't screw it up. John doesn't think like anyone I've ever met.*
>
> *I better get going. I miss you. Write me tonight, before you go to the club. By the way, I still haven't approached Mom and Dad about your idea.*
>
> *Love*
> *Jeanine*
>
> *P.S. Amelia and I have decided from the pictures and all you've told us that we'd most like to meet: Brian, Lieutenant Prather, and Joe Shifrin.*

Brian seemed complimented to be listed first among such impressive company. "Geez, what a nice person Jeanine is," he said. "Tell her I said thanks. And I hope I meet her and Amelia next year."

"I sure will, Briney. We could have a hell of a time. You and Elaine both can come down for a few days. It'll be wild. Jeanine would love Elaine, I'm sure. And Amelia is one of the neatest chicks I've ever met."

"You might not like John Teeter," Joe said quietly. "He sounds considerably different from you, Brian, and me—and any of us who are over here. I don't mean to doubt Jeanine's judgment, but this philosophy guy may think he's intellectually and ethically superior to anyone so lowly stationed in life as to be a soldier over here."

"Well, dammit, Joe, we may have to have your ass with us in case he mounts a serious intellectual and ethical attack on poor Brian and me," I said. "Would you and Jill come down to Louisville, too?"

"Possibly. I mean, sure."

"Well, sounds like a done deal to me," I said, genuinely hoping that all of this would occur in a year or so. "Hey, Brian, you gonna let me see what Elaine wrote, or is it too filled with sex?"

Brian seemed hesitant. "I haven't read it myself. I'll do that, and if I'm still in the picture I'll maybe let you read it. I sometimes feel a little stupid actually letting you guys read her letters."

He then reversed his field without any warning. "I don't want you to feel inferior or anything. I mean she knows stuff about me that you guys maybe shouldn't know, and I'd hate for you to be jealous."

"Yeah, you're right. We hadn't even thought about that," Joe said earnestly.

Brian disappeared into the mailroom and locked it.

"Well, if there's pictures in that damn letter, I wanna see 'em, and they better not be stuck together," Top said, obviously in a better frame of mind from listening to our inane conversation.

Again the room got quiet. Upon completing the 1049, Shifrin began typing a new company roster on a legal-sized A. B. Dick stencil. His old roster lay on his desk with a thousand little penciled changes and notations. His company roster was updated in pencil each morning from the morning report and was perfectly accurate. I found him, and the way he worked, fascinating.

While I waited for Brian, Lieutenant Prather came into the orderly room, sat at Top's desk, and scratched furiously on a note pad while Top relocated himself on the desk corner and talked to Sergeant Kulp, who had come to discuss losing Ghent.

Chief Donaldson strolled in and thumbed through a pile of magazines. Meanwhile, two brand-new guys stood signing in and waiting for Top's orientation. Toby Randall, a recent arrival and serious party-lover from the equipment platoon and San Jose, California, had come in to sign out for his half day off and was just hanging around, shooting the breeze. Karch was in his office with Mr. Snyder, leaving Frank McCollough leaning against the Table of Organization and Equipment board, which was nailed to the wall. Finally the mailroom door opened, and Brian emerged.

"Well," I said, "am I going to get to read this one, or are you just gonna give me the highlights, which you ought to know pretty well since you were in there so long?"

Brian glanced around and reddened. "I guess you can read it. It's short. She had to get ready to be in a wedding when she wrote it."

I felt an adrenaline surge. I was about to read an immensely personal message from the great Elaine. As I took the letter, I felt as if I was touching something written by an angel. The envelope and stationery were yellow, she had used a fountain pen with peacock-blue ink, which was unusual enough itself—though it was obviously her trademark. Every letter he'd gotten was the same. And magically the scent rose from them, as though she'd just perfumed them that day. All the other perfumed letters seemed to have nearly run out of gas by the time they arrived, but not Elaine's. She had the touch. I gazed at the envelope and the return address, then pulled out the letter and gently unfolded it:

July 11, 1967
Dear Briney,

I just got back from Mary Lu's house. What a chaotic mess! In case you've forgotten, Saturday is the day. Mary Lu Kingman becomes Mrs. Robert Sheffield.

Mary Lu's choice of her sister Susan for her matron of honor was sheer genius on her part (even though they can't stand each other, as you know) because neither Bev nor I feel the least bit hurt being bridesmaids. Oh, Sweetie, I wish you could be here, it's gonna be the greatest weekend of my whole life.

*I guess I spend as much time thinking about you and
praying for you as I do anything else. I only want you back.
You say that if I'm still available when you're back we'll see
what happens. I want you to know that I cannot wait for that
day.*

*Mary Lu and I talked about you for an hour the other
night, and as happy as she is, she suddenly burst into tears.
And I, imagine this, I was comforting her, telling her that
you were okay and didn't have it that bad, like anything in
Vietnam could be good. Oh, damn, Briney, I miss you so
much.*

*I better go now. It's already midnight and I have to be up
at six. I'm crying now.*

I love you.
xxxxx,
Elaine

I was touched. I mean, not knowing what to expect, I felt like I understood
instantly the way they communicated. I was happy for him, though I felt a
certain envy—not over her but of the way they trusted each other and looked
forward to making everything work. Jeanine and I were a few significant
steps behind them.

"Well, come on, Kitzmiller. Read the damn letter to us, or let's have
McClain do it," Top demanded.

I could tell that Brian was really embarrassed, and I was the one who'd put
him there. Elaine had become, to a degree, the first lady of the 209th. In the
previous weeks Hobson and I had urged Brian to show off her picture so many
times, literally everyone had seen it. As he made the rounds at mail call,
inevitably someone from the various platoons would ask about her. Brian was
in conversations daily about her and whether she'd wait for him, and how
they'd probably get married eventually. Mail clerks were universally
popular, but Elaine seemed to help Brian make friends more quickly than
anyone else.

"I tell you boys what you ought to do," Top said. "The PX has got an offer
where you can take a wallet-size picture and get it enlarged to a five by seven
for a buck. You oughta go and have your chicks' pictures enlarged. Then you
could tack 'em up over your bunk. Maybe then you wouldn't have to be

pullin' out your wallets all the time. If somebody wanted to see one of them broads, they could just walk through headquarters platoon and not bother you."

"That would be a good move for you guys," Shifrin agreed. "And the rest of us, too, as neither of you has contributed much to the aesthetics of our barracks. There's McClain's ten-dollar radio and Kitzmiller's picture of the '63 Bears, and that's about it."

"Hey," Brian said, "that photo's no Miss April, but it's still a nice picture of the team that just happened to kick the Giants' ass for the world championship that year!"

Shifrin frowned and shook his head, but I knew he thought it was funny.

"I agree with Top," I said. "I think we ought to get enlargements made of the chicks' picture. You gonna do it?"

"Ah, I don't really think so. I only got this one. Suppose they lose it?"

"Well shit, have her send you another one," Top said.

"I don't think she has any more of these. And this is my favorite one of her. What the hell. I might do it. Hey, look at this." As if he were trying to change the subject, Brian began fumbling with a large box that had come in the mail for the entire unit. "Let's see what we got to read this month."

Each month we'd get a box of brand-new books from the Department of the Army. I had an arrangement with Brian that he would never take the box to mail call before I had a chance to go through it with him and Shifrin. Anywhere from sixty to eighty books came in each shipment, from the classics to best-selling fiction or nonfiction, to cheap sex books, though not the pure filth with no titles that Karch enjoyed. We'd usually take two each, then pass it on. Our choices eventually got circulated anyway, but the idea of being first was truly exciting. When the three of us were through, *To Sir with Love, A Farewell to Arms, To Kill a Mockingbird, Hot Rods to Hell, Paper Lion, Good-bye Columbus, In Cold Blood,* and *Lady Chatterly's Lover* were in a pile on Shifrin's desk.

"That ought to hold us," I said.

Prather came over and picked out two from our pile.

"Hey!" Brian protested. "That what they teach you OCS guys, to invade the enlisted guys libraries?"

Prather squinted slightly at Brian but said nothing. Then as he walked past us, he suddenly grabbed Brian in a headlock.

"I mean it's sure okay with me," Brian added, "but I hope these guy's feelings aren't hurt too bad."

We'd each seen one particular book that made us smile among ourselves. I had put it near the top as a trap for Chief Donaldson, who, sure enough, perused the box, then nonchalantly stuck the blue-covered book in the shirt pocket of his jungle fatigues.

Throwing discretion to the wind, probably because Prather was there, I strolled over and fumbled through the box. "Say, Chief," I said innocently. "That wouldn't be the only copy they sent of *Defile the Haughty Virgin* you stowed away there, would it?"

The chief reddened. Suddenly, Top burst out into ferocious laughter and in seconds the whole room rocked.

"Fuck you!" Donaldson spat. "I got work down at the motor pool." He stormed out, and I thought everyone including Karch and Prather were going to have a hernia from laughing.

"Well, Andy," Prather said. "You damn well better hope ol' Donaldson never becomes company commander, because your ass will be a buck private faster than you can shit on malaria-pill day."

"Hey, Andy?" Brian asked out of the blue. "What the hell did Jeanine mean by 'I haven't approached Mom and Dad with your idea,' anyway?"

I had never mentioned it to anyone other than Jeanine, and I pondered the wisdom of answering in front of everybody. I did anyway. "I asked Jeanine to meet me for R and R in Honolulu."

"Man," Brian murmured, "what an unbelievable idea."

"Yeah," I answered. "About time for a break. I been here around five months now."

"I was wondering about that the other day," Brian said. "Man, congratulations. You're almost short."

"So I'm thinkin' I'd like to take my R and R pretty soon. Everybody says Honolulu is not a good place if you're single and don't have a girl. So I started asking Jeanine about six weeks ago if she'd like to meet me there in August or September, if it doesn't screw school up too bad, for seven days and the best time of her life—not to mention mine."

"What's Jeanine been saying about it?" Shifrin asked.

"At first she called it greatest idea ever. Then she got a little cold on the idea, mainly because she's thought too much about what her parents are going to say. At this point I figure I got a little better than a fifty-fifty chance."

Top was nodding. "If I was you fellas, that's definitely what I'd do. What the hell you gonna do in Bangkok or Singapore besides catch the damn clap? Sydney'll be nice when they get the hell around to openin' it. Now if I was young and single and still handsome and didn't have no tasty morsel to invite to Hawayah, I'd go ahead and take my chances. Hell, them countries is light-years beyond this one as far as decent places to have fun and get your noodle wet. But what the hell? If you got it, and it's waited for you all this long, you'd better think of gettin' on with it before you flat-ass lose it. Hell, McClain, Jeanine's twenty-one. What the piss has she got to lose? Her ol' man and ol' lady'll get over it."

"Well, she figures she has plenty to lose," I said. "For one, they're paying for most of her education. Another is that they're a fairly close family. And even though she's got a sense of adventure, she's worried about hurtin' them."

"Ah, hell." Top waved his hand. "You can get around that shit, surely. Hellfire. That's what I think I'll do. Meet ol' Betty Jo there. Man, even her fat ass sounds good."

Not long after that a grumbling Brian and I went down to the PX and ordered our pictures. When we returned to the orderly room, Top had a *Life* and a *Time* magazine open on his desk.

"Every time I open a damn magazine there's more about the goddamn war protesters," he muttered. "I never saw nothing like this in my fuckin' life. Shitfire, what do they think, anyway? That everything in life is free?"

"That's your communist infiltration," Chief Donaldson answered. "Shit, you don't think they got those stupid young punks right where they want them?"

I might have given this line of reasoning some consideration had anyone but Donaldson brought it up.

"We had a couple of guys in basic that up and left for Canada," Brian said. "They could never come home. Can you imagine that? Never have the right to come back to the United States?"

"That's the way it should be," Top said. "We couldn't fight no wars if people had the right to decide whether or not to fight in it. Shitfire, in my day, everybody wanted to serve. Now I guess times are so much better that there's a shitload of cowards and softies out there who figure they'll raise hell and stick together and they won't have to go. I guess we'll see about that."

Brian shook his head slowly. "Too late to do us much good, even if they were successful."

"I don't think many of us would be here if we'd had the choice," Shifrin said. "Even some of the gung-ho people—"

"Ah hell, Shifrin, that ain't the issue," Top said. "Hell, I wouldn't be here myself. This ain't like World War Two, when the whole free world was dependin' on us. It's more like Korea. But the goddamn issue is, when your country calls you, you got to go. We may not like it, and we got the right to question it to a degree, but in the end we gotta go. Every boy turns eighteen is gonna face it. We take our country for granted, but for my money she's the best in the world. We owe this to her and to the other little chickenshit countries we support and trade with and protect. Hell, this should be a goddamn free world, and no fuckin' Russian, no fuckin' Hitler, no fuckin' Ho Chi Minh is gonna fuck with us or those poor bastards we protect."

"You think we'll be in wars all the time, Top?" Brian asked. "Taking up for somebody weaker who's our friend? Is that what we should be doin', or should they be fightin' their own wars?"

Top looked confused. "You know, Kitzmiller, despite what I just said, I ain't sure I can answer that one hundred percent. I suppose that if they're our friends and they don't wanna be taken over by the commies and they ask for our help, then by God we oughta kick the shit outta whoever it is that's fuckin' with 'em. But I gotta be honest. I don't wanna go to no more wars. Hell, this is my third, and I'm damn lucky it's an assignment like this. I get pissed when I think about France in World War Two, who we saved and then they shit in our face. Or this country. I ain't sure the South Vietnamese are givin' it their best effort."

"Top, be honest. How long do you figure it'll take to win this war?" I asked, expecting to hear him say nine or eighteen months.

"McClain, let me tell ya somethin'. I ain't in Intelligence. Never have been. But I do know a little about fightin', and I do have connections. And I'll flat tell you somethin'. I don't like this, not one fuckin' bit. Number one is, we ain't takin' ground and holdin' it. From what I'm hearin', we're fightin' fierce battles, like Junction City One and Two. We take the ground one day, and a month later—sometimes a day—it's Charlie's again. That ain't how it's 'sposed to work.

"Number two is, and I don't begrudge you boys this one fuckin' bit, but this one-year tour-of-duty shit? I ain't sure that works. Now when we was island hoppin' back in '44 and '45, we knew we not only had to beat the Japs today but tomorrow, too, and the day after that, until either we was all dead or we won the whole Pacific theater. That was the mindset. We wasn't goin' anyplace. They might pull us after six months and give us a few weeks to get our health back, but basically we only went home to the women and beer after it all ended, after we'd beaten the Japs, period. And the Japs had the same rules. And now the same goes for Charlie and the North Vietnamese Regulars. They ain't done fightin' till it's over. You see what I mean, boys? They know they got to keep killin' and killin', and *we* know we only gotta last twelve months, then we're home free. Compared to World War Two, this is the country-club approach. We're fightin' more to stay alive than to win.

"Another problem with the one-year rotation is this—if they got a half million men here in July of '67, then it don't take a fuckin' mathematician to figure out that they're gonna need a whole different half million to take their places by July of '68. Plus more to take the place of the shitload that's gettin' killed, wounded, hurt, sick, the incurable clap, and all that shit." Top shook his head sadly. "After a year you figure a man is gonna know what the hell he's doin', so they replace that guy with a total green kid, and you know what happens?"

"The overall efficiency of the effort never seems to grow but more or less hovers," Shifrin said.

Top nodded. "I was gonna say the situation has a tendency never to quite make it out of the fucked-up range."

"And three is: We don't know Charlie from the South Vietnamese allies for shit. I mean we probably got Cong workin' in our fuckin' mess hall. These damn South Vietnamese don't seem to have their heart in it any more than we do. In fact, not as much. And boys, I'm gonna tell you somethin' else. We ain't able to use our main strengths to their maximum effectiveness. See, in my view, artillery and air superiority is what's ultimately gonna win it for you. And we got it. It ain't even a question. But it ain't doin' the good it should for us because of the fuckin' jungle and the tunnels. We not only can't see Charlie for shit, but when we do spot him and call in strikes, we still don't see him! He's covered with the thickest jungle in the world, and even if we put our bombs and shells right on top of him, because the jungle is so damn thick, what woulda wiped out everything within a two-hundred-yard radius for sure might not hurt Charlie thirty yards away. Then he's got all them tunnels. We're not sure about whether we're killin' him or not. You mark my words, boys—nobody, and I mean *nobody*, will ever be dumb enough to take our ass on in a desert! It'll never happen. You just saw what happened with Israel and Egypt. This shit here, though, I ain't sure about. Congress don't give up on us, though, we should win her. I just don't know how long it'll take."

Shifrin had gone over to Top's desk and begun thumbing through *Life*. "There may have been quite a bit of opposition before we entered World War

Two, but once we were in, the support was almost unanimous. This isn't the same."

"Yeah, fuck it!" Top said. "I'm damn sick of wars. Hell, I'm sick of foreign countries. But if our own people are so dumb that they don't think we need to stop the commies here, the commies'll take more and more until the whole continent of Asia is communist. Then you got to contend with protectin' Europe and Australia, and pretty soon you're either gonna have a world war or you're gonna give in and lay down."

"So at least we're doing some good for these people," Brian said.

"I hope, anyway," Top replied. "But I half think these people don't give a shit one way or the other. They're sick of fightin', and they really want to be left alone."

"I don't think the protesters even know much about the South Vietnamese people's attitude," Shifrin responded. "Imagine if they did, how much worse the protesting would be."

Chapter 12

Toby Randall was already recognized for his laziness and anti-army attitude. He had made his mark as a true company clown. Over a two-week period he had teased a Vietnamese KP so mercilessly that she had finally come after him with a knife. This had everyone in the mess hall in stitches except for the lady herself and Mess Hall Sergeant Irwin Helton. In Randall's short stint with the company, he had run down the food constantly—which we all did, but he was dumb enough to do it in front of Helton and the cooks. Not five days after reporting for duty, Randall held up his hamburger between his thumb and forefinger (they were always small) and yelled to our table, "Hey, McClain, Brian! I thought they were servin' lunch, not holy communion!"

Helton came for Randall, who barely made it out of the mess hall without getting hurt.

Randall's most recent escapade elevated him from the status of clown to folk legend. At 0400 hours, Frank McCollough, who was driving the KP run that week, woke Randall, designated shotgun for the trip down the isolated country road we took along the outskirts of Bien Hoa. Randall, as usual, had a hangover. McCollough, a dependable, well-prepared soldier, was on the wagon.

McCollough brought his M-14 but no ammunition, thinking that Randall would bring the required two magazines, which held twenty rounds apiece. Unfortunately Randall had fired several magazines on his day off with a buddy from another unit who had access to a jeep. The last time he had requested more ammunition, Randall had felt closely scrutinized by Sergeant Tibble, so he decided he would do without.

He decided not to inform McCollough, who, he was sure, had enough ammo of his own. Besides, Randall had been on the run several times now and considered it safe—even fun. The KP run had gone smoothly for months, so no one really took it seriously or saw it as much of a risk. Had McCollough realized that his shotgun had no ammunition, he would have awakened as many of us as necessary to get the rounds. But he didn't, and despite being pissed at Randall all day, the two were back together that evening recounting the whole story at the EM club.

Brian and I persuaded Shifrin, Glasscock, Hobson, and Champion to join Randall and McCollough at the club for the original version before it became too skewed with added details.

"The truck we usually use on the run was undergoing some big-ass repairs in the motor pool," Randall said. "So McCollough here is forced to drive that zero-zero-three-nine junker that must've fell into Camh Ranh Bay when they shipped it over. So I'm watchin', and ol' McCollough almost gives up on startin' her, but she finally kicks in, which, of course, was our undoin'."

"The damn battery was damn near juiced when I got it to kick in," McCollough added. "Shit, imagine havin' zero-zero-three-nine with fuckin' Randall for your shotgun. That's some bad-assed luck."

"So we rumble on out," Randall continues, "and as we turn off One and head down the road to Bien Hoa, McCollough slams on the brakes to avoid hittin' a dog."

"Couldn't have been a dog, man," Champion said. "Gooks eat dogs. You ever see a dog around Bien Hoa?"

"I know a fuckin' dog, George," McCollough said.

"Remember those skinned, chocolate-covered dogs they had in that window in Saigon?" I asked McCollough.

"Sure, but they haven't killed 'em all."

"Anyway," Randall said loudly to shut us up, "McCollough stalls the truck, trying to save Old Yeller's life. And unbelievably he gets it goin' again. By this time, I think it's safe to say, McCollough ain't too happy about his choice of vehicles. So he goes, 'The next fuckin' time we stop, I'm gonna rev this bitch up to as many rpm's as it can stand, to keep from stalling and charge the battery.' So in no time at all we're done with the town part of the trip, and we're on that ol' dirt path in the boonies, headed for where we pick up our lady gooks.

"Now I gotta tell you that this is an unusual morning. The whole damn sky is lit with flares, and there's heavy-ass automatic-weapons fire everywhere, and I mean damn near on top of the road, too. So as we get within a mile or so of our destination, we forget about the truck's problems and start wondering if we should even be out there. McCollough thinks out loud that maybe we ought to turn around, that they can always send somebody after dawn. Then we remember that that couldn't work 'cause by then the gooks will be all scattered back to their villages or houses in Bien Hoa, and we'll never be able to round 'em up. So we proceed, only slower.

"We pass this flare-lit area, and then I mean we hit some deep-ass darkness. You know there's a reason ol' Mama Cass said that the 'darkest hour is just before dawn.' We go much closer to gunfire than I ever dreamt we would. Then I'll be damned if we don't drive through an artillery barrage that had to be our own stuff being poured right down Charlie's throat. One round, I bet a one-five-five, explodes and the concussion damn near blew us off the road."

Even though the incident had taken place over twelve hours before, I could tell by the way Randall was gripping his beer, he was still shaken.

"We both had had it by then, and McCollough goes, 'Fuck this shit!' And right then and there, we come on a horrible shock—I mean ghastly, too. There's this body, a human body, sprawled in the middle of the road. In our beams it's easy to see the gook had bled all over the dirt trail. McCollough hits the brakes hard to keep from running over him and—you guessed it—stalls out the engine."

"'Oh dear God, no!' I yell," McCollough adds.

"So while McCollough works at startin' the truck, I get out real slow to have a look at the body. I'm shook, too. The guy's wearin' black pajamas. He's been shot several times, and he's good and dead. I know he's a VC."

McCollough jerked a thumb at Randall. "He's tellin' it so cool *now*. Hell, he comes runnin' back to the truck and gasps, 'He's shot to fuck! Let's get out of here!'"

"Of course that's utterly hopeless—"

"—because the truck won't even turn over at that point." McCollough cut back in. "So I inform asshole here that we'll have to run for it. And—"

"—to give him a magazine for his M-14." Randall grinned sheepishly. "Which I ain't got. I knew he'd have a shit fit, too."

"First he looks all over the cab of the truck like some miracle will happen. 'Our Lady, Queen of Bullets, where are you?' Then he quietly informs me that he hadn't brought any ammunition. I couldn't believe it. A guy riding *shotgun,* and he brings a rifle with no bullets. I go, 'What? You goddamn idiot! What do you mean you don't have—"

"I knew he wouldn't understand," Randall said.

"Understand? I still think you're an idiot."

Randall was eager to continue. "I go, 'Hey, Frank, man, I'm sorry.' I mean, I couldn't afford Captain Karch finding out I sorta wasted the shit. I can't risk the article fifteen. I meant to ask to borrow yours last night, McClain, but I was too drunk and forgot and fell asleep. Anyways, I tell McCollough, 'Come on, man, let's go. This truck is too big a target.'"

"Dumb ass." McCollough shook his head.

"So we stew about it for another minute, but eventually genius here realizes we got to go, too. So the plan is that we run all the way back to Bien Hoa, on the road we came on. We figure by the time we get there the sun will be coming up, and either we'll get a Lambretta back to Long Binh, or we'll hitch a ride along Highway One with one of our trucks or jeeps. At that point we're about eight miles from here."

"At least," McCollough said.

"Then," Randall continued, "two bright headlights round the last bend we took and bear down on us, fast. We're about to jump in the brush and hide when we realize it's a damn jeep with two MPs. I mean we're not even aware that these parts of the boonies are ever patrolled by the MPs, or even Bien Hoa itself, at that hour.

"We're pretty damn relieved to see them. I mean, you can imagine. Till the bastards say they knew about some shit goin' on that morning on our particular trail and that there might be a truck or two of ours out there. Also, the one guy spouts somethin' about our safety, but you can tell they're both lookin' at the situation as a pain in the ass. They don't give a shit about safety—well, *my* safety—'cause at that point they inform us that they'll take McCollough back to our unit, or at least to where they can get him a ride on another American vehicle, and they tell me that I gotta stay with the truck.

"'Stay with the truck?' I go. 'What the fuck are you talkin' about?' And this prick goes, 'Government property, and you're designated the shotgun, the protector, of the lives and property assigned to this mission, your idiot KP run.'

"I go, 'What the fuck, man, the son of a bitch won't start. How is it gonna get stolen?'

"He goes, 'Watch your language, punk. You heard me. We are the sole authority in a situation like this, and you're gonna do your job and stay with this vehicle.' Then he cites army regulations, MP policy, US Army Vietnam policy, even Vietnamese law. And, I mean, I start to realize that I'm gonna be stayin' in this truck, two hundred yards away from a firefight, while all these other bastards, McCollough included, even though he did protest for me, are gonna leave.

"Man, I was about to cry. This fuckin' MP dick was passing out a death sentence to me, Toby Randall, age twenty.

"The other one goes, 'You can bet that firefight will be over at first light. The airbase is only five miles from here. Besides, the brunt of it must be a mile away.'

"'Bullshit!' I go. 'Tell it to the fucker who's layin' right here in the road!'

"'I said the brunt of it, asshole,' the guy goes coolly.

"The argument goes on. Then I gotta tell the MPs that I don't have any ammo. I'm humiliated, and those pricks can't believe it. They jack me off about it for a coupla minutes, then they give me three magazines of rounds. Then the short one, the one with the big mouth, tells me he's gonna write me up and give his report to my company commander."

"That statement freezes me," McCollough said. "I mean, Karch has always had so much faith in me, I can't imagine what he's gonna do when he finds out I went on the run trustin' Randall."

Randall shook his head in mock disgust. "Aw, fuck you. The next I know, they're leavin' me. I mean, can you imagine?"

"I couldn't believe it, either," McCollough said. "So I tell Randall we'll be back in no time for him."

"Yeah, thanks a lot, dickhead. You coulda refused to go."

"Hey, the faster I got back, the sooner we're both out of it. Besides, I was goin' right back through the bad part of the battle."

"Yeah, right. And I'm all alone in the middle of the night, not two feet from a freshly shot-dead gook. So anyway, I watch in utter hopelessness as they leave me. I'm torn between the dude's callousness toward life and the absurd fact that the army would have a rule somewhere that would require a human being to stay with a disabled, worthless piece-of-shit truck during a firefight. I'm doubting seriously that the MPs have their facts straight."

"I doubt if they did," Shifrin said.

"Then I'll file a formal complaint on those turds, too," Randall vows. "So then I look at the dead gook, and I get scared. I mean, I'm havin' a damn panic seizure. I get back in the cab of the truck on the shotgun's side, and every second is like a minute, with a horrible life of its own. So I guess I'm in the truck for about four minutes, almost getting back some nerve, when I hear something. I freeze. I hear it again, not far off in the bush on the driver's side of the road. I'm tryin' to tell myself that it's an animal and nothing to be concerned about, and as long as I stay in the truck with my loaded M-14, I'll be okay. But I can't convince myself of that. I'm sure the sounds are human. I do not budge. Then it happens—shots. Five or six shots right into the side of the truck. I got to tell you guys, I shit my pants, bad. I grab the door handle and open it, and for a split second I think, 'What if the gooks are on this side too? I'm dead.' But it's my only chance. I roll out of the truck and land pretty hard on the ground. I lie there for maybe three seconds in a kind of fear that's more like passing from one life to the next. Then another barrage of shots are hitting the truck. God only knows how I didn't get shot, but I'm on my feet and running for Bien Hoa."

"Holy thit, Wandall, did you thoot back?" Hobson asked.

"Fuck no, man. I had no intention of fighting or hiding—only running. I ran with everything I ever had. I could feel all that shit sliding down my leg past my knee. Then I remember that a loaded M-14 weighs a good ten pounds. I don't need ten pounds, I need to fly. So I threw the fucker away. I glance over my shoulder, and I'm sure there's at least two guys chasing me. I go and go, no slowing down. Like hundred-yard dashes piled on top of one another. I ran track in high school, the four-forty, and I tell you I bested my time, combat boots, shit, and all.

"There's nothing left to me, and I know I'm slowin' down, but I keep going. Then, with dawn just beginning to show, I hit the fringe of Bien Hoa. I look back and don't see anyone. Then, I get sick and puke, 'cept there's nothing much down there to puke. And I tell ya, I'm thinking that I may have actually killed myself running. I keep wondering if I'm just gonna fall over dead. My heart is pounding, hurting, and my lungs are like fire. My stomach and my side are splitting, and my legs are rubber. I got on one knee, afraid that if I laid down I'd never get up. I finally start walking again, toward the center of town where I'm sure it's safer. I see gooks starting to wander about, and that wasn't a bad feeling, really. My fatigues are soaked through, and with my moaninglike breathing, these people are looking at me like I'm a spaceman. I gotta tell you, I was amazed at my recovery. I mean in no more than a couple of minutes, I'm almost okay. Of course I'm still loaded with adrenaline.

"'You're okay,' I'm telling myself. I jog a fairly long stretch, rest a few seconds, then go some more. Eventually I'm to Highway One. I'm in luck, and it takes me no time to flag down a five-ton army truck, and these two guys can't believe my story. When we get within a mile of here, all of a sudden the one fucker goes, 'What the fuck is that smell? Hey, you shit your pants, didn't ya? Ah, fuck, man, we gotta be in this cab all damn day.' I mean I'm torn between gratitude, anger, and humiliation, but I hop out and thank those bums. Then I walk on in the gate and head home."

"Meanwhile, I got half the company ready to go rescue his ass," McCollough said.

"Yeah, well, I know, something is probably going on about me. But I got to get clean, and I don't want anybody seeing me this way. I sneak to the showers and heave my pants into a burning pot of shit outside our latrine. I'm happy there's soap in there on the floor. When I get finished I use my shirt for a towel, and I'm tryin' to get to the barracks and get changed when all of a sudden fuckin' Top sees me from down the company street and yells for me to report to the orderly room this second, just the way I am." He chuckled.

"When Karch sees me, he can't believe it. 'This is Randall?' he asks Top 'cause he ain't really that familiar with me.

"'Yessir,' Top goes.

"'Randall, where the hell are you comin' from? McCollough said you were back in the boonies with the truck.'

"I'm stuttering' my ass off. 'Yeah, Top, they hit me. Fuckin' Charlie shot the truck up with me in it. I had to get out of there.'

"Fuckin' Karch goes, 'All right, watch you language there. You're okay? You're not hurt, right?'

"'I'm okay, sir, except that I'm a little sick,' I go.

"'Hell with that,' Karch goes. 'You're goin' on the detail to recover the truck. And it better be there, soldier. The MPs told you to stay with it, didn't they?'

"For the first time I'm thinking court-martial. 'Yessir,' I go, 'but I got hit. Gooks, lots of them, firing on me. I had to get out!'

"'Why didn't you come right here and tell us you were here?' Karch asks. 'You fuckin' think it's your day off or something? Where are your pants? Why are you using a shirt for a towel?'

"And I'm still so shook, I can't think of anything. No lies even. I go, 'I kinda shit my pants, sir.'

"Top gets this grin on his face, and Karch looks at him, and he gets a little smile goin', too, the motherfucker. That's it, though. They don't say anything else right then.

"I get dressed, and when I return there's two jeeps with four guys each, a deuce and a half with ten guys in the back and two in the front, and a three-quarter truck with a shotgun. Everybody's armed to the teeth. "'Course I got no gun and no ammo—again."

At this we all burst out laughing.

"So Top draws me another M-14 from the supply room and four more magazines. So I got a rifle and eighty rounds. There's a total of twenty-three men, countin' Prather, who's commanding the expedition, and his fearless driver, McClain."

I smiled and nodded, though I had been plenty nervous. We had ridden out in a small convoy, with a sense of injustice and determination about us. Despite being scared, I never felt stronger or badder the whole time I was in Nam. We were out to recover our truck, and God help anybody who got in our way. Of course no one expected combat. We had determined by radio contacts that the firefight had subsided, and the infantry had the area secure after dishing out heavy casualties to Charlie. Still, this was, given our normal routine, as close to a planned combat mission as we were ever likely to experience.

We got through Bien Hoa and were on the narrow boonie road, which I had never seen from this direction with the sun up. Somehow it appeared less intimidating. We rounded a curve, and suddenly there loomed our truck. We slowed, half expecting an ambush. Prather ordered us out of the vehicles, and eight men proceeded on foot to check out the area around the vehicle. Not having a book to go by, I'm sure this was all unprofessional and dangerous. But it felt well-directed and caused me to feel like a real warrior.

"Jesus God!" Prather exclaimed.

The truck was riddled by bullets. We never counted the holes, but I'd bet that at least two hundred rounds had been fired into it. For some reason they had not hit the gas tanks. The tires were flat, and we couldn't haul it back with our tow truck. Eventually a smaller detail of men returned with tires and towed it back. No one ever saw the dead Viet Cong.

Randall figuratively and literally had dodged a bullet. He was in the clear, saved by the simple fact that Karch never learned that he had ridden shotgun with no ammunition. The long-awaited report from the MPs never came, perhaps because they had not acted appropriately, either. Both Karch and Top considered the order to stay with the truck improper. Even if it had been correct, no one begrudged Randall his life. For a while a lot of jokes about blackmailing Randall swam about in our circle, but his secret was safe with us.

Later in the week I received a letter from Jeanine that gave me my biggest rush in Nam. She agreed to meet me in Honolulu in early September. Her parents were not thrilled about it, but they saw her as an adult, she said, and they trusted her judgment. She wrote: "I wouldn't care if you invited Brian and Elaine like you mentioned. That way I might tell Mom and Dad that I roomed with her. But, whatever happens, looks like I'll be there."

Physically, I was in a Third World country ravaged by war, with a climate that rivaled hell's; mentally I was as happy as I could be. My heart was full of genuine love; my mind was filled with lust for my bouncy, honey-colored Jeanine and her creamy-soft riches.

When I told the guys, everyone seemed delighted for me, but I couldn't help detecting some looks of envy. Both Brian and I had our girls' pictures hung above our beds. In the evenings a steady stream of guys complimented me on my luck as they filed by. Jeanine may not have been the beauty Elaine was, but she was damned pretty, and I was as proud as I could be.

The more I thought about it, the more intrigued I was by the idea that Brian might invite Elaine, and the four of us would spend seven unimaginable days in Honolulu. Brian, however, was surprisingly cold on the idea. First, he claimed he wanted to take his R and R well after the halfway point in his tour. Second, he felt that while he might in time set up a similar rendezvous with Elaine, he wasn't sure it would work out as well with four people. He was quick to add, though, that he'd give anything to meet Jeanine and that he was sure that Elaine would like both of us. He went on to explain that Elaine's parents were stricter than Jeanine's and that she was a year younger and probably more submissive to their wishes than my Jeanine.

I was perplexed, but I kept pounding him with the idea of at least asking her. In a short time many of our buddies began pounding him, too.

"Come on, Bwine, you'd nebber hab a better time dan wiff Andy and Deanine, and you know it. Dut doe ahead and atz her. Tee what happenth," Hobson urged him.

"Sounds like an interesting time to me," Shifrin would agree. "You might be amazed at how much better your time would flow and how much more fun you guys could have if there were four of you."

"Hell, Kitzmiller, you can only screw so many times," Randall pointed out. "I think you'd have a shitload more fun with four of you to do all the other shit that Elaine's gonna wanna do anyway—tourin', gettin' rays, shoppin'—that shit."

Brian relented. "Yeah, you're probably right. I'll write her about it. I don't think she'll do it because of her ol' man and ol' lady, though. They're different. Of course so are mine—who the hell knows."

Chapter 13

During my first six months, of our roughly two hundred soldiers we never had more than six black people in the entire unit. By the time I left, there were only ten. I was surprised to learn later that such small ratios did not exist in combat units.

In late May we had gotten a flabby, cantankerous, white cook who called himself Big Daddy LaForte. He was from West Georgia, though he claimed to be an army brat who had lived all over. A wild man nearing forty, Big Daddy fit in our barracks pretty well at first. Everyone seemed to like him because he was a true clown. He knew literally thousands of dirty jokes, and he drank like a fish. A lecherous character, he constantly wanted intricate descriptions of our girlfriends' bodies and how they acted during sex. Beyond that, his everyday conversation was an endless variety of stories where he or someone else had outsmarted the army and gotten away with something unthinkable.

Though a lot of guys felt he was a loudmouth with zero class, he did not seem capable of making enemies. When he felt he'd pissed someone off, he'd simply hand him a beer and say, "Ya know ol' Big Daddy jus' carryin' on with ya, don't ya? Huh? Ya know ol' Big Daddy jus' tryin' to make ya laugh, don't ya?" And when someone would respond positively, Big Daddy would add, "Why, hale yes ya do. Goldarn ya. Big Daddy don't really give a shit whether that little woman of yours screams 'Geronimo' or not when she comes. Hale no, he don't. Big Daddy don't give two shits whether that fine hunk of butt ya got back in Ohio got a pussy tighter than Rocky Marciano's fist. Hale no. Big Daddy jus' wanna be your bud. Wanna make you feel at home overseas. What the hale's wrong with that? Huh? Ain't a fuck of a thang wrong with it, now, is there? Now sit yore ass back down here and tell me, that little crack of yours ever give ya a yeller shower?"

Some people, including Shifrin, ignored him completely, but generally Big Daddy was good for laughs and just one of the many types it took to make up a unit in the army.

About two months after Big Daddy had been with us, a skinny black man arrived from the States. A tired man who looked aged beyond his fifty years, he, too, was a cook. Will Cleveland was his name. Will was quiet, frail-looking, and overly polite. He went out of his way to be pleasant and seemed to agree with anyone on just about anything he said. I thought he was one of the most likable people I'd ever met. In his twenty-ninth year of the service and with an upcoming pension, he was nonetheless deeply worried about what the future held for him when he was done with the military or, perhaps more appropriately, when the military was done with him.

One of sixteen brothers and sisters who were mostly sharecroppers, Will had had a hard life. He'd fathered two children. One had died before reaching her first birthday, and the other was killed by a truck at age eight. He was from a rural area not far from Vicksburg, Mississippi. He said once that he "spected" he had been to a couple of years of school when he was very young. "Undastand, that was even before the Great Depression. A long time ago. And I had to help the fambly so much by workin' that whatever schoolin' they was, all I know is that I missed the most of it." One of the saddest sights I ever witnessed was when Richio, another cook, read Will a letter from his wife—my first encounter with illiteracy.

Will Cleveland was the first black we had in headquarters platoon, the division of the company where you'd expect the least trouble, given its composition of clerks, drivers, supply personnel, and cooks—generally the people who worked the closest with the management of the company. But trouble began after Will had been with us only a couple of weeks.

Our mess sergeant, Sergeant Helton, decided he wanted all of his crew at one end of the barracks so that when they got up at four-thirty, they would be less likely to disturb anyone else. Will, reassigned the open bunk above Big Daddy's, began to move his belongings.

Brian, Glasscock, Hobson, Shifrin, and I were lounging around in the mess hall, and we heard one of the cooks, Private Dewey Huffman, jovially inform Big Daddy, "Daddy, looks like you're bunkin' with the nigger."

Huffman's calling Will Cleveland "the nigger" sent an icy premonition down my spine.

"The fuck I am," Big Daddy replied.

"Well, the fuck you ain't," Huffman replied. "I jus' came back from the barracks and seen 'im setting up the empty bunk atop your'n. Ain't gonna hurt you none. Jus' funny, is all. All your rantin' about coloreds, and now you got one in your damn bunk. Hee hee! The US Army, one big ole meltin' pot, yessirree."

Big Daddy grabbed Huffman by the top of his apron. "Let me tell you somethin', boy. You don't know fuckin' Big Daddy from Adam if you think I'm gonna bed down with a goddamn boothead. Big Daddy done served his country proud—proud!—in this man's army eighteen years, and I ain't bunked with one yet. I ain't even bunked next to one. You mark my word, boy, ain't nobody here man enough to make Big Daddy do somethin' he don't want. Hale no! I'll whup the man's ass, be he sergeant, captain, colonel, general. And I'll tell you somethin' else, boy. I'll shoot a fuckin' black man don't know his place!"

"Jesus," Brian whispered. "Can you believe that?"

"Ah, hell, he's as likely as not to just be cockin' around," Glasscock answered.

"Bullshit, Bobby," I said. "The fucker's serious."

"Oh, thit, Andy," Hobson said with a laugh. "Big Daddy is tho full of thit. Whath he gonna do? He ain't gonna do nuffin'. He'th dith bullthittin', fuckin' around wiff ol' Huffman, who ain't too bright, thath whath he'th doin'."

"Damn," Brian said. "I don't think he is. Man, I never figured anybody we had in the whole company was really that prejudiced. I mean, the way everybody works together and all"

"That's sort of naïve," Glasscock said. "Shit, Brian, some of these guys been prejudiced bad all their lives. You don't realize it 'cause everybody works together, but everybody's *got* to work together or they get their ass busted. Not that it ain't good for everybody to cooperate, then go back home and say, 'Hey we did it, we got along.' That's a damn good occurrence because ain't neither group, Negroes or whites, is gonna go away."

"I think Big Daddy is serious," Shifrin said suddenly. "And if he is, there could be an ugly situation."

"Yeah, well, Top and Karch aren't gonna stand for that," I said.

Glasscock chuckled and shook his head. "Shit, Andy, do you think Big Daddy even cares about them? I mean look at him—a fuckin' E-five, and he's been in damn near twenty years. What a loser, a big, dumb redneck lifer who couldn't make it in a million years doin' anything else. The army's the only reason that glob of shit's not in jail."

As much as I thought I liked Big Daddy's crazy personality, I found myself agreeing with Bobby. I felt disappointed in Big Daddy, and just that quickly I no longer felt any trust in him. This stemmed from *more* than his being openly prejudiced toward Will, though that was the biggest part of it. But also, I now saw him as a bully, and I detested bullies.

I glanced at Shifrin, whom I'd begun to see as a more intellectual Prather. "What do you figure about Big Daddy, Joe?" I asked, because he was not one to volunteer much unsolicited conversation, and he had already expressed an opinion.

"Well, I'm sorry to say it, but he sounds like an asshole. Worse than that, he sounds like a bad person, someone who gives his part of the country a bad name. I mean, you can find a lot of good Southerners who may not know all the answers but who give a shit about their fellow human beings and don't have the viciousness in their heart to hurt or humiliate anyone."

"Well, in your book, is he a radical or just a hick?"

"I'd say he's a radical. Extremist behavior is extremist behavior."

"What's your take on radicals?" Glasscock asked.

"I don't wanna get into it. It's no more than my personal feeling. It doesn't mean I'm right. Let's go over to the movie."

"We'll go in a second," Glasscock said. "I really want to hear your opinion."

Shifrin squinted up at the ceiling fan, then said as if he were being truly burdened, "Nice to know I made it as somebody's sociology prof, even if it's Glasscock's. Look, I don't claim to know everything about every kind of person, but I don't trust radical behavior. It's too illogical. Radicals are not true thinkers. They're not stable. They're not negotiators or the kind of give-and-takers we need not only to flourish but to survive. The rare ones with some intelligence are either psychologically or emotionally flawed, I think. Most of them, though, are simply followers with ordinary IQs and extremely low self-esteem. They hide behind the shield of their cause and need the shelter it gives them from thinking and working with their fellow human beings. It makes them feel like somebody to be reckoned with.

"They are incapable of hearing anything but the drumbeat of their hard-core stance. They become followers and sacrifice their individuality, which in my book is perhaps the greatest gift in the universe. And by doing all that, they put themselves at risk that they will ruin their lives."

I had never thought about extremism or radicalism. I understood that some people hated others but had made little attempt to understand it. I had only recently been introduced to the term *hippie*, and I wasn't sure I grasped how much of their attitude was related to anything truly political, or even what *political* meant beyond, say, Democrats and Republicans. Everything Shifrin said was new and educational. He planted a seed, and soon I found myself reading everything I could in the magazines and newspapers. In time, I guess

I looked at issues with Shifrin's slant on them even more than Lieutenant Prather's.

At age twenty, I had something of a complex about people who'd been to college, probably because of Jeanine. I was impressionable and easily influenced by anyone who had been educated, especially Shifrin, who sounded like Solomon every time he opened his mouth. I wasn't alone in my perception of him. Top and Karch had more respect for him than they did for each other. Shifrin never got excited or raised his voice, which gave his brand of logic stunning credibility. His theories were for me easy to embrace, especially in relation to the extremists we were reading about in *Time* and *Newsweek* and now were experiencing in Big Daddy.

"Well, Big Daddy's an asshole," Bobby said, "and likely to fuck himself up a whole lot more than what he can do to poor ol' Will Cleveland. But I'm too short to give a damn."

We left the mess hall in silence and joined Randall and McCollough, and the seven of us headed for the movie barn to see, of all things, *Born Free*. We had a couple of beers during the show, then went over to the EM club, where we ran into more of our company mates. We all drank too much, then headed back around eleven. I had this slight sense of guilt about being away from the company, yet I think we all believed the Big Daddy episode would be over when we got back.

We were wrong. When we returned, Tony Richio was only too eager to fill us in on what was happening. Trouble had started hours before, when Big Daddy had taken the bunks apart and moved Will's outside the door. Richio, who had been reading a *Playboy* in his own bed, decided he'd better do something, so he left and found Sergeant Helton. Helton was not somebody to fool with. Even though he was renowned for sticking up for his cooks, he demanded their absolute obedience and respect. He had a hair-trigger temper and a wicked passion for fighting.

When Richio approached him at the NCO club and informed him about what was going on, Helton blew a gasket. He returned to the barracks but couldn't find Big Daddy, who'd gone for some libations of his own. Helton stormed around screaming Big Daddy's name, then ordered Richio to refit the bunk adapters, and the two of them put Will's bunk back in place. Steaming, Helton told Richio, "Somebody better tell that fat piece of shit nobody steps out of line like that in my fucking platoon. I'm not going to be made out to look like I'm not in control. I will kick his ass up one side this barracks and down the other if he even looks crossways at Cleveland. You got that, Richio? I'll be back in a coupla hours, and there better not be any shit!"

Helton's threat got to Big Daddy, but not in the way intended, because Will's bunk was back on the ground outside, the mattress sprawling in the dirt.

Will Cleveland entered the barracks, walking slowly. I always had the sense that Will just wanted to do his job and stay out of the way. That evening he had volunteered to help with some "light cleaning," which had lasted past eleven. He had to be up at five. Stone silence fell on the entire barracks. Most of us were sad and ashamed. Will stopped at the end of the barracks, not grasping fully what had happened and looking for his bunk.

"This can't be happening," Brian muttered.

"No, it isn't," Shifrin said. "At least it won't go any further. We won't let it. Let's set that bunk back up."

Brian pushed the door open hard and, along with Hobson, who had decided to join us in case trouble developed, began to bring the bed back inside.

"Hey, maybe we shouldn't be setting it back up here, with this maniac LaForte," Brian said. "There's plenty of room down in our section for another bunk."

"You're probably right," Shifrin agreed.

"Hold on, guys," Richio said sternly. "Sergeant Helton said us cooks had to be together and that his bunk assignments were final. We got to set it up here."

"Hell with that," Brian said. "Will shouldn't have to be around a guy that prej—that messed up."

"Then Big Daddy wins," McCollough said. "That's not right, either."

Amid the arguing, a quiet, shaky voice began. It was Will's, and it riveted us. "This ain't for me. I ain't gonna be part of no trouble. It ain't good, and there ain't no good can come of it. I get along fine with ever'body. I don't have no enemies, and I don't 'tend to at my age. I don't mind to sleep outside. If it rains, I can jus' drag my shit down to the latrine an' sleep."

Stunned silence prevailed. Then Randall, who had stolen out to get George Champion, returned with him. George was one of my close friends. He hung around in our gang mostly, but he had some black friends in the 96th with whom he spent time, too. He played ball, drank at the club, went to movies, and shared stories of home and of his one semester of college with us. His sense of humor made fun of other people and himself with such a clever mix, no one ever seemed offended. He was anything but a pushover, however, and could become angry if he felt he was being screwed because he was black. George could also become deeply philosophic, and I felt perhaps for the first time that if a guy like George could be so troubled by the overall picture back home, then the state of affairs were probably a long way from being right.

"What is this shit?" George demanded. "Who the fuck said you weren't sleepin' in here, Will?"

Will said nothing.

"Fuckin' Big Daddy," Glasscock answered for him.

Brian stepped forward and gently put his arm on Will's shoulder. "That's not gonna happen. If anyone goes it will be Big Daddy. Or all of us."

"Yeah," Hobson added. "If you go thleep outide, then we all will, and that ain't gonna happen." This brought a momentary smile on some faces because Hobson was not even in our barracks to start with.

McCollough had placed the bunk adapters back onto Big Daddy's bunk. Then as he and Hobson picked up Cleveland's bed so it could be fitted as the top bunk, Big Daddy crashed through the screen door. He never gave anyone a chance to speak. Squinting and enraged, he shouted, "Just what the fuck is goin' on? Get the fuck away from that bunk, McCollough!"

"Aw, hell!" Richio said, banging out the door. "I'm gonna get Sergeant Helton."

"What the fuck you think you're doin', boy?" Big Daddy barked at Hobson, who had lifted one end of the bunk and looked like someone with his hand in a cookie jar.

"Jitt puttin' dit bunk togetter, Bid Daddy."

"'Jitt puttin' dit bunk togetter,'" LaForte mocked him. "You take your fuckin' hands off my equipment, you nitwit, you Babel-touched, God-scorned-and-stricken, mumbo-jumbo moron." With this he grabbed the grinning Hobson but couldn't dislodge his grip on the bunk. The two jostled with the bed as Hobson smirked, and then suddenly Big Daddy's rage peaked, and he slapped Donny in the face, then kicked him.

"You fuckin' redneck," George snarled, starting for them.

"Idth otay, Deorge. I don't need no one to fight my fighth."

"This isn't about you, Donny!" George said. "It's about us!"

"Then come on, black boy," LaForte said. "I'll whip your ass, too. I'll whip all your asses." Big Daddy cocked his fists, and the muscular George Champion, with a ferocious look on his face, did the same. Shifrin tried to step in between, but George yelled to let them settle it.

Hobson was the one who wouldn't let it go. "Otay, Bid Daddy, I'll jut put dit bunk back up here while your doin' dat. While you're dettin' your att kicked by the whole barrackth."

LaForte grunted as if something had exploded in his gut, then reeled and threw a punch at Hobson, who, with his magical athletic moves, turned his head and caught only a brushing of hair from Big Daddy's forearm. Then Hobson, using much of Big Daddy's own momentum, grabbed his arm, turned him, and stepped forward quickly, which tilted Big Daddy off balance. He then gave the awkward, grossly overweight man a shove toward McCollough's bunk, and Daddy toppled over it backwards, landing on his head.

At this Randall began shouting in a sportscaster's voice, "I don't believe it! Big Daddy has gone down! The Kokomo Kid, the white Cassius...Muhammed Ali has put Big Daddy LaForte on his ass!"

Hobson was still grinning, and Randall was laughing, but no one else saw humor in the situation. Big Daddy scrambled to his feet and screamed, "Motherfuckers!" Grabbing a bunk adapter—a two-foot metal pipe—he lunged toward Hobson, then cut unexpectedly toward Randall and swung mightily.

Randall ducked away with a millisecond to spare. "Goddamn, LaForte!" he yelled.

We closed in on Big Daddy, and he swung again. The weapon came within an inch of my face after it had bounced off Randall's shoulder, and out of reflex, not courage, I grabbed it. Champion, enraged, punched Big Daddy hard between the eyes. The flabby cook fell backwards as I wrenched away the pipe.

Shouts came from outside. "Fight! Fight! Headquarters platoon!" In no time twenty-five people jammed into our barracks from the side door to watch. Then the front screen door burst open, and in stormed Sergeant Helton. His rage matched Champion's and LaForte's.

"What the fuck are you doing?" Helton screamed. "Are you out of your fucking mind?"

"It's takin' this whole barracks to take me on!" screamed LaForte. "You started it, so go ahead and join in! I don't give a fuck! I ain't bunkin' with no nigger!"

"The hell you ain't! You'll bunk with whoever the fuck I say, you big, fat, stupid, son of a bitch. I make the rules, you fat fuck. You got a problem, you shoulda come to me. Now you don't do what I say, I'll put your fat crybaby ass in the hospital."

"I ain't afraid of you, Helton! You're a big fuckin' bag of wind. You motherfucker, you come on me, you're makin' the biggest mistake of your life. I'll fuckin' kill you tonight! I'll cut your balls off and throw them on this tin roof, and if I don't do it tonight, you can start counting the days 'til I do!"

Helton threw a haymaker that caught Big Daddy square in the face. His nose flattened, and the blood shot like ketchup onto the front of his T-shirt. Daddy was obviously shocked. Then Helton delivered an even stronger blow to Big Daddy's head, then another, and Big Daddy hit the ground hard. A noncommissioned officer beating the crap out of one of his men was serious beyond words, as was Big Daddy's assault with a steel pipe.

LaForte was out of his league. Hobson, Champion, or Helton could have beaten Big Daddy a hundred out of a hundred times. But that was not the issue. Big Daddy may have been a physical wreck, but he was psychologically unbalanced and dangerous; Helton, too, was unstable, always seeming capable of much anger and little fear. Rules of fair play no longer applied. Big Daddy grasped the wooden two-by-four beams and stood with great difficulty. His pulpy face was covered with blood, and he looked like the cover of a professional wrestling magazine.

"Sergeant Helton," Big Daddy's voice gurgled through his mouthful of blood. "I hope you've written your slut mother and your slut wife today, 'cause you ain't gonna see tomorrow."

"You fucking dirt!" Helton spat and headed for his prey again. This time though, Richio and McCollough grabbed Helton, and though he thrashed wildly and shouted threats at them, they had good grips under his arms and one leg and were not about to let go. LaForte made a move toward the restrained Helton but stumbled to his knees, gasping. Hobson and I moved to stop him. To our relief, Top entered, then Karch.

Top pulled up short. "What the hell—?"

"I ain't bunkin' with no nigger," LaForte managed to say.

"You idiot fuck! You will do what I say!" Helton yelled.

"Shut up, Helton," Karch shouted.

"I'll kill this Helton fucker!" LaForte screamed back. "He had no call to put a nigger in my bunk! He's signed his own death warrant."

"The hell with you, you redneck motherfucker!" Champion yelled. "Who do you think you are?" Then, pointing at Will, he said, "This man wasn't doing anything but what he was told."

"That's right, LaForte! And I gave him the order!" Helton said. "You don't like it, tough shit! Your whole body'll look like your bloody pigface."

"Shut up! Shut up, Helton! Shut up, LaForte! Shut up, Champion!" Karch bellowed, his face even redder than Helton's. "Shut the hell up! Now!"

"Hey, Captain—" Helton started to say.

"You heard your company commander!" Top came in. "Now you all shut the fuck up and listen!"

Karch got on his soapbox. "The fight is over. Every man not assigned to headquarters platoon, get out now! Move!" Then, looking at LaForte, he said, "You will not disrupt this company's mission because of your personal hatred. This is a war zone. The 209th's place here is well established. We cannot function except as a team. I would've thought you might grasp—"

"Captain Karch, it ain't right." LaForte interrupted.

"Shut your fucking mouth, soldier. I'm the only one talking, you understand? If I say so, then you can talk. But until that time shut your fucking mouth!" Froth shot from Karch's lips. "Your days are over as an E-five, LaForte. Your days are over in this unit, too, if I have any say about it. Send your ass up to Charlie country to cook for the grunts, and see how you like that. Top, is there a place this man—this *disgrace*—can bunk tonight?"

"Down in the asphalt platoon, sir."

Karch glanced around. "McClain, McCollough, and Richio will move your shit to the asphalt platoon, where you will remain until 0700, when you will report to me in my office. You are not to leave that barracks even to take a piss until that time. Whatever injuries you sustained, we'll worry about after your meeting with me. Helton, you will report to me at 0730, and you are not to leave headquarters' platoon even to take a piss until that time. Do you understand?"

"Sir, I got two men missing from my rotation. One's on R and R, and one's got the clap."

"I do not give a shit! Every cook will report to the mess hall at 0500 or whenever the hell they usually start. I'll have the CQ see to it. Do not open your mouth again, Helton."

Putting LaForte in the asphalt platoon had seemed prudent, but it turned out to be a huge mistake. After we moved LaForte, McCollough and I stayed under the pretense of visiting with our buddy Jack Yoder. We watched from several bunks down as Big Daddy consumed another half pint of whiskey within fifteen minutes and began yelling and screaming obscenities about the injustice done to him.

The only black man in the asphalt platoon, Specialist Henry Wood, was a good worker and had never caused a bit of trouble, but he was eerily quiet and a loner. His nicknames included Henry the Hermit and Mute Spook. He rarely showed any emotion, and in the harsh working conditions of the asphalt plant, his demeanor was interpreted as bitter discontentment. The small group of people he worked with believed he had no patience with anybody, especially white people. At six feet tall and about 190, he was extremely intimidating. Brian was one person who had a rapport with Wood, but even George Champion questioned Brian on why he would ever waste his time making friends with a man who walked around with a chip on his shoulder.

The fact that LaForte garnered sympathy in the asphalt barracks, then ignored a black man's presence and ranted about "niggers" did not sit well with Henry Wood. In no time he was pacing his area, throwing equipment and cussing crazily to himself. Then suddenly he rammed his fist into a locker door.

Several soldiers quickly got the message that Big Daddy's raving was insensitive and disrespectful to Henry Wood. But several others appeared to think that Wood was eavesdropping on their private conversation.

"Go ahead, Big Daddy," one of them urged.

"Noooo, you don't go ahead, Big Daddy! Motherfucker!" Wood declared. "You and anyone stands wich you is white-trash shit and is gonna kiss my motherfuckin' ass or get his fuckin' head split!"

We froze, shocked at the suddenness of the crisis.

"You say what, boy?" Daddy said.

Henry Wood strode rapidly down the aisle, looking straight ahead.

Big Daddy stood. "I ain't afraid of your black ass, boy. Come on, men, let's get ourselves a jig thinks he can scare us. Hey, now, if you smart you'll get your black ass back to your bunk area. I ain't in the mood, boy. You understand?"

Wood lunged at Big Daddy and delivered a barrage of heavy punches to his head and shoulders.

LaForte screamed, "You goddamn nigger! I'll burn your ass like we done in—" Big Daddy was on the deck again. He had sustained a rocket blow to the mouth, and his words became garbled.

"Now wait a minute," said Frick VanLewellen, a large, hostile man who saw himself as everyone's boss though he still maintained the rank of private first class. "You gonna beat an ol' man when all he wants to do is talk? Huh? Is that what you think you're doin'?"

Henry Wood, now beyond rage, grabbed an M-14 and, using it like a baseball bat, beat VanLewellen senseless in seconds. Stunned, the forty-plus witnesses watched in horror before anyone interceded.

Once one guy grabbed Wood, several followed, and they wrestled the rifle away from him before any more damage was done to the incapacitated man. Everyone panicked. Wood was perceived as an animal, a killer who had to be contained. One man shouted to tie him with a rope. Two more grabbed Wood where they could. He did not struggle but rather slipped into something of a catatonic trance, which I found all the more terrifying. Shortly thereafter Top and Karch arrived, along with Sergeant Bliss and Lieutenant Prather.

Karch was incensed, and his mood grew uglier when everyone tried to talk at once. Though he got the gist of what had happened and could have shot Big Daddy, he surprised everyone with his next move. He decided that his best strategy was not to mess with LaForte anymore now, but rather to lock Henry Wood in a conex. Conexes were common in Nam—large metal boxes with sturdy corrugated metal walls and a door that could be locked. Used for shipping and storing supplies, they had no openings other than the door, and no ventilation was possible. Any time a person might spend inside a conex, open door or not, was stifling. We had two in the company area. The larger one was right behind the mess hall.

As the procession out of the asphalt barracks grew, so did the onlookers from the rest of the company. George Champion suddenly began a tirade about what Captain Karch was doing and was ordered to shut up. Will Cleveland just stood there, sadly shaking his head.

That night was unlike any we'd ever imagined. I believed Karch sensed the air of fear, of riot, of anarchy, but was determined to do what he felt he had to do. As with Helton, he could not tolerate a situation he did not control. He was wound too tightly and became too paranoid under stress. In an unsettling affair like this, he was at his worst. The company watched in disbelief as Karch directed six men to imprison Wood inside the conex. Even soldiers who had no use for Wood were silenced, sensing that a man could die in there—an American GI, dying at the hand of his own company commander.

In his most intimidating voice Karch then addressed us. "Every man report back to your barracks and remain there until reveille. Anyone wishing to join Specialist Wood in the conex can be standing here in thirty seconds."

"Man, what next?" Brian mumbled.

Slowly, in defiance, the men began to shuffle away.

Back in headquarters platoon with the lights still on, we all felt a sense that something else would happen, and no one did anything more than sit on his bunk. Brian looked at Will. I could sense their uneasiness.

"Hey, Will," Brian said, "It's gonna be all right. Big Daddy is gone. We sure didn't need a guy like that."

Will Cleveland, however, was not to be consoled. Slowly he shook his head in despair. "Put that man in a conex? Send the man to war, then go put him in a conex when he take up for hisself and maybe get a little out of line? Ain't right. He's only one man. You mean to say forty white boys there, and they couldn't a got it settled 'fore somebody got hurt?" Again he shook his head. "Seem like my country wanna put the black man to war to keep the Vietnamese free but don't really care about the black man bein' free. It ain't right, Brian. Ain't your fault, but it ain't right."

Now that the victim was someone other than himself, Cleveland seemed to care a lot more about the issue. "It just seem like this world's blowin' up all over—nobody likin' nobody, somebody always wantin' to bust somebody else's head or kill 'em, and they don't even know they name or know nothin' about 'em."

The heat of the night seemed to intensify. Half of the troops, maybe more, had been drinking, and the groups had remained together. Guys began to blurt out their opinions. Many more than any of us would have guessed sided with Big Daddy, or at least Big Daddy's choice not to bunk with someone he didn't care to.

I had a sickening feeling that we had somehow ventured off the well-traveled highway of our routine onto a terrifying unknown side road—I only prayed that we would find our way back. Long minutes passed, shouts could be heard emanating from the asphalt and maintenance platoons. The rivalry between these two barracks made the night even more volatile. The maintenance platoon complained frequently that they had the hardest row to hoe because they were frequently asked to work extra hours. But the asphalt platoon felt they had the hardest labor to perform compounded by the difficulty of breathing in the heavy cloud of dust that always hung over the plant when it was fired up. The platoons had had their run-ins before, and this seemed like the perfect time for their emotions to boil over.

George had slipped back into our barracks, and fearful for Wood's life, we were debating whether to awaken the company commander of another unit. Then, to our horror, someone outside yelled, "Hey, black boy!"

Everyone poured into the company street and then behind the mess hall, where we saw Mitchell Stone, a huge farm boy from the maintenance platoon, stomping the side of the conex wall.

Stone was a drunken mess. "You wanna come out here, boy? You wanna fight somebody fair, you caged gorilla?"

George Champion walked silently from the crowd, then rushed Stone and tackled him. The two rolled ferociously on the asphalt pathway. Several men began cheering for Stone.

Next Eddie Battle, a Spec 4 who drove a Euclid dump truck, looked around, grinning, then rushed to help Stone. From nowhere Hobson moved into Battle's path like a free safety closing on a receiver. Battle didn't see Hobson in time. Donny lowered his shoulder and exploded into Battle's chest. In an instant Battle lay groggily on his back with the back of his head split open on a prime example of our unit's finest product, an asphalt street.

Someone from the asphalt platoon yelled, "Nigger lover!" And just as quickly someone from the maintenance platoon yelled, "Shut the fuck up, asphalt asshole!"

The two platoons, some ninety men, now stared coldly at each other. As the two combatants clawed at each other with Champion clearly getting the upper hand, voices barked to let 'em fight. I felt with every instinct I had that a full-scale brawl was about to ignite. Karch and Top reappeared, with a vengeance, along with every officer and NCO we had in the company.

Lieutenant Prather and Lieutenant Thornberry got Champion and Stone separated. When the two were standing, Stone made the mistake of lunging toward Champion again. Karch, who seemed by now to carry nothing short of a mob mentality himself, kicked Stone's legs out from under him and landed a ferocious boot to his kidney. Then in true New York cop fashion, Karch grabbed a loose arm, bent it hard behind Stone in a hammerlock, and shoved with all his might. Stone screamed as if he were on fire, and then we heard the muffled *pop* of breaking bone.

Karch turned to face the company. "Anyone else?" he asked angrily. "I'll tell you something, gentlemen. If someone wants to come up here and go a round with me, this is your chance. Because after the next time I send you to your barracks, anyone caught outside is gonna be court-martialed. Then you can have the disgrace and lifelong repercussions of being court-martialed in a time of war, which reeks of treason or some other form of cowardice."

He ordered the platoon sergeants to write up anyone not in his barracks in sixty seconds. Then, to his surprise and chagrin two jeeps full of MPs arrived.

I could feel the men around me breathe a collective sigh of relief, but Karch looked angry and shocked at the intrusion. A company commander could lose a lot of ground in a situation like this, where he couldn't consult with or coach his most loyal men about how to remember an incident. The cops stayed long enough, I felt sure, to sense that Karch was sweating it. Some of the MPs stared openly at him and would not look away. I always found it ironic that a PFC or Spec 4 MP could make an officer's life miserable. The conexing of Wood was far from regulation and far from necessary, and the ranking MP wanted to know what in God's name was going on.

Karch recovered and offered him a detailed story. We couldn't hear exactly what he was saying, but his gestures were convincing even without the words. Then came the inevitable: To our great relief the MPs took the handcuffed Henry Wood with them. They also took off with Eddie Battle, Mitch Stone, and Big Daddy heading for the field hospital, where VanLewellen was already being treated.

At first no one could figure out where the MPs had come from. Very few people knew how to contact them. An unwritten rule said that each company would take care of its own problems. Sergeant Bliss later informed us that Top, unbeknownst to anyone else, had argued vehemently with Karch for several minutes over what they were doing to Wood. He felt that this was the type of decision that could get them both busted. When Karch would not heed Top's demands, our first sergeant had marched into the orderly room, ordered the CQ out, then called the MPs. Almost simultaneously, Stone was attacking the conex.

Whatever the consequences might be later for Top if Karch found out, I guess he didn't care. He'd done an admirable thing, and I never forgot him for it. Karch later claimed that he had not intended to leave Wood in there for long, but when the MPs had arrested Wood, he had ceased sweating and did not look good.

Once again we found ourselves in our barracks, and though lights out had been ordered, a single bulb burned hanging from its cord near one end of the building. As if God were determined to punish us all, Sergeant Helton now carried on much the same way Big Daddy had. His wrath, however, centered on Big Daddy, whom he swore to beat to death.

"Come on, Sarge," McCollough urged him. "Let it go for now. It'll all work out. You can only make it worse by not turnin' in."

"You guys listen to me. I'm only gonna say this once," Helton seethed. "You just watch what I do to that fat piece of shit. You understand what I'm sayin'?" He spat on the floor. "Shit! I'm in as deep shit as that son of a bitch, and I'm just doin' my job. Imagine, in up to my ass, and all I'm doin' is my fuckin' job. Fuck! Let 'em bust me back to E-five. Let 'em take my mess hall away and then see what happens. Hell, let 'em try to get somebody who gets his job done like I do. Keep the cooks goin' all the time. Toughest job in the army, I tell you that. Keep the chow rotated in and out right without it fuckin' rottin'. Keep shit clean like I do. Make good meals for the men like I do."

At this Brian glanced at Randall, who rolled his eyes. This was unfortunate, because Helton already hated Randall's loudmouthed, cooler-than-thou attitude. Helton got up casually, walked over to Randall, looking straight down at the floor all the way, and then delivered a horrid forearm blow to Randall's jaw. The surprised surfer went down like a sack of potatoes.

Even in the midst of this chaotic evening, Helton's reaction seemed incredible. Randall was the cockiest guy we had, the guy with pizzazz, the guy who was not afraid to say anything, the guy who had as many girls writing to him as Prather, and the guy who had pictures of them—one of them naked—plastered all over his locker. But Randall, as his performance on the KP run indicated, was not a fighter. He was a talker, a convincing intimidator, but in reality he could no more defend himself than Big Daddy.

"You fucking asshole, Randall! You big-mouth punk! I'm gonna punch every one of your fucking teeth out!" Helton drew his fist back again, and I, desperately wanting to be a peacemaker, jumped on Helton. I got a lot of help, which was good, because Helton became incensed with me.

I thought the night would never end. I had imagined fighting in Vietnam, but I never believed I would see it happen among ourselves. Despite what I had believed in the months before, that my army unit would somehow list with my school, my church, my Boy Scout pack, my high school baseball team, I knew differently now. The stability of the unit and all of its characters, perhaps the one truth we held on to even more than knowing that someday we'd be going back to the world, now seemed fatally eroded. I knew our company would never be the same again.

Chapter 14

"Talk about a couple of section eights," Brian almost yelled, shaking his head. "God, those guys were sick! Ambulance drivers? Son of a bitch!"

I stacked my Carling Black Label can precisely atop the skyscraper we were building on our tabletop, early in the evening, at the EM club. Eight days had passed since the riot, and Brian and I had had the afternoon off. We made the mistake of catching a ride into town on an ambulance. "I can't say I'd want my life depending on those guys."

"You think they were fucked up?" Glasscock asked.

"Had to be," Brian said. "I mean you shoulda seen their eyes."

"They told you they threw some wounded Vietnamese guy out?" Shifrin asked.

"Yeah, just like that," Brian said in disgust. "And said they'd done it before, too."

"Well, what actually happened?" Glasscock asked.

"Apparently these two get called to a spot about three miles north of the 90th Replacement Battalion, where some signal corps guys are stringing some phone lines and get into a firefight after Charlie pops up out of nowhere. Anyway, three of the signal guys get hit but none real bad. The signal guys shoot one VC, but he *is* hit bad. Mason—the driver with the big mouth—goes through the list like he's reading a duty roster for a pathologist: 'sucking chest wound, large facial intrusion with half of jawbone missing, hole in thorax region of throat.' You wouldn't think they'd have even done this much, but the ambulance guys load this Cong in the back and are gonna take him to the field hospital. Then they find out that the signal guys had casualties. Mason has a cigarette clamped between his teeth the whole time he talks, and matter-of-factly he goes, 'So, we didn't have room for everybody. As you can see this ain't a fuckin' bus. So I look down at the dink and go, "Hey, sorry, man, we got some real people who need to go," and me and Phoebus here dump his ass out on the ground and load the signal guys in.' Mason is laughing his ass off, then goes, 'Of course we was soon to find out that the worst off was this fucking new guy—we call 'em FNGs—when he sees all this blood and dried guts and catches the general aroma of our limo. He blows his cookies all over the back. So if it smells unusually peculiar, please accept our apologies.'"

Brian's eyes seemed to double in size as he emphasized his story. "And, I mean, I'm lookin' around this big green hot box of a vehicle and smellin' all these terrible smells, like burnin', rotten, limburger cheese and dead fish, and seein' all this blood—some that looks damn fresh along with a whole bunch of faded blood and even some black gooey puddles of it that have half dried. And I mean it's gotta be a hundred and forty in the back, and I swear I start thinkin' that *I* might faint. But I'm determined to hang in there when all of a sudden ol' Andy here goes, 'Hey, guys, pull over. I'm gettin' kinda hot.' And of course they're really laughin' their asses off at that. I mean, no kiddin', Andrew? I noticed, too, that you didn't have your ascot on or your carnation."

Brian had everyone looking at me in hysterics, as usual, and of course he wasn't finished. "'Aw, shit, the air conditioner's broke,' that Mason guy goes, so they pull over, and we hop out. They're laughin' hard again, goin', 'Hey, guys, anytime you're hitchhikin', anytime!' The other one—Phoebus or whoever—goes, 'Yeah, you rear-echelon motherfucks!' And then Andy—"

"Shut up, Brian, you dickhead," I said. "Shit, I was roastin' in there, and I can't stand the smell of puke. God, I can't imagine those guys drivin' around in that boxcar all day."

"So what happened to the gook?" Glasscock asked.

Brian shrugged. "When we got back, I told Top about it, and he starts this big-ass lecture about that being part of war. But he did the call the MPs and tell them there might be a wounded VC real close to that part of the compound, so they could check it out. Then he tells us that some oriental guys will spend their last moments waitin' to get one last shot in or a grenade pin pulled. It's like that's what the point of their whole lives is, according to him. Top's still got all the answers." Brian shrugged at Glasscock. "All I can say is, hell of a half day off."

"You guys get laid?" asked McCollough abruptly.

"Nah," I said. "Hell with that. All I need is to get the clap right before I go see Jeanine next month."

"Ho, shit! That's right. When are you goin'?"

"Exactly three weeks," I bragged. "I can't believe it. Honolulu, no less."

"That's even nicer than Saint Louis this time of year," Randall said.

Shifrin asked if Jeanine seemed excited about it.

"Sorta. I think she's nervous. Her letters are gettin' kinda weird. She'll go on about it in one and not mention it in her next. I know she'll dig it, though. Everything will straighten itself out." I had been firing off a letter to Jeanine every day, while she maintained her every-fourth-day pace. "Just like a pitching rotation," Brian would say. "Jeanine writes on three days' rest."

"Well, fuck a duck, McClain gets his ashes hauled by the love of his life," Glasscock said now. "His own little round-eye, right on the beach in H-lulu. Keep the sand out of it."

"Out of what?" Randall asked.

"What'd you ever decide about goin', Kitzmiller?" Glasscock asked. "We ain't talked about this shit in two weeks."

I had been frustrated with Brian and his continual nixing of my idea. I saw this as the first time that I had resented anything about him, and though we continued to hang around, I was offended, maybe even a little hurt, so I hadn't mentioned it to him in several days. I was eager to see what kind of bullshit he'd spew forth.

Brian looked at me with all the innocence of an altar boy. "I was going to tell you this afternoon, but then the ambulance ride came up and all," he said to me and not to Glasscock. His voice then took on a more serious tenor. "I asked Elaine point-blank a little over a week ago, to come and meet us in H-lulu. She had written to me that she was going to be visiting this chick friend of hers who goes to Saint Mary's of the Woods and lives in Sacramento. I asked her to extend her vacation a week. I figured that if she wanted to, she could get around her parents easy that way. But she didn't even try. She just told 'em, and she's coming." He looked back at me for my reaction.

"You scrawny bastard!" I yelled. "You little punk!" I was elated. Brian was going with me! Elaine was going to be there! Jeanine would love it. The sudden idea of the four of us in Hawaii—partying, drinking, surfing, making out on moonlit walks—overwhelmed me. Then the thought of not having to do all the processing and shitting around for two days by myself and of not having to travel alone hit me. Even that stuff would be fun now. I had worried too about Jeanine's getting bored or being uncomfortable with the situation. But I knew Elaine and Brian would keep that from happening. "Oh, man! This is great! You dumbass, I knew if you'd ask, it'd happen."

"Yeah," he said, "I kinda thought it might, too. I mean, I knew my chances were decent."

"Dat's too muth," Hobson said. "Thit, thath tho cool. You futters are gonna hab a time. Man, oh, man!"

As we partied on—the first time since the night of the endless riot—the idea became more and more glorious. I suddenly realized how badly I wanted to fill in all the voids with Jeanine. I had been plotting for months about how I would get her to agree to marry me someday. Never for an instant had I downplayed the importance of her having fun every time we were together. This was perfect. Brian and Elaine were coming into the picture at exactly the right moment.

"Well, I think it's a good move," Shifrin said. "And I admit I'm a little envious of you guys."

I was all grins, but Brian seemed distant. I punched him. "Unbelievable, Briney. We're going! They're coming! Jesus!"

"Hey," Shifrin said tugging at my shirt-sleeve. "Whatever happened to that philosophy grad student that Jeanine was so impressed with?"

"I haven't heard, Joe. And to tell you the truth, I don't much care," I said happily.

"I don't think you should, Andy," Glasscock said from across the aisle. "I never knew a philosophy major that had a big dick. So you're safe. Even you."

We laughed a lot that night. As we drank, oblivious to how we'd feel the next morning, we did what most drunken young soldiers do. We got loud, then we got philosophical.

"Love ain't the big issue, man," Randall said. "That's for ole-timers and ugly people. Life is about gettin' laid as much as you can by as many fine-lookin' broads as you can."

"Ah, Randall, you're such a shithead," Brian said, almost asking for it.

"You know what you are, Kitzmiller? You're out of your league. You're pussy-whipped by that chick because you couldn't get another one like her in a million years."

Brian seemed unusually defensive. "Randall, I can't even begin to tell you what a ridiculous—aw, who cares?"

"I till tink ith reawy gweat, Bwine," Hobson said. "Futt ol' Wandall here. He'th dit dealous."

"Yeah, fuck Randall," McCollough agreed. "He does all his thinkin' with his dick. Most of us are smart enough to let it make only ninety-five percent of our decisions. The other five percent allows me to see what you're talkin' about. Yep, love is indeed fucking wonderful."

"Oh, McCollough, you're such a hopeless romantic. Anybody got a bag for me to puke in?" Randall asked. "Or the back of an ambulance?"

"That was some unbelievable shit," Glasscock said. "I can't believe Top thinks those crazy bastards are just part of the war."

"Hey, they are," Randall said. "I don't disagree with Top about that."

"You can fuck this whole fuckin' activity, man—this police action or whatever you call it," Champion said. "I can't believe I wasted a year of my life in this godforsaken place. There ain't no good reason for us to be here."

"Hey, George," McCollough said, "the commies are for real, man. And they're relentless in what they want to do. Would you rather fight them over here or in San Diego? That's what it comes down to."

"Bullfuckinshit."

"I'm not shittin' you, man. Like ol' Truman or Ike or whoever the fuck ever said it, countries are like dominoes. One falls, then the one next to it, and on and on. Hell, Hitler proved that."

"You really believe that?" Glasscock asked.

"Yeah, I really do,' McCollough said. "And obviously so does Johnson. So do fuckin' Congress and most Americans."

"I'm not sure about public support," Shifrin said quietly. "It's not there among people our age. I think a certain amount of public reticence, reticence spawned by ignorance, is being mistaken for support. I'm not sure that even half of the population really backs this war right now, and if it goes on another year, it will be way less. At least, that's what I believe."

"How can you say that?" Brian asked Shifrin. "What do you mean, half? Man, I bet it's eighty-twenty."

"I think you'd be surprised. On the campuses I don't think it's ten-ninety. And it's getting worse. This isn't World War Two, and whether you realize it or not, it took Pearl Harbor before Americans got behind that war effort. People are better informed now and a hell of a lot more likely to express disapproval with their government than in 1941."

"That's bullshit, Shifrin," Brian said. "In spite of the protests, most people back us. Most guys our age would join us if they got drafted or if it got worse and they thought we needed them."

"I hope toe," Hobson said.

"Hey, guys," Shifrin said, leaning forward on his elbows. "That's not true. This war is being debated and denounced every damn day."

"Who cares? It's not that important," Brian said. "We'll have it won before most of our friends even graduate. The bottom line is, we had to come and we came. We were gettin' drafted in droves, and a lot of us enlisted to get a better job. What choice was there if you weren't in school? Those guys back home aren't going to be exempt forever. Everybody has a two-year obligation. There's no way out, except to ruin your life. Sometimes you have to pay a price to live in the best country in the world."

"And that best country sometimes has to make sacrifices to help the rest of the world make it through," McCollough added.

I agreed with that, but I was curious about what Shifrin would say. He looked at McCollough, then at the Empire State Building of cans we had growing. "I guess that's what I basically believe, too. There's honor in serving your country. But not everyone agrees with that. Not everyone agrees with their government, and they shouldn't be forced to act against what they believe. I hope Brian's right about winning within a year. I saw Westmoreland on TV around Christmas time, and he predicted we'd be here another year."

"Well, Mr. Rich Ivy League Jewish Boy agrees with us, even at our low-ass level," McCollough said.

Shifrin took the jab well and smiled. "I'm not rich, I'll promise you that. You've got more, I bet, than us."

"Hey, bullshit, Joseph," McCollough said. "My dad owns a gas station. I don't think he ever brought home more than eight grand."

"And my dad's a tailor for a small men's store in New York," Shifrin replied. "I don't think he's ever brought home eight grand."

We sat a few moments in silence. I would have bet anything that Shifrin was from a big-bucks family.

"How'd you get through Columbia?" Champion asked.

"I was fortunate enough to get some scholarship money, but mostly I busted my ass. I worked thirty hours a week the whole time."

"Wow! You're our only college grad who's not an officer," Brian mused. "In fact, other than George here—and, of all people, Randall—you three are the only ones left who have any college at all. Out of two hundred and four of us."

"Top was bitchin' about it the day you went in front of Karch for the first time," I said. "It didn't strike me as that weird then, but now, shit. What's goin' on?"

"Where are all the college guys?" Brian asked.

"Where are all the *rich* kids?" Randall asked.

"Think about that," Champion put in. "I know of no one in the company who isn't just a plain ol' everyday Joe, poor as hell."

"Now that we find out about Shifrin not being rich, I believe you're right," I said. "Where are all the rich kids?"

"I wonder if it's different in the other branches of the army," Glasscock said. "Like, say, the signal corps, artillery, medics, infantry, finance. Or what about the navy?"

"I guess I figured rich guys, educated guys, fuckers with good jobs, they'd all be mixed together," Randall answered. "Or—and I'd kinda like to know this—if it's just us."

"Yeah, us poor dumb assses," Brian said.

"You're a dumb ass, Kitzmiller," Glasscock said, tilting back his can. "A dumb ass that just happens to have a tough broad for a girlfriend."

We were nothing if we couldn't change the subject on a dime. "Anybody who likes the Red Sox is a dumb ass," I added. "Shit, how long before that inevitable losing streak that puts their ass in the cellar for the rest of the season?"

Brian squinted at me. "Suppose it doesn't happen. Suppose they hang in there. You ever think of that, you stupid shit?"

"You wanna bet on it?" I said, and then in my alcohol-aided excitement I figured I'd better give a little something away, to make it seem fair. "I'll bet you ten bucks they don't finish in the top half of the league. And I'll bet you twenty and give you two-to-one odds they don't win the American League."

"As Cheedah would say, 'When do you get paid?' You're on, Mr. Know-it-all."

"When you got to center all your hopes around Carl Yastrzemski, you'll crash sooner or later," I said.

"I'll take Yaz any time. In fact I'm not so sure he's not the best player in the American League."

"Yeah, count on it, Brian. Sheesh, you're dense."

"Yeah, Bwine. Yad ain't no Mittey Mantle."

"Is that right?" Brian said. "Well, you go ahead and yuk it up. Especially you, Andy. You and your Senators and A's! You really know your baseball history. 'Hi, I'm Andy McClain. Oh, ah, Ted Williams? Yeah, let's see, I've heard of him. Wasn't he the guy that Jerry Lumpe took over for on the A's? Oh, no! He was that limey fucker who was in the Profumo affair."

Shifrin spat a spray of beer.

"Yeah, Brian, that money'll come in handy when we get back from Hawaii," I said. "Don't think I'm gonna buy your damn beer, either, just because your ass is out of money. Wait 'til Elaine hears about this bet. Brian Kitzmiller, a young man who knows where to invest his money. 'Hi, I'm Rico Petricelli, shortstop for the worst team in baseball in 1966, and I'd like to tell you about a wonderful investment opportunity.'" I burst out laughing.

Brian seemed to be enjoying this as much as anyone, and the way I saw it, he should. When Brian was having a good time, he enjoyed being argumentative, and he didn't mind taking the entire group on, no matter what the subject. He was impossible to fluster, and what he lacked in facts, he made up for with his off-brand humor.

"Hey, Brian?" Randall asked. "How come Yaz holds his bat that way? Is that from screwin' in light bulbs, his off-season job?"

"You referring to number eight, McCollough?" Brian answered. "A man destined for the Hall of Fame?"

"Shit."

"A man on his way to winning the triple crown?"

"Oh, shit. I'll take some of that action, too," I offered.

At last call, as so often happened, Brian and Bobby Glasscock were arguing about yet another completely absurd subject—electric trains.

The next few days went quickly as my anticipation rose to unprecedented heights. Never had I looked forward so much to anything. My thoughts, my visions of Jeanine were constant. I saw her as I drove Lieutenant Prather around in Bien Hoa. I saw her when I was in the mess hall, at the EM club, playing basketball, and when I woke up to take a piss in the middle of the night. I got especially nervous about getting in an accident or shot. I couldn't bear the thought of anything keeping me from that week. I found myself exuberant to the point of obnoxiousness.

Compared with my excitement, Brian was surprisingly calm. I guess I was beginning to get on his nerves with my endless questions and pressure about what we'd do when. "Hey, Brian, you figure it'll be a good idea to go surfing on our first day?"

"Jesus, Andy, how should I know? Why don't we just let it happen? Shit."

"Might impress 'em," I went on playfully, intending to aggravate him. "My nickname back home happens to be Surfer Joe."

"In Louisville? Well, that figures. Every time I've ever crossed that river it's so full of oil and scum you not only could surf on it but you could walk across it. Which is bad news for us Hoosiers. And that only means you'll be on your ass in the Pacific Ocean. Or under the Pacific."

"Does it make any sense to have Elaine and Jeanine meet in L.A. so they can fly together? Maybe get their flights booked all the way back to Chicago, too?"

Brian looked pensive and stared blankly.

Still in my childlike character, I raised my voice so I was almost yelling, "I said, does it make any sense to have Elaine meet Jeanine in L.A.?"

"Look, shithead, maybe we should leave well enough alone, okay? Elaine's already got her plans made, and I kinda feel iffy about the whole episode. You know her parents can't be digging this, really, so don't make more chores for her."

"No problem. Forget I—" I decided to change the subject for my own good. "Can you imagine watchin' a John Wayne movie and those guys gettin' ready to leave Iwo Jima for a week in Hawaii to meet their girlfriends?"

"War's come a long way," Brian said, not able to suppress a grin.

I spent most of my time trying to figure out what Jeanine was thinking. Where did I fit in her plans? What would this week in paradise do for us? Did she love me? I was sure she wasn't as fired up about the trip as I was. I knew, however, with all my heart and soul that once we were there, she'd have no doubts.

Suddenly I felt good about just being me. About half of my tour in Nam was done. I had a girl back home whom I dearly loved, who was coming to meet me in Honolulu for a week of romance, laughter, and sex. I had a future that included college on the GI Bill, and I had some damn good buddies and the respect of my bosses. I felt lucky and plain good, so good that I was actually starting to look handsome to myself.

When the wait got to be under seven days, I felt giddy, almost reckless, though I'd have to say I was pretty nervous too. Nothing mattered now, but the countdown of days until R and R, and then I would feel luckier than the guys even leaving to go home for good.

Chapter 15

The letter came two days later—a mere letter, like so many others that had arrived in the past months. I should've sensed something was amiss when I put it under my nose and detected no trace of perfume.

> *August 2, 1967*
> *Dear Andy,*
>
> *I know you're all psyched up for Hawaii, but I'm afraid you're going to have to forget it. In fact I'm afraid you'll have to forget a lot more than that.*
>
> *I expect you're sitting there wondering what has transpired. Well, Andy, a lot has happened, and I'm afraid this letter is actually overdue. I've been too naïve, too cowardly until now.*
>
> *For starters, I've grown to love someone else. I've mentioned him a few times to you before—my good friend John—and to tell you the truth he has brought me out of my childhood, a place I'm only too glad to be done with. If this hurts you, to an extent I'm sorry, but then you've not been up-front with me, and you know it. Andy, why didn't you tell me everything about that stinking, corrupt, criminal war you're in? John and many of the people I've met through him have filled me in on about the military and about Vietnam, and it is too much for me to stomach.*
>
> *I'm very disappointed in you. Why didn't you ever mention the children who are being burned and killed by the war machine you so proudly serve? Have you seen them? Have you heard them scream? Did you think that I, or any other responsible woman you might take to your bed, would*

never know about the thousands of innocent people who are being slaughtered? In the name of fucking freedom? More I'd say in the name of lining the pockets of big corporate scum, and politicians and generals. What was in it for you, Andy? What did you want in exchange for your crimes and your sins against the human race? Medals? Money? Glory? Pussy? Oh, does that word shock you from sweet, innocent Jeanine? Or were you just a pawn, too dumb or too cowardly to say, "To hell with you! I'm not going to murder babies in the name of Fucking Old Glory?"

Andy, it hurts—hurts that I ever let you touch me. I thank God, if there is such a being (and if there is I'm sure he's inherently sadistic), for John. John, John, John, a human being who actually uses his intellect first. Compared to him, you are a child.

No, I won't be in Honolulu with fucking Elaine and Brian. I prefer instead to heal. And to live. And to expand my mind. Andy, did you ever read anything other than a fuck book or the sports page? Do you, or any of your heathen friends, even know who Sartre is? Or Nietzsche? Will you ever know anything? Will you at least know to stop killing someday?

I hope you can live with what you have done.
Jeanine

My heart shriveled. I thought, *I'm still here. Alive, standing here. I can see, I can hear. This is the most ungodly event that's ever happened, and I'm still standing here with Shifrin and Brian and Top, and they don't even know. Everything is so much the same, only so horribly different.*

I walked outside without a word. I'm not sure why, but I had to read it again. I had to see if, by some miracle, it didn't really say what it did. I couldn't comprehend that she had written this letter, but the handwriting was hers. I remembered suddenly the blandness, the self-righteousness, the sort of anti-Andyness of her previous three letters and her growing disdain for the war before those. The clues had been there. I could've seen them if I had wanted to. *Oh, God,* I thought over and over, *this couldn't have happened.* I looked at the date: four days before. What she had been doing since then? I wondered. Did she have any regrets? Maybe she'd written again, maybe to say she'd overreacted. Then I read the last two paragraphs again. I knew I was through.

Brian came out. "I can't talk!" I nearly shouted as if I were telling him to stay away. "It's over. I—We'll talk later." I stifled tears and walked away. When I was forty yards down the company street, I turned back and said to my friend who was still frozen in place, "I won't be going with you, buddy."

I lived an afternoon of hell. Prather and I drove around in silence for nearly three hours, from one site to another, while my hands grew cold and then numb on the steering wheel. My mind wandered, and from time to time I couldn't remember where to turn or where we were going. Prather still said nothing, allowing me to figure out the route for myself.

Reading that letter filled me with the most pain I'd ever endured. The worst I'd ever allowed myself was perhaps someday to be tearfully pushed away; instead I was smashed by a piano hurled from fifty floors. I was experiencing a living death, stark and excruciatingly mean, and meant from the heart to destroy.

I wondered if Prather had any clue. Then at four we stopped in front of a seedy-looking place in downtown Bien Hoa. He put his hand on my shoulder and said, "Come on, Andrew, you need a drink."

I wanted a drink but not to talk. I was coming out of shock, and the pain was intensifying.

"I'm sure it's bad. I'm sorry," Prather said, looking at me briefly, then paying for our beer.

"I love her so much, and she hates me. I got no idea what I'm going to do." I waited for his response, but he said nothing. I continued, hoping I wouldn't sob. "It happened so fast." I took the letter from my pocket and handed it to Prather. It seemed so light for something so awful.

Prather bent forward and looked me in the eyes before he began reading. "I realize that this doesn't mean shit to you right now, but we all lose someone we love at least once. I'm damn sorry, Andy, but you've got so much going for yourself. You'll be all right. You don't see it now, I know."

"She asked me about the babies we were burning. What the fuck is she talking about? I got no idea where they're getting all this shit."

"It's the antiwar movement. They're making us, Johnson, McNamara, the administration, into criminals. It's on all the campuses around the country."

"I gotta write to her," I said.

"Do what you feel you should. She sounds like a messed-up chick. I'd bet this John guy is calling the shots. He's older. Younger girls want somebody they can be dominated by, if you ask me."

I thought about this for a few moments, not really believing it. I recalled an instance from my weekend pass in St. Louis with Jeanine. She had walked over to the mirror above the dresser in our motel room. She was naked. "Mirror, mirror, on the wall, who's the fairest of them all?" she asked softly, in a child's voice.

I walked up behind her and nestled my face against her head. "The fairest?" I repeated. "It could only be you, my lady Jeanine. Only you."

That moment seemed so incredibly stupid to me now—not only how embarrassing sweet-talk can seem after the couple parts company but the word fair. The fairest? Homonym or not, the word stuck me as particularly ironic.

"This guy has done the equivalent to her of what they're accusing us of—being brainwashed," Prather continued. "In a sense he's brainwashed your girl." In a rare moment of animation he spat on the floor. "A fucking philosophy major is perfect for the part, too. Most of them are weirdo know-it-alls. This guy spouts all his existential shit, and it's his way into her pants. We're over here, in this forsaken place, and this coward fuck back home is picking us apart, telling our girls that we're murderers. And then fucking them. And if this ass-head has his way, he and others like him will do all they can to make us into criminals when all we're doing is what we thought was right."

He paused for well over a minute. Neither of us spoke, and I began squeezing my beer can, slowly creasing it.

That night I was treated like someone who was mourning the death of someone close. Everyone tried hard to raise my spirits. In my experience, no one seemed to garner more respect and consideration than a guy who'd just received a Dear John letter.

We went to the club, but the music haunted me. So the guys and I headed to the command bunker.

On the way, Brian came up and put his arm around my shoulders. "Andy, I can only imagine what it's like. God, I'm sorry."

"Thanks, pal," I said faintly, and for the first time since I'd read the letter a tear started down my face. I turned away. "I'm sorry I won't be going to Hawaii with you." I managed to say after a few seconds, realizing he probably saw me crying then wondering, *So what if he did?*

"I been thinking, Andy. Why don't you go with me anyway? I'm sure Elaine won't mind."

"No, no, I couldn't. I wouldn't feel right."

"Don't be crazy. You'd have a great time."

"No, with Jeanine not there it would kill me. I'm not sure I'm even going to go on R and R, for the whole year," I said solemnly.

"Andy, why don't I call it off, the trip with Elaine? She's not even thoroughly comfortable with it. You know, her parents and all. Then you and me can go. Hell, we'll have a super time."

"God no, Brian. I couldn't do that. I want you to go and be with Elaine."

"We could go over and just hang around on the beach and check out the chicks. Go to Pearl Harbor. Hit the night places. Do some surfin' like you been harpin' on, check out Honolulu. Man, it'd be wild. Let's do it, Andy."

"You're crazy. No way."

"All right. Let's go to Singapore. It's sposed to be unbelievable."

"No way, man."

"Bangkok. Come on, let's just go, Andy. It'll help you get over it."

"Brian, man, I'm never gonna be over her. Now shut up about that shit."

"Sometimes it's a better situation to be with your buddies—"

"Shut up about it. I ain't goin' no matter what! To any of those places! Not now! You got an obligation. You got to see Elaine. Do you understand me, you shithead? I'd be very disappointed if you didn't go." I grabbed him by the shoulders and shook him. "Don't you fucking see what just happened to me? Do you want that, too? Don't be stupid, Brian! You can't replace something like—" I had to stop.

We climbed the sandbags, and once atop the bunker, everyone expressed some well-meaning theory.

"You know, Andy," Shifrin said, "the day I read the letter where she first mentioned Teeter, I had this feeling that he wasn't going to do your cause any good. You just know a guy like that's not going to be in our corner, and you could also tell that Jeanine was pretty impressed with him."

"The bastard's an existentialist," I said sadly.

"I'm not surprised," Shifrin answered. "She must've filled you in on quite a bit about him."

I pondered this a moment. "I don't even know what the fuck an existentialist is," I said. "All I know about 'em is that I put 'em in the same category as the Viet Cong and the Nazis."

This got some laughs. The guys didn't really want to be somber. "Yeah, except more spineless, two-faced, uglier, and lower than slime," Bobby Glasscock said.

"Well, hell, yes," Brian added. "Ho Chi Minh is a fucking existentialist himself, a big one, too. He's president of the Asian existentialists for the extermination of red-blooded, beer-drinking, All-American boys, the fucker."

They went on with a twenty-minute barrage on existentialists, but I'm sure Shifrin was the only one there that had any idea what they were. And he was the only one who never said a word.

I tried to blend in, hoping that my friends could keep me afloat. But I couldn't get into it. After a while I didn't feel like doing anything except getting off by myself to see if I would die. When ten rolled around, I simply had to get away. I bummed a couple of Marlboros and matches from George and bounded down from the bunker.

I wandered down the company street. I felt relieved that no one followed me, but I guess I wasn't surprised.

I headed through the motor pool and wandered through the trucks, jeeps, dozers, graders, rollers, tankers, low-boys, and various pieces of asphalt equipment. I climbed into the seat of an asphalt spreader. I had no idea how it operated, even though it played such an incredibly big part in our company's mission. I stared at the manufacturer's nameplate, which, unlike so much other military equipment, still stood out prominently. *Barber-Greene.*

I wondered about Barber and Greene and how long they'd lived, if they were still around, and what their lives were like. I wondered if they had met someone early on like I had, fallen in love, then married and had little Barbers and Greenes. Of course they had. These guys were important. They'd founded a company, and the government and many others, no doubt, were buying their stuff and shipped it all over the world.

I envied everyone who had kept his relationship together, but especially Brian. Because of Elaine's picture, she was the most popular girlfriend of the whole cluster of companies along the south end of the Long Binh compound. He never worried about losing her. Their love seemed to get stronger. Elaine's letters—at least the ones I had read—had a different tone to them than Jeanine's, almost as if their relationship were more perfect than anyone else's. She never even mentioned the war in any terms other than the way we thought of it—as something we had to make it through. Their biggest problem was their parents.

Perhaps an hour or so later I clawed at my shirt pocket and pulled out a Marlboro. I smoked on rare occasions when we were drinking, but I was not really addicted. I sat there on the Barber-Greene asphalt spreader, smoking, crying, and wondering what could be done. I was out of my league, competing against college kids and the faculty, pitted against the ones who specialized in logic and reasoning, life and truth, right and wrong. Without wanting to be there or knowing anything about it, I was suddenly on the other side of the fence of a major political issue—the unpopular side, the uncool side.

My eyes filled with tears, and then, for the longest time, I cried.

Over the next few days my life operated on automatic pilot. Work was my only real solace. I wrote to everyone who was writing me and told them the news. This was a horrific chore, but the alternative was worse, because I was still getting interim mail—especially the daily letters from my mom and dad, who adored Jeanine and talked about her and me in the present tense. Because I still loved her, I simply explained that Jeanine had fallen in love with another person and that they probably had a heck of a lot more in common than we had, that he was there, and I was here, and that I understood and wished her all the happiness in the world.

This had become my standard story to my buddies in Nam, too. Some told me that I was a good person—too good for her. That was okay to hear, but I sure didn't feel it. Many of the guys told me she was a worthless slut. I didn't like that, either. Nothing I heard matched anything I felt.

In an effort to understand Jeanine's attitude toward the war, I reread many of the letters from my friends. My buddies back home were still friendly toward me, though they seemed increasingly baffled about our presence in Southeast Asia.

Suddenly I couldn't stand to listen to the music on Armed Forces Radio: "Strawberry Fields", "Happy Together", "California Nights", "Respect", "98.6", "It Takes Two", "Can't Take My Eyes Off Of You." Before, they had given a special meaning to everything I was missing and yearning for back in the good ol' USA. Now they inspired only despair and loneliness. Instead a country tune played in my mind, its refrain haunting me: "And if there's time before I pull this trigger, Laura, tell me what he's got that I ain't got." I can't say that I ever contemplated suicide, but I was well aware that I was in uncharted territory for me, territory that drove some to end their life.

I became increasingly withdrawn and finally had to write to her.

August 10, 1967
Dear Jeanine,

There are moments that happen that you can't believe. I couldn't believe it when I came down on orders for this place. I couldn't believe it the first time you told me you loved me. And I couldn't believe your letter last week.

Jeanine, after the wonderful times we've shared, I don't understand how you could write what you did. I know the anti-war sentiment is pretty big right now. Believe me, I've never seen children burned or being hurt, I know it happens but I believe it happens because of the Viet Cong and the North Vietnamese Regulars. They are making life in the villages awfully bad for the South Vietnamese people.

That's really why we are here, to help them become free, like we are.

At least that's what I believed and still believe. Maybe, and I know this is possible, you know a lot more than I do.

Jeanine, I love you very much and I always will. Please, I want you to know that I forgive you and I thank you for everything that has made these past two years the best of my life.

I love you.
Andy

Far-fetched or not, I half-expected to get a letter from her, and I imagined myself forgiving her, holding her on the beach some thirty days hence. When none arrived, loss and depression robbed me of the one necessity I needed to keep me going—hope. I learned quickly that without hope, life is bleak and meaningless.

Chapter 16

On the morning Brian was to leave for Hawaii I purposely avoided him. I was elated for him but at the same time so painfully jealous, I did not want to see him off. While he was gone I found myself alone more than ever before. For consolation I frequently wandered zombielike to Elaine's picture, just to stare. I couldn't seem to get enough of her, especially those incomparable eyes, filled with cheeriness, highlighting a face that radiated life at its highest state. Brian was one lucky dude.

I wondered about their time together in Honolulu. I thought about the sunsets, the deep-blue waves, the beach, dinner, wine, and whatever wonders Brian was enjoying with her in their room. I tortured myself with the certainty that I had already lived the highlight of my life—the weekend Jeanine and I spent in St. Louis.

One afternoon a couple of cooks wandered in to the barracks and caught me staring at Elaine's photograph.

"That's some hunk of butt, ain't she, McClain?" Ira Jaffe asked. He was the new guy that Big Daddy had been traded in for.

"She's pretty cool, all right," I answered, feeling a little pissed that Jaffe would blaspheme such a being, let alone invade my reverie.

"Well, Kitzmiller's gotta be gettin' his brains fucked out about now," Richio added. "That's always bothered me, that a kid like that could have such a perfect broad. But the little bastard's done it, and my hat's off to him. He's a better man than me. I know from livin' in the same barracks it ain't his pecker, so he must have a hell of a long tongue."

"Yeah," I muttered, wishing these bozos would evaporate.

"Hey, what the hell you doin' here this time of day?" Jaffe asked.

"Prather's got a meeting with Karch and Colonel Gallagher. Tomorrow they go to a big-ass meeting with General Yates from Group. They're trying to make sure they have their shit together."

"Cover-your-ass Karch," Jaffe said. "That dude's a real pistol."

"Yeah."

"So they don't need you this afternoon?"

"Not right this second," I answered, reddening slightly.

"Man, you got it made, McClain. I shoulda thought to brown nose some dumb lewey when I first got here," Jaffe said, testing me.

But his timing was rotten. By then I was in a terrible mood. I began to spit my words. "Get outta my shit, Jaffe. Go make some more fuckin' slop for us to suffer through or buff your bishop somewhere."

"Hey, Andy, calm down, man," Richio said, looking surprised at my wrath.

"Yeah, man, I was only jackin' around," Jaffe said, holding up his hands.

Richio spoke to Jaffe as if he were referring to Scripture. "Andy got a bad Dear John from his girl. We shouldn't be messin' with him."

"There ought to be a law against firin' on guy's chicks when they're at war," Jaffe said, indignant.

"Yeah, thanks," I said, quickly realizing I needed to simmer down. "I'm sorry, too. I don't see how you guys do as good as you do with all the limitations you got. We all know that."

"I gotta tell you, man, I never seen you like that," Richio said. "I guess in time this place gets to all of us."

"I guess, man," I mumbled.

"Tell ya what," Richio offered. "You wanna coupla hits of pot with us?"

"What?" Marijuana was something I'd read and thought quite a bit about. I was aware of its booming popularity at home and in Nam. Supposedly the infantry guys, particularly in the 1st Cav, were smoking it. But I had never actually seen any here, though I suspected it had to be around.

"No, I mean, thanks anyway," I said.

"Man, you don't know what you're missin'," Jaffe said. "It's around, you know. I know three different guys from three different companies in the 96th I can cop it from."

"I really don't care, is all. Thanks, I tried it once in Saigon," I lied.

"With Prather?" Richio asked, his eyebrows shooting up toward his hairline.

Now I'd screwed up, almost painting myself in a corner. "No, not with Prather."

"What do you mean? Why would you be in Saigon without Prather?" Richio asked.

"Prather and me were in a bar," I said, as if some spirit was forcing the words out of me. "I was having a beer with him, and he struck up a conversation with a coupla Aussies. Some guy came in and said there were some gorgeous Red Cross girls, Americans, down the street at another bar. I wanted to see if they were really there. I mean, you always hear there's American chicks over here, but when's the last time you saw one? Anyway, Prather's deep in thought, looking at his map, and I tell him I'll be right back. So I go in this place, and I'll be damned if I didn't run into this buddy of mine from basic—Maynard Clanton. Of course the girls weren't there. Maynard followed me out into the street and asked me to come down the alley. He pulled a joint out of his shirt. We had been drunk a few times, and he was a good guy. Anyway, I took a coupla…drags, and that was that. I had to get back to the other bar because of Prather. I mean, it wasn't anything."

"Prather didn't smell it on you?" Richio asked right away.

I shrugged. My shoulders felt tight. "Never said anything. I'm sure he didn't. But, hell, he went to the University of Missouri. I'm sure he ran into it a time or two."

Jaffe looked skeptical. "I can't believe you'd do it on duty and not do it now. Aren't we your buddies?"

"I *am* on duty. Look, I tried it—on the spur of the moment. Anyhow, I thought then, that it was dumb—I mean risky. I don't really intend to do it anymore, at least over here. But don't worry, I don't care what you guys do."

Richio laughed and punched me on the arm. "Yeah, we're real worried you'll turn us in."

I forced a laugh, then wandered out of the barracks and onto the company street, under the baking sun. I was angry at myself for lying and putting myself in jeopardy for no good reason. I was angry, too, that Richio and Jaffe had bugged me and forced me out into the heat. All I wanted was some peace, for chrissakes. I couldn't find it anywhere.

The week dragged on. Without Brian even our own little clique seemed less harmonious, out of touch with one another. Shifrin was absorbed in the book he was reading. Hobson would go off and shoot baskets, then disappear until the next day. Bobby was short and spouting off about it to the point of being truly obnoxious. Randall had sandbag duty every night as a punishment for a second article fifteen he had gotten, this one for insubordination. McCollough would trot off to the movie by himself. After a while I realized that the guys were trying to give me a little space. I appreciated it, but with no Jeanine at home and without Brian around, I was as lonely as I could be.

Prather was the only exception. He surprised me when, during one of our talks, he told me that his fraternity would have been lucky, even honored, to have me. This remark was unsolicited and, coming from him, made me feel pretty good.

During Brian's week away two more horrific fights broke out. Both stemmed from long-standing feuds, but I believed the chaos that had erupted during the racial incidents had contributed to our unit's turbulence. In orderly-room conversations both Karch and Top confirmed that in-fighting had become one of our biggest problems.

One brawl resulted in the grisly beating of Denton Farling, a private who was incapacitated for two weeks. Because no weapon was used, no serious charges were filed, although Captain Karch bumped both combatants down one grade in rank and cited each man with an article-fifteen violation. Then Karch called a surprise formation after lunch. With everyone sweltering under the midday sun, the captain delivered a five-minute tirade about our recent conduct and the stupidity and destructiveness of fighting.

"I'm going to tell you men a little bit about General George Armstrong Custer and his methods. We remember Custer for his one all-razing defeat, but he was a hell of a great leader. In the 1870s, a man who disobeyed orders, who failed to get a job done, who fought his fellow soldiers, or who didn't give a fuck was stripped to the waist, tied like a flattened spider to a wagon wheel, and given twenty-five ferocious lashes with a heavy leather strap. Then his head was shaved. Imagine what kind of pain we're talking about here and how long it would take for those bruised splits of the skin, those swollen burns to heal."

Despite the heat, we remained attentive, almost as if Karch was about to enact a similar policy. "Custer had little problem with discipline in those days, and I cannot tell you how many of the company commanders around here, including myself, would go back to corporal punishment in a second.

"I could take you to some of our ally's compounds and let you see how the South Vietnamese officers handle their fuck-ups. They spend eight hours tied down, naked and on their back, on a metal roof. You're lucky in the US Army. We'll take your pay, your rank, and even lock you up with the animal scum that somehow got in the army and now occupies our stockades, but we won't beat you."

Despite the fear, I could sense a slight feeling of relief around me.

"But we expect more from you. Most of you would never be whipped or fried on a roof even if those penalties existed. Most of you are damn decent soldiers who have common sense and pride and want to bring honor to yourselves and your country."

He then shocked everyone by calling Private Farling to the front of the formation and ordering him to take his hat off. Farling's face was mostly purple, and swollen to nearly twice its size. His eyes were blackened slits, and his lips had swelled to a dimension and shape not unlike a crescent roll. "Face the company, Farling."

Karch let the scrutiny and discomfort simmer. Farling had been out of shape to begin with, so he looked nothing like a soldier. "This man," said the captain, "disgraced himself in all ways possible. For the next fourteen days he will lounge on his fat ass under a ceiling fan while the rest of you pick up his slack. He doesn't give a good shit about you, though, I assure you. How do I know that?

"Just take a look at how much he cares about himself," Karch said. "No pride, no common sense, no esprit de corps. Just a man who couldn't handle his beer and stood up when he should have shut up."

When Karch dismissed the formation, most of the company seemed to get the message—no one wanted to put himself in the same category as Farling. The men were angry with the private for the injustice of our having to do his work. The captain had fulfilled his purpose.

Shifrin, handling mail call in Brian's absence, handed me a postcard from Honolulu. It simply said, "Andrew, Unbelievable.—Specialist Kitzmiller."

The picture showed the beach at Waikiki, with the Diamond Head Peak in the distance, the beach that I had dreamed of all year. I was disappointed that Brian hadn't written more, but I suspected he was half trying to be funny and half wanting to spare me details, which would surely hurt. I was the only one to get anything from him during the week he was gone.

A second piece of mail was from my buddy Danny Burdette, at the University of Kentucky. We'd exchanged letters every six weeks or so since I'd gone in the service. I always enjoyed hearing from him. We'd gone to four years of grade school together, then all of high school. He was funny, a beer drinker, and as loyal as the day was long, plus he loved sports. In short, he was a pretty good friend. In my mind he was more of a party student than anything else, but his luck with girls was only mediocre.

August 24, 1967
Dear Andy,

I'm really sorry to hear about Jeanine. I started to give her a call, but I didn't. I don't know man, I sorta sensed it might happen sometime.

I gotta tell you this, and given what you're going through with Jeanine, I apologize about the timing. It's important to me that you know where I stand because we've been friends forever. I don't want to piss you off or offend you, but I don't have anything but bad feelings about the war over there. Andy, if I get out of school and the son-of-a-bitching "conflict" is still on, I'm not going. I can't. To me, it isn't an ethical situation. And certainly nothing to risk getting killed over.

None of this means I feel any different about you.

Cats weren't much this year. You remember what a letdown '66 was. But we got some big guns you're gonna be hearing about soon. Write these names down, you mercenary bastard: Casey, Issel, and Pratt. Gonna be champs again! Soon!

Gotta tell you one other tidbit. Maybe the world's not so bad. Remember Gwen Nordquist, class of '65, that everybody drooled over? Tall and lean and wore knee socks all the time? Blonde, third in her class, sang at weddings, perfect heinnie, the chick that nobody we knew had a chance at? That Gwen Nordquist? Well, I fucked her. I swear, man. Last weekend. I didn't write about her before, but I been out with her some five or so times. I have no idea where it'll all lead. Damn Andy, who would believe it? Me, of all people. Guess she's dumber than we thought.

Don't get your ass shot, buddy. Sorry about Jeanine again; I know you don't believe this, but there's still plenty more.

Your buddy,
the Gwendolyn Conquistador,
Daniel

I sat for a time. I guess I sort of suspected his feelings about the war. A month ago, I'd have been pissed at him, but given my present mental state, I was grateful he still considered me a friend. I was shocked about Gwen, though. She was pretty special, and I couldn't believe that she'd fallen for Dan. Not that anything was wrong with him. There was just too much right with her.

As I thought about Dan's letter, I felt increasingly bitter. Everything had changed in one short year. A summer before, I seemed to have no choice but to serve in Vietnam. Now growing numbers of guys were forging a way out and enjoying ecstasies that we could only drool over. And many of those same people were building the case that we were the scum of the earth.

How could this be happening?

Chapter 17

The seven days Brian had been gone seemed like weeks. I hugged him, then got him in a headlock and told him he'd stuck me with one son of a bitch of a week. His return was memorable for another reason too. Never had there been a more anticipated return from R and R. I guess I hadn't thought enough about what a favorite Brian had become because he was mail clerk and because of his girlfriend, but all the guys from all the platoons seemed thrilled to see him. Questions flew, because Shifrin was right. Elaine was the Betty Grable of the unit. Everyone wanted to know what happened, down to the last detail, and Brian would be faced with the grilling for days. It started with Top, who bombarded poor Brian before anyone could get in a word.

Top looked up from his desk, and a huge smile split his face. "Well, well, look who's back from Hawaya," he said, leaning back in his chair. "Specialist Four Brian F. Kitzmiller. Kitzmiller, you owe me a report, son—a full report, too. If it wasn't for your ol' first sergeant lookin' out for your ass, I don't think you'd a got any farther than Vung Tau. Now don't you, even for a second, think of holdin' anything back. You understand me?" This was the kind of exchange between Top and Brian that we hadn't seen in months.

"Yes, Top."

"Well?"

"Well, what, Top?"

"Well, how many damn times did you get your damn noodle wet is fuckin' what. How much mud did you get for your turtle? Damn, Kitzmiller, do I have to start right back at square one with you?"

"No, Top." Brian hesitated. "Well, let's just say I had one great time in one tremendous place for a week and sort of leave it."

"No, we ain't gonna sort of leave it, Kitzmiller. That ain't what the hell we're gonna do at all."

"Well," Brian said. "I really had fun. I think I'd go back any time. The climate was warm but not the real muggy, thick heat like here. I mean, ninety degrees there feels a lot different, maybe like seventy here. Plus we had air-conditioning. The beaches were really nice. I thought Pearl Harbor was fascinating, and eerie. Did you know oil is still bubblin' up from some of those ships?"

"Kitzmiller?" Top asked, his patience nearly gone. His fists were on his hips, and he was squinting at Brian in a way that reminded me of a Popeye cartoon.

"Yes, First Sergeant?"

"Did you get laid?"

"Well, you remember the first day we talked about this stuff, and I kinda—"

"Kitzmiller? How'd you like a little KP tonight? They say it's the perfect remedy for jet lag."

"No, Top. No, thanks."

"How'd you like to fill me a coupla hundred sandbags along with your buddy Randall?"

"No."

"Did you stay in the same hotel room with Elaine?"

"Well, yeah," Brian said with a laugh.

"Was it day or night when you got in?"

"I got there at around six on a beautiful morning. She got there about four hours later. She couldn't believe how nice a day it was, either."

"Now hold it. I don't intend to waste no time on what ain't right to the point." He shook his head. "What was she wearing when you met her at the airport?"

"A white sundress with a pattern of little red flowers, and she had a red ribbon in her hair. How's that?"

Top nodded slowly and winced a bit. "Damn nice sight, I bet. Short dress?"

"Yeah, and she had white sandals on, too."

"Kitzmiller?"

"Yeah, Top?"

"What fuckin' color were her fuckin' unmentionables?"

Shifrin, Prather, and I broke up.

"Way to be dainty, First Sergeant," Prather said, laughing as hard as I'd ever seen him laugh.

"Well, now, the man is damn near engaged to the young thang," Top said soberly. "I ain't about to insult or be disrespectful to no man's future bride by callin' 'em drawers or panties. That wouldn't be right. Wouldn't be good for my man's morale. So what about it, Kitzmiller? How long did it take for you to get into 'em?"

Brian reddened but smiled. "Well, Top, let's just say we checked into our room early, like one-fifteen. I didn't waste any time. I'd say by one-thirty I was somewhere in the vicinity you're talking about. And that, First Sergeant, will be the extent—"

"Whoa! All right, Kitzmiller, one-thirty! That's my boy. You only wasted fifteen minutes. How long then before—"

"No, Top, that's it. That's all I'm sayin'," Brian said, laughing. "It's too personal. It wouldn't be good for my morale for me to have to talk about it."

"Why not? It's gonna be all you're thinkin' about for the next seven months, and them thoughts is what morale is all about. You might as well fill your pals in on all them good thoughts." This was the first time any of us had heard Top use the term *pal* when referring to his men.

"Well, we had a nice time. Certainly was worth doing." Brian's face flamed. "Shit, what am I supposed to say?"

"What the hell are you 'sposed to say? What the hell do you think you're—all right, skip the details. How many times did you do it?"

Brian smiled. "Ah, twelve, maybe fourteen. I forgot to count."

"Fourteen? Damn, Kitzmiller, you set over here for six damn months gettin' good and seethin' horny, then I send your ass over to Hawaya to get a job done, and you only do it twice a day?"

Brian shrugged. Then with all the conviction his baby face and 145 pounds could deliver, he said, "Well, Top, you got to remember it takes a hell of a woman to handle me, and I guess I was afraid I might do some serious damage if we did it any more, with the way I am and all. That's why I stopped after the first day."

Top broke up. Probably a whole half minute passed before he could continue. Then he hammered on and on but got no more significant details.

Later at lunch with Hobson, Shifrin, and me, Brian was somewhat looser but still remained vague about the details of his R and R, even about details not related to sex. One guy after another came by the table and asked how Elaine was, and those who knew Brian better dug for a little personal information. Brian was cordial and even extroverted but did a good job of dodging the questions. I admired him for this and felt guilty about discussing Jeanine more openly than I should have. *God probably punished me,* I thought.

At mail call Brian was asked if he and Elaine got engaged. "No, just a hell of a great time is all. Maybe later, if I'm lucky."

"You figure you'll be lucky?"

"I hope."

"You were lucky in Honolulu, right?"

"Yeah."

The worst of the grilling came that evening at the EM club. Bobby sat at the head of the table and demanded to be referred to as His Shortness. Brian really let go that night, drinking as much as I'd ever seen him drink. At first he dispensed information grudgingly. He tried and tried to change the subject. Then for a while he answered every really personal question with, "Let me have another beer and maybe I'll tell you."

After a couple of hours, Brian simply couldn't withstand the bombardment he had taken all day. Glasscock, Hobson, McCollough, Randall, Champion, and I continued to put him through it. Shifrin sat quietly, speaking only when spoken to, and seemed to waver between laughing with us and coaxing us to show Brian some mercy.

"Is Elaine a screamer?" Randall suddenly asked.

"No, Randall, you shit-hook."

"Did you eat her?" Bobby asked. "I mean, you don't have to answer, but...well, did you?"

Brian became caustic. "Oh, man, geez...I might have." He raised his eyebrows.

"Oh, Bwine, you wady kilwer, you," Hobson said.

"I might be sometimes," Brian replied.

"Wath thee kith like?" Hobson wanted to know. "Doth thee keep her mout open thum? Doth thee like to frenth a wot?"

"Well, of course. She kisses like a complete angel. Her perfume is the scent of an angel. Her hair is the satin of an angel's. And, yes, she frenches like an angel."

"Ith thee dentle or kind of wild?"

"She's real gentle. Really gentle, like an angel, and she's real wild."

Shifrin asked his first question. "Does she like to hold hands?"

"That's kinda personal, isn't it?" Brian answered, and I busted out laughing as I had done in the days of old.

Shifrin smiled but wouldn't break his stare.

"Yeah, Joe," Brian answered. "She does like to hold hands, and so do I."

"Did she bring stockings and garter belts and high heels?" Randall asked.

"Well, geez, she didn't bring that stuff specifically for that, but she did have some high heels. And that was sorta nice. She looks pretty great in high heels."

"And nothing else, right? I mean, that's what we're talkin' about—California style, high heels and naked."

"Damn, Randall," Brian said, "I think you need to fill some more sandbags. How can you sit there and harp on the same shit, man? I can't get away from it, but you're the worst, you and fuckin' Bobby."

"Hey!" Randall shook a finger in Brian's face. "In the fraternity of man, you are fucking obliged to answer these questions the best you can, man. Now, California style or not?"

"Piss on you. I'm not answering that. Let's just say we didn't do it Kentucky style."

"Oh," Randall said without missing a beat, "you mean you didn't take your dog tags with you."

"Eat it, Randall!" I shouted, throwing an empty beer can at him. "Man, you are one nice guy. We ought to get the chaplain to write a prayer of thanks to the Lord for the day we got your ass."

"Oh, Andy," Randall said dramatically, putting his hand on his heart. "Let me be the first to apologize. Fuck, you Midwestern and Southern guys are like biblical characters, man. Or monks. Or out of Grimm's fairy tales. Man, get fucking real. 'Does Elaine hold fucking hands?' Damn!"

"I'm not from the Midwest or the South, Randall, and I asked that question," Shifrin pointed out.

"Hey, Joe, I fucking know you did, man, and I would specifically address that issue to a greater degree, man, but I don't want you assignin' my ass to guard duty next week, when I get off sandbag duty."

"Speak your mind, Randall," Shifrin said. "If it's your turn, it's your turn. I don't play favorites or get even, but if I was to start—"

"I'll vouch for that," Brian said. "Joe doesn't play favorites or God. But I would."

Randall ignored Brian. "Aw, come on, Joe. It's been terrible, even when I ain't got some sentence to serve out. I've had some kinda fuckin' duty every damn night since I been here. Surely you can skip my ass. Fuck my turn."

"Hey, learn to be a good soldier, like us, and you won't have to worry. Right, Bobby?" I asked the drunken-faced Glasscock.

"I'm too fuckin' short to give a fuck," he said, slurring his words. "But I will say this—Randall, you're one dumb motherfucker if you fuck with the company clerk. And that's what the fuck you're doin'."

"Hey, Bobby, I ain't fuckin' with nobody. I ain't even addressing Joe. I'm asking Brian some simple, highly proper questions about his vacation, man. I got a little side-tracked, but I ain't fuckin' with Shifrin. Man, what a bunch of old ladies."

"You are fuckin' with Shifrin," McCollough pointed out. "You're makin' out like his question was a pussy question. And I agree with Bobby. The company clerk is one of maybe four guys you don't mess with. Your own sergeant, the first sergeant, the company commander, the head cook, the mail clerk, the supply sergeant, and the company clerk. Hey, you know that guy…or know of him, that guy Papadopolous, the company clerk from A Company of the 96th?"

"I met him," Brian said.

Shifrin nodded too, then said, "By the way, that was about eighteen guys."

"Well, that fucker," McCollough said, oblivious to Shifrin's remark, "would put a guy he didn't like on leave on the morning report and then bring him back again in six days or so, and the poor bastard never even knew it, never knew he'd used up six days of leave and could never get it back. Even if the guy caught it later, how in the hell could he ever straighten it out? He couldn't. Just out that many days vacation. Unreal…"

"Man, I never heard of such shit. Joe, you ever do that?" I asked.

"Nope."

"Could it be done?"

"I suppose. I'd think it would be caught fairly easily the way they go over the morning reports at Battalion. I mean, a guy doesn't just go on leave over here. It would be easier in the States, I'd guess. A lot easier." Shifrin spoke with his normal low-key erudition. "Just have to slip it by the company commander. You could probably do that with an extra page, or a late entry, after he signed it."

"All right, all right, Joe. Please don't pick me up on any leave I didn't take, and do what you can for me," Randall said solemnly.

"Damn, Randall, you're gettin' worse off all the time," I said, feeling giddy. "Sorta like my truck driving, or ex-truck driving uncle. And he's in jail."

"What happened to him?" Randall asked.

"Poor fucker. Drunk on his ass during an ice storm in Wyoming, near Casper. Anyway, he was doing about ninety miles an hour when his exit came up. Fought it well, almost had it, then—ended up takin' the last three rooms off a motel."

The guys laughed hysterically. Then Randall ended all the digressing. "All right, Kitzmiller, let's get back to the issue we were discussing. Red, white, or black? What color high heels did Elaine wear naked before you, kid?"

"Ah, man," Brian groaned, cradling his head, "why did you have to be stationed here? Shit."

"Come on, dammit! Why is this like pulling teeth? We're your fuckin' buddies. This is part of us being fucked over in Nam together. What we can tell each other about the ass we've had. That's all we got to look forward to—or back to."

"This will be my last answer. Red. She brought red ones to go with this cool-ass dress she brought over for our last night."

"Oh, man." Randall fanned himself. "Patent leather?"

"Either that or she'd spit-shined the hell out of them. Now you wanna talk about something red, let's talk about the Red Sox still being in the race," Brian said.

An hour passed. Brian was good and drunk

"Man, fourteen timeth," Hobson said. "Wed patent weather thooths, reawy tan kin, and bwonde haiw tieth back. You awe my hewo, Bwine."

"Well, Donny, I'm glad, too. Yeah, you guys woulda fuckin' been proud of me. Fourteen. I shoulda done it more, but we ran around too much, wastin' time seein' shit and being on the beach and shit." He laughed, glassy eyed. "Man, we had fun."

"Man, Andy, that shit's all over the company. I just had Troyer, the new guy in dispatching, ask me about Elaine's red shoes. I mean, this guy's been here three weeks. Shit."

"Brian, forget it," I said. "You're my hero."

"Damn, what an asshole. Why would I *do* that? Man..."

Brian indulged in self-recrimination about his loose lips, but other than that, he was back to his old self, concerned about my broken heart. The next night we took in *The Happening* at the movie barn, then went for a long walk around the complex. We climbed the command bunker and looked out over the darkness at the flares drifting miles away.

"Any word from Jeanine or back home?" he asked.

"Nah, but I feel better than the last time we were up here. I mean, most of the time I feel completely gutted, but other times, I have this feeling I'm gonna make it. I probably could fall in love again, only I don't think I'll ever feel the same way about anyone as I did about Jeanine. And Prather's right—I'm much better off for having had her at all than not. You know, the old 'better to have loved and lost—' God, if I'd only gone to school with her."

Brian thought for a good while. "Well, of course you're better off. And as bad as you feel, you will find an even better Jeanine. You mark my words."

"Do you think you could find a better Elaine?" I asked.

He stared intently at the stars. "Well, if I had to, I guess I think I could come close. I believe there's more than one person that each of us could be happy with. It isn't like God is a matchmaker and says, 'Jill is for Joe, and that's it. Paula is for Paul, and that's it,' you know? I think it's our job to find 'em."

"Yeah, I guess I believe that or something like that. I don't believe Jeanine will ever find anyone who will love her as much as I did, as much as I do, though."

"You don't absolutely know that," he said, surprising me a bit.

I shrugged. Several seconds passed and then I asked, "Brian, do you believe everything happens for a reason?"

"Sometimes I do, and sometimes I think they happen because we prepare ourselves well, so when the right opportunity comes, we can take advantage of it. I know that's part of it, anyway. Like Prather will get a real good engineering job back in the States because he went to the University of Missouri and because he served with the Corps of Engineers over here.

"But I guess God does play some role in teaching us, and perhaps His way is by sending us certain experiences in life. Like maybe Jeanine, for you. Like maybe she taught you how to love and be a good, caring person, and that was all she was supposed to do. And maybe it ended badly for you, and that was supposed to teach you strength and that you're still supposed to love her. I'm proud of you 'cause you do even though she did that horrible shit. Love her, but move on and be happy again someday."

He looked at me, and his eyes were full of thoughtfulness and compassion—a look I didn't see every day with all his banter and joking and bullshit about the Red Sox, and I was touched.

"I'll make it, Briney," I declared. "It may take awhile, but I'll do it. I don't think you understand fully, though, what the hell it feels like. In some ways you've got it made more than anybody, with Elaine waiting for you and with nearly half your time done over here now."

Brian stared curiously at me as if I was missing something. "Andy, can you think of a girl back home, maybe someone you were good friends with and always attracted to, or someone you had a big crush on?"

I thought about that. "Well, yeah, there's a few chicks from high school I had crushes on and one from work. I had a big crush on Gwendolyn Nordquist, but my buddy Danny got to her first. But yeah, sure."

"Well, why don't you pick out four or five and write to them? Maybe it'd be better if you did 'em one at a time. That would get you through your tour— or almost, if you went through five of them. Knowing you, I bet that they would write back, war or no war. And you could kinda get something started. Not everyone feels the way Jeanine does. It might be something to take your mind off—" He held up his hand. "—a little bit, off Jeanine and give you something to look forward to."

My initial reaction was anger. I couldn't just pick somebody out of the air who'd be able to take Jeanine's place. But before I could even verbalize that thought, I realized that Brian was right. Jeanine was gone. Other girls were out there and whether I cared for them or not did not make it a worthless endeavor.

"Well, I guess it's maybe better than doing what I am doing," I said quietly, "which, along with grieving and feeling sorry for myself, is absolutely nothing. This way I could try to get over Jeanine and also work on something new, along with grieving and feeling sorry for myself. I might think about that, Briney."

"With some girls," Brian added, "I would think they'd be curious as hell just to be writing you. Then before they know it, they got a crush on you, and you're ready to go home and have a blast on your thirty-day leave in your new '68 Mustang, with three or four new girlfriends. I think it's a cool plan, and because I thought of it, it will work and once again you'll be in my debt."

"Yeah, right," I said.

I got off two letters that week though I had to push myself because I thought I sounded corny and because I was flat scared. I had chosen Linda Carson, an old buddy with a wicked throwing arm from my neighborhood. In the old days, she and I had busted about forty factory windows with some green apples from trees right outside the factory's fence. I always thought she dug me, and when I had seen her last, she looked good.

The other letter had gone to Kathy Springer, a girl I was in a play with in high school. She was a year younger, and I really dug her. She thought I had done such a good job with my role, she planted one on me at the cast party. We were always pals after that, and I knew I'd like to see her again. They both seem sort of insignificant compared to Jeanine, but sending the letters had put some excitement back in my life.

A few nights later Brian and I were on the bunker roof, waiting for the gang, and I told Brian about the letters.

"God, Andy, that's great!" He clapped me on the head. "Damn, I'm proud of you."

I pulled a beer out of my jungle fatigues pants pocket and opened it with a can opener I had in my shirt pocket. "You know," I said after a swig, "there's this other girl I been thinking about—not that there's anything wrong with Linda or Kathy. But this girl is unreal. I had the worst crush on her you can imagine. A lot of other guys did, too. She was valedictorian of our whole school and captain of the cheerleaders. She was goin' to the University of Chicago the last I heard. Anyway, I found a way to get introduced to her—she was a year older, like Gwendolyn—and we talked for about thirty seconds. Then another time I called her and talked maybe two minutes on the night of the second Ali-Liston fight. Anyway, I been thinking about writing *her*. I mean, what the hell? The worst she can do is not do anything."

I was actually pretty sure that I wouldn't do any such thing—that Brian would say something sensible, like not to waste my time. I should have known better; his eyes were aglow.

"Andrew, I think you should do it. Man, it wouldn't be right not to. I mean, think how many guys never take the chance. And if you don't take the chance, you'll never know. And you know what else? Suppose it's a hundred fifty years from now and you're six feet under in a box. Maybe God doesn't let us in heaven right away. Anyway, you're down there, and you can't even scratch your jawbone. All you can do is think, and all you have is what you did when you were above the ground, walking around. And you say, 'God, I'd give anything to be back for just one day walking above the ground again, living life to its fullest.' And you're proud and sad about your time above the ground. 'Man,' you think, 'so much I did up there was great. All the opportunities I had that I took advantage of and all the great events I made happen. Of course I missed a lot of opportunities, too, that I can never do anything about.'"

I chuckled, and Brian continued. "Then you remember this one earth-shattering chick, the most perfect creation you ever saw, and God gave you maybe a one-in-fifty chance or, heck, maybe one in eight or maybe one in four. But you didn't do shit because you didn't have the balls. Seems pretty dumb now. Some other asshole got her, and one day you saw the guy, and he didn't really seem to have anything, overall, on you. He just had the courage, even though it was hard, to take his God-given chance.

"And you think that maybe that's why you're stuck in this hole, not knowing if you're ever gonna get out. Yep, maybe you're stuck in that hole because God wanted you to prove your courage and win her and make her happy and secure and feel love. He wanted you to take all your chances at the stuff you thought was wonderful, and He even filled you with burning want and awe. But because you didn't, hey, you didn't go to hell, but you didn't go to heaven, either. You're just stuck in that hole forever. Because even in heaven they don't want guys who are too boring to take those chances the good Lord gives them no matter what the odds. And the only way to beat the odds is to play the damn game all the time and then quite naturally to get better at it." He nodded.

I caught myself with my mouth half open. "You bastard, Brian. Now I *have* to do it. It'll damn near be the hardest shit I ever had to do, too. I don't have the guts for it, but now I gotta do it anyway. All I had to do was keep my mouth shut. I shoulda known not to ask you, of all people. Damn."

Then we broke into laughter.

Brian continued smiling. "What's her name?"

"Steffie Kissinger," I said, again expecting him to laugh.

"Steffie Kissinger. Stephanie," he repeated as if amazed. "Man, you just know a chick with a name like Steffie Kissinger is gonna be cool."

"Ah Brian, man, I'm not sure where to begin."

"Look, numb nuts, you begin exactly like you did with Linda and Kathy. They all process the communication the same way. If we had three jars up here, each one with a brain in it, we couldn't tell Steffie's from Kathy's from Linda's. Or Elaine's from Jeanine's, for that matter." He thought for a few moments. "It's exciting, isn't it?"

"Yeah," I admitted, but fear of rejection still plagued me. "I just hope they don't all accuse me of being a war criminal for driving Prather's ass around."

"Well," he said, smiling wryly, "you know how chicks are these days."

The next afternoon I showed him the letter I had written and then rewritten three times until it sounded somewhat smooth, for me:

September 5, 1967
Dear Steffie,

*For some weeks now, I have wanted to write this letter.
I'm hoping you remember me. I felt like the whole time we
were in high school you were the one person I wished I could
have known better.*

*I don't mean for this to sound corny and if you want to say
I had a crush on you, I did. But my feelings were different
from that, too. You seemed so vivacious and genuine and I
guess I just wanted to make some kind of impression on you
other than what everyone else did.*

*As I write this, I am sitting in a jeep at my army unit, the
209th Engineer Company, in South Vietnam. If you want to
know exactly where that is, if you have a map of Vietnam find
Saigon, and a little to the northeast is the town of Bien Hoa.
We're very close to that, at an army base called Long Binh.
I actually don't have it too bad over here. I have been in a
few dangerous situations and I have seen some limited
action but I don't have to fight for a living and having met
several people who do, I am very thankful.*

*I've got around six months to go before I come home to
Louisville for a thirty-day leave. Then I'll have another year
and a half somewhere in the States. After that I'm done, and
I'm pretty sure I'll either start school at UK or U of L.*

*I recently broke up with my girlfriend at U of L, or she
broke up with me, sometimes 10,000 miles and twelve
months is a bit much. I never really thought, of course, that
I would ever write to you, as I sort of believed that Jeanine
and I would get married. But I still thought of you, maybe
because in my way of thinking you represented the best that
any of us could hope for if we were fortunate enough to make
it back. I'm not a presumptuous person and I don't want to
be a pest but I thought if you're back home in Louisville,
maybe at spring break or even next summer, we could get
together for a few drinks or dinner or something. Also,
sometimes I go to Chicago to see the White Sox or Bears and
I know there are so many cool things to do there like the Art*

*Institute and the Museum of Science and Industry and all the
places downtown, that I've never been to.*

*Well I've got to drive to Saigon, my lieutenant and I have
to meet with some civilian engineers about a stretch of road
we're building through some real swampy slop. You
wouldn't believe how fast we can build roads. Maybe I'll
end up majoring in some kind of civil engineering myself.*

*I'd really love to hear from you, Steffie, and I understand
if you have a boyfriend or you're not comfortable with
something like this just showing up in your box. By the way,
didn't you have Mrs. Harrington for English? Whatever you
do don't show her this. I've forgotten an awful lot about
adverbs and I hate to admit, I also forgot how to among
other infractions not split an infinitive.*

Your friend always,
Andy McClain

Of course the letter was ridiculous and corny, and I had no intention of
sending it. And of course Brian laughed his ass off but called it perfect.

"Plus you worked in some crap that proved you weren't a dumb ass, or at
least a complete dumb ass," he pointed out. "You don't talk like a guy who'd
know an infinitive from a damn comma."

I shrugged, feeling sheepish. Since hanging around with the guys in the
army, my language skills had tarnished. "Do you think it's…pretentious?
Should I rewrite it?"

"'Pretentious'? You're starting to sound like a professor!" Brian hooted.
"No, don't touch it. I'm not sure you could ever duplicate that again, so you
have to let it go."

In a four-beer fit of recklessness I dropped it in the mailbox.

My project turned out to be one of the strangest endeavors of the year.
Linda wrote back wishing me luck but informing me that she was engaged to
some guy who managed a restaurant and was twenty-nine. She never
mentioned any feeling about the war, but she said she'd pray for me. Kathy
also responded, but she asked, "How could you be there when you could be
in school? What is this fantasy some people have with war? I'm concerned
that in time you may look back on this and be ashamed of it."

To my amazement, Stephanie came through:

September 16, 1967
Dear Andy,

I was quite surprised at your letter just showing up in my mailbox. Of course I remember you, you were a friend of Wade Timms and he was quite impressed with your sense of humor.

I'm a junior now at Georgetown University, near Lexington. I left Chicago, I really loved it, but my parents seemed relentless about my going closer to home and I decided to appease them when they offered to pay for graduate school. I'm majoring in History and Fine Arts and I may go to law school.

I'm sorry you had to go to Vietnam. I'm really sorry. I can't believe you're over there and so many of our classmates are getting shot at and killed. I have thought about it a lot lately, and I feel like we should pull out now to save lives. I don't blame you, though. It wasn't your fault. Of course I'll see you when you're on leave, I'll definitely be in Louisville next summer though I'll probably be in Fort Lauderdale next spring break.

Please take care of yourself.

Peace,
Stephanie

Brian read the letter with absolute awe. "See, Andrew, you dumb-shit, you're irresistible. And you've got something started!"

That same day Bobby Glasscock left for the States. He had raised hell and been drinking all night, so that when he left for the 90th Replacement Battalion, he was still blitzed and bellowing, "Short, you motherfucks!" at nine-thirty in the morning. We all shook his hand and laughed gleefully because he was about to experience what we all yearned for—the day we went back to the world.

"Hey, Captain Karch! I'm too short to take a shit!" Glasscock yelled upon seeing him head for his jeep with McCollough.

Karch simply waved and looked away quickly, pretending not to hear what Bobby had yelled.

I sighed deeply, almost feeling good. Hope burned inside me where there had been nothing but despair—beautiful, dream-spawning, life-restoring hope. I had it again, and for that I was grateful beyond words.

Chapter 18

Two days after I got Steffie's letter, I came in at lunch from a hot drive on which Prather and I had seen a gruesome accident. A two-and-a-half-ton army truck had smashed a Lambretta, killing five Vietnamese. I was still shaken from the experience. I walked into our barracks with a glass of ice water from the mess hall. I had no appetite; I just wanted to relax, have a smoke, and collect my wits before Prather and I hit the highway again.

As I took a long drink, allowing some icy water to slop down the front of my neck, I was startled to see a heavyset soldier lying on the top bed two bunks down, leering quietly at me. I could tell instantly he was new in-country—uniform was too green, with not a hint of fading from the harsh washings the Vietnamese gave our clothes. I had an immediate dislike for him.

"Hi," I said, peering into his intrusive stare.

He nodded ever so slightly but said nothing. This angered me.

"You a 'cruit?" I asked, meaning to sound disrespectful.

"Maybe," he said.

I had never encountered such surliness from a new guy of any rank, including colonel, and I felt somewhat unnerved by it. He scowled almost, even at rest, with an air of disgust one might expect from a short-timer of the most obnoxious variety, like a Huffer or Bobby. I guess I expected everyone to come here with the same fears, reverence, and stupid questions that I had had. I turned away thinking, *The hell with this guy.* I put on a fresh shirt and left the barracks without saying another word.

I ran into Shifrin on the company street. "Joe, who's the new dipshit?" I asked bluntly.

He smiled knowingly. "His name's Ron Noonan. He arrived this morning, and you're the first guy besides me to meet him. Brian was getting the mail, and Top was down at the motor pool. I processed him as quickly as I could because he gave me the creeps. I sent him right on up to battalion. He's slated to work there as a pay clerk. At least he'll have a job outside the company area."

"Well, that's damn good, except the sonofabitch will be in our barracks," I complained. The finance slot placed him with us.

Shifrin nodded. "Yep. He says he's had experience in construction and some background in soils analysis. He could fill a critical position for us. He's going to apply for it, too. If Noonan can impress Prather he's a cinch to get the job, what with the shortness of *our* soils guy, Rafferty. If he becomes the soils guy, he'll be transferred over to asphalt."

Given my first impression of Noonan, I wasn't surprised to see him sitting with a couple of asphalt guys I couldn't stand at chow that evening. Later, he was at the EM club with the same guys, and he got pretty drunk. It seemed strange that he had avoided us and made friends with guys from another barracks first.

The next day, Noonan continued to sneer at everything. His new friends had given him impetus. I tried pretending that he didn't exist that morning, but I couldn't because of his long scrutiny of Elaine's picture. *Yeah, take it in, fatso,* I thought. *You'd never have a chance at a chick like that.*

That afternoon we learned that Noonan was from Indianapolis, of all places.

"Hey, Brian," said Shifrin, "looks like you've got one of your buddies here. Class of sixty-five, White River High School. Know where that is?"

"Sure," Brian answered. "Not far from where we live. Wow! I haven't even met the dude."

"Yeah, well, don't get your hopes up," I told him. "This guy's got the personality of a shit sandwich."

"Give him a chance," Brian said. "You're just jealous because Top was out of the orderly room, and Noonan didn't have to go through his orientation."

"Nobody should miss that," I agreed. "Especially the first person through here who actually deserves it."

Right after lunch I stopped by the barracks to change shirts, a habit I was developing. Prather had been ordered to meet with the brass at 18th Brigade Headquarters.

Back in the barracks, I was in a hurry. Brian came in and threw some unclaimed letters on his bed while he fished around for something in his locker. I started to say something irreverent about the Red Sox when I noticed

Noonan, evidently taking some extra minutes for lunch break, stroll into Brian's area.

"So you're from Indianapolis, huh, Kitzmiller." His remark was a statement, not a question.

"Yeah, sure am. Noonan, right?" Brian looked a little surprised but extended his hand cordially as he did with all the new guys.

The gesture annoyed me. I buttoned my shirt and glanced into the tiny mirror hanging on my locker door. I could see them releasing hands. Then Noonan mumbled something about the northside, and Brian laughed.

"Well, you're welcome to have dinner with Donny Hobson and me under our flag in the mess hall tonight. It's next to Kentucky's, though. I hope you don't mind," Brian said loud enough to harass me.

Noonan didn't answer. I thought he was really an asshole now, but I didn't have the time to take in any more. As I briskly made my way down the bunks, I heard Noonan's voice boom matter-of-factly, "I see you know Alice Ann O'Neal."

I stopped briefly. I had no idea who Alice Ann O'Neal was, and I wondered how some girl I'd never heard of could be the topic of a new man's conversation with Brian. Then it hit me as I looked around and saw their focus. Noonan was referring to Elaine's picture.

"What?" Brian asked.

"Alice Ann O'Neal from St. Elizabeth's. Goes to Purdue now," Noonan said. "Pretty easy mark for jocks. You've had some of this? Obviously, or you wouldn't have her senior picture blown up and over your bed. I'll be. Small world. I wouldn't have thought you were her type."

"Wait a minute, man. You're not talking about the same person. This is my girl, Elaine. She goes to St. Mary's of the Woods—"

"Bullfuckinshit!" Noonan exclaimed, laughing.

I was riveted to my spot. All sense of urgency about Prather and his big meeting had abandoned me.

"I know this fuckin' broad," Noonan continued. "This is Alice Ann O'Neal. I might even have the same picture right here in my wallet." He began fumbling through his billfold. "If not, I can sure get one. She had to get an extra fifty of these printed, I remember, to give to all the guys she knew. She gave me one, man."

"Look, dumb ass," Brian said, his face beet red, "you've made a mistake."

"The hell I've made a mistake." Noonan shook his head as if in disbelief. "What is this Elaine shit, man? I got no fucking idea what you're up to or what kinda phony crap you're trying to pull off, but I've known this chick for years."

"You're mistaken," Brian said angrily, "but I don't have time to argue with you." He stormed out after scooping the letters off his bed and glancing down the row of bunks at me.

"Bullshit! You're fucking bullshit, man!" Noonan bellowed almost joyously, determined to get in the last word.

I cut over to the company street to intercept Brian on his way to the orderly room. Surprisingly, he turned the other direction and walked briskly toward the asphalt plant.

When I jogged into the orderly room, Prather was fuming. "Dammit, you knew we had to leave five minutes ago."

"Ah, I had the shits, sir. But I'm okay now. Sorry." My own words of deception surprised me.

Prather said little to me after his scolding except to comment on the weather. The afternoon saw the temperature hit 107 degrees, and the shrill sun seared us through the heavy, sticky air. In the silence I could feel a seed germinating inside my brain that was about to explode, but I refused to acknowledge it fully.

"Shit," he said as we arrived at brigade headquarters. "I'm already soaked through. We might as well not have even wasted the time changing. I'll never live east of the Mississippi again. I hate humidity. I'm moving to Colorado or Utah when I get out."

"I think I might, too, sir," I said, not giving any thought at all to what such a move would mean to me.

"You okay?" he asked.

"Yeah."

Prather looked at me for a moment as if he were half expecting me to change my answer. "Well, if you got the shits, it's probably better if you drive to that transportation company a mile back. It's so concentrated with officers here, that I don't even know where the EM's shitter is."

"I'll be okay. If I need to, I'll drive back to the trans company. Kinda makes me understand what it must be like to be colored in the South, though."

Unlike his usual manner when he was uptight, he followed with a jibe. "Now don't go promoting yourself, Andrew. The black brass doesn't want you in the officer's shitter, either."

A colonel suddenly appeared and returned our surprised salutes. "Lieutenant Prather?"

"Yessir."

"Come on in. General Yates is actually in for once and is eager to see you. This will be a chance for you to take some credit for the fine job the 209th has done." He took Prather by the arm, and I headed for some shade. "Son, no, come on in. We've got a waiting room in here, out of the heat."

"Yessir." I walked into the compound of Quonset hutches, which were air conditioned. I couldn't believe it. This was my first encounter with air-conditioning since I'd left the States.

Prather disappeared around a corner, and I relaxed, savoring the chilly air. I could have stayed in there for the rest of my tour. Then I started thinking about Brian. How could Noonan have mistaken Elaine for Alice Ann whoever? Too weird. After several minutes, the other side of the situation hit me, the side I had tried to ignore. Could Noonan be right? No, of course not. Brian had gotten letters two or three times a week since he'd been here. He'd just gotten back from R and R with her, an R and R that I was supposed to go on.

I thumbed through a *Sports Afield,* reading about retrievers. I loved dogs. "Teddy Bears that came to life," Brian had called them. I looked into a black lab's morose, intelligent stare for a long while. Those eyes were communicating with me. Why, I wondered, had Brian gotten so angry? Why had he turned away from me in the company street? Something bad had happened back there, and I was beginning to feel a mixture of confusion, anxiety, and anger. Damn! I flung the magazine to the floor. Then, looking around in embarrassment, I scooped it up. Something horrific was occurring. I could not shake the feeling. I prayed that I was wrong.

At 1900 hours, Prather was still beaming because of his meeting. Karch, who had waited long for recognition, was taken aback because the big brass were focusing on Prather. Top believed the brass was flattering Prather to get him to extend. Nonetheless, in keeping with the spirit of the day, upon our return Karch informed Prather that he had personally recommended him for the Bronze Star for meritorious achievement. I felt proud of Prather, but I was anxious about Brian.

Top caught me by the shoulder as I started down the company street. "You better get with Kitzmiller tonight. There's some shit goin' on about Elaine that I don't understand. The new guy, Noonan, seems to be stirrin' it up. If that fat fucker thinks he's gonna come in here and cause some shit for my guys that I've had all year and are doin' a good job, he's gonna find out that he'd rather stick his peter in a wolverine's mouth."

"What's goin' on, Top?"

"I ain't sure, but I don't want Kitzmiller fightin'. I'll work on the situation from my end. I can make a new man's life miserable, but I can't protect Kitzmiller and baby-sit him for any shit that he might've brought on hisself."

Top's ire suddenly vanished. "Better watch out for Kitzmiller's best interests tonight. You stay outta trouble, too. Let me know if you find out any details."

When I walked into the barracks, Brian was sitting on his pillow with his back against the wall. He glanced up at me and then away. Shifrin, McCollough, Squires, and Richio were with him.

"Well, I wouldn't worry about it then," Richio said. "This guy's obviously got his facts mixed up. Screw him. Forget it. Sure seems sure of himself, though."

Shifrin stood silently looking at Brian as if to say, "Defend yourself, man."

"What's going on?" I demanded, sounding angrier than I was. "What is this shit, Briney?"

"You heard him," Brian said softly. "He's apparently got Elaine—" Then he said annoyed, "You fuckin' heard it. You were there. Why are you even asking?"

"Well, shit…" I started to say, grimacing.

Hobson came in, the door banging behind him. For the first time I could remember, he didn't have his happy, childlike grin. He looked somber and hurt.

"Well, there's no sense letting this matter ruin our evening," Shifrin said. "Let's go to the movie. Come on, Brian. *A Fistful of Dollars,* is showin', and your old hero Rowdie Yates is in it."

"All right," Brian said, "but I don't want to hear one fuckin' word about this fuckin' bullshit."

I had intended to point-blank ask Brian the most direct question I could think of, but I hesitated. As we neared the movie barn, however, I couldn't stop myself. "Brian, I know you don't want to talk about it, but, shit. There's nothing to it, is there?"

Brian turned and glared at me. "How could you even ask me that?" He spat. "Ah, piss on the movie." He turned to go, but Shifrin grabbed him and turned him back. "Come on, he believes you. We all do. Forget it. And shut up, Andy."

Like a scolded child, Brian shuffled along into the makeshift building, turned down a row of benches, and plopped down, ignoring everyone. Something was wrong with him, something bespeaking guilt. I kept thinking that if there's nothing to it, wouldn't he look at it as funny? Why would it make him so mad? I felt afraid—afraid for my friend and for his future. He still had another six months to endure.

In a *Fistful of Dollars,* Clint Eastwood's character gunned down four men in an early scene in a four-on-one showdown. I found myself imagining that Noonan was the fifth man—a pompous dirtball to be blown away with glee.

After the movie, Brian's mood had lifted, and he insisted that we hit the club. I began to believe that the incident was merely a fluke. We had several rounds, then headed back to the barracks.

My blood began to boil as soon as we got there. Noonan was seated on Brian's bunk with two of his brand-new asphalt buddies, Ken Weathers and Gordy Prackle. Noonan took a long pull from his beer, then emitted a repulsive sound. His whole countenance reflected a most satisfied look.

Before Noonan or Brian could say a word, Prackle asked incredulously, "Kitzmiller, what is this shit, man? I can't believe it. Noonan here says he knows Elaine, and she ain't Elaine. And you ain't her boyfriend. What the fuck, man?"

Brian reverted to his rage. "Get the fuck out of my face, Prackle." He put his finger an inch from Prackle's nose, even though the guy outweighed and outmuscled Brian considerably. "You believe whatever you want. Okay? I got nothing to prove. You want to believe Noonan, you go ahead."

"What are you so uptight about, man? I'm only askin' what the circumstances are." He smiled at Noonan, then turned back to Brian. "You wouldn't lie to us about servicing this girl, would you, Kitzmiller? You wouldn't—"

Cutting him off, Brian shoved him and said, "I never talked to you about servicing anybody, asshole, and you know it."

McCollough rushed between them. "Don't be stupid, man!" he yelled at Brian.

Prackle, however, was not about to retaliate. He just stood there laughing. "What'd I do?" he asked innocently, looking around at Shifrin and me. "What'd I do?"

To my chagrin twelve guys from other barracks filed in after hearing the shouts. Randall was with them. This incensed me. "I'll tell you what you're doin'," I shouted. "You're stirrin' up a bunch of shit that you got no business stirrin' up."

"Hey, fuck, McClain," Prackle said. "You can say I'm stirrin' up shit, but the way I see it, I'm just trying to get to the bottom of somethin'."

"Bullshit," Shifrin said, coming in on my side. "Nothing productive can come out of this. You're all drunk. And you—" He turned on Noonan. "—you've got to be the biggest disappointment I've seen as a replacement. What kind of team person are you? No one even knows you yet, and you've begun some ridiculous smear campaign. How are we supposed to depend on you if we ever get hit?"

Noonan grinned broadly. "Hey, Shifrin, we aren't talking about what kind of man any of us is. We're talking about a bullshit situation that I'd like to get fucking resolved. If there seems to be widespread interest in it, well, hell, that's not my fault. I guess it just means that some of the boys around this place wanna get to the bottom of it, too." He laughed. "Sure looks like I came around at the right time. Right after Kitzmiller's bogus R and R."

"Hey, jerk—" Brian began.

"None of this is worth it," Shifrin said, his voice rising. "He says something, Noonan, and you say something else. One guy's word against another's. It's best that we just leave it there and forget it."

"Hey, wait a damn minute, Shifrin. That might be a good idea if we had no way to prove anything. But I can have a picture over here in a week and a letter from Alice Ann herself." Noonan grinned again.

"Well, dith who in dah futt hath Bwine been whiting to all dit time, and who hath been anterring back?" Hobson asked.

Noonan looked at Hobson, tilting his head and raising his eyebrows, which infuriated me. Before I could jump in, Noonan answered. He began to mock Hobson's speech impediment, but after glancing at Hobson's muscular forearms, Noonan changed course. "Hey, mitter, what would *you* do, man? This girl happens to be a friend of mine. Kitzmiller has been tellin' everybody in Vietnam he's fuckin' her. And this lie has made him some sort of hero."

At this Noonan jutted his jaw and said to Brian, "You sorry dipshit." Then giving the comment a couple of seconds to sink in, he continued to address Hobson. "I ain't got a clue what *you'd* do, man, but this is what *I'm* doin'."

"Fuck you," I said.

"Hey, fuck you, boy," Noonan replied, standing up, his hands balled into fists.

I felt a surge of rage and fear. I knew in a couple of seconds I'd be in a fight, maybe getting hurt, but I didn't care. My desire to pummel this cynical bastard was so great, any sacrifice seemed worth it. But it didn't happen. Brian jumped up.

"Fuck you!" he shouted. "You fat piece of shit!"

"Hey, dipshit," Noonan shouted back, "I don't have to take that. I'm not claimin' to be corking Alice Ann. I doubt you've ever been out with her, let alone seen her naked. And I promise you this: I'll get the same picture, and everyone'll see. You're the one who'll have to do the explainin' and probably the fightin', not me."

"Oh," Shifrin said, "what an honorable human being you are. Excuse me for not noticing."

Brian stood, his face ashen. "I can't believe anybody would come into this unit and make accusations and enemies before he even knew anybody. Not over here anyway."

"Hey, right's right, man. It don't matter where." Noonan laughed smugly. "I'm letting anyone who wants to read Alice Ann's letter. Go ahead, dipshit! You lie and threaten my ass. Very soon it'll all sort out."

"That would be interesting," McCollough said, looking at Noonan with a little gleam in his eyes.

I couldn't believe it. McCollough had been our buddy all year. "Hey, what are you sayin'?" I demanded.

"The truth will be all that matters," McCollough said. "Somebody's gonna be mighty embarrassed over this, and we need to find out who. I mean, you agree with that, don't you? Even Brian agrees with that. Don't you, Brian?"

Brian looked down at the dust cover on his pillow and mumbled, "Sure. Sure I fucking do."

Randall, who had come in with the recent mob, looked from Brian to Noonan, then back to Brian. "I'll tell you what. The motherfucker who's lyin' here really, *really* needs to have his ass kicked. If it's fuckin' *you*, Noonan, I feel sorry for you 'cause this whole company will lynch your ass. If it's—" He looked at Brian sadly and shrugged.

Brian shrugged back, then said wistfully, "I wish Bobby was still here."

The comment made no sense and surprised me, as if Brian thought Glasscock carried away some secret magic that would have made everything okay. I never felt Bobby was that close to Brian, certainly not to the degree that Shifrin, Hobson, or I were. If anything, Bobby's presence would probably make the situation worse because he was a cynic. The absurdity of Brian's remark told me that events would probably get worse.

"Why don't you dut tell Ewaine what gowan on and tee if thee hath any ideath?" Hobson suggested at chow the next morning.

"Yeah," Brian said, looking away. "I might just do that. But to tell you the truth, I don't really want to start my day off thinking about this bullshit and that asshole." Brian nodded in Noonan's direction. He sat in the midst of an ever-growing group of guys who nosed out trouble and chased after it. "It's just a funny situation."

Shifrin gazed at Brian for several seconds without saying anything.

"Yeah," I agreed to break the tension. "Of all the bullshit crap. Ah, hell, you know the truth. Don't worry about it."

"I'm not worried about it," Brian said, his mouth full of greasy bacon and eggs.

That afternoon Prather and I rolled in at three in the afternoon, and the lieutenant sent for Noonan. Prather hadn't said a word to me all day about it, so I naturally figured Noonan had made it as the next soils analysts. If the guy got promoted, he'd move to another barracks, and maybe Brian's problems with him would be over.

They met in the officer's section of the mess hall. Curious, I hung around, with a Coke in my hand, peering through the door from the last table in the enlisted man's section of the building. I didn't care that they could see I was watching.

Noonan sauntered in with his already familiar swagger and confident air, but he was no match for Prather's coolness.

"Afternoon, sir," Noonan said without saluting.

"Afternoon, Noonan," Prather began, then launched right into business. "I considered your request for my soils job, and I'm afraid I'm gonna have to reject it."

Noonan's jaw dropped. "Sir! Why? I mean, I want the job, and I'm qualified. I've worked some road construction, and I got a good feel for what you need. Look at my scores."

"I don't care, Noonan. I don't give a fuck if you're a CE from MIT. I don't want anything to do with you. I don't want you in my platoon."

"What? Sir, you don't know anything about me." He glared over Prather's shoulder at me.

"I need team players in my platoon. You go ahead with your pay clerkin'. The way I see it, you got it made, no matter what."

"But, sir, pay clerk ain't gonna do squat for me. I figured that training and experience with the soils job would help me a lot when I got back in civilian life. I mean, I really want that job. I am a team player, and I'll do a damn good—"

"That's it, Noonan. I have no intention of discussing it further." Prather stood and put on his cap.

Noonan looked crushed but only for a couple of seconds. Then he surprised me again with his boldness. "Sir, does this have anything to do with Kitzmiller lying about fucking that girl I know back home?"

Prather's eyes seemed to bulge, and his skin reddened. "What did you say to me, boy?"

Noonan smiled. "Sir, I mean, you said it to me, too. *Fuck,* that is."

"I could court-martial your ass for talking to me that way. I suggest you apologize, or I'll put you back at E-one. I'm not so sure you deserve the rank of Private E-two."

I snickered openly, so that Noonan looked away from Prather again and glared at me. Prather ignored my behavior, his eyes continuing to burrow into Noonan's.

"I'm sorry, sir," Noonan said.

"You better be sorry, soldier," Prather fumed. "I'm not dignifying that question with an answer, either. This is war, Noonan. You may have a candy-ass clerk's job, but a time will come when you'll need to depend on the men you serve with. If you're going around weakening this team, then you're gonna make one shit soldier when we need you the most. Do you understand me?"

Noonan looked away in disgust, then turned back to Prather. "Yessir."

"Good. I suggest, too, that you lose some weight. Those pay vouchers can pile up and exhaust a man in your condition."

Noonan's face turned scarlet. He glared at Prather but looked away when Prather would not break eye contact.

I was as happy as I could be.

Life almost returned to normal for the next nine days. If anyone questioned Brian, he largely shrugged it off. He got one letter from Elaine during that time. As I watched him reading it, I could feel myself believing he had been telling the truth. I would have been won over for sure had he let me read it. He didn't share it, though. He only reported to a few of us gathered in the barracks that she had said the usual, along with some references to Hawaii, then quickly changed the subject to gloat about the American League.

"We got the Twins, the bad-assed Twins, in the last series of the year, and I tell ya, it's gonna happen," he said.

"Well, the White Sox may be nearly out of it," Champion said, coming over, "but those same Twins may have something to say about that, not to mention the Tigers. In fact, I gotta go with the Tigers."

"The Twins got it," I said. "Too much power."

"Bullshit, man," Brian said. "I notice you haven't had too much to say about Yaz in the past few weeks."

"Yaz had one great year," I admitted. "I was wrong about that."

"You were wrong about the Red Sox, you dumb shit."

"Maybe. They haven't done anything yet."

Brian looked at me with great surprise.

"Well," I corrected myself. "They have done something. In fact quite something. They've surprised—"

Noonan entered the barracks, followed by Gordy Prackle and six others from the asphalt platoon. He held up a pink envelope in his right hand. His chubby face wore a grin, and the gap in his front teeth seemed bigger than I had noticed before. *Shit,* I thought.

Prackle spoke first. "You guys know Luke Martin, the mail clerk over in A Company of the 96th?"

"I doe him," Hobson replied. "I pwayed tum ball wid him a coupla timeth."

"Well, that's right," Prackle said. "Plus he's become our occasional drinking buddy down at the club. Anyway, when Noonan wrote Elaine—or let's just say the girl in question—we figured we'd better find a way to get around our own mail clerk. So Noonan, with a little help from me, had the girl in question write to him in care of old Luke Martin of A Company." The asphalters beamed. "Smart, huh?"

Brian's gloating expression disappeared, and he said solemnly, "I would never have not delivered a letter to anyone, even if it had my death warrant in it."

"It does," Noonan replied, smiling even more broadly. He gazed around at his audience, then confronted Brian. "You gonna stick with that same horseshit story, Kitzmiller?"

"I don't have to take this," Brian said and headed for the door.

I watched as he stepped out into the company street, only to stop as a group from the maintenance platoon headed for our platoon.

"There he is!" a voice shouted.

Noonan stepped outside. "I think you ought to stay, Kitzmiller. I got a letter from your girlfriend." Then he yelled to the advancing troops, "I got it! I got it! Come and listen. Kitzmiller's been lying his ass off."

Brian reentered the barracks, and Noonan cheerfully reeled and rushed after him, laughing. "Where were you going, man? Don't you want to hear this?"

"It's bullshit," Brian said as Noonan's entourage surrounded him. "Yeah, I'll listen to it, but it's all crap."

"I hardly think so," Noonan said. He pulled the folded contents from the envelope, then held it momentarily as a magician might. "Lookee here, guys," he said, bobbing his head with his mouth open, and held up a photograph.

Everyone stared at the identical picture that Brian had been carrying around with him the whole time and later had blown up—the same picture that hung over his bed. On the back of Noonan's picture was penned, *Good luck, Ronnie, and thank you! Alice Ann.* The gathering was speechless for several seconds, then the murmuring began.

"Jesus!"

"Holy shit!"

"I'll be fucked."

Brian glared at Noonan, who said viciously, "You fucking dipshit."

"Eat shit, you fat sonofabitching slob motherfucker," Brian shouted.

Noonan laughed as a guy might when he's play-fighting with a girl who gets mad and starts landing painful yet relatively harmless blows. Then he continued to emcee his little show. "Listen to this, guys. This is *her* letter—Alice Ann O'Neal's. She says, *Dear Ronnie*—the little twat always called me Ronnie—'I can't believe your letter. First of all, let me say that I'm concerned about you and will pray for you. I hope time goes quickly for you over there. Please be careful. What you told me was *very* upsetting.' Look—she's got *very* underlined. 'The idea that some stranger would have my picture and pretend that he was having a relationship with me is pretty scary and weird, too. I don't know Brian Kitzmiller, and the snapshot you sent doesn't ring a bell. The idea that this person claims to have been to bed with me really angers me. I am wondering if I should write your general and have this phony prosecuted.

"'Angela Cooke called Dick Richardson, a friend of hers from St. Sebastian. Dick informed her that Kitzmiller was real shy and never went out or did much of anything with the guys, and as far as he knew never even had a date. A complete weirdo, in other words. Then Angie—can you believe her nerve?—actually called his parents, and before they realized that maybe they were spilling too much info, they as much as confirmed it. When Angie told his mother what her mama's boy was up to—'" Noonan grinned, his eyes beaming. "'—she couldn't believe it and hung up.

"'I wish I hadn't told Daddy. He's really pissed off. Plus a couple of my closest friends—I'm sure you know Allan Thomas and Steve Virtucci—say they would like to have a little talk with Kitzmiller. And I won't be surprised if they do if he ever shows his face in town again. God, I feel like the girl in that stupid song 'My Boyfriend's Back', with all of you willing to defend my honor.

"'Well, Ronnie, do what you can to expose this phony. I never dreamt I would have my reputation fouled halfway around the world by some creep I don't even know, in Vietnam no less.'" Noonan sped up, twirling his hand as he read. "'Be careful, Ronnie, for God's sakes be careful over there. Thanks, thanks very much. Yours in appreciation, Alice Ann.'"

"Wow," someone uttered.

"What about this shit, Brian?" Randall demanded.

I had been watching Brian as Noonan read. He had looked at the floor most of the time and was as red as any human I'd ever seen. I bled for a trace of something to cling to and was glad to hear Brian's faint, "It's bullshit."

"Thath good enough for me," Hobson said.

"Me, too," I agreed, knowing full well it wasn't and that it would take a miracle to change things. I wondered if I had been right to jump in.

"I think it's good enough for all of us," Shifrin said.

I could have hugged him.

Shifrin glanced at Noonan. "It has to be. It could be a mix-up, or maybe you're the one—"

"Wait, wait a damn minute!" Richio yelled. "Dammit, Shifrin, it's more than some kind of fucking mix-up. There's something big, something huge here. Look at these fucking pictures. This is the same girl, by God. Hell, it's the same picture. Anybody think it ain't?"

No one answered. It was clearly the same girl.

"Then Noonan's lying!" I found myself yelling. Again I knew I was a hairbreadth from a brutal exchange of blows. "We don't know how he got this picture or if this letter actually came from Elaine." I was getting some incredulous stares. "Hey, shit, I can't explain what's goin' on, but why do we take this guy's word over Brian's, who we've known all year? I was set to go on R and R with Brian and Elaine. I mean, fuck."

"How 'bout it, buddy?" Randall asked Brian.

"I don't know what to say," Brian said, "but it's bullshit. I've known her for years. It's bullshit." With this he rose and headed out the door. "I gotta take a piss."

"Holy shit, man," McCollough said, his eyes following Brian's exit. "Unfuckingbelievable!"

"Let's go get him and get a beer," Shifrin whispered to Hobson and me. I was only too glad to leave.

"Holy shit," McCollough said again as we paraded out.

For two days controversy raged. Everyone was talking about it. Noonan's evidence seemed overwhelming, but some guys still had enough plain decency to stand back and watch, out of respect for the mail clerk who had grown so popular over the months. Captain Karch and Top were fed up with all the uproar.

Brian withdrew and seemed not to want company. Then, during the afternoon three days after Alice Ann's letter, Shifrin intercepted me as I was about to enter the orderly room.

"This episode has taken another unbelievable turn," he said, taking my elbow and steering me out to the company street.

"What could be worse than what's already happened?" I asked.

Joe shook his head. "Captain Karch got a letter from Brian's mother."

I winced. "But Brian would have had to—"

Joe shook his head and gestured toward a patch of shade, and we headed there to talk. "Mrs. Kitzmiller had typed the envelope with no return address so that it would pass through Brian's hands. Anyway, Karch read the letter aloud to Top and me while Brian was up at battalion. Basically she apologized for seeming overprotective if not neurotic, then said that Brian had written several days before about a new guy from Indianapolis who had created a set of unfathomable circumstances for him. He informed her that he wouldn't be writing every other day for a while because he had a lot to do. He also said not to worry, that everything would work out. She went on to tell our commanding officer that some girl had called—"

"Alice Ann's—I mean Elaine's friend," I said, feeling sick.

"Yes. And that she accused Brian of claiming all sorts of sexual perversions that could not possibly be true about her friend."

"Oh shit!" I said.

"Mrs. Kitzmiller then went into this spiel, which Karch read most sarcastically. She told the captain that Brian had never really dated anyone and that he had never even been to a high-school dance. She begged him to look after her son."

"What's Karch going to do?" I asked, remembering how the captain had humiliated Private Farling before the whole platoon.

"Nothing that I know of but talk to Brian. But that's not—"

Relief flooded me. "Well, as long as nobody finds out—"

"That's not the worst part. None of us realized it, but Chief Donaldson was, as usual, sitting on his fat ass outside the orderly room. He went down and told Helton at the mess hall, and word's spread all over. Noonan, Prackle, they all know. Noonan's even saying that Kitzmiller is going to be court-martialed on the charge of 'impersonating a fucker.'"

"What's Brian say?" I asked.

"Nothing, except that he's innocent and I'm free to believe whatever I want."

I hurried to the barracks. I was in an awful mood, and I can't say why I expected anything different. I felt like a fool for sticking up for Brian. He should have told me the truth, especially since I had come close to defending his honor with my fists.

Though it wasn't even four-thirty, I found Brian sitting alone on his bunk and looking dejected.

"I gotta know what the hell is going on," I started in impatiently. "I'm the last to have a clue."

Brian looked up sadly, then stated matter-of-factly, as if he were telling me the score of a Red Sox defeat, "There's no Elaine, Andy."

"What?" I asked angrily. "What the fuck do you mean?"

A small grin momentarily crossed his face. Then he looked gloomy again. "Elaine. I made her up."

"Damn you, Brian!" I shouted. "What kind of an asshole do you take me for?" I turned for the door.

"Wait a minute, Andy. At least let me explain. I never planned—"

I was in the company street. "Son of a bitch!" I yelled at the top of my lungs, and when I saw faces turn my way, I began to run to the basketball courts, then continuing another eighth mile to the EM club. Instead of going in I veered into Delta Company, of the 96th's motor pool, where I certainly had no business. I sat on the running board of a five-ton truck. Never had I felt more betrayed. *My God,* I kept repeating. *This is too much.* I picked up two handfuls of dirt, and for no reason began rubbing it on my face. Then I buried my head in my hands. I hurt—perhaps not as badly as from Jeanine's good-bye, but something like it. Why had Brian misled me and everyone else? He certainly hadn't needed to. Everybody liked him.

I could not pinpoint the exact mixture of sickening emotions churning inside me. I should have been angry with Brian, but I wasn't sure if I really was. The situation seemed too grave. I didn't know what to do, and I had no idea what Brian would do. I knew only that life was going to get very rough for him—Noonan would see to that, along with most of the unit. How in God's name could a snake like Noonan have come out of nowhere to bite him?

That night I slept in the maintenance platoon, in an empty bunk next to Hobson's. In some ways I was letting myself believe that I was the one who was hurt. For the next twenty-four hours I couldn't bring myself to talk with Brian or even be around him. That was a mistake.

The next few days were pure hell for Brian, as I had guessed. The first mail call was one of the worst spectacles I'd ever witnessed. The old maxim about not messing with the company clerk, mail clerk, or head cook was out the window. Everyone seemed to enjoy humiliating Brian, including guys like Randall, McCollough, and Richio. In the process they lost my respect and friendship.

"Hey, Brian, you gonna read anything from Elaine to us today?"

"Hey, Brian, what color panties did you say Elaine had on when you met her at the airport in Honolulu?"

"How many times did you say you nailed her? Sure hope you remembered the rubbers."

"Hey, Kitzmiller, you fuck Miss October? I mean, like before you got engaged to Elaine, of course."

It tore at me, and I never went to another mail call. My letters, of course, wound up on my bunk.

Roughly twenty-four hours after his admission to me, I knew I had to hear Brian out. I was by now sick about ignoring him. I tried to justify that mistreatment by reminding myself that it had been only one day, but I was not successful. I felt like a first-class traitor. In the early evening I looked for him. He was nowhere to be found, which was unsettling.

I was wandering around between companies when Top ran into me.

"McClain, I been looking all the hell over for you." He shook his head sadly. "Your buddy's got hisself in one hell of a jam."

"I know. I can't believe he made up all that stuff about Elaine."

"Me too, son, but that ain't the fuckin' half of it. He's put in a 1049 for the infantry, and Karch is gonna sign it, sure. The captain's gonna give him one chance in the mornin' to back out, but that'll be it. Karch is in a bad mood about the whole damn company. I think deep down he likes Kitzmiller, but that side ain't showin' much today. He said somethin' about it bein' time for him to learn the consequences of what he done." Top took a breath as if to give me a second to catch my sinking heart before it hit the ground. "He'll be out in the boonies inside of two weeks."

"What the hell does he mean, 'it's time for him to learn the consequences of what he done'? What has Brian ever done but a damn good job and conduct himself, as Karch would say, 'accordingly.'"

"He got caught in a big ass charade is what, McClain," Top said. "That other stuff can't undo the lies."

"I can see that, but what about—"

"Brian goes to the infantry, I'm afraid he ain't gonna come back. I know you heard me babble on about it before, but it's the damn truth. And I never seen a case quite like this. I seen boy soldiers before, I mean real boy soldiers. Seen 'em in World War Two mainly, when everybody was clamorin' to get in, at all ages. You know, kids lookin' a hell of a lot more like they're closer to the eighth grade than they are to being a man. When the shit hits, their chances ain't as good as a man's. And I got to remind you that men—*men*—are dyin' out there. Seasoned infantry, rangers, marines…whole companies are gettin' wiped out in one battle. Every day, them guys are gettin' sniped and steppin' on mines like they was cow shit on a farm. He ain't right for it. He ain't got the tools to cope with it."

"Can't you stop it this time?" I asked, already knowing the answer from the Ghent episode.

"Hell, no, I can't stop it. Try to scare him is all I can do."

"Damn, Top, this is one terrible situation gettin' worse by the minute. You gotta do something."

He rolled his eyes. "I am doin' somethin'. I'm lookin' all over for your ass. That's about all I can think to do. You're his best friend—you and Shifrin and Hobson. It's really up to you boys to stop it." Top paused as I looked down. Despair rounded my shoulders.

"Now, McClain," he said, "I know you've had a bad series of weeks, son, but you handled 'em well, and you'll live to see the day that you laugh at this shitty year. But Kitzmiller ain't gonna get that chance unless you—you—do somepin'. I'm afraid it's on you, son. It ain't on me."

I didn't like what he was saying because I knew it was true. "What can you do about the harassment?"

"I can't do shit about the harassment," Top said without hesitation. "Karch don't care about no harassment in this case, believe me—not after Kitzmiller sat face-to-face with him and showed him Elaine's, that bitch's, picture and claimed he was screwin' her and gonna marry her. Then lied to him about what a fine ol' time he had in Hawaya with her.

"I ain't none too impressed with it, either, but with me, at least at this point, I figure the embarrassment of being found out is plenty nuff. He's only a kid, and he's a good kid. I figure he's learned his lesson. Besides, McClain, I seen too many boys like that die already."

I folded my arms and turned away for a few seconds because I thought I might be getting misty-eyed. "He doesn't deserve this shit. Most of what he told Karch was to answer the same old questions to get the captain off his ass." When I turned back I fumbled for words. "Ah, man, Top. I keep hopin' we'll find some missing piece here, like at least some other girlfriend, just not the girl in the picture. I mean, I'm hopin'—"

"Hell, McClain, Kitzmiller lied, never figurin' that anything could come of it. Ain't no missin' piece gonna come out of it—*ever*."

Chapter 19

I searched and searched: the barracks, mess hall, showers, shitter, EM club, movie barn, basketball courts, command bunker, orderly room, and the barracks again. As sunset approached I climbed the command bunker one last time. Brian wasn't up there. I turned and surveyed the entire area, somewhat surprised at how much I could see from only ten feet up.

Damn, I thought, feeling unbelievably guilty, *why did I desert him yesterday? What kind of friend would do that? What must he have been going through the past twenty-four hours?*

Something caught my eye. A quarter mile down, on one of battalion's bunkers, I could see someone alone in the haze. I studied him for a minute, noticing the way he was sitting. It had to be Brian.

I walked over to him. I wanted to run, but I was too scared. The situation was weird, delicate, terrible. I climbed the bunker slowly. Brian continued to stare to the south toward Saigon.

"I wondered if you'd ever notice me," he said quietly.

"Well, shit, yes," I said with a nervous laugh. "I saw you a long time ago."

"Did you bring any beer?"

"No, but I will. You promise to stay right here, and I'll be back in a jiffy. Promise?"

"I'll be here. I don't have too many places to go, you know," he said. "But, Andy, I don't want you to bring anyone else. I don't want to see anyone else."

"Okay."

When I returned with a couple of six-packs of Black Label, I was so nervous I gulped down most of a can, while Brian took a sip. "This should be one of the happiest times in my whole life," he said. "The Red Sox won the pennant on Sunday."

"Yeah, I know. Man, that had to be the greatest pennant race in history. Four teams down to the final series and three alive on the last day."

"Yeah," he answered with a sigh. "I even sent Yaz a postcard. Hope he doesn't think it was dumb."

"Oh, no, I'm sure he'll love it. I'll bet you're the only one who thought to do that."

He didn't look at me, but he did smile.

"Hey, look, I'm sorry about yesterday," I said, seeing this as a good time to inject my apology. "It came as such a shock, and I kinda lost my senses for a while."

"Yeah, well, I'm sorry about the whole fuckin' affair. But that was bad, Andy. That may have been the worst of it." He stared to the south again, and I felt chilled inside. Then he let that part of it go. "I mean, I didn't intend for any of this to happen. It all started so innocently. I was just tryin' to get by Top. He had me scared shitless that first afternoon, and I remembered the picture. I've carried it sorta for luck and maybe a little morale booster for almost two years."

"Where'd it come from?" I asked.

"I found it, actually. See, I used to sweep the stands out at CYO field on Saturday or Sunday mornings after football games. That was how I paid for most of my tuition at Saint Sebastian. One Saturday, I happened to look down, and as I kicked this half box of popcorn, I suddenly see this, this unbelievable face. Even on the concrete in the midst of all that shit—popcorn, cigar butts, and paper cups—it jumped at me. I picked it up, and I'll be damned, but I couldn't take my eyes off her. I'd never ever seen her in person and still haven't. Probably best I keep it that way."

He grinned slightly. "I had absolutely no idea who she was, but she like represented everything I had ever imagined. I felt dumb, smiling at this beautiful angel, so I put her in my pocket and kept working. But I felt like I'd found something private and personal, something that was meant for someone else but was mine now, and I thought of it like some illegal treasure.

"Every now and then I would take the picture out, and the same feeling would come over me again. I started to wonder what she was like. I thought about her and nothing else. I imagined that she was my date for that night. This went on and on, and I started falling in love with the girl in the picture. I thought of her as Elaine, which is a classy name I love. I sort of gave her a personality. I know you're thinking that this is the weirdest shit you've ever heard and that I'm some kind of psycho."

"No, I can see doin' somethin' like that. I mean, I had this unreal crush on Hayley Mills three, four years ago, but when I started going out with real girls, I sorta put her on a back burner. I probably coulda had her if I tried," I added, and we both laughed.

He got serious again quickly. "You gotta understand this about my old life, Andrew. There were no real girls and no real life. There just couldn't be. I suffered, trapped, in a hopeless situation. My old man was off the deep end. I'll never know if he hated me or was an idiot or some kind of insane. But he was a religious-fanatic asshole with a personality that would make Helton seem cordial.

"Both my parents believed that no one should even be around members of the opposite sex until they were eighteen at least. They were against everything—dating, smoking, laughing, driving—anything that they didn't see as somehow honoring God. I'm sure it pissed Him off, because after all we were created in His own image and likeness and I'm sure he wouldn't have lived that way."

He took a swig. "We came down from Fort Wayne—I never mentioned this to you—at the beginning of my freshman year, so I was separated from the kids I knew growin' up. We arrived in Naptown, and naturally I had to go to an all-boys school, and I had this ten o'clock curfew, so if I went to a football game I couldn't go to the dance afterwards. My old man is one of those people who thinks the devil invented dancing—even square dancing, not to mention slow dancing or our kinda dancing. And because I wasn't permitted to get a driver's license, let alone a car, and because I was so fucking humiliated, I had a hard time asking other guys for rides to stuff. By the time senior year came—well, shit." He looked anguished. "Most of the time I just didn't bother going to anything or doing anything."

"God, that *would* sorta ruin high school," I said. "Where was your mom in all this?"

"My mom is a nice person. She loves me. I never doubted that. But she never uses her brain, and if my old man told her Jesus would be there in the morning she'd go along with it. She is his slave. She tells everything she knows about me and my sister to my dad every time he got home. Mom was scared to death of him but thought that was the way marriages were supposed to be. You know, like some fuckin' moralistic Henry the Eighth who wouldn't actually kill you, only make you wish you were dead.

"But that wasn't all about her. My mom is afraid of everything—germs, people, dogs, traffic, bugs, Castro, the Mafia, neighbors, God, priests, hot days, cold days, burning leaves, sports, everything. She believed her sacred duty was to protect me, so it came easy for her to fall into agreement with everything my old man came up with."

He shook his head. "I'm sure not surprised she wrote to Captain Karch. Probably the first mom ever to write to a C.O."

"Anyway, my old man was one violent bastard. He beat the shit out of me so many times, I lost count after a thousand. I can't remember a week going by where he didn't at least hit me. But the worst shit about him was his ranting and raving. He was always in a rage—not angry, not irritable. He was those when he was asleep. This man was in a constant rage. He never stopped yelling at me and Megan. He never stopped bitching and digging at my mom. I'd wake up, and the first thing I'd hear was him downstairs screaming at my mother about what an irreverent, disrespectful, rotten son I was. This man was full of hate. He hated Protestants, rock and roll, young people, Catholics who wore tight clothes or short dresses, his bosses, and his parents. He was a complete and total terror."

"Did any of your buddies in high school know about this?" I asked.

"I was way too embarrassed to talk about it. No one from school lived anywhere near us, which was probably good. I used to think that if I ever so much as brought a friend home with me, my dad would probably smack me in front of him.

"I got some shitty grades one time, and first he threatened to take me down to the principal's office and offer to beat me right there in the office. Then a light goes on in the creep's head, and he tells me that he's not above beatin' the crap out of me in front of the whole school." He laughed nervously, I could tell he half expected me to, also.

"Brian, man, I'm surprised you didn't slug him or shoot him," I said. "That bastard deserves to be in jail or the nut house."

"I got to admit I was too intimidated by him or maybe by the situation. I mean, it could so easily get out of hand, and that'd completely ruin my life. I'd have no future. He was a big strong guy, and he told me more than once that he would rather see me dead than not turn out right."

Brian had begun to sweat. He wiped his forehead with his sleeve, chugged some Black Label, and continued. "So I hung in as best as I could. Besides, I had a plan," he said proudly. "And my plan was what I lived for, and I didn't want to fuck it up."

"Yeah? What was it?"

"I decided to live despite him, to win by lasting him out. Of course I knew I couldn't live in his world, which happened to be a part of the real world, so I made up my own world. Not that I ever told lies, until here. I just lived in a fantasy. Then I created my simple plan and stuck to it. He wasn't going to take my life and make it his.

"I would come home from real school and go up to my room and shut the door, where I had my own dream high school, in my own city, with my own dream experiences. I lived in a fun place in my head, and I created everybody around me. We won the state in football and basketball, and the chicks all dug a character who resembled me. It was beautiful. I lived in my imagination constantly—at school, at work, wandering around, and certainly when I was around my parents. That was what got me through it.

"The actual plan part of it I concocted when I was fifteen. I was going to be my own person no matter what, and I was. My father never got control of my mind. I decided that I would make three simple goals for my first eighteen years: one was to be alive and a whole person, still me, on my eighteenth birthday, on freedom day. Second was to have my high school diploma from that excellent high school. That was no small accomplishment, you know, like it would be where you and Steffie graduated from."

I couldn't keep from laughing.

"Third was to somehow figure out how to get a driver's license. That wasn't easy, but I did it. In fact I reached all three objectives by the time I was seventeen and a half. I was so fucking proud of myself. I knew I could survive. I'd shut up and wait till I was eighteen, then leave the house on my birthday like I was going to the drugstore, join the army, and never look back.

"But I caught a real break when my old man signed my papers, waivin' my being seventeen. I told him I wanted to go in and serve my country the way everyone in our family always had. It killed my mom, but what the hell. I was goin' to do it in a few months anyway. So the way I figured, I'd join and do three years instead of two, to stay out of Nam."

He laughed. "Then I'd start college somewhere using the money from the GI bill. Pretty cool, huh, for a trapped, lost soul with no hope? Anyway, I didn't want to come to Nam, but I did. But then I lucked into this unbelievable job here, and everything seemed so within the reach of the plan's final phase." He awaited my reaction.

I shook my head in genuine amazement. "Incredible…I mean, I can't believe the obstacles and the bullshit you overcame. You sucked it up without going nuts or exploding, then you escaped. And it's gonna work—your plan. You're way more than eighty percent way there already!" A brilliant idea occurred to me. "I'm goin' to school too when I get out. Maybe we could do it together!"

He grew glum again. "I fucked up, Andrew. I destroyed my great effort. It wasn't completely my fault, but I can't undo it and I can't live it. I suppose you've heard, I'm pullin' a Ghent. I'm putting in for the infantry. I gotta get out of here, buddy, and this is the only way. I can't take it here."

"Brian, that is not the only way—"

"It is. I saw you watchin' mail call at noon. Well, it got a lot worse tonight. Noonan wanted to know if I had anything to tell my girlfriend, that he was writing her tonight. Then Lauck suggests that I make a tape for Alice Ann. And Richio starts goin' apeshit, sayin' what a great idea it was. I swear I'm so close to sluggin' one of those fuckers, but I don't want to get busted up before I go where I'm going. Maybe I'll start torchin' their mail." He looked down.

"Brian, listen. It's really bad now, I admit. But it can't get any worse. What you're proposing, though, isn't the answer."

"Andrew, it's the only answer." He rubbed his eyes, then looked at me, almost begging me to understand. "You can't know what this is like. I never felt like I had any real respect. I spent my whole life in the background, trying not to bring any attention to myself. Every time I thought of being with people my age I felt so embarrassed. I didn't want to be around anybody. It wasn't till here, here in fucking South Vietnam, that I ever felt like the person I was supposed to be. I was *somebody,* the mail clerk, the guy everyone wanted to see because everyone associated something good with me. And I was Elaine's boyfriend. I mattered. I was someone people came to for advice, and it was something to be my friend. I had actually made it as a real person. I never had that."

"Brian, you didn't need that stuff—I mean that Elaine stuff. It wouldn't have mattered."

"Maybe. Maybe not. But you gotta believe me. I never planned to tell everyone that the girl in my wallet was my girlfriend. But when I saw Top for the first time, I panicked. I figured him for a real bully, not the decent guy that he is, and it scared me, made me think of more harassment, of going through that kinda shit every day. Then I remembered the picture. When it shut everyone up, it felt like magic."

His eyes filled with pain. "I didn't mean to be a fake. It just happened in an instant, and when I saw it was working…well, when Top was asking me point-blank and all you guys were laughing at me, why wouldn't I say that we—me and Elaine, who didn't exist anyway—had done it. I had no time to think about it. If I'd said at that point we hadn't done it, wouldn't that have kinda left me where I'd always been? Probably a lot of guys lie about it. I guess I figured what's the difference."

He stopped and thought. "The idea I slandered her is really bullshit. I mean, I didn't really see her as anything but a figment of my imagination. I never meant to hurt her, whoever she was. I never even thought about that. Jesus, God. Ah, Andrew, I never dreamt this could happen in a million years."

We sat silently. I couldn't think of anything to say.

Brian finally spoke. "You know, I didn't like what I was doing. I kept lookin' for the right time to get a *Dear John*. Just when I was ready, I'll be damned if Jeanine didn't come out and send you a real one. After that, I never happened on a good time to get out." He stopped as if he were searching for something.

"Brian, what about Hawaii? What if I woulda went with you?"

"Andrew, that was what I wanted. That woulda been perfect. You needed to go and get outta here and have a good time, and I coulda got out of it by then, the easiest way. At the last second I would have gotten her cancellation and her good-bye. By then we woulda been perfect for each other. Two buddies who had just lost their chicks out tomcattin' for a couple more. I wouldn't have felt guilty anymore, and you and me woulda had a week of drinkin' and chasin' girls. Man, it woulda been great. Instead of the shit time I actually had," he said dolefully.

"What? You didn't like Honolulu?"

"I found it too hard to do by myself. Gorgeous girls were everywhere, but I was afraid to talk to them. I did eventually try it…"

"What happened?"

He hesitated. "After half my leave was up and I had gotten pretty bored and disappointed, I was lyin' on the beach and finally got the guts to talk to this girl sitting a few feet up from me. She was cool, with this ungodly perfect tan. She was blond and tall, like five-nine. I really thought she was a knockout."

"So," I cut in, "you naturally wanted to pick her up and screw her."

"Well, sure, but just as much—well nearly as much—I wanted to be like friends with her too. But she was really cruel and tough, though sort of funny in a way."

"Like how?"

"Well, I asked her for a cigarette—"

"You don't even smoke!"

He blushed and pointed for me to pass him another can. "—and she blew me off. To be honest, it kinda hurt me worse than I had imagined."

"Chicks do that all the time. Surely someone with your wit and quickness could handle it."

"Maybe in the right circumstances. It wouldn't have been that bad if you or Hobson were there. But the way she did it, she coulda been an assassin.

See, at first I'm sittin' there scared shitless, and I keep stealin' a peek up at her and those long brown legs. She was slick and smooth, all covered with oil. Anyway, finally I decide I have to make a move. It was killing me. She's reading, but I bet she was aware of me."

"What was she reading?"

"Well, I think it might've been *Defile the Haughty Virgin,*" he said quickly, and I broke up.

"So, anyway, I asked if I could have a cigarette. And she goes, 'Help yourself.' So I did. Then I asked her if I could sit down for a second and she shrugged like she didn't care.

"Well, she let me sit there for a good three minutes, which seemed like an hour, and ignored me. I feel like I'm sitting on a block of ice and not her beach towel. Finally, I go somethin' like, 'Pretty cool place.' She looks at me. I'm like tan in the face and arms from here, but I'm sunburned bad on my back and chest. She goes, 'Oh, you're not from around here? I sorta figured you were a surfer.'"

I laughed unintentionally, then so did Brian. "I'm sorry," I said. "When I think of a surfer, I think of someone with long hair who looks like Randall."

"That's okay. Anyway, I'm so excited and scared, I didn't realize that she was jackin' me around. We get to talkin', and she tells me she's a student at the University of Montana most of the time, and she's workin' as a waitress and just hangin' out only for the summer and maybe the fall. Her name is Heather. Then a couple of her girlfriends join her from out of nowhere. Shit.

"Right away she starts gettin' weird, and everything she does makes them giggle. She finds out I'm from Nam and have to go back, and she starts askin' me all sorts of questions like, what's it like to kill somebody with my hands, and if napalm is jellied gasoline, can you eat it and just stupid kinds of shit like that. She goes on and on. I'm kind of speechless and don't want to be there anymore, but I feel dumb about getting up and moving. And, I mean, you never know, I might have been doin' good."

At this we burst out laughing again, and Brian laughed as hard as I've ever seen him. I begin to think I've got a chance of keeping him in the company, if I can keep his spirits up.

When he got himself under control, he continued. "So, simultaneously with jackin' me around, they're having a regular conversation going on among themselves too, and that gets weird and pretty crude. One girl says she saw some guy naked the past night, sleepin' on their apartment floor with some other girl they were lettin' crash. Heather asks the girl tellin' the story if she saw the guy's cock. The other one goes, 'Yes, I certainly did.' And Heather asks if his dick was beautiful, and the other one goes, 'I'd say so, in an aesthetic sense, much as one would admire the Washington Monument.' Then, laughing her ass off, Heather goes, 'Does that sound familiar, Brian?' And I look down like I'm checkin' myself out, and I go, 'Well, yeah, it does. Thanks for noticing.' And they all cracked up."

I was in hysterics at Brian's storytelling.

"Don't roll off the edge, you stupid shit," he said, pointing to the corner of the bunker. Then, "Hey, I'm telling you about the worst moment of my life before a few days ago, and you're laughing your ass off at me. Thanks for the understanding, Mr. Compassion."

I sat up, and he continued. "Then, and this is where she really electrified me, she goes, 'Do you have a shower in your hotel room, Brian?' And I go, 'Sure.' And she goes, 'I'd like to take a shower. How would you like to soap me all over and help me take a nice long one before I go to work?' And my jaw about hits the sand, and of course I go, 'Sure.' And she goes on in some pretty exciting detail about that for a while, with her friends laughing it up, and then finally she goes in sort of a mock sorry voice, 'Oh, no, look at the time. Darn. Oh, Brian, I'm so sorry, but I got to go, but I really have enjoyed meeting you, though. I love the way you smoke.'

"She gets up, and the three of them, all grins and snickers, start walking off, and she turns and goes, 'Listen, I really hope you get laid while you're here in the Pineapple State.' Then they're gone. And that was that. I didn't see them again. And I really felt stupid and kinda washed out, but in a way I was relieved that they were gone. After that I was too shell-shocked to try it again."

My mind teetered between sympathy and recognition. Finally I said, "Hey, you did good, man. The only important issue was that you had the guts not to let an opportunity pass you by. Exactly like you convinced me about Steffie."

He took a deep breath, then lay back and said, "I hope it works out with you and Steffie."

"Yeah, me too," I said quietly, then looked at him. "Brian, I got you to thank for that chance. Listen, man, I can't let you do this infantry shit. We're too good of buddies."

"I know we're buddies, and we always will be, but, Andy, I got no choice. I'm gettin' the fuck away. I'm a villain now. It's not the losing of so many friends—which is horrible—it's that they've become instant enemies, almost like I raped somebody's little kid or something. I can't face doin' any more mail calls. If they want to bust me they can. Nothing they can to do me is worse than this. I especially can't stand to think about being around Top. I mean, he believed in me."

"He's one of the ones who's really in your corner right now." I decided not to enumerate his allies at the moment. "How did you fake the letters?"

A smile crossed his face. "I wrote 'em every other day in the mail room. Dopplemeyer was right: You can do almost anything in there. I had my own little space that I didn't have to share with anyone. Early on I wrote my aunt Rose and told her that I had met a nice lieutenant nurse that had treated me for ant bites, and she was complaining that they didn't have any classy, feminine stationery for her to write her boyfriend, who was a lawyer and an older guy. I told Aunt Rose I wanted to do something nice for a very nice nurse who was too down to earth to ask anyone back home to help. So she sent me a couple of boxes of that yellow stuff I been using. My little sister, Megan, gave me a Schaeffer cartridge pen the day I left, so I could write to her, and from time to time I would have her send me little boxes of peacock-blue cartridges. Peacock-blue ink was Elaine's favorite, you know."

"I knew that," I said.

"So I just made 'em up every other day in the mail room. I got the perfume from Megan, sent her some money, and told her I was going to play a practical joke, which I guess I sorta was. I decided always to do as good a job as I could, in case I wanted to show the letters to someone else, like I did you and Joe now and then. I'm good at imagining stuff. I might be able to write a book or two. I even had Megan send me stamps, 'cause of our letters goin' free. Shit, just try to find a stamp around here! I drew my postmarks with a compass. I was so damn meticulous, no one could ever tell." He smiled wistfully. "Anyhow, that's how I did it, and you already know why. I swear I never meant to gain anything."

"I believe you."

"That's means an awful lot, Andy."

"Okay, one wrong is enough," I said sanctimoniously. "Another one is not going to make it right."

"Where'd you ever hear that?" he asked.

"Come on, I'm being serious now."

His face changed suddenly. "I thought I knew about humiliation before with my old man. I never understood how much worse it could be when you do it to yourself, when you destroy your own integrity. If I thought I knew what absolute misery was, I was wrong there too. I'm not even sure that out-and-out death wouldn't be better. Certainly just the chance of dying is better. I gotta go, Andy. I wish I could go tonight. I don't want to see another soul from here ever again. Except you."

"Hey, Shifrin and Hobson, Top, Champion, and Prather? They'll understand. And they care about you," I said.

"I can't imagine ever looking Prather in the eyes. As far as Hobson and Shifrin, man, I can't tell you. Hobson is my good friend, and I really let him down. He was so proud of me. He would only believe the best about me." At this Brian choked back tears.

"It's okay, Brian. That's precisely it. He is your friend, and he'll still believe the best about you. Once those guys hear what you've told me, they'll understand, and so will a bunch of others. And the ones that don't, fuck 'em. They're not our friends."

"I can't face those guys—I can't. It's not going to happen. They'll always know, and I'll always know. I can't walk around this company knowin' what everyone is thinking."

"It doesn't matter what they think. You can't worry about what people think."

He shook his head. "If it doesn't matter what other people think of us, then why do we worry about protecting our reputation or getting an education or getting chicks to like us or persuading people or about the way we look or first impressions? What the fuck people think is everything, you dumb shit! I mean, I even care about what Alice Ann O'Neal thinks. Oh, man. The real person in the picture comes to life and hates me after all those months of loving her. I'd have given anything to have really met her. Now, if I ever do, it'll be—Well, it'll be gruesome. You tellin' me that doesn't matter?"

His voice rose, and he was truly angry. "You saying you don't care what Steffie Kissinger thinks? You hardly know her, and you're madly infatuated. You're damn near in love, and I guarantee you, you do give a shit about what she thinks."

"Yeah, I do. There's still a chance there," I said solemnly. "But let's say my glorious quest doesn't work out. I'm not going to fret over what the hell she thinks. It really doesn't matter that much."

"You saying it doesn't matter to you what Jeanine now thinks of you? She thinks you're a war criminal. You saying that doesn't bother you? Andy doesn't care what people think. What a unique, cool, tough dude."

"All right, damn it. It *does* matter what people think, but if you can't control it, you don't go ending your own life. Brian, you can't go to the infantry because of Alice Ann and Pigface Noonan and what some of the guys in our company think. Let *them* go to the fucking infantry and get shot to pieces if they don't like *us*."

"Maybe, I don't feel like I deserve this job anymore," he said. "And maybe I really owe my country and the guys already out in the boonies my direct support."

I was getting angry. "You sound like Ghent, and that logic got him nowhere with you, remember? Damn it, Brian, this war is a special kind of event. We all have one job and only one job: *survive* until your year's up. That's your real duty. You go out there in fuckin' Indian country, your chances go down dramatically. Throw in the fact that you're not a trained infantryman, and your chances almost don't exist."

"What would you do?" he asked.

"I-I'd stay, and I'd just get through it. It has to get better. I'd stay with you guys, my buddies, and I'd make it. It might be hard...Fuck, I don't know. I sure wouldn't go to the infantry, though."

"You sure as hell might. To get away from this place, if that's your only hope of transferring, you damn well might. A 1049 for anything else would be turned down in a second. But one for combat gets approved instantly. Those are my choices. I can't face this mess. What I did was really bad and stupid, and what I'm living now is hopeless. I've even thought a couple times that my plan is gone, and I'm not sure that I even want to live."

"Ah, shit, Brian, please. It could never be that bad."

"Yeah, it could, Andy."

I was shocked, but I guess I shouldn't have been. I was afraid, too. I felt that the burden of the entire process of persuasion was on me and no one else. I began to speculate about possibilities, commitments I hadn't thought out. "Look, what about this? I will extend six months to cover the rest of your time. I'm here through August or so, and you go home in March. That gets you through it."

"Andy, that's bullshit. You're not going to spend another day in Nam because of me. I wouldn't stand for it."

"Now, listen. We both go to school when we get out, which is about three months apart. We go to the University of Kentucky or at Indiana U or somewhere. UK is the chick capital of the world. We get an apartment together. It would be unreal. We'd have a blast. We'd have cars and already be twenty-one. We could get jobs like at the student hangouts, the bars. We'd have it dicked. Plus we'd be gettin' an education."

He snickered. "Well, I'm glad you worked that last fact in somewhere. We might want to consider that. Look, I'm going to take my chances in the boonies with the grunts. That's that. I can't get around these people here. When we get out, if you still want to, I would definitely consider something like that."

"Brian, it won't be that bad here after—"

"Andy, my troubles are only beginning here. On top of the guys here now, every time a new guy comes in he's gonna be filled in on this crap—each and every new guy. That's probably a hundred new people I've never even met that will be laughing at me, constantly riding me, trying to pick a fight with me when they're drunk. I'm not wasting one fucking day. I'm putting in my 1049 in the morning, and that's the end of it."

At this he turned and covered his face with his hands. I had never seen him cry, and I wasn't good at consoling him. But I stayed with him for a long time.

Chapter 20

Karch met with Brian at seven the next morning. Prather wanted to hear what was going on as much as I did, so we hung around the orderly room, pretending to be studying some prints and a map. Shifrin tapped away at the morning report, and Top puffed on a cigar while he stared at the previous day's *Stars and Stripes*. McCollough sat cleaning his shotgun while he waited for his boss. I'm sure Karch knew we were there and was out to make certain we heard every word for reasons I'd have never given him credit for. After the usual moments of ignoring Brian for effect, he stopped shuffling papers and began in earnest.

"I have here, Kitzmiller, in my hands, your insane request to join the 9th Infantry Division." He paused, and we heard him light a cigar. "I'm a busy, busy man, son, and I do not intend to fuck around all morning with this. I hope you understand that this is a serious document, representing the most dire consequences that you will ever face in your life."

"Sir, I fully—"

"Shut up, Kitzmiller. Your entire existence is boiled down to this one fucking moment in time. Do you understand me?" he asked tersely.

"Yessir."

"If you tell me to go through with it, I will sign this, and you'll be as good as dead. You will sacrifice the rest of your young, precious life because of an idiotic decision based on total immaturity and a huge dose of self-pity. This is wartime, Kitzmiller. We don't grant requests to change our venue every time we're caught lying about all the ass we've had."

I grimaced, imagining Brian's embarrassment.

"Sir, I feel that I have an obligation for more hazardous duty. I'm no better than those who, for some reason, were chosen to be in the field, while I wasn't."

"Uncle Sam didn't give you this duty because he liked you or figured you couldn't make it out there," Karch said angrily, punctuating his words with a

198

finger stabbing the air in Brian's direction. "You enlisted and signed up for it, and you got it because you gave an extra year of your life to the government to stay out of combat. That was smart, Brian, damn smart. Now you want to undo that and in the process kill yourself? I suggest you get out of here and resume doing your job."

"I am going forward with my request sir," Brian said, beginning to sob.

"Kitzmiller, you fucked up. You lied to Top and to me and to your buddies who still genuinely care about you. You lied to guys you didn't know. Despite your appearance as a youngster, you wanted everyone to believe you were a Casanova. You tried it and obviously liked it. You got away with it for a while then you got caught. Now I suggest you take the consequences for what you did. Suck it up like a man. Now get out of here and get your ass back to work."

"Sir, I have the right to request a combat assignment," Brian said shakily but with determination. "I want to go ahead with my request."

Karch's face and neck turned dark red. "Let me tell you something, boy. I have a directive as company commander to approve without question requests for combat. The infantry is being blown away, burned up, shot to pieces faster than they can be replaced, and the army is telling us to stand back and let you fuckers come. My immediate superiors don't feel that way, nor do I. But I'm not going to get my own ass in a sling because I resisted you on this. I am simply trying to convince you to save your own life. You want to live, don't you, Kitzmiller?"

"Yes, I do, sir. I—"

"Then get out. One day you'll enjoy all those pleasures of the flesh that you so ardently long for. One day you'll be a boyfriend, then a husband and a father. You'll probably have a bunch of girls just lay down for you while all of that is shaping up. You don't want to miss that, do you? Now what's it going to be, Kitzmiller? I've taken all the time I can on this." He lowered his voice and said more softly than I'd ever heard him speak, "Please, make the right choice. What's it going to be, Brian?"

I began to pray and could feel myself shaking during the short silence. "Sir, I am staying with my request for the 9th Infantry Division. I have that right. I appreciate your concern, but I am requesting the infantry."

"Very well. It's done." I heard the sound of paper being whisked across the top of a desk, followed by an angry scrawling.

The captain left from his office and handed the document to Top. "This goes in with the morning report, Top. Not at noon, but with the morning report. I want a list of four solid candidates for mail clerk on my desk at

1800." He strode over to Shifrin's desk, glanced at the morning report, signed it, then motioned for McCollough, and the two left for the day.

After he was gone Top groaned. "You gone and done it, Kitzmiller. You gone and wasted yourself."

I waited for Brian to cry.

"Top, can I be excused for a few minutes?" he asked, barely audible.

"Kitzmiller, I'd just as soon you stay here. Let's talk about this. It ain't too late. I'll still tear the fucker up and tell Karch you changed your mind."

"If we did that, I'd just be back tomorrow or the next day to put it in again. You can see that, can't you?" he asked sadly.

"Top's right, Brian," Shifrin said, ignoring Brian's question. "There's no reason for you to get yourself killed over this. You know you've still got friends here. This'll all quiet down in a few days."

"It goes in with the morning report, Joseph. You heard Captain Karch," Brian stated flatly, then brushed past Top and went out the door. "I'll be back with the mail," he called back.

Prather had an idea that surprised me on a couple of counts, not the least of which was he had begun to seem a little distant with me and I was glad to feel his concern for Brian. "Top, how about letting Shifrin handle the mail this morning? Let's see if we can get Kitzmiller to go with us. In the meantime, you hang on to that document until we get back."

I was also astonished when Top consented and even more amazed when Brian agreed to go with Prather and me.

When I pulled out, I headed for a site near the new army headquarters in Long Binh, but Prather corrected me.

"Saigon," he ordered.

"What?" I said, not believing my ears.

"Let's go to town. Not Bien Hoa, but the real town. Let's check out some of the sights we've never seen and maybe hit a bar or two. Hell with it. We deserve it. Right, Brian?" he asked over his shoulder.

"I guess so, sir."

"Good," Prather said. "And it will just be our little secret. We'll hit a couple sites and check the plant out when we get back. We'll work a day the way Chief Donaldson does every day."

I drove the jeep to Saigon. Brian sat in the back without saying a word. When we got there we endured the traffic jams and meandered through the narrow side streets, taking it all in. As always, I felt overwhelmed by the sheer number of people, people who by our standards had nothing, yet who pressed onward as full of purpose and urgency as people would anywhere in the States.

I knew Saigon some, though most of the time I still felt like I was lost. But I never felt any panic when Prather was with me. I felt good just driving around like a tourist without that imaginary clock constantly counting down in my head. The day was cloudy, and for a change it actually felt cool, compared to what we were used to. Eventually, we wound up on To Do Street, which was famous for its bars, hotels, cafes, and shops. It attracted an international mix of people, including journalists, higher-ranking military leaders, politicians, investors, economists, government officials, professors, and ambassadors, along with people from the seedier side of life—prostitutes, black marketers, drug dealers, alleged agents of various intelligence organizations, gamblers, and even mercenary recruiters.

We wound up in one of To Do's dingier bars. Prather was his usual quiet self for the longest time, and I wondered if he had anything cooking in his head. We sat and relaxed at a table, enjoying a couple rounds of beer.

As the beers took effect, Brian became talkative. "This is a big-ass city," he said. Prather looked at him. "I mean, in comparison to Bien Hoa."

"It's a big-ass city compared to anywhere, with around three million people, I think," Prather said. "Brian, you're in the most famous red-light district this side of Bangkok, and from what I've heard, you'd have to go to Hong Kong to equal it."

Several women sashayed by our table, in dresses not only hauntingly short but of a quality more decadent, more Western, than what you'd see in Bien Hoa.

"You can say what you want about the Far East, but sex is a lot easier here than say—in New York. A lot cheaper, too," my lieutenant mused.

Time passed. I wondered if Prather intended to get Brian laid or would work some miracle of persuasion, but I was disappointed in both respects. When Brian spoke, Prather listened to him intently, but for the longest time the conversation never drifted to Brian's situation.

As we drank and discussed what little we knew about the Orient, a Caucasian man dressed in a white jacket approached us. He had an unusually pointed nose and chin, and his features were so chiseled that he looked like a guy who might appear in a movie to make it seem more grotesquely real.

"Good day, gentlemen." He spoke softly with an obvious French accent. "A fine day, no? I could not help but notice you had drank, ah, more than ze couple, and you look as though you might be in ze market for a service. No? Perhaps some form of entertainment. Maybe you wish to gamble? Eh?"

"No, no," Prather answered. "We're taking in the sights a bit, and we'll be leaving soon. Thank you, though."

"You know this place is a little special, and I thought perhaps that was why you were here. If not, you should know that—" He looked around nervously. "—this is a place where if one would have ze desire, well…could this be of interest to you?" He unfolded a flyer of sorts, which matched almost perfectly an ad in a French magazine—or at least a magazine printed in French—that we'd seen before. It read:

American GI Is This You?
Are you tired of the army but not the war? Are you sick of meager pay? Do you yearn for the *true rewards* of a soldier of fortune? Put your skills to work. Many operations, many countries to choose from.

Prather began to chuckle. "No, I'm afraid that's not us. I guess we're tired of *both* the army and the war."

"I see, I'm so sorry. I am only in ze business of arranging meetings, you understand. Now, there must be something, some pleasure I can arrange for you, or you would not be here, no?"

"Look, sir," Prather answered. "We just stopped in for a drink. I don't believe we will require your services. Thank you, though."

"Ah, yes. Only I find it a little strange that you would be here in ze middle of ze morning. If you come with me, I will take you to ze most beautiful women you will ever see—more beautiful than in all of Paree."

"That will not be necessary. Now if you will excuse us."

"Whatever you say, Lieutenant. Perhaps you are—and understandably so—worried to talk to a stranger. But you and your young men have nothing to worry about. You can say anything you want in here—anything."

"Well, if that's the case," Prather said, now clearly annoyed, "would you mind leaving us the fuck alone?"

"Certainly, sir." Then he startled us. "Would you be interested in leaving the country?" He looked at us eagerly. "I am one of only a few men in Vietnam that could get you to Hong Kong or even to South America, where you would be safe and able to start over in life. Who knows? Someday you would be able to return to the States when this is over."

"Yeah?" Brian asked. "How much?"

"To Phnom Penh, Cambodia, or maybe Bangkok? Five hundred American dollars. Of course you would be responsible for travel beyond there. Now to go to a place, say, like Hong Kong—one thousand American dollars. That would include a new identification, including passport. Any later commercial airfare would not be included in that price. You are interested, no?" he asked Brian.

"I should be but I'm not," Brian replied. "I was just curious as to how it worked. I never imagined such a way out existed."

"Anything in ze world is possible, my friend. You need only two possessions—desire and money, no? You are not obligated by your existence in the world to fight for your country. That is only in your mind and in ze minds of those making you do it. In fact most of ze world thinks that you are crazy for being here. I can help you—all of you."

"We're too damn short to desert," I said. "It would be stupid. I'm down to five and a half months. Lieutenant here has less than three. And Brian only has six months. Besides, we're with the engin—" I stopped and looked uneasily at Brian, who grinned. I felt like a huge idiot.

The Frenchman sighed. "You wish maybe to see a cockfight?"

At this Lieutenant Prather burst out laughing. "Man, you are the consummate salesman. No, I'm afraid we can't help you. But nice of you to stop over. Have a nice day."

"You think about it, yes? I can arrange anything you wish today," the Frenchman said, then drifted away.

"Well, there was a way," Brian said. "Except I only have six hundred bucks saved—well, crap, only four hundred after Hawaii."

"Aw, hell, Brian, that guy's a con man," Prather said. "You know there aren't many chances to get out like that."

"Did I mention Cheedah's out of Nam?" Brian asked. "I got a postcard from him a couple of days ago. He has to serve four more months in the prison at Fort Leavenworth, then he's out of the army on a DD. That would be another way out. Seems like everyone's out that doesn't want to be in."

"A dishonorable discharge is no way out, either," Prather said. "That guy is a worthless thug."

"Look, dammit, why don't you stay with us?" I said quickly, as if I had been waiting all morning for that opening. "Six months is not a long time. You'll get out alive. That's what matters."

Brian looked at me with an expression that said, *Don't start that again.*

"He's right," Prather finally said. "And I've got to say that most of what

Karch said today was right, too. Brian, you are at the edge. This is a reprieve, your only one from the ultimatum you got this morning. Please take it."

"I can't, sir. I appreciate what you're doing for me. I was glad to get the time away from the company, and I knew you guys would try to change my mind. But I won't. I won't."

At that moment I was convinced nothing could be done. Brian was going to the ground war as an infantryman.

The few days between Brian's request and his departure were sadly memorable. During a ride to a site inspection, Prather confided his initial intentions for that afternoon in Saigon. "I thought we'd get Brian drunk and maybe even laid, but I felt lost with him." He shook his head slowly. "This may shock you, but if I were in his shoes I might do exactly what he's doing. Your good name is irreplaceable."

Meanwhile, Shifrin took over the mail duties, and Brian focused more on typing reports and duty rosters. To my disgust, the hecklers were relentless. Some were surprised by Brian's decision, but others used it as an inspiration for further insults. One of the worst offenders was Sergeant Helton, who seemed to hate Brian for the whole affair.

"Well, good afternoon, Specialist Kitzmiller," Helton began when he'd see Brian in the lunch line. "Look who's here. Our platoon's answer to Audie Murphy. Kitzmiller's gonna earn himself a Combat Infantry Badge and a couple of rows of medals to impress Elaine. Hey, why go to all the bother? Just go down to the PX and buy 'em. Step aside, boys, we got a real man in the chow line now! You'll write us, won't you, when the number of gooks you've killed exceeds the number of women you've laid?"

Noonan remained the ultimate scourge. Late one evening, when Brian attempted to sneak into the barracks, Noonan took a cigarette from his mouth and blew a long, steady stream of smoke. "You know, Kitzmiller, maybe you could explain something to me. If you didn't have the guts to stay here and face your lies, how the fuck are you going to face combat situations?"

"I'll just pretend that Charlie is your fat, fuckin' ugly ass."

To most of this, though, Brian withdrew and would not respond. He made every effort to stay away from everyone, and many times I couldn't find him. Often I found myself angry at him for acting like a child, being a martyr for what he had brought on himself; but mostly I felt sick. As the days passed, clearly the tension from the his fellow soldiers and his increased fear of what was to come made him nervous, even ill.

When he was with his friends—provided no one else was around—all he wanted to talk about was the World Series. The Red Sox got behind but then miraculously caught up in games, tying the series. When it came down to game seven, as much as I liked the Cards, I found myself rooting for Brian's Sox. Bob Gibson, of course, knew nothing about Brian's impending departure for the infantry and in the seventh game dominated the Red Sox, pitching his way to his third win of the World Series and the 1967 World Championship. Brian slipped that much further into gloom.

Brian's defeat was Prather's victory, and in celebration the lieutenant handed out beer and cigars to everyone he saw. When he made this offering to Brian, Brian said, "Sorry, sir, but the way I see it, that would be like drinking to Ho Chi Minh and his boys."

Then came huge shockers on back-to-back days. At noon the day after game seven a letter arrived from Green Bay, addressed to Brian and me.

"This looks like Audrey Glasscock's writing," Brian said, turning the envelope over. "But she forgot to put their return address on it." He tore it open.

"Read it out loud" I said.

"'September thirty. Dear Andy and Brian, I don't know if you remember hearing about me, but I'm Bobby Glasscock's wife. What I have to tell you is the worst nightmare of my life. Bobby was killed.'" Brian looked at us, horrified. "Jesus, no."

"Oh my God," I said.

He continued, stuttering, obviously shaken. "'H-he got home a few weeks ago and was having a blast. I never saw him drink so much. He went out the other night with two of his best buddies from the plant. He didn't even bother to have dinner. Then, at around three in the morning, it happened. The police said he was driving too fast. He lost control and ran off the road. The car hit a tree, and all three of them were killed. I really don't know what to do, but he talked about you two constantly, ever since he got back, so I figured you'd want to know. The funeral is tomorrow. Please pray for Bobby, because I'm not sure everything he did was pleasing to God. And please be careful over there and when you get home, too. Life is too precious. Thank you both for being his friends. Audrey Glasscock.'"

Brian sniffled and wiped his eyes with his forearm.

"God…" I managed to say, fighting tears.

"Man, to make it all the way back," Brian said. "He had it made."

"I can't believe this."

"God, I feel so sorry for her," Brian said, shaking his head. "All he ever wanted was to work in that shit paper plant and watch the Packers and have a good time drinkin' with his buddies and spend time with his wife."

We were consumed with depression, and later that evening it hit me: If I felt this bad for Bobby, what would it be like if Brian got it?

The next day we rolled in at noon, and after I dropped Prather off at the officers' hooch, I went with Shifrin and Hobson to fetch Brian and head to the mess hall for lunch. We had to escort him, or Brian wouldn't even eat. As we left the orderly room, Mitch Woodson ran up the street. He was full of grease, and his fatigues were stained a filthy brown from his months of labor as a mechanic, not unlike Hobson's. "Hey, did you guys hear about Ghent?" he asked, out of breath.

"No. What?" I asked.

"There's a guy over at the 96th who's good buddies with some guy who was in the same grunt company as Ghent. He got zapped, man, last week. He's dead. They said he caught the first shot of an ambush. Charlie plugged him right through the eye, man. He never knew what hit him. He went to swat his face like a bee flew into it, then just collapsed."

I felt numb. Ghent had had that country boy's savvy, and as time had passed, I found myself believing that he'd adapt and make it. I looked at Brian, who was ghastly pale.

He shook his head, then said sadly, "It's like nothin' is right anywhere in the world right now. It's like watchin' somethin' go down the toilet. It swirls around lower and lower, and nothing can stop it. God, I can't believe all this."

He disappeared, and I didn't see him again until the next morning.

That day I began a ritual, a daily exercise that I was to become addicted to until I left Vietnam. Sergeant Miguel Delgado, a former boxer, had returned from his temporary duty pushing jungle and brought two punching bags with him—a heavy bag and a speed bag—with the works, including hand wraps and bag gloves. Nobody knew Delgado well. He'd be gone weeks at a time, and when he returned he might have anything from battlefield souvenirs to black-market items to miscellaneous crap he won at poker.

Now, he rearranged some bunks at the far end of the equipment platoon and hung the bags. Top happened to come in during the preparations and commented, "This might be good. Might cut down on all the fightin' for the guys to have somethin' to beat the crap out of."

At first the bag attracted a lot of interest, but after a couple of days I was one of the few who used it. I returned four times that afternoon and evening to work out. The sessions were as exhausting as wind sprints. Delgado gave me lessons on punching and protecting myself from wrist sprains. More than once, as I blasted away, I pictured Noonan's face turning to pulp before me.

Chapter 21

Brian's orders arrived within ten days. He was to leave the next morning for the 90th Replacement Battalion and then ship down to the delta immediately. When he actually saw his name in black and white on the orders, he rushed outside to compose himself.

I walked away and kept walking. Champion tracked me down to tell me Prather had taken off by himself with the jeep. Of course that was the first time I'd done anything like that. It could've been serious if Prather wanted to press it. I didn't care, at least not at that moment. Luckily Prather understood. He asked me in that humble way of his not to let it happen again.

Brian had the rest of the afternoon off, and surprised us by going into town by himself.

In the evening we got together for our last party. Again we chose our own company command bunker. Donny Hobson was not with us—he could not be found—and I felt awful about it. Shifrin, Champion, and I toted up a case of beer, and I added a bucket of ice from the mess hall. Despite our companionship and the beer, nothing could cheer up Brian, who sat facing the south, looking entranced. George, Joe, and I had made small talk for nearly a half an hour when George finally addressed Brian.

"What do you see out there, Brian?"

He answered without turning. "The delta, George, the Mekong Delta. My new place of residence somewhere down there fifty, a hundred miles or so."

"Lot of swamp, lot of rice paddies down there," Shifrin said.

"Yeah, I almost wished I'd have gone up north somewhere where there's mountains. The central highlands are a lot prettier. Maybe coulda got in the First Cav or maybe even the 101st."

"Not so sure, man," Champion said. "Seems like the farther north you are, the closer you are to North Vietnam and the NVA regulars. I wouldn't wanna much fuck with those dudes."

"Well, from what I hear the NVA gets around," Brian said. "I'm sure they're in the delta, too, but maybe not with as much force."

"Well, up north you got ant hills the height of a man," Champion said. "I wouldn't want to see the kinda ants that live there. Plus you wouldn't dig those airborne guys or the air cav guys, either. Bunch of gung-ho dicks."

Brian shrugged. "I guess…"

"You scared, man?" Champion asked.

"I'm scared shitless, George."

"Well, I guess everybody who's ever faced combat has been," Shifrin said. "It's only normal. You'll be—"

I waited for the finish of the sentence, which I thought might be something like, "You'll be okay" or "You'll be in good company," but it didn't come. I looked over at Joe and was shocked to see the most stable, logical person I'd ever known biting his lip, fighting tears.

Brian sensed it, I'm sure, but he never stopped looking south. After a while he said, "I think what scares me the most *is* dying. I can't deny that. I really want to live. But I'm also worried about how they'll accept me and if I'll have balls enough to do what I'm supposed to do out there. You know, like when we first come under fire. I can't describe how I feel tonight. It's the worst I've ever felt. But I can't help thinking that as bad as I think life is tonight, when I'm actually going through the shit, I'm going to wish I was back here in this exact place and time, even under these shitty circumstances, even with these exact feelings. How much better will this seem when Charlie's tryin' to kill me?"

"Those are very valid feelings," Joe said solemnly. "But given that you actually have to do it, you'll be better off once you start because you'll be living it and getting it out of the way."

"Yeah," Brian said glumly. "You're right. If I'm gonna get back to the States, I've got to get through it, and the sooner the better." He looked at each one of us for several seconds. "God, I wanna make it back."

"Brian…" Shifrin said.

"I just want to be free and be my own person. I never had that," Brian continued over him. "I want to be able to pursue my own dreams and live the way I want. I'm gonna do what I have to. If in the process I help these people get their freedom, too, that'll really be great. But I got to tell you that I'm not thinkin' about anyone but myself right now."

We sat for several minutes. I was suddenly seized by anger. "Do what the fuck they tell you, okay? I mean, all this 'alert-alive' shit they're always talkin' about? You gotta do that shit, okay?"

"Yeah," he said. "I'll do what they tell me, believe me." He shifted around uncomfortably. "You hear from Steffie?"

I sighed. "Yeah, as a matter of fact, I got another letter from her today, while you were off. I was surprised. It's the third one. I mean she doesn't talk like she's gonna be my girl or anything, but she seems interested in my well-being and, who knows, rooting for me, maybe. At least she doesn't seem to hate us."

"That's all right," he said.

A minute of emptiness passed. Then I remembered something I'd meant to ask days before. "Hey, Brian, speakin' of that kinda stuff, remember you tellin' me the other night about goin' to grade school in Fort Wayne and how much your friends meant to you, that you had to leave, that sort of changed your whole life?"

"Yeah."

"Well, I got this original idea out of the blue. Was there some chick that you were real good buddies with back in those days?"

He smiled at his own words of only weeks before. Then the question actually seemed to fascinate him. "Yeah, I guess. Sure…And I half thought about that before, I guess."

"Well, who were your favorites?"

"Well, my sweet pal Brenda Dunleavy, who I'll always love, and Rita Zimmerman and Karen Farmer. I went to grade school all eight years with them. We were good friends, sorta—as good friends as you can be with girls in grade school. I used to walk Brenda home in the eighth grade, even though she lived in the opposite direction from us. Man, I really had a crush on her."

"Well, why don't you write ol' Brenda Dunleavy a letter? You know, it worked on Steffie, and that was a real long shot. What the heck do you have to lose?"

He thought a few moments, then answered, "I might just do that."

Shifrin jumped in quickly. "Man, why didn't we think of that before? That's a great idea. You're a very convincing writer. Look at all those state capitals that answered you. Your record is without equal."

Brian smiled. "Get real, Joe. I found out from that Bernie Cobb guy, the mail clerk of B Company of the 96th, that a lot of companies did the same shit with the state flags and all. We're not the only unit that has them, like we thought."

"So what? What's truly significant is you didn't know that when you did it. You wrote those governors like you owned them, and your message was very persuasive and expressed extremely well."

"I guess that's true." Brian chuckled. "And I still know Brenda's home address, if she still lives there. Yeah, I just might do that."

"Your ass go to Bien Hoa today?" Champion asked.

"Yeah, by myself. I never thought in a million years that I'd go to a Vietnamese town by myself. Funny, it doesn't seem all that dangerous anymore."

"What'd you do?" I asked.

"Well, the other night when we got back from Saigon, I was thinkin' that there's a couple items I ought to take care of before I go out in the boonies. The first was, well, in case this is my last chance—or only chance—" He blushed and shifted around. "—to get laid, I went to a whorehouse. I walked around for about an hour and a half before I had guts enough."

"Well, shit, man, that's okay," Champion said, grinning, as were we all. "Did you like it?"

Brian looked south again. "Ah, I guess. I was kinda nervous about bein' there by myself and all. The whorehouse part was upstairs in that building next to the Sunset Strip Bar. A family lived downstairs. It sure wasn't romantic, and I kinda felt real cheap afterwards, too."

"Was she cool?" Champion asked.

"Yeah, she was good-lookin'. Not like the ones we saw in Saigon though," he said looking at me, "but damn cute."

"Then what did you do?" I asked.

"I came back, only to the compound but not to the company. I went to a big PX down by the hospital. I didn't even know about it. I felt like I found Macys. Kinda walked around some more after that."

"What was the other—item?" Shifrin asked.

"Well," Brian said, his smile sheepish, "in case this is my last chance, too, I sorta decided to go to confession. Seemed like a good thing to do at a time like this. I mean, you never know. I'm not sayin' one religion is better than another, but I think it's good to go back to what you're most familiar with."

"Always good to set matters right," Shifrin agreed.

"Brian, Brian, *my man,*" Champion said. "He gets hisself laid by a whore, and then goes to tell God he was sorry for his sins. Man, that's *vintage* Kitzmiller."

"Well, George, I guess it's good to get them in the right order," Brian said, and we all laughed.

After another uneasy silence Shifrin spoke. "You know, Brian, that's not as good as it gets—paying three dollars to a prostitute, I mean. Like Karch told you the other day, you have so much more to look forward to. I know you did what you did this afternoon for a reason, and in a small way I'm glad for you. But I want you to realize that later on, today's experience isn't going to mean much. I hope that came across right. I want you to feel better about the whole situation with women and all."

Brian was rubbing the lid of his beer can with his thumbs. "I know that," he muttered. "You know, Joe, in a way I was thinking about that while I was walking around afterwards. I felt so weird, like I'd sold my soul. I was searching for something else to dwell on. And I sorta got to thinking that sometimes the smallest experience can mean so much…even when it's not with somebody you're in love with or even know. But still, it can seem like a big deal, and it tells you a lot about life."

Brian seemed to grow mystical, and his eyes took on a faraway look as he related the story to us. "Something happened to me once, something you guys might really think is nothing, but it was monumental to me, and I couldn't get it out of my head this afternoon. During my junior year, my old man must have been stoned or asleep this one time, but he gave in, and I actually went to a football game down at IU with two friends from St. Sebastian's. I can't imagine many prettier places than Indiana University.

"It was early November, and right after the game was over we tried to get in this place called Nick's, which is like the number-one student bar in the whole world. I didn't have a fake ID, but the two guys I came with did. I sure didn't want them to be dragged down by me, so I suggested we meet out front of Nick's at six or so. That'd give them a couple of hours to drink, and then we'd go get a pizza someplace else and head home.

"The weather turned nasty, and what had been a beautiful morning turned into a cold, drizzly afternoon. Around four-fifteen or so I started walking up Third Street. Because of the weather, I guess, there wasn't much traffic, football Saturday or not.

"I remember being alone, standing out in front of a place called Swain Hall. Way off in the distance was this figure walking down the sidewalk toward me. The wind kept getting colder, but I was diggin' this fresh woodsy smell from all the oaks and maples and sycamore trees lining both sides of the street. All of the colored leaves were gone by then. Only some brown ones were left, and with all those limestone buildings on my side of the street, everything seemed gray, almost like there existed no other color: gray buildings, dark gray trees, wet gray street, gray sidewalks, gray sky, gray everything, except for this approaching person who was wearing a bright yellow jacket. I kept watching and waiting, hoping that the person in yellow would turn out to be a girl.

"The figure got closer and closer, and finally I saw it was a girl and not only a girl but an incredibly pretty girl with dark brown hair and beautiful brown eyes and dimples. Then—and to this day the whole scene doesn't seem real—I got nervous. It's just me and her. As she walked by, she looked right at me, and I couldn't think of anything else in the world to do, so I just smiled at her, and...and she smiled back. And it was this *wonderful* smile, a smile right from heaven, filled with happiness and complete trust, and I, like, exploded inside. She continued down the street, and I continued standing there. But in that one instant, that one indescribable moment, damn, I felt as if she'd given me this, well, this perfect gift. And I got to tell you I never felt better in my whole life. And today, after Bien Hoa, I kept thinking about that day and that girl, and if I had to give one of the experiences up, then or today, I guess I decided I'd always keep that smile."

He looked at Joe. "So, I mean, just based on the way I felt, I think I know what you're saying." No one said anything for quite a while, and, again, though he had turned away from us, I knew Shifrin was fighting back tears.

In the morning I was uneasy, unsteady, as if the earth was shifting under my feet. I persuaded Brian to eat with Champion, Shifrin, and me. Again, to my total disappointment, we couldn't find Hobson. Most of the guys had the decency to leave Brian alone on his final day, but the exceptions set the tone.

"Lover boy!" Sergeant Helton greeted Brian as he came down the chow line. "Mr. Kitzmiller, tomorrow you'll be shooting gooks, puttin' ol' Charlie in his grave, makin' the little dink motherfucker sorry he was ever born. We'll all be better off—"

"Why don't you shut up, Helton?" I said.

Helton reeled, his wrath shifting, causing me to gulp. "McClain? Are you talkin' to me, punk?"

"It's his last day, man. Can't you just let him be?" I asked angrily.

Helton's mouth hung open as if he were astounded. "Who the hell do you think you are talking to me that way? I am the mess sergeant of this fucking company. I'll mash your goddamn face in, you officer-driving piece of shit." He started to come around the line, fuming more and more with each step. "Talkin' to me that way! A fuckin' punk talkin' to me that way!"

In my numbed state of terror, I wondered if there was a way in hell that I could hurt Helton even a little before he beat me half to death. I couldn't think of any, but I was mad enough to do what I could. Then I lucked out.

"Helton, you asshole! You're about to lose another stripe! You wanna fuck with somebody, fuck with somebody your own size." Top had entered the mess hall without our noticing him. "You're one sorry excuse for a human being is all I can say. The next fight you get into, I promise you, you're going to the damn stockade as a buck private. And then I'll railroad your ass out of this man's army, and you can go be a fuckin' bum on skid row because there ain't any jobs out in the world for a man who can shovel shit onto trays and call it food, and that's all the fuck you can do."

Helton's face turned deep red. He stopped in his tracks and for an instant looked as if he'd cry. "I can't believe you, Top. I never thought that you weren't in my corner." He stood a few seconds, seemingly in shock. Then he continued, "Okay, if that's the way you wanna play, First Sergeant, like a stuck-up, phony-ass officer would—like Karch would—hey, then that's fine." He strolled into the bowels of the kitchen, still muttering to himself.

"Well, I'm startin' everybody's day off right," Brian said as Top made a stumbling apology to the rest of the cooks.

As we got to the end of the chow line, Will Cleveland came from behind it and addressed Brian. "I just wanna say good-bye, Brine. You one fine young man, and I enjoyed servin' with you, and I'll pray for you out there. I'm sorry 'bout what happened, and I don't see why you have to go, but I want to thank you. You the best mail man I ever saw. A good frien' too." At this he extended his hand, and Brian shook it.

"Thanks, Will," he answered softly. "That means a lot to me, a whole lot. Good luck to you, too."

We ate quietly. Brian was in no mood to talk. At Noonan's table and the tables around him, I overheard constant joking, with innuendoes followed by boisterous laughter. Someone said, "I wonder how long before he's got that picture out, tellin' those grunts that he's corkin' ol' Elaine."

After chow Brian scrambled through his locker and half unpacked his duffel bag to remove something that he thought he had on top. In frustration he began throwing his equipment.

"It's all right, buddy," I said, putting my hand on his shoulder. "I'll wait for you at the orderly room."

"Andy, hold it," Brian said suddenly calmed. He was gazing at Alice Ann's picture, which still hung above his bunk. Gingerly, he took it from its small nail. "I'm sorry, Elaine. I never meant to hurt you." He handed it to me. "Take care of this for me, buddy. I can't throw it away myself, but I never want to see it again."

"Okay, Briney," I said, almost choking.

"I-I slid the original, the one out of my wallet, through the grill into Donny's locker a couple of days ago. I can't really say why."

I lost my chance to drive Brian, when a truck actually from the 90th Replacement Battalion happened in with two new men. We stood there, six of us, with nothing left to say but good-bye.

"Well, this is it," Brian mumbled. He shook hands with Shifrin, Top, Champion, and Prather. Then he faced me. "Thanks, Andrew."

"Be careful," I said. "For God's sake, be careful. You'll make it. I know you will. Remember UK or UI. We'll make it happen, Briney."

"IU," he corrected me, then suddenly became talkative. "Sure we will, and it'll be the best time we'll ever, ever have."

"You bet it will." We shook hands, then awkwardly hugged each other.

"Listen," he said nervously, "I wrote a letter to Brenda Dunleavy last night. I couldn't sleep after all, and since I knew I wouldn't probably have my final unit address for a few days, I gave her this as my address. If she writes, forward it to me like I showed you."

"I will," I said, wondering why he was telling me and not Shifrin. "Me and Joe'll make sure you get it. Just be careful. We'll be in college in less than two years, and we'll laugh our ass off about today. Maybe right there at the old bar at Nick's"

"Yeah," he murmured, his eyes filling with tears. "Tell Donny good-bye, and…and I understand, and to write to me."

"I will, Briney."

He climbed into the truck, and within a minute disappeared down Highway One.

Chapter 22

I hadn't realized how much easier Brian had made my life until he was gone. For me, losing a friend with whom I had so much in common, a person I was completely tuned in to, literally made me feel as if I were being deprived of half of myself.

When I hit the mess hall one evening later in the week, I half expected to see a fierce Helton spitting on my food. Instead I saw Donny Hobson for the first time in three days, sitting under the Indiana state flag, eating by himself. He appeared to be in a catatonic trance, looking only at his tray. During the past days, I had been sure I was going to chew his ass out or at least make him feel guilty, but the instant I saw him all such thoughts left me.

"Donny. Donny, man," I said.

He looked up with the eyes of a bloodhound.

"Can I sit here?" I asked, not even believing my own question.

"I reawy don't cawe," he said quietly.

"Donny, how could—I mean, Jesus, I wish you'd been with us the last few days," I said uneasily. "Brian's gone. Damn, I wish you could've been there and seen him off."

"I couwun't do it," he said simply.

I took a deep breath. "It's okay. He asked me to tell you he understood. That was his last request."

Donny's eyes were tearful. "He wad my bet frien'. I mean, I dew dat you two wath clother, but dat wath otay. I din't want to tee him doe away. I dut couwun't. I din't wanna tee him befow he dot—befow he died."

"Donny! No, God, no, that's not going to happen!"

"Tumpting idn't wite wid me wite now. Tumpting idn't wite wid all dith moddewfuttin' thit. I'm afwaid of mytelf, afwaid of what I might do. I dith need to det away." At this he got up, leaving three-quarters of his food, and wandered out the door.

"Donny," I said, then let him go.

I felt lost. I looked up at the colors of the state that I'd been conditioned to ridicule while I was growing up. "He's nobody's Hoosier," we said of someone who'd made a smart move. Now that banner—Brian Kitzmiller's flag—seemed like the largest, most revered piece of cloth in the world. He was responsible for all of them, but this one was *his,* the one he sat under every chance he got, and it belonged to Donny, too. How appropriate also that Noonan couldn't care less about such a symbol. Without warning, my contemplation of the navy-blue standard with its bright yellow stars and torch suddenly brought tears streaming down my cheeks. I got up quickly, not believing my lack of control, and darted out of the mess hall.

That evening was one of loneliness and utter depression for me. Shifrin wanted me to go to the movies, but I told him I was tired. I stayed in the barracks and tried to read *To Sir With Love.* I had a rotten time trying to concentrate and switched to *Candy.*

Much later in the evening, a couple hours after lights out, Noonan returned with a pair of his buddies from asphalt. They, too, were pretty new, and I didn't know them. All three of them were plastered, and they'd returned to finish off a bottle from Noonan's locker. They sat on the empty bottom bunk beneath Noonan's. Wide awake, I lay completely still and listened to the conversation, which Noonan dominated with one of his typical tough-talking stories.

I'd already heard some stories from Noonan's Indianapolis days, in which he and his buddies had made someone pay dearly just for being alive. I was having an increasingly difficult time just being around the guy. I thought that his stories were mostly bullshit, but whether or not they were true, he was despicable.

"Get this," Noonan began. "I'm out one night with Crazy Dominic the Dago and my main man, Al Paff. Paff's the baddest dude in Naptown. I don't think you'd find anybody that'd say he ain't. So we're out lookin' for a little fresh ass, and we've probably drunk a case apiece, gettin' ready to do some serious drinking. We're cruisin' the north side in my four-twenty-six Dodge. It's a sixty-three, a hemi. Got her jacked up on blocks at home.

"About ten or so I see this blonde who looks like Jayne Mansfield, I shit you not, God rest her soul. So I slam on the brakes, don't even park the fucker, and hop out. Later Paff goes, 'Man, I didn't even see the bitch, and you were out of the car.' That's me. I got a bat's radar for fine pussy. Anyway, I go right up to her and sorta introduce myself. She's with this fuckin' dork who, in the course of the conversation, turns out to be a college guy, goin' to Butler. I'm like just turned seventeen. So I go to the chick, 'Hey, why don't you come along with us, get some real dick?'"

His listeners laughed.

"Hey, I ain't shy, so I go, 'How 'bout it? Ain't nothin' says you have to be with a pussy.'" Again, more laughter.

"I can tell she's groovin' on me some. But college boy makes himself a big mistake. The sorry bastard calls me a heathen. Me, Ron Noonan! Imagine that! So I sorta stroll over to him, and I can tell he's about to shit his pants in front of that beautiful dish, and *bam! bam!* motherfucker! I break his head. I really paste it for a good twenty seconds.

"The broad tries to pull me off him, and ol' Dominic picks her skirt up all the way north of her linen. It's pretty funny. But, anyway, between that and me doin' such a good job on her date, she ends up cryin', kneelin' on the ground, tryin' to fix his face. Shit, you shoulda seen it.

"Anyhow, we get some booze—little one-fifty-one, some Jack, some tequila, and another case—and go over to these broads' apartment. There's these three hot broads that we can hit up anytime, one was a cheerleader at Ripple. We fuck 'em and roll on, even though they're like beggin' us to stay.

"By then we're fairly drunk. It's about three-thirty or so, and I don't remember all the details, but the next shit I know, we're into it on the west side with these six niggers. Yes, you heard me right, six jamokes, and it gets a little hairy, but in the end we smoke their ass for 'em, too. And that ain't all that easy to do 'cause they ain't all that easy to hurt by hittin' 'em in the head. Shit. You just gotta be smarter when you fight a nigger.

"So then we're cruisin' again, and Dominic goes, 'Hey I'm fuckin' hungry.'"

I stared at their glowing cigarettes. *God, what a turd,* I thought. *What a phony-assed pig.* It made me sick that he led the case against anyone's deception, let alone Brian's. I stared and stared at those glowing orange tips. It occurred to me that this had to be what hell was like, living with absolute vermin like Noonan for all eternity.

A couple of days went by, and we had heard nothing from Brian. I assumed that he was in some sort of orientation and training course. Hobson continued keeping to himself.

We were at the club, which was unusually packed for the first time in a while, and among others, Noonan, was having himself another wild time. I sat with Shifrin and Champion. McCollough joined us around nine, but I chose to ignore him for as long as I could. I drank quite a bit and then had a heated conversation with McCollough about his actions during Brian's crisis. I contended that he was a cheap friend. He argued that he was only being logical, that even Brian didn't have the right to mislead us, and that if he felt Brian was lying, he had the right to question the story. It didn't mean that he didn't like Brian or even imagined it could lead to the infantry decision. One's normal function was to pursue truth, he said.

"You make me want to throw up," I said, though I knew full well he had some points.

McCollough was anxious to make up. He must have missed us, after all; we were his closest friends. But I was equally determined not to forgive him. I pointed out that curious or not, when the crisis got to a certain point, we owed Brian, our good friend, extra considerations and loyalty. If McCollough had wanted to take Brian aside and discuss whether Elaine was really Alice Ann, then that was one scenario, but to join in with a group of vigilantes led by some fat new turd was missing the point of true friendship.

We went back and forth, and finally Shifrin surprised me by joining my side. "McCollough, you have to understand that sometimes friendship transcends logic. If you care about someone, you have to put yourself in his place, and if you wouldn't mind a pack of wolves down your throat and your buddies joining them one by one, then and only then can you join that pack."

McCollough refused to get angry but remained adamant that he was innocent of any disloyalty and that he intended to write Brian as a friend. At that assertion the silent George Champion rolled his eyes in disgust, slid his chair back, and left the building.

"Who can blame him?" I asked self-righteously, staring at McCollough.

After a while I noticed that Hobson had entered the club. He stood off to the side with a beer, neither at the bar nor at a table but seemingly within earshot of Noonan's group. We motioned for him. I was sure he saw us but he remained aloof. Shifrin suggested we leave him be for a few more days.

McCollough went up to buy his third straight round as if it were his penance to buy until we liked him again. On his way back he passed by Noonan's table, and Prackle grabbed him. McCollough stood at their table for a couple of minutes, sometimes laughing, sometimes just listening. When he got back he sat down slowly.

"Man," he said, "I can't believe that Noonan fucker. Prackle grabs me, and they're fuckin' around, feelin' no pain, and Prackle gets Noonan to tell me what he plans to do. Poor Brian. I hope Noonan's only shitting around."

"What, McCollough? What did the asshole say?" I asked impatiently.

"Well, when Brian got to his new unit, Noonan told me that he'd know his new address because he had to forward some pay records. Said he was gonna write to the company commander, the first sergeant, the squad leaders, the supply sergeant, the company clerk, the mail clerk, the mess sergeant, any curious machine gunner, any interested rifleman, telling them the whole story about Brian and Alice Ann. He said there's nowhere in 'Nam that he can go where they aren't gonna know what a phony shit he is."

I felt myself redden. "That fat fucker's had it!" I said, shoving back my chair.

Shifrin grabbed my arm. "No! Don't! You can't—"

"The fuck," I said.

"Andy, listen to me," Shifrin hissed. "If you get in a fight, your job, your pretty damn special job, your rank, your money, and everything is jeopardized. You can't win. Why crawl to his level and let him do that to you? Those letters will never leave here. I'll intercept them, and once I do, I'll take them to Top and Karch. I'll take them to the colonel if I have to. I wouldn't even have to open them. Let him explain to the brass what he's doing, writing to all those people. Let me tell you," he said with unShifrinlike emotion, "Karch is not happy about this whole affair. I'm sure he had a soft spot for Brian and feels like Noonan basically took someone out of his orderly room. He's not letting on much, but I promise you he is not happy with what happened, now that he's had time to think about it. I guarantee you that Top hates Noonan, and his days here are not going to go well for him. He'll have to tear up the letters and is liable to get busted, and for sure won't get promoted. And he'll get a shitload of extra duty. I'll see to that myself."

I had been punching the heavy bag for several days. My hands felt as if they were actually alive, and my arms had a power in them that I'd never known. Sure, Shifrin made sense, but I wanted to fight. "He can't do this shit. He can't go so far as to fuck Brian over again! Dammit, Joe, what if that dirt-that-walks sends the letters off from another company, like they did with Alice Ann's letter and her answer?"

"Let me worry about that," he said, though I could tell he was thinking about it, and it was disturbing him.

We sat silently. Suddenly McCollough said, "Believe me, I can't stand the bastard."

"Well," I said bitterly, "That's sure interesting, McCollough, because you chose—you fucking chose him over Brian."

"Andy, I never chose—"

"Brian's in the infantry. Mr. Fatshit is here, and we're living with him every day!"

McCollough shook his head sadly. "You and Hobson and Champion, and you, too, Joe, have to learn to look at matters—"

"Oh, fuck you." I looked over to where Hobson had been standing. "Hey, where'd Donny go?"

"He left," McCollough said. "I tried to talk to him on my way back from Noonan's table. He snarled at me like a dog would and walked out. I tried to tell him that I was no friend of Noonan's, but he wouldn't even talk to me."

"You figure Hobson heard what Noonan said?" Shifrin asked.

"He had to have," McCollough replied.

"I gotta get out of here!" I almost yelled, looking back over at the table.

"Good idea," Shifrin agreed.

"Let's grab our beer and go," McCollough added.

"Hey, don't do us any favors," I said to McCollough. "Feel free to join your buddies."

"Come on, Andy," he said.

We walked and walked, the three of us, around the 96th, back past the signal companies and all the way down by the hospital and big PX that Brian had talked about, then back around it all again. Shifrin worked hard to settle me down, claiming that he was certain he could get Noonan's ass scorched if he mailed the letters. He told us calmly that he knew most of the 96th's mail clerks fairly well and that he was pretty sure he could count on them.

Still I couldn't be consoled. I had become hateful. I suddenly felt no fear and craved the taste of blood. My attitude was horrible, and my words had turned to a punk's. I knew I had become what I had looked down on all year, but still I couldn't imagine doing anything differently.

When we got back to the barracks we were shellacked with sweat and decided to hit the showers. When we returned, Noonan was up in his bunk, snoring heavily. I realized that he was not with any of his close friends when he was in our barracks. I put on a T-shirt and pants and was debating fighting him. I had learned some practical lessons from Top about survival and fighting. I began putting boots on. A tremendous advantage went to the warrior with shoes—especially combat boots—when your foe was barefoot.

Shifrin sensed what I was doing in the dark, in an instant he sat next to me.

"Listen to me, Andy. Get those off and get some sleep. Remember what we talked about. Don't let him off the hook."

I took a deep breath. I knew a fight in the middle of the night that interrupted sergeants' and officers' sleep alike was worse than a morning skirmish. "Okay, Joe," I said, "I won't. But I'm wearing my pants and boots to sleep in case—"

"In case of what?"

I smiled like a grade schooler. "In case I get up late and don't have time to dress before I take Prather to Brigade."

He got up. "Don't—please don't disappoint me. I've already seen one of my best friends destroyed this week." He squeezed the back of my neck.

I settled back, feeling somewhat touched. I knew Shifrin's friendship was a privilege and shouldn't be taken for granted. Still my thoughts bounced back to Noonan—grim, vicious thoughts. *Yep,* I thought, *come morning I'll mosey over there and start it. What a way to start a day. Walk over and start swinging from the heels 'til I got knocked out or pulled off.*

I was suddenly very pleased with myself. Growing up, I'd been picked on a few times, but I had never bullied anyone. I couldn't even slap my dog the time she grabbed a steak off my plate. Now I was going to be a bully, or at least try to be, and I was going to enjoy it. I listened to Noonan's snoring and snorting, which sounded like a wild pig. He was in trouble. Yessir, real trouble. Joe would understand after a while. He'd come around. I drifted off, exhausted, half drunk.

As near as I could figure, about thirty minutes passed. I was in a deep sleep, yet I heard the screen door next to my bunk squeak open loudly, then slam. I saw the lights go on. I struggled to wake up but couldn't quite break the barrier of sleep, not until I heard Noonan's bunk hit the floor and the sound of Noonan's nearly naked body smacking the concrete after falling nearly five and a half feet. Then came the yelling and his screams. Startled, I was now out of my bunk.

Hobson!

"Det up! Det up! You modderfutter! Det up and fight, you futting coward peat of thit!" he yelled as if he were insane. Rather than starting the usual clamor and scrambling, guys woke up and sat transfixed, horrified. Hobson was a man possessed.

"Hey, hey, man, what's wrong with you?" Noonan pleaded loudly.

"Det up!" Hobson replied, kicking him.

"Ow!" Noonan wailed. "Come on, man. I don't want to fight you!"

Hobson grabbed him by the hair and one ear and lifted him, squealing, to his feet, then punched him in the nose.

"Oh, man! My nose!" Noonan cried frantically. "I just had an operation a few months ago. Leave me alone!"

"You donna wite Bwine's new company? Id that what you donna do?"

Shifrin started down the aisle, but Richio cut him off. "Hey, Joe, let 'em fight. Let 'em work it out." Shifrin backed off.

Hobson slapped Noonan hard.

"Hey, please, man, I don't want to fight."

The scene was pitiful, and I was shocked. I knew Donny could handle Noonan, but I sure thought the loudmouth would stand up for himself.

"Tho you're donna wite tum wetters?" Hobson smashed Noonan's mouth then threw a wicked left hook followed by a hard right-left combination, which led to an absolute frenzy of shots.

Noonan feverishly tried to block the assault, but when he covered the front of his face, Hobson's hooks easily found the side of his head. When he tried to block the side blows, Hobson jabbed and threw straight overhand punches. Noonan dove to the floor to escape the punishment.

Hobson put his foot in Noonan's face and shoved him on his back. "Det up and fight!"

"No, man, please!" Noonan's lower lip began to quiver, which truly enraged Hobson.

"You did all dat howible futting thit? And you're not eben a man?" He kicked Noonan viciously in the jaw, then dove on the shriveling troublemaker and began pummeling him.

Noonan bellowed, "Get him off me!"

Hobson grabbed his hair again and began slamming Noonan's head into the concrete floor. Noonan screamed.

"Donny! Donny! You'll kill him!" Shifrin yelled. "He's not worth it!"

Hobson was indeed insane. I grabbed him under his arms, but his strength was not human, and his rage seemed to add to his weight. He continued to pound Noonan's head into the floor. Richio, McCollough, and Shifrin joined me, and together we pulled him to his feet.

"Come on, Donny!" I pleaded. "You got to stop it, man! You'll kill him!"

Donny shoved me hard into a locker, then flung the bigger Richio off and smacked McCollough in the mouth. Joe then stepped in front of him. "Okay, Donny, you did what you wanted. You beat him badly. You humiliated him, and now everyone in the company will know what kind of a coward he really is. Let it go. Let it go before any of the brass gets up. There's no one here who won't say it was anything but a fair fight. But if you go on you'll only ruin yourself."

Suddenly, Sergeant Helton, a man who had no control over his own rage, slammed in from the NCO barracks. I fully expected Helton to yell and Hobson to answer and the two to engage in a life-or-death struggle. Unbelievably, nothing like that happened. Maybe Helton had a sixth sense, like the instinct leopards have around lions, but he seemed to see something in Hobson that even he wanted no part of. Carefully, even respectfully, he assisted us in persuading Hobson away from the quacking, sobbing Noonan, out the barracks rear door, and back down to the maintenance platoon. Then, without any ire toward me at all, he agreed with Shifrin. To keep Donny out of trouble, we had to get Noonan down to the field hospital to get the back of his head stitched.

I thought the unpleasant task of driving Noonan was mine, but McCollough, seeing an opportunity to placate me, offered to do the job.

By dawn everyone knew. In addition to his swollen face Noonan had a mild concussion and a sprained shoulder. Karch was in a corner. His no-fight edict had to have teeth, so poor Donny got busted pack to PFC and put on shit-burning detail for two weeks.

Hobson bided his time, and daily life returned to normal. But Hobson's assault into Noonan's life was far from over.

Several days after the fight, when the shaken instigator was fairly well healed, he strode out to the latrine while Hobson was working off his extra-duty sentence.

Donny Hobson had planned for that moment, each day dumping most of the rancid contents of each container into one giant vessel he was saving. He used kerosene on the emptied ones, and each morning had several pots belching black smoke, so no one suspected his plan. Late each evening, on his way to the showers, Donny dumped a gallon or so of water in his concoction to give it a mudlike texture and to increase its volume. That morning while Noonan took care of his business, Donny, waiting outside, set his emptied pots afire, then with Herculean effort pulled his huge project from beneath the last hole. When Noonan stepped outside, Donny accosted him. McCollough and I, along with nine others, saw the whole incident.

"Dood morning, Mitter Noonan," Donny said. "Tum ober here. I dot tumtping for you, tumpting weawy yummy."

Noonan looked in horror at the caldron of shit and turned to run, but Hobson collared him within ten steps. Putting Noonan's still-sore arm in a hammerlock and gripping a clump of hair, Donny led his victim close to the brimming, eighteen-inch-deep pot of excrement. "I'm donna div you one tantz to do the wight ting. You kneel down and tubmerd your head in the thit—"

Noonan yelled no at the top of his lungs and struggled mightily, while we began to laugh like kids at a circus. Hobson's timing was perfect. As Noonan lurched upwards, Donny doubled him over with a mighty blow to the solar plexus. Then he grabbed Noonan from behind, by the scrotum and the collar, and half picked him up, half marched him to the container. Noonan crumpled next to it, screaming in agony. Wrestling him with fierce determination, Hobson finally got Noonan bent over the short barrel, then kicked one of his legs away and plunged his head into the fetid stew. Hobson held him down for a good twenty seconds. When he finally released him, Noonan was coughing, gagging, and pleading for help. Then he began retching and soon vomited.

We made sure Hobson didn't go any further. Laughing uncontrollably, he first rubbed his hands in soft dirt, then went back to his burning.

Shortly after that, Noonan, deeply shaken, stumbled into the orderly without even cleaning up. I jumped in right behind him, determined not to miss anything. The morning was still young, so Karch had not left to begin his day. I was afraid that Donny would lose another stripe, but as Noonan blurted his tearful story, Top suddenly burst out laughing, as did Prather, Thornberry, Shifrin, McCollough, and I. Nobody laughed harder, however, than Captain Karch.

"Noonan," the captain began, "I have waited all year to relegate this top-priority assignment, and you're the man to do it. I expect a full report by eighteen hundred hours highlighting any differences between army food and human feces." He could barely get it out, and when he'd completed his sentence he roared along with the rest of us. "I suggest you get your ass down to the showers before you report to work. Of course those creeps at battalion might not notice any difference in you at all. As a matter of fact, I'm not sure I do."

Noonan mumbled something about being sick and writing his congressman. He turned abruptly to leave and in the process almost ran into me. His stench was overpowering.

"Don't touch me, you shithead!" I shouted, jumping backwards.

"'Shithead'!" Karch echoed loudly, then broke up again. "McClain, I'm gonna put you in charge of nicknames. Your spontaneous accuracy is without equal."

I had never seen Karch quite like this. As Noonan stomped out of the orderly room, then down the company street, Karch followed him outside, his mood suddenly and terrifyingly changed.

"Remember this, boy!" he bellowed at the top of his lungs, though Noonan was barely twenty feet away. "He who lives by the sword, dies, always, the same goddamn way! Remember it well, you disgraceful piece of shit!"

Noonan paid dearly for his cowardice. After the fight, he lost his status as a bad boy and became a company joke. If he'd stood up for himself either time, if he'd thrown only one punch, he wouldn't have been beaten up any worse than he was; but now everyone could see that Noonan was guilty of the same crime he had accused Brian of—being a phony—and most of the guys who had hung with him every night shunned him, ridiculed him, and simply shook their head whenever he appeared.

Hobson had always been perceived as a happy-go-lucky sort with many friends in all the platoons. Before, those of us who played basketball regarded him as some sort of sports god, but now he became a hero to an even larger group of men. Such comments as "Damn, that Hobson may be one goofy-looking, goofy-sounding dude, but is he bad or what?" were voiced throughout the unit.

Though he still chose solitude, he was in an improved state of mind and relentless in his bullying and cruel jokes with Noonan, doing everything from dumping several quarts of urine on his mattress and pillow to shoving his tray in his lap in the mess hall. These acts brought every reaction from laughter to silent amazement from those who witnessed them, as if by some sense of fairness, Noonan, the tall-talking cynic, was not to be exempt from his own brand of justice.

Chapter 23

I had begun worrying that something dreadful had already happened to Brian when we got his first letter. It was addressed to me. I tore it open and read it instantly aloud to Joe and Top in the orderly room. That evening I reread it to Donny, George, McCollough, and Joe on—again—the rooftop of our bunker.

> *10-22-67*
> *Dear Andy, Joe, Donny, Top & George:*
>
> *Sorry I haven't written. I've really been busy. I went thru this training program they got for us dumb asses volunteering. I learned a lot about compasses, strategy, and how to use an M-16, but a sergeant who seemed to know his shit said the training was too watered down to be worth anything because they never got the personnel or time to make it good.*
>
> *I got assigned to a rifle squad in C Company, 2nd Battalion, 4th Brigade of the 9th Infantry Division. These guys are really edgy. They think they're jinxed. Last month they really took some bad casualties, six guys got killed and fourteen wounded.*
>
> *Some of guys think I've put them at risk by volunteering. Top, get this: my squad leader said that if we got into the shit, he was gonna feel my gun barrel afterwards, and if it was cold he was gonna cut my lungs loose and pull them out my ass.*
>
> *It's kind of funny—back at the 209th we had an almost all-white company, except you, George, and Will, and the couple of guys in asphalt. Out here it's like thirty percent of the guys are colored.*

I've already been out on patrol for six days. I've never been so hot or thirsty, but after the second day I was too damn tired to care. The mosquitoes are unreal down here, I'm eaten to shit. I hate to sound like a true grunt, but you REMF dudes don't know how good you got it.

It's so weird out here, especially at night. I got freaked out. One night we slept on our backs in a circle, helmet to helmet, so no one could sneak up on us. On patrol we took a couple of sniper shots, but no one got hit. We never even got off a shot at the sniper—no one could figure out where he was.

Oh, well, got to get my gear figured out and ready for tomorrow. I'm wondering if you have had a letter from Brenda. The more I think about it though, the more I'm sure it won't happen. No big thing. "Don't mean nothin'," as they say. Take care, you guys. I miss you all.

> *Your buddy,*
> *Brian*

"Man, the little fucker's already out there and doin' it!" Champion exclaimed.

"Yeah," I answered. "It's sure good to hear from him. I'll write him and tell him about Noonan's misfortunes."

Hobson shrugged, his face wistful. "Dat futter wadn't donna dit away wid id forever. Maybe he'll doe to da infwantry now, too."

"When are you going on R and R, Andy?" Shifrin asked me suddenly.

"I don't know. Maybe this month, maybe never." I hadn't felt like going anywhere since Jeanine had screwed up my original R & R plans. Now that Australia was opened up, I was tempted to go there.

"Why don't you see if Steffie'd meet you in Hawaii?" Champion asked.

"Well, if she would, I'm pretty sure I'd go." I laughed, but the very idea sent a chill all the way down to my bowels. "But I don't know her well enough. Asking her would be, like, inappropriate."

"Shit, man," George countered, "chicks have changed since you been over here. A whole new culture of wild, psychedelic, promiscuous chicks are influencin' 'em all. But, man, you got to have balls. Ain't nothin' possible without balls."

"What do you think, Joe?" I asked, looking for a voice of reason.

Shifrin shrugged. "She's *your* dream, Andy. You play it however you want. Only make sure you do something. I've known too many guys who've never had the guts to take *any* shot."

I left, frustrated by my inability to make a decision. I knew Steffie wouldn't meet me in Hawaii, and asking her would make me seem presumptuously stupid, killing any long shot with her I had. Although I would've taken Jeanine back in a second, Steffie filled my daydreams and had come to represent femininity on a grand scale. I found myself constantly comparing the two girls. My mom used to talk about the special rewards God had for the good and the faithful, and that was how I saw Steffie—occupying a higher place in heaven than Jeanine. I thought about how beautiful Steffie was and how popular she had been in high school. She was everything I had believed Elaine to be, and I had a shot, no matter how slim.

Unlike Jeanine and that asshole John Teeter, Steffie didn't hate everybody over here. *I feel something terrible and immoral is going on in Vietnam,* she had written. *I also believe that you and your fellow soldiers are merely doing what your country has asked you to do, like all those who served in previous wars.*

In my imagination, she would be so impressed with me as a person, so consumed with lust, then head over heels in love, we never had to talk about the war *ever,* or at least not until we'd won and it started making sense to everyone.

I had faith in my belief that we were there for a good reason, but Steffie's letter got me wondering. Was it possible America wasn't doing the right thing? What did they know back home that we didn't? The college students could benefit from a genuine exchange of knowledge. We were just the morons being spoon-fed the Stars-and-Stripes version of the war, along with our narrow-minded superiors' interpretation. I yearned to know someday precisely what was true.

George and even Joe had planted a sense of urgency—if not despair— within me, and I decided that doing nothing would be intolerable. I could wait no longer; the chances she'd have a boyfriend by the time I returned stateside would be astronomically high.

An almost unbelievable scenario unfolded in my mind, which became an obsession, then a done deal. I would fly to Honolulu on R & R, then, against all regulations and dressed in civilian clothing, catch a plane to California. My adventure would cost at least three times more than flying in uniform as military standby, but I didn't care. At San Francisco International I'd nonchalantly visit a john, change to my uniform—making me eligible for inexpensive military standby—and fly to St. Louis or Chicago, then on to Louisville.

A trip to the mainland would make me officially absent without leave, and if caught, I'd have to convince a jury that I had not deserted. At best, I'd lose my rank—I'd just been promoted to Spec Five—and some hefty pay; at worst, I'd be busting rocks at Leavenworth.

Before I could implement my plan, I'd need phony orders in case anyone at the airlines counter wanted documentation for my request to fly standby. (My R & R only covered my flights from Saigon to Honolulu.) Orders weren't hard to fake, but I didn't want to be the one to do it. Instead I contacted my friend Harry Blakemore, at the headquarters of USARV, the main army headquarters in Vietnam. The four times I'd seen him in-country, he said he could get me anything, from fake leave orders to a Bronze Star. I sent Harry the possible dates of my departure, and he sent me four different sets of orders with different dates. It was cake and it happened all too soon.

Within ten days, I found myself in a bathroom stall in San Francisco's airport. Changing into my uniform, I was overcome with a sense of guilt so strong, I decided I needed a beer. As I strolled through the terminal, I drew stares from young people. My palms began to sweat. This felt like my AWOL experience at Ft. Leonard Wood, only this one would last longer than thirty minutes.

I darted into a pub in the main terminal and ordered a Bud at the bar. Down the counter from me, two marines built like fullbacks were hunched over their drinks. One was around six feet two and 210 pounds. A nasty scar switchbacked across his cheek and disappeared under oily brown hair that surprisingly reached his irate brown eyes. The other guy appeared to be a couple of inches shorter but was built even more powerfully, weighing probably 220 or 230.

"Look at this fuckin' army boy, Brubaker," the taller one said.

"Well, well," the other one replied, his veiled blue eyes scanning me. He brushed his thinning blond hair back, then spat on the floor as if to acknowledge my existence with something appropriate from a marine.

I hadn't consorted with the marines before, but I sure recognized the mentality.

"Say, man," the tall one said. I looked at his name badge—Wagner, it read. "Where's your infantry badge?"

"I-I was with the engineers," I said quietly.

"Sappers? Combat engineers?" asked Wagner.

"Construction," I managed to say. "Roads mostly. Cleared land and jungle."

"That's pussy shit, ain't it?" Brubaker wanted to know.

I shrugged, feeling deeply disappointed that this could be happening.

"Whole army's a bunch of pussies, you ask me," Wagner said with conviction.

"Hellfire, Wags, this dude ain't even in their infantry. A stinkin' R-E-M-F. Ever hear of the DMZ, rear-echelon motherfucker?"

"Yeah, sure. You guys had some bad shit up there. We followed a lot of it in the *Stars and Stripes.*" I blushed from my stupid words.

"And all that time we thought nobody cared!" Wagner said sarcastically. "Here we had a bunch of REMF pussies rooting for us like we was in the pennant race."

I surprised myself by blurting, "Hey, fuck, you guys. My best buddy's in our infantry, all right?" I chugged my beer and made for the door. "Hey, fuck this. I don't need this shit."

"Damn, Wags, must've been something you said," Brubaker said with a laugh.

I began walking up and down corridors, past gates and counters, looking for another bar—some quiet place to work the courage up to purchase the standby ticket.

As I neared the baggage-claim area and an oblong red light that I mistook for a bar sign, I saw seven scruffy-looking young adults yelling angrily at a couple of sailors. One protester in particular caught my attention. Somewhere in her midtwenties, she was extraordinarily attractive, but her finely chiseled features were twisted with anger. A black headband tamed her golden-brown curls as she stomped around and waved a small poster that read Out Now! The letters were painted in what looked like dried blood.

Certain the sailors had done something to incur the protesters' wrath, I intended to mind my own business.

As I skirted the group, however, the five guys and two women behaved as if they had been waiting for me and solely me all their lives.

"Where do you think you're going?" the pretty lady asked as if she were a teacher admonishing a first-grader.

I did not break stride.

"Hey, fucker!" she shouted. "I asked you a fucking question!"

Never had I heard a lady shout an obscenity before, let alone publicly and at the top of her lungs. A couple the guys stepped into my path. I tried to walk around them when the girl grabbed my arm, stopping me. "Are you mute, soldier boy?"

"I've got nothing to say to you, miss," I said, and flung her hand off me.

She grabbed me again. "You proud of these?" she asked, thumping my ribbons. She jabbed a finger at my National Defense ribbon. "Is this for slaughtering farmers? Burning babies? Bombing schools? You fucking war pig!"

"Leave me alone," I said angrily, beginning to feel awful. I looked around for a security guard or a cop, but all I saw was a guy at a rental car booth leaning forward, elbows on the counter, chin in hands, enjoying the confrontation.

"You're not accountable for what you've done, is that it, coward?" she challenged.

"You don't know anything about me or what I did," I grated. "I was in an engineer unit that builds roads, all right? It's none of your business, though, what the hell I did."

"Fuck you," she said, sneering. Her lips drew back over white, even teeth. I looked at her face. She was so beautiful.

"Genocide is every citizen's business," one of the guys said. "You're part of the killing machine."

I had to get to Kentucky to see Steffie. I shook my head in disgust and tried to walk away. The girl reached for me, but I deflected her wrist with my arm.

"Did you hit me, soldier-pig?" She stepped in front of me and spat into my ribbons. At this I grabbed her upper arm and flung her to the side and took two steps, only to be blocked by one of the guys.

He had a waist-long ponytail, shiny and straight like a model's. He was skinny, maybe five foot ten and a hundred and fifty pounds. "You fucking kill babies, and now you beat women," he yelled at the top of his lungs. "Try shoving me, you murdering roach!"

Six or seven people had gathered to watch as the young militant worked himself into a fury, hating me, humiliating me, screaming so loudly that my ears had begun to ring. "You coward pig. How do you like it now? Murderer! Killer! Hit me pig! You sniveling coward!"

He seemed to be screaming directly into my soul, causing me the greatest discomfort I had ever known. Not one foot away he raged, the noise like a G force. I felt as though my face were contorting.

For a millisecond my accuser was distracted—just long enough, for me to move with all the quickness I possessed and catch him full in the mouth with everything I had. I crouched, preparing to slug it out with him, but to my utter surprise he hit the floor and skidded, flat on his back. I had really hurt him.

Someone grabbed me from behind, and another one began pummeling me. The lady was kicking me. Somehow I managed to back up and topple the guy holding me on to the baggage tram. Flailing away, we ended up on the floor. Now two protesters were punching me from above while another kicked me in the head from the side. The guy beneath me tried to pin my arms to my sides, but my hand found his crotch, and I had him in a death grip. I prayed I wouldn't lose any teeth or an eye. I knew they were going to beat me senseless, but I was amazed that I had no fear, only rage.

Brubaker and Wagner came from nowhere, two overpowering men whom thirteen months of combat had prepared well for savagery. Bodies flew, including the beauty's.

When I struggled to my feet, Brubaker had his foe on the ground smashing his head into the marble floor, and Wagner kicked a curled, prone body again and again as the onlookers backed away in horror. With the three of us in uniform on our feet, three of the protesters, including the second woman, ran out of harm's way, then stopped. The guy I had hit was now trying to raise himself to hands and knees. Wagner kicked him hard in the face, and the guy's head bounced sickeningly on the floor, leaving him unconscious. Wagner kicked him again in the kidneys and the ribs.

"Hey, man." I went to grab Wagner, but I must've taken a more severe shot to the head than I remembered and staggered into him. He shoved me away and kicked his man again, this time in the thigh. Meanwhile Brubaker was beating my first opponent's mercilessly, having grasped the fellow's ponytail in one hand and driving his giant right fist into the young man's face.

The security cops who were nowhere for me now came running in droves. Two each restrained Brubaker and Wagner, and another, probably sensing that I was several notches down the danger scale from my comrades, simply placed himself between me and the carnage. I began to feel incredibly weird and deeply saddened.

"Fuck with us, you hippie scum, and you will fucking die!" Brubaker kicked at a head as by now three cops him pulled back. "Cocksuckers! You want some more?"

"You'll go to jail, son, if you don't cool it," a heavy cop in his late forties said.

"*Us?* Well, fuck you!" Brubaker yelled. "You can put us in fucking Alcatraz. Where we been, jail ain't shit."

"Put these clusterfucks in jail," Wagner yelled. "Fuck, man, we just come back from the fuckin' war, and they gang up on our buddy." I did a double-take at the word *buddy,* then studied the victims. Two of them lay writhing on the floor, clearly needing an ambulance. Two other guys looked shell-shocked. The last fellow was the exception. The lenses of his wire-rimmed glasses were steamed from the his body heat and sweat, and his shoulder-length hair was a tangle. He looked like the quintessential young philosophy prof, John Teeter's twin, maybe. "You should take these dogs to jail and shoot them in the morning," he shouted, his finger jabbing the air.

"What the hell happened?" a security guy asked him. "What the hell are *you* doing here in the first place?"

"We have a right to be in this airport, and we have the right to challenge these killers of the Vietnamese people." He raised his voice even more. "If these pigs are not arrested, we'll make sure this whole situation will be on page one of every newspaper in this asshole country."

"Sir," an older officer replied with elaborate patience. "Just stand back and let us do our job. We need to get help for your injured friends."

The beautiful protester sat on the baggage carousel, sobbing loudly while the other woman tended to her. Both her lips were split, and her nose spewed blood. "Oh, God," she wailed. "They *hurt* me! They *hurt* me. Oh, God!"

"You guys better leave," a younger guard told us.

"Leave? What the fuck are you talking about?" the philosopher wanted to know.

"It was a seven-on-one fight when we got here!" Brubaker said. "A fight these pussy hippies started."

"I want to press charges," the philosopher yelled.

My heart sank.

"We better hold these guys," one guard said to another. "Call SFPD."

"Hey, we just did what we had to do," Brubaker said.

Brubaker, Wagner, and I began edging away and in no time were walking fast. A couple of guards looked ready to stop us but didn't. We broke into a jog. I had no clear idea why I was doing what I was doing but I felt I needed to get out of the airport quickly.

"Let's grab a cab," Brubaker said, and we climbed into one that had just deposited its passengers at the curb.

"Take us downtown," Brubaker told the driver.

I looked out the back window, to see two guards emerge from the terminal. Instead of being headed for Georgetown, Kentucky, I was a fugitive from the law and an AWOL soldier. I wasn't sure I had the money to fly as a civilian, and I was afraid to go back to the airport period, let alone in uniform.

What now? I wondered. My face hurt like hell, and I felt both eyes swelling fast and throbbing.

"Hey, man," Wagner said.

I realized he was addressing me.

"We decided we'd buy you a drink. Thought maybe we got off on the wrong foot. Good we decided to do that, huh?" He smiled a gap-toothed grin.

"Why is it that the marines always rescue the fuckin' army?" Brubaker asked, then chuckled. "Hey, army boy, you really creamed that one dude. I'd of never guessed you had it in you."

"I had no choice," I muttered.

"You coulda run," Wagner replied. "You guys are good at that."

"Well, thanks for your help."

"Your face is sure gonna be pretty in a couple of hours," Wagner said. "Welcome home, motherfucker."

"If we was smart, we'd fly to Australia or New Zealand and start over," Brubaker added. "This don't feel like home anymore."

"Our fellow citizens spit on us now when we come home," Brubaker said mournfully.

We pondered the awfulness of this fact for thirty seconds. I was too scared to think clearly, but I knew something utterly terrible had happened. I looked at the men who had labored through an unspeakable year of war for their country and began to feel like an outcast in America. In less than one year we had become contemptible, real villains. The hurt was unimaginable.

Like it or not, I had to get out, change clothes and get back to the airport. Would I go to Hawaii or Kentucky? I had to get out. I felt uncomfortable with my new chums. I didn't want them to know I was AWOL.

The cab driver broke in. "You know, fellas, I was never in the service. I was Four-F, around Korea time. But I tell you, I honor what you guys did for us."

I wanted to thank him, but knowing what the marines had been through— I had noticed in the bar that Wagner had a Silver Star, a Bronze Star, and a Purple Heart, and Brubaker had a Silver Star and a Purple Heart—I did not feel it my place to. After a few seconds Brubaker said, "Thanks, man."

"We ought to go Haight-Ashbury, man," Brubaker said. "Kill us some fuckin' hippies."

I smiled to acknowledge the absurdity.

"No, I mean it, man. Cut their fuckin' hearts out."

We hit downtown 'Frisco, and Brubaker yelled, "Let us out here, man, at this bar."

"Hey, I got it, man," I said, and pulled out my wallet. As I paid the fare and tip, a stroke of genius struck me. "I gotta get back to the airport. My brother is picking me up in fifteen minutes."

"Hey, fuck," Wagner said. "You come with us and get fucked up. You need somebody to watch out for you."

"No, I can't, he's bringing my chick, too. Thank you, guys. Thanks a lot," I said sincerely.

"Well, fuck," Wagner said. "Watch out for your ass, army boy."

"I will," I said. "Thanks again."

I went in the airport far from where I had come out. I shot into a restroom, where I inspected the wreckage of my face. I looked a lot like Farthing had after his beating. *God,* I thought. *I can't let Steffie see me like this.*

As I changed quickly back into civilian clothes, I decided to call her, then get back to Hawaii on the next plane and lick my wounds for the remainder of my R & R. Unbelievably, someone had left a San Francisco Giants cap hanging on the peg in the stall. It was somewhat worn, but I didn't care. I put on my sunglasses which I had safely stowed in their hard case. When I looked in the mirror, I was satisfied that I'd be difficult to recognize.

My watch read seven, which was ten in central Kentucky. Do-or-die time. The time to buy time, to grasp hope, to make a connection with her. The real birth or death of something would come later.

Her phone rang. I realized how little I wanted to talk to her. I'd have been scared shitless under the best of circumstances, but I was still shaky and dazed from the fight.

"Hello?" an angelic voice answered.

"May…may I speak with Stephanie?"

"This is she."

A tide of bodily fluids and solids surged through me. "Steffie!" I tried to sound enthusiastic and happy. "This is Andy McClain. How are you doing?"

A pause. Then, "Andy, where are you?"

"Hawaii," I said. "This place is really cool."

"Well, that's really nice," she said slowly, nearly stammering. "You mentioned in your letters you were going somewhere for R and R. You still have to go back, right?"

"Yeah, I got ninety-nine days when I get back. Won't be long now."

"No, it won't. But be careful."

"Yeah, I will. There's all kinds of stories about guys making it till their last day, then getting za—becoming a casualty. I'll be okay, though."

"Hawaii, huh? What've you been doing?"

"Uh, mostly just hanging around. Taking it easy." I couldn't think.

"Are you by yourself?" she asked.

"Yeah. At one point, when Jeanine and I were still goin' on, I was going to meet her here, along with my best buddy and his girl." I suddenly realized that I had inadvertently told part of the Elaine fiction. "But then the debacle with Jeanine came up, and, well, I still could've gone with Brian, but I didn't."

"Oh, your friend who volunteered for combat, how is he?" she asked, and I reported the contents of his letter.

"I think *I* have problems sometimes," she said sadly. "My God, that's so terrible."

"Yes," I agreed softly.

"How are you doing?" she asked.

"I—I'm okay. I kinda got into a little scrape awhile ago—anyway, that's nothing. I'm gonna be fine, Steffie. The worst times are behind me, Jeanine included. I can last fourteen more weeks. I get around quite a bit with my lieutenant, and that's somewhat dangerous, but we're a good team. We know what we're doing, and we're lucky."

I tried to ask her about school, about the courses she was taking, and what was happening in Kentucky and Chicago. But I found I wasn't paying real attention to her answers. I was thinking too many moves ahead. My stomach was in knots. Everything seemed so strained and formal.

"God, this must be costing you a fortune," she said suddenly, and I knew our chat was nearly over.

"Well, that's okay. It's not much. I guess you got to study, though."

"Yeah, Andy, I ought to go."

Now or never to propose some bullshit story of how I was going to be in Kentucky the next day. I stooped to get one last look at my face. My left eye was nearly closed. Shit, I knew I couldn't possibly do it.

"Well, thanks a lot for writing me. That's meant a lot. I was really excited, especially the day your first letter came." I paused awkwardly, not even sure how to close. "I look forward to seeing you. I'll call you when I get home."

"Okay," she said. "Please be careful."

"I will. Take care, babycakes," I suddenly said, vaguely trying to emulate Randall, whom I no longer liked but still thought was a cool guy.

"'Babycakes'?" she said with astonishment and probably offense.

"Just an expression one of the California guys calls everybody," I said with surprising coolness despite my intense blushing.

A harrowing silence followed.

"Well, bye, Stephanie. See you soon," I managed to say with a little laugh.

"Good-bye, Andy."

"Fuck!" I yelled the moment I hung up. "God, am I a dumb ass!"

I went back to the original lounge. The bartenders looked at me suspiciously but left me in peace. I chewed three aspirins and drank three beers.

In two hours I would be on the plane to Hawaii—in civilian clothes. Deeply shaken, I would call my mom who had written me almost daily, and get my head together. I had spent a fortune, been beaten and spat on and raged at, and had risked my honorable discharge to make a three-minute phone call that I could have placed from Honolulu.

Chapter 24

On the flight back I concocted story to tell the guys, about a fight involving marines and some civilians in a free-for-all in a Honolulu bar. I thanked God for my bruised hand—at least I could say I got some shots in. I told the entire truth to Shifrin, Hobson, and Champion when we were alone in the barracks.

"You paid three hundred extra dollars to make a phone call?" George hooted. "Damn, man, I coulda tol' your ass the wires were hooked up between Hawaii and Kentucky."

Shifrin was somber. "I'm so sorry, Andy. I'm not sure I'll even wear my ribbons when I go home."

"I will, motha fuck," George said. "Nobody's gonna spit on my ass and get away with it! What's wrong with those people anyway? Spit on our ass."

"I can't tell you what it was like," I said, and saw the pain in their eyes. "I don't even want to think about it. Man, it's like, two, three years ago we were all in high school together, and now they're on the right side of the fence, and we're some other…terrible place."

"Better we all keep our mouths shut about it," Shifrin said. "What you did was a crime."

"Yeah, a little crime, but still a crime," I agreed.

"No, a big crime, Andy," he told me. "They'd have nailed you for desertion."

"Okay," I said, half smiling. "I didn't desert, really. I mean, I know what was in my heart. But don't worry, I won't tell anyone. Except Brian."

I decided I also needed to write Steffie an especially clever letter, but I felt I needed to let a little time pass, to let the "babycakes" gaffe recede in her memory.

"We got another letter from Brian," Shifrin told me, and dug it out of his locker for me to read. The week that I had been "vacationing," Brian had been deep in the boonies.

November 8, 1967
Dear Guys:

I'm back in base camp again. I'm sorry I didn't write while I was out, but I've learned to carry only what I absolutely need. Some bad shit happened out there. We were in two bad fire fights. Tony Carter, this colored kid I didn't like much, got hit the first day and lost half his arm. I couldn't believe his screaming and all the blood. I froze during the whole fight, too. I was in bad shape. Near the end, I remembered what Sergeant Banks (his first name is Ernie, can you believe that?) told me he'd do about feeling the barrel of my '16. I put my gun above my head, pushed it on automatic, and shot off a whole magazine. Then, several rounds popped into the ground all around me. God, it was bad. We got out of it, though.

Sgt Banks sent three guys, Philpot, Jackson, and Dumire, to try to hit the gooks' flank, and they must've surprised them. Only Dumire got zapped. Not too long after that we called in fighter planes, F-100's, I think. They were unreal, they came in so fast and low then got up so high before their one napalm bomb even hit. God Almighty, it was the scaredest I've ever been. I kept saying, I'm not really here. I couldn't do anything.

The next day though, we caught two gooks in some thick shit. We'd finished lunch, and I'd nearly fallen asleep. Sgt Banks thought they had fucked up and didn't see how many of us there were. We got fired on, and we all started firing from everywhere. I may have hit one, I'm not sure. Anyway, we checked it out, and we killed them both.

Each day I got sick. I thought I was losing my mind. I'm less afraid of dying than I am of being that afraid again. I'm not shitting you, that kind of fear takes you to some horrible place you can't imagine, and I'm not so sure I can keep coming back from it. My feet are all fucked up from being wet the whole time. You wouldn't believe the smell. I hate this fucking shit, man. I did a dumb thing.

I keep thinking about IU or UK, Andy. God, what a deal that would be. If I make it, man, I promise you I'll be there.

Your friend forever,
Brian

I cringed. No one much said much after I handed the letter back to Shifrin. Brian was into it now, and I wondered if I'd ever see him again. If I could find a way to visit him before I left, I would do it.

Eight days passed, then we got another one. The penmanship was horrible and tough to read.

16 November 1967
Dear Guys,

Back again. I ain't sure what to tell you. I fell asleep when I had guard duty on our perimeter, out in the boonies. Fuck, I do it every time. I'm too fucking tired to stay awake when it's quiet. It's a kind of tired I can't explain, beyond exhaustion. I'll nod off, then for a while I fall into a deep sleep. Anyway, this Murdock asshole came to relieve me and caught me asleep. He slugged me in the mouth and broke one of my front teeth. The next morning he made a big-ass episode out of it in front of everybody. I got the shit beat out of me.

That isn't the half of it though. That afternoon we got into it bad with Charlie. Murdock got wounded bad in the chest, and another guy, a good dude, Howard Browning, got killed. I got into the fire fights full-fledged this time. I finally could do it that day. I really hated the little bastards for all the hell they were putting me through, and I got the feeling that the only thing left for me was try to kill some of the fuckers. I also told myself, Hey I might die, but if I do, so fucking what? It can't be worse than what I'm living. I'm sure I hit a couple of them this time, and still pretty sure I got one the last time, too, like I told you.

I been thinking, Donny, about what you did to Noonan. I laughed my ass off. But you know I feel bad. You told George the night of the race riots you never let anybody fight your fights. I should have done something before I left. I been thinking a lot lately about that fat fuck. Someday he may be real sorry he fucked with me. You tell the bastard if he's smart he'll keep his name out of the phone book.

Bad shit. All this fucking shit is so bad. I don't give a fuck about anything but saving my own ass. I got a few buddies now. I don't feel like that Augie fucker we met, Andy, but I can understand him some. I wrote my mom three times since I been here, but it bums me out. Started smoking, too. Every little diversion helps, and I got to admit, I enjoy it. There's other shit being smoked around here, too, and I've tried it. Man, it's weird, but like calming. I got to go. Going to drink as many beers as I can. I'll catch you next time, you fuckers.

Peace,
Brian

Brian was changing with each letter, and I found it hugely depressing, almost like watching someone drown. I wondered what he'd be like in five months. My God, here was a kid who three months before had been arguing about electric trains!

Shifrin, Top, Champion, Hobson, and I discussed Brian every day. We'd answer questions about Brian from other guys, and I was surprised that a fair amount of interest, even concern, had developed among his former cynics.

Time went by. Prather was short now, much shorter than I, and alarmingly nervous. Many times he called off afternoon plans that he had made only that morning. Captain Karch informed me that after Prather left, I'd probably be used as a "swing driver" with no official assignment to any officer. I was somewhat relieved; I didn't want to get stuck with Prather's replacement, some new lewey who was reckless and didn't know his ass from Twiggy's. Prather never took unnecessary risks, and that was part of the reason we were both around and healthy.

As I drove Prather to the sites, back to the plant, through Bien Hoa, and occasionally to Saigon, I found myself continually wondering what Brian was doing. My own fears seemed petty compared to what I knew he was going through. I might look at my watch and think, *Ten-fifteen. I wonder what Brian is doing right this second. I wonder if he's in the shit.*

I asked Top if I could use a couple of days of leave time to visit Brian. He replied, "No way in hell to get you there, son."

Hobson became more and more detached. We could hardly recognize him. One evening I happened to be walking past the basketball court. Hobson appeared, just out wandering, and passed his former kingdom. Several guys were playing from our company and the 96th. They shouted for him to join them, even pleaded. But he would not even look their way.

Chapter 25

Two full weeks had passed since we'd heard from Brian, but I was more concerned about not hearing from Steffie. Ten days had passed since I'd written the letter I hoped would redeem my blundering in San Francisco.

At about four I bounded into the orderly room. The generator was down, disabling the ceiling fans. Top, sitting at his desk and slowly puffing on his cigar, was shrouded in a huge blue-gray cloud. His squarish face looked almost surreal, as if he were dead and looking back at his murderers from the next world.

I rounded the corner and saw that the mailroom door was open. I was startled to see Captain Karch facing me from a rarely used desk slightly catty corner to the mailroom. His expression puzzled me.

"Need to see Shifrin, sir," I mumbled in case he was waiting for an explanation. I entered the narrow space between the orderly and supply rooms. Shifrin stood motionless at the sorting boxes. One unopened letter lay at his fingertips on the small work top. His eyes were as red as a swimmer's, and his cheeks glistened with tears. I froze, understanding everything.

"Joe?"

"It happened, Andy," he said simply. "We just found out. He's gone."

"No! No, it can't be!" I burst into sobs.

"Yesterday," Joe rasped. "Top contacted Sergeant Major Rollins a few days back, and Rollins contacted another sergeant-major friend with contacts in the 9th. Brian showed up on the casualty report right after that."

"Dear God, no!" I cried, beginning to feel a larger wave of despair.

"He was hit in the stomach and near the heart. He died on a Huey en route to the hospital. I guess he never lost consciousness till the end, so he was aware of everything."

I slumped and grabbed the old sagging two-by-four. "Joe," I said, crying, "Joe, man, he never had a chance out there."

"I wanted to think otherwise, but you're right. He was...done the day he left."

"Jesus." I looked at Shifrin for help.

"Andy, look at this?" He pointed to the solitary envelope.

I wiped my eyes and squinted, trying to read through the blur. I judged it to be a fairly long letter from its thickness. The return address read:

> *Brenda S. Dunleavy*
> *107 Bryan Hall*
> *McNutt Quad*
> *Indiana University*
> *Bloomington, Indiana 47401*

"Turn it over," Joe said.

Printed in tiny blue letters on the back were messages spaced randomly:

> *Remember in the eighth grade, in February, when we got snowed out of school and went sledding? You remember what you told me, Brian Kitzmiller?*
>
> *Does your hair still sort of curl up on the sides?*
>
> *I still have the poem you gave me in the sixth grade. You're lucky I didn't give it to Sister Mary Elizabeth!*
>
> *Write me soon. See you when you get back. xxxx.*

I swallowed. "Jesus Christ, Joe, he never even knew."

"No. Imagine how happy it would have made him." He couldn't continue.

Karch appeared in the doorway. "Why don't you close it up for today, Shifrin?" He looked at me. "I'll drive Lieutenant Prather myself if he wants to go anywhere. You two get out of here."

Shifrin nodded.

"Thank you, sir," I mumbled.

Karch, who never offered an explanation or apology for anything, added, "I couldn't stop him, you know. And whether or not you believe it, I did my best."

I considered this, and it hit me that of all the off-the-wall bullshit Karch had come up with, he probably really had done his best in this case. "I know, sir. You did the best you could," I managed to say.

If Karch's reaction surprised me, it was nothing compared to Top's. He had remained shrouded in the cigar smoke. I could see that he, too, had been crying. He spoke to us without looking up. "I never had a son. Got two girls..." His chest heaved, and his voice broke. "Eighteen and a half years old! Goddamn, he was a good kid."

I went outside into the blazing heat. Shifrin walked ahead of me as I wandered aimlessly down the company street. I realized that when I had come to Nam in what seemed like a century before, my only thoughts had been of getting it over quickly and returning to Louisville, pursuing my relationship with Jeanine, working, going to school, following baseball, merely being a happy young man. I had no expectations of making friends, of having any good times, or of doing anything that I would ever regard as special.

I could see now that I'd undergone huge changes that had radically altered my perspective. I believed that because I had lost the best friend I'd ever had, my life back home would never measure up to my days in Nam when Brian was alive.

The loss I felt was far worse than what I had gone through with Jeanine. The finality of it was so hopelessly stark.

Ahead, Shifrin had veered into the barracks to change into a T-shirt, and I walked slowly, waiting for him. Suddenly, I saw Noonan coming toward me. I was surprised to see him at that time of day because he had two hours of duty left at battalion. I had not spoken to him at all since our first day, not counting the yelling sessions. The sight of him appalled me. I never dreamt I could feel what I did toward a human being, but my sense of Noonan was that he was no more human than a leviathan cockroach. I stood with my hands on my hips as he started to walk around me, pretending I didn't exist.

"Noonan!" I said with no real control of the words flying from my mouth. Our eyes met, but he continued to walk.

"You miserable piece of shit!" I screamed. "Stop, you scumbag coward! You son of a bitch! I hope the fuck you're happy, you motherfucking idiot. Brian got zapped. Do you fucking hear me?"

I charged at him and grabbed him by his shirt and slapped his hat off, then shoved him hard. "Do you fucking hear me? You douche-bag pig! Brian's dead! Do you understand what I'm saying?"

A wild look rose in his eyes as he backed away. "I didn't have shit to do with it, McClain."

I shoved him hard into the drainage ditch, and he slipped awkwardly on the rocks, then fell full on his back.

"You asshole!" he yelled. "I don't have to take this!"

I stood with my fists clenched and my gut on fire. I had no blood in my system—only adrenaline. I crouched to dive on him just as Top grabbed me by the arm and pulled me to him. "Let it go, son. Ain't nothing can be accomplished like this."

Then Shifrin was at my side. "Come on, Andy." He grabbed a handful of my sleeve and jerked me away.

We passed the night in utter solemnity at the EM Club. Joe and I ran into Donny and George, and McCollough found us. We drank many beers that evening, as we had so many times before, only no one laughed or spoke of home or the future.

"He had it made, man," George kept saying, shaking his head slowly. "This was what Nam was supposed to be for him, not what he ended up with."

"I dew he was dead the day he weft," Hobson said.

"I'd convinced myself that he'd beat the odds," I said. "I mean, there was something about him and the way he won people over." Suddenly I yelled, "Goddammit!" and slammed my fist on the table. The empty cans hopped in all directions. Heads turned my way. "Son of a bitch," I moaned.

Shifrin looked pensive. Finally he said, "Damn, he was a good person. I had hope, too, but I didn't like what we were reading in his letters. I mean, they were into it every day."

Hobson was silent. After a few minutes he said in a cold, hard tone, "He wad our buddy, an we wet him down."

"Donny—" I started, but my words became mangled. I could only put my hand on his shoulder.

Hobson had a way of turning a deaf ear and disappearing if someone disagreed with him or tried to console him. In an instant he was gone, having mumbled something about Brian's being cheated out of eighty years.

"God, as if this wasn't bad enough," Shifrin said, his worried eyes following Hobson to the door. "We better keep an eye on him."

I glared at Joe, and he read me instantly. "Andy, I don't want you or Hobson or anybody else to take this any further. Please."

"Shifrin," Champion said solemnly, "we're damn good friends, and I respect you, brother. But I got to tell you that as far as Noonan goes, the motha fucker deserves what he gets. It's dudes like him that put hate in the world. This planet would be a whole lot better off without him. And I got to say this, too—I don't give a fuck what happens to him. I don't even care if he dies.

Happenings got a way to even themselves out. The world just lost a damn good dude. Now it owes itself an asshole."

"I don't give a damn about him, either, George," Shifrin answered without hesitating. "But I do give a damn about you and Hobson and Andy. The way I see it, if something happens to any of you, you will regret it, maybe for the rest of your lives. Just how much are we going to let this bastard hurt us?"

"Shifrin," McCollough said suddenly, "that fat pig got away with murder."

"That's right," George said.

"No court anywhere in the world would agree," Shifrin said.

"You saying Brian wouldn't be alive if Noonan hadn't done what he did?" McCollough yelled.

"No. But that doesn't make it murder—not in the third degree or the fiftieth degree. Brian chose to go. And remember, the only possible crime, the one of slander, was never even committed here. What Noonan revealed was true."

"Well, that's fucked," McCollough said vehemently. "It's still murder!"

I began to wonder if his objections had ulterior motives.

Tony Richio suddenly appeared at our table. "Listen, guys, you gotta do something. Hobson's in the maintenance platoon. He's painting himself up with that black-and-green infantry shit, you know—camouflage grease."

"What?" Shifrin half stood.

"And he's saying shit like, 'This is war, and it's Noonan's night to kill or be killed.'"

I hurried blindly along with the others. By the time we got to the maintenance platoon, word was already out. Hobson stood in front of a two-foot mirror, admiring his ghoulish appearance. The Rolling Stones blared from his PX stereo. He must've just set the needle on "Paint it Black."

"Donny, man, what're you doing?" I asked.

He did not respond. I noticed he was wearing a pistol belt with a bayonet affixed to it.

A new guy, Jamie Healy, sat on his bunk, transfixed in horror. "What's with this guy?" he whispered to us. "He just asked me if I had a jar big enough to hold a human heart."

"Where's Noonan?" I asked.

Healy jerked a thumb over his shoulder. "I heard he ran up to the NCO's hooch when he heard about Hobson. I guess he's up there now."

"Come on, Donny," I said.

Top crashed in the door. "What in the hell?"

Donny did not respond.

Top could not be intimidated. "Listen to me, soldier. I got Noonan up in my barracks having what looks like a nervous breakdown. Tommorah I'm gonna contact Sergeant Major Rollins about getting him the fuck transferred. You are not going to go near him. You understand me?"

When Donny held his silence, Top grabbed him by his pistol belt—with bayonet—and unhooked it. He folded them, tucked them under his arm, then grabbed Hobson by the back of his collar and scooped a towel out of Hobson's locker. "You and me are goin' to the showers, Hobson. You're gonna get cleaned up and get to bed!"

Donny complied in a detached manner.

"He's crackin' up," Shifrin said quietly.

The next morning Top worked quickly. He had Noonan cleared to "hold" for a few days at the 90th Replacement Battalion. When all the red tape was cut through, he would be reassigned.

Before Noonan was to depart, Karch called him in. I was waiting for Prather and watched the entire scene, with Top and Shifrin.

Noonan stood awkwardly before Karch. As usual Karch took his time shuffling papers, freezing his prey. Suddenly he cleared his desk, cramming everything in a drawer, save one sheet of paper.

"Noonan."

"Yes, sir."

"Do you know what you are, boy?"

"No, sir."

"You're everything a normal young man would detest and avoid. You're dog shit."

He stopped to light a cigarette, then settled into a hard twenty-second stare. Noonan fidgeted and looked down. Karch blew out a cloud of smoke, then continued, "Accordingly, I have decided to remove you from the company of these young Americans who serve their country and rely on each other as teammates, as friends, and as men. I am not protecting you. I'm protecting them. A real man was not made by God to live alongside a cancer like you. Do you understand what I'm saying?"

"Yes, sir."

"I'd like to read a note I'm affixing to your 201 file. God help you if you lose this file or if this permanent letter disappears from it. And we will check with your next company commander and personnel sergeant up there, like you thought to do for Kitzmiller, to make sure he'd feel welcome. It says—" Karch looked across at Noonan, then back down at the letter, "'—Private Noonan is no longer a welcome member of the 209th Engineer Company, Construction Support, Long Binh, South Vietnam. He is a disease on the morale and effectiveness of this unit. He is a self-centered, immature coward who shows no sign of responsibility or intelligence and no regard for his fellow soldiers. He cannot be relied upon to perform normal duties. Perhaps permanent duty as a mess boy with a couple of hours set aside for latrine maintenance would best fulfill his potential, if you have someone to ensure he washes his hands between jobs. My sincerest apologies for allowing him to become your problem.' Does that sound reasonable?"

Noonan sniffled. "No, sir. It's not fair."

Karch again stared hard at Noonan, who now sobbed openly. "Get out of my sight, you waste product."

"Yes, sir." Noonan picked up his 201 file and turned to walk outside.

"Go get your shit," Top told him, "and be back here in ten minutes. I'll drive your ass to the 90th myself."

A few minutes later, Prather strode in the orderly room. "Okay, Andy, let's—"

Pop! Pop-pop-pop! The muffled sounds of shots sounded from a barracks. We looked at one another in horror, then sprinted for headquarters platoon.

Noonan lay dead in a lake of blood on the floor, half of his skull blown away. Donny stood ashen-faced off to the side still clenching the M-14. Top approached him.

"Give me the rifle, son," he said.

"Tay away," Hobson replied, backing up.

I walked up to Donny, somehow knowing he would not shoot. "Please Donny." I gently put my hand on the piece and took it.

Hobson began to sob. "He wadn't going to det away wid it. Doe and be a clerk tomewhere elth? And dut det away wid ebryting."

Shortly after some MPs and two lawyers from the Judge Advocate General's office took our statements, Hobson was led away in handcuffs and, unbelievably, Prather and I left for Saigon. He was scheduled to meet one last time with civilian engineers—an appointment he considered nonessential but one I knew he felt he owed Karch. I was a near lunatic, and the lieutenant seemed all nerves. In the past weeks he had become aloof, as if we enlisted men, with our ever-increasing personal problems and immaturity, were beneath him. With that attitude—coupled with his increasing short-timer's anxiety, not to mention what had just happened—he was insufferable.

My thoughts were not on the road, and my navigational skills, along with my learned ability to run with the diverse Vietnamese traffic, were not with me. On Highway One I nearly collided with a three-quarter-ton truck, which pulled out in front of me from the transportation battalion.

"Goddamn, Andy," Prather yelled. "Watch what the fuck you're doing!"

That upset me more, and events intensified once we were in the city. I missed my usual turn, and we became mired in Saigon traffic. I darted down a narrow street that I mistakenly believed would lead somewhere recognizable. Suddenly we were lost a long way from the center of town. Prather sat steaming, not saying a word, as I continued to make one wrong turn after another.

"Damn it, Andy!" he finally exploded. "We going to do this all fucking day? I'm pretty sure you've got us in the off-limits part of town. Jesus!"

Tears were in my eyes from the loss of Brian and now Hobson. I could not believe my life. "Sir, I don't know what else to do. We're bound to see something we know."

"Look!" He pointed ahead, where two MPs had stopped alongside of the street. They seemed to be studying an alleyway whose entrance they had blocked with their jeep. "Let's ask them how the hell to get back to Highway One, at least."

I pulled in behind them after a civilian on his bicycle almost hit me. Prather saw that as my fault, too, and by now he was really furious. He jumped out of the jeep and walked over to talk with them himself. This irritated me. I could not believe his callousness. I decided to get out and take a short walk to show my displeasure and to stretch my legs. I slung my M-14 over my shoulder by its strap, grabbed the only magazine of ammunition I had brought, and I stuffed it in the back of my belt.

I was surprised at the overcast sky, since the rainy season was over. I walked down the street and looked around. We were still in Saigon, and the street was lined with small stone structures and huts, unlike any Bien Hoa neighborhood I'd seen.

Suddenly, eight Vietnamese kids surrounded me and began yelling and jumping up and down. "GI, you got candy?"

"GI, you got cigarette?"

"GI, you want pussy?"

"Shit, get away," I half mumbled.

I decided to head back to the jeep when I realized that one of the kids was pretty big—probably fourteen or fifteen years old—yet carrying on like the children. Then he became aggressive.

"GI, you show me rifle?" Before his question even registered, he had wrenched my weapon from my shoulder just as another kid grabbed hard on my other arm.

I couldn't believe it. The kid had my rifle. "Fuck!" I yelled, swiping at him amid the small bodies that now separated us.

He grinned nastily. Suddenly, almost as if he were a magician, he produced the magazine that had been pickpocketed from me, and in a second he loaded the rifle.

"Hey!" I yelled. "Give me that, you son of a bitch!"

He laughed and began to dance with the rifle. "Wock and woad, mothafuck! GI, no gun! GI, no gun!"

I was astounded at my stupidity. Prather appeared at my shoulder.

"Sir, get the MPs!" I said.

"Gone," he answered grimly. "This part of the city is off-limits."

"Give me the gun!" I yelled at the kid.

"Fuck you, fuck you, fuck you!" he said with a high-pitched laugh, causing the children to laugh, too.

"God damn it!" Prather yelled.

I refused to look at him, knowing he was screaming at me.

"Give me the gun!" I yelled. I caught the barrel with only half my hand, and the kid easily ripped it away.

"You touch, you die," he squealed. Then, laughing, he waved the rifle menacingly in large figure-eights that crossed our path.

The children had moved away. "GI, American GI, numba ten thou. Time to die, GI."

Suddenly Prather stepped in front of me. He had drawn his .45 and pointed it directly at the kid's chest. "Drop it and *di di! Mau!* Drop it, you fucking asshole!"

The kid grinned fearlessly. Suddenly he half opened his mouth and began to make a whining sound. I could see that the safety was off. He eyed Prather like a cat about to pounce, then he made a lightning-quick move. I saw his smile turn to anguish before I heard the four shots and saw the smoking holes high in his chest. He fell instantly onto his back. The children screamed and ran away. Civilians stopped and looked, terrified. Some then ran, some still gawked.

Prather knelt by him, his hand on his rifle, which was frozen in the kid's hands. When he tugged on it, the boy seemed to tug back, but after a few seconds the kid's hands went limp. Prather lifted the M-14 away and handed it back to me. "Let's go!"

"Those MPs—"

"Go! Go! Just get us the fuck out of here!"

We sprinted to the jeep, and I sped away. After a mile or so, I stopped. "What do you want to do?" I asked.

"I-I don't—" Prather was a white as a ghost. "Just go! Can't get arrested by the dinks or the MPs. We're liable to get lynched or shot. Drive!"

I sped through unfamiliar streets and felt as though a huge net were closing on us. Prather held my M-14 as if alert for a fire fight. I drove and drove, making turn after turn, wishing Prather would say something. Finally I recognized a major street, and within a minute we were downtown and then on To Do Street.

"Sir, are we going to the meeting?"

"No." He did not look at me.

"You want to head back?"

"No. I've got to have a drink."

We sat at a bar on To Do Street. "God," he groaned after two shots of Jack Daniels and two beer chasers. "I was so sure I'd make it out of here without killing anyone. God!" He sniffled. "How could you—I mean, what were you thinking about?"

"Shit, I'm sorry. I didn't feel any danger, and I'm so messed up over what happened to Brian and Hobson—even Noonan—that I wasn't paying attention. I'm really sorry."

He rubbed his eyes with the heels of his palms. "I can't believe I killed him."

Into my mind shot miasmic images of Hobson sobbing, crying, "Det away." Top's head in the cigar smoke. Noonan and the kid both shot four times, lifeless. I glanced at Prather, my mind shifting back. "It happened so fast. You did what you had to do. Otherwise we might both be dead."

Prather looked at me coldly.

I said resolutely, "It was my fault, sir. You told him to drop it. He understood you. I'm the one who put us—"

"You have no idea what I'm going through."

"Look, sir, I'm sick about it, too. But we couldn't afford to take the chance. You had to shoot him."

"A fucking kid," Prather groaned. "I killed a fucking boy. My God." He covered his face with his hands.

I had put Prather, my hero, in a tragic situation that he would struggle with forever. I wanted to say I'd have done the same thing, but I didn't honestly know what I would've done. I got a lump in my throat and began to tremble. Everything in my world was fucked.

"God, I wish I'd only shot him once. Maybe we could've saved him."

Several minutes of silence passed.

"I think I'm going to report this," he said, sounding not like himself, cool, but like a scared 'cruit.

"Yeah," I murmured, thinking about what might happen to me because of losing my rifle.

"He was dead when he hit the ground. I blew his heart out. I-I was thinking of reporting it to the MPs, but maybe I'll only tell Karch. Right. I'll report it to the company commander."

That evening Prather came and got me out of the mess hall, and we met Karch in the officer's hooch. Lieutenant Thornberry handed me a beer from a barrel full of iced cans. I described how I had lost my rifle. Karch lit a cigar and searched my eyes, then listened intently to Prather's apologetic version of the story. I felt chills and genuine sorrow for the victim when Prather described his death. When the lieutenant almost broke down, Karch seemed pissed off.

Silence followed.

"Sir," I said, "the whole incident was my fault. I had horrible feeling about what that kid might do, and I'm pretty sure we had no other way out of it. I can't explain what happened to me. I put Lieutenant Prather in that—"

"McClain," Karch interrupted, "that was dumb, a rookie mistake—and you're anything but a rookie. But I'm not sure you should've been out there today, given what has happened with Kitzmiller and Hobson and Noonan. That's our fault. It's understandable that you might have some sort of lapse from your lack of focus. Nonetheless, in time of war soldiers have to suck it up and go on.

"Lieutenant Prather," he continued, "you and I have gone through a lot this year. I've never seen a better company-grade officer than you. Given the circumstances, I feel you did what was necessary to ensure your safety and your driver's. I'll mention it to Gallagher in the morning if I still feel like it. I can't imagine any dire consequences from this. As far as I'm concerned, that kid was a VC who, for whatever reason, was out of his head. Who even cares? But you acted courageously and in accordance to the situation."

Then came the shocker. "If anything, I'll recommend you for a bronze star for valor. Let 'em know what kind of men come out of this unit."

Chapter 26

December arrived, my first Christmas season away. With two months to go I should have been excited, yet my sense of guilt over Brian and Hobson left me depressed.

Lieutenant Prather left on the twelfth. After spending the better part of a year together, day in and day out, twelve hours a day, he simply shook my hand, wished me luck, and walked off without even making eye contact. I was crushed.

Lieutenant Thornberry took the reins of the asphalt platoon temporarily, but he, too, was short and had his own driver. Top put me in charge of the mail and made me interim assistant company clerk and, since I still had access to my jeep, "swing man-errand boy." I was not comfortable performing what I saw as Brian's job and hoped I could simply finish out my days in the orderly room. Top himself was to rotate back to the states on December 20, and he announced that Sergeant Vic Matthews would take his place. Although no one could replace Top, I liked Matthews. An E-7 and not officially a first sergeant, he was full of jokes and more of a soldier's man than any other non-com I'd known.

On December 16, Top hugged me, promised, "Everything will turn out in the end," then left Nam for good, in time for Christmas with Betty Jo and his daughters.

A letter I received later that day proved him wrong.

> *Dec 11, 1967*
> *Dear Andy,*
>
> *I hope everything continues to go well for you. I have some news that I hope you will understand. I have started seeing someone, and I feel it would be unfair to you and to him to continue our correspondence or lead you on about*

seeing you when you return. I'm sorry, I truly am. I guess
part of this is that I don't feel there is any real future for us.
I don't mean to hurt you. I am sure that you will do quite well
in the world and that you will meet someone special.

Please be careful in your remaining weeks. You have so
much to look forward to. God bless you.

Peace,
Stephanie

Again a paralyzing depression swept over me. I felt completely alone in the world. I had clung to the thought that maybe I might make it without falling further into despair. But futility and hopelessness overwhelmed me. I broke down, fell to my knees, and cried, "God, what do you want from me? Do you hate me? Have you sent me to hell without letting me die first? How much more do you think I can take?"

In January, unsettling rumors began to circulate about activity on the Ho Chi Minh Trail. "I'm telling ya," McCollough said, "I'm hearing around various headquarters that there's like this huge gook buildup that's growing like cancer. They've found elephants within fifty miles of here. Fuckin' elephants! They're using them like water buffalo, to drag shit down the Ho Chi Minh Trail and through the boonies—big guns and tons of ammo. We're hittin' 'em where we can, but they're mostly invisible."

I thought it just my luck that I could have done the whole year and never really felt threatened around our location…and now, with only a month to go, something big was possibly afoot. God, how I wanted out!

All hell broke loose on January 30, 1968. In an almost choreographed move the North Vietnamese regulars and the Viet Cong attacked nearly everywhere. The American embassy in Saigon fell to the Viet Cong for only a few hours, but those hours shocked the world. Long Binh, our home, the site of the largest American concentration of troops and as large as a medium-sized town, was hit in several places.

Our lives changed in an instant. We became, in a strange way, brothers. Fist fights stopped. The club closed, the movies stopped, and our half days off were suspended. We couldn't go to town except on official business.

More rumors flew: Charlie's got nerve gas; Charlie's got anthrax gas. We cleaned our weapons and practiced putting on our gas masks. The NVA has planes now, bombers. Long Binh's got the most trucks, most of the supplies, and most of the ammo. Charlie wants our ass. Man, we are in some serious shit.

Bien Hoa was hit, both the town and the air-force base. Then, right after midnight on the third night of Tet Offensive, I was awakened in my bunk by a light. The illumination was outside, and my sleep-fogged brain wondered if it was sunup, but the color was too weird, too white-orange and brilliant.

"What the—?" someone said before the concussion—an ear-shattering noise such as I never knew existed. Our lockers slid along the concrete floor. Glass cracked and fell.

"God what is it?"

I thought somebody from Russia or China had done the unimaginable, dropped a nuclear bomb.

"Get under your bunk!" someone yelled.

"No! No!" I shouted. "Get outside and into the bunkers! Take your rifles!"

In seconds I was outside in my boxer shorts and T-shirt, gripping my loaded M-14, kneeling in the same ditch I had knocked Noonan into, waiting in the rat poison and expecting to be incinerated. We moved like zombies along the ditches. Gradually a freakish form of curiosity cracked my all-pervasive terror. We gawked, slack jawed, to the northeast, where a quarter of the sky shimmered orange, rimmed by the velvet black of night. And in the center of the brilliant topaz some miles away was a giant mushroom cloud. Nuked! Atomic bomb! Had to be!

I knew we were goners. Would it be heaven or hell? Oh, my dear God, I am so sorry for my sins. Thank you for saving us, dear Jesus, I want to be with you in heaven.

"Look, look up!" Thousands, *millions,* of tiny orange sparks slowly descended toward us, as if the heavens were falling in unimaginable splendor. The orange slowly lost some of its intensity.

Then it happened again. Where the sky had been orange, it suddenly flashed white. We were bathed in radiance, and then came the concussion, even more brutal than the first. Entire sections of corrugated metal slid off the roof of the mess hall and crumpled to the ground. I pressed my face in to the ditch to protect my eyes. The white slowly shifted to orange, and I looked up to see a second mushroom cloud dwarfing the first.

Oh, God, how could they? Why, why do we have to die? Just when I was convinced my life had ended, a resonant voice cut through the air.

"All right, men, listen up!" Sergeant Matthews calmly walked down the company street, dressed in full combat gear. "I've been on the radio all night.

There's no nuclear attack. They've hit the ammo dump. The biggest fuckin' ammo dump in Nam—hell, maybe in the world. Those are pads of thousands of artillery shells being blown to kingdom come. The ammo dump is a good four miles from here, so we're far enough away to be safe. It may burn and go on like this for some time, so stay calm."

I felt as though I'd been rescued from a burning building. My heart still pounded, but at least I knew we had a chance.

"Get dressed," Matthews continued. "Helmets, rifles, what ammo you have, and bring your gas masks. No lights. We're under full red alert. Long Binh is being hit in several places, and Charlie has likely broken through in a couple. Don't worry about that—hundreds of men are being trucked to those spots. Come first light, Charlie's ass'll be up. Our assignment is to man this sector. With the 96th, the signal corps boys next door to us, and the transport companies down the road, we'll have a couple of thousand men manning the short fire-bunkers on our front.

"Once you're dressed, report to the command bunker, and we'll tell you where we want you. You'll be on your belly for most of the night, no more than a couple of yards from your buddy right up there on the perimeter just overlooking Highway One. We'll all be behind the concertina wire. Actually, a piece of cake, boys. Just follow orders." He strode on to deliver the same message to the asphalt and maintenance platoons.

I dressed quickly, anxious to get where they needed us, eager to be part of a long line of armed soldiers in case Charlie tried to infiltrate or overrun us. As I struggled awkwardly with my pistol belt, which had ammo pouches, my gas mask, bayonet, and canteen affixed to it, I heard many whispered questions, but no one made jokes.

I heard someone sobbing in the dark, then, "Come on, man, you got to go. You can't stay in here." The same voice whispered to me. "Hey, Specialist McClain!"

I recognized the speaker as a new guy, Private Ross Haberstitch, who'd been with us for two weeks. "You gotta help me with this 'cruit."

I made my way toward them. On the floor between two bunks lay a soldier still in his underwear, crying. He was Private Gordon Streeter, another scrawny eighteen-year-old who'd only arrived that afternoon.

"Hey, man, what's wrong?" I asked. He was curled up on his side.

"I-I can't go," he said, crying. "I don't want to die."

"You ain't gonna die," I said. "Come on, man, I know this is a hell of a first night, but you'll be okay. Come on now, we need you, and you need us."

"I can't. I don't want to be here."

"You *are* here though," I said sternly. "Get your shit on!"

"I don't want—they got bombers. We're gonna get bombed."

"No, Streeter," I said with complete conviction, ignoring that three minutes before, I'd thought the same. "We've got total air superiority. We own the sky. No one can bomb us. But they can mortar us, and if some kind of incendiary round hits these hooches, this is the worst place you can be. Come on, man, we'll help you."

"He's right, Streeter," said Haberstitch. "Specialist McClain's been here a year. Listen to what he tells you. That's the way, man. Get your shirt on. Where's your weapon?"

Streeter curled into a tighter ball.

I grabbed him by the shoulders and gripped him hard. "Get hold of yourself. You're gonna be fine, but you got to listen. Get this shit on, and when we get up there, go the hell where they tell you, stay down and be alert. You remember all those rounds you fired in basic?"

"Yes..."

"Well, this is what that was for," I said. "Don't let fear turn to panic. That's the only way you can die. Stay on top of it. Okay?"

We helped the kid up, and he got dressed quickly, fueled by his fear. We started out, and Streeter tripped going out the door. "Damn it," I said, "tie your boot laces."

He moved to do so, but Haberstitch and I were already on the ground at his feet and in the light of the orange haze wrapped his laces and tied them for him.

When we got to the command bunker, Sergeant Matthews, who had returned to his position, sent Haberstitch and Streeter to a spot on the line about eighty yards away. I was summoned to the command bunker—our old party bunker—with Matthews, Lieutenant Thornberry, and Captain Karch.

Karch put his hand on my shoulder. "McClain, I want you as my personal runner with Colonel Gallagher. You know the compound like you've lived here your whole life."

"Okay, sir," I answered without thinking.

"You know where battalion's command bunker is, right?"

"Sure. In front of their Headquarters Company."

"Right. Colonel Gallagher's in there. We've all got radio contact, but in times like this we use a runner to confirm or change actual messages. If Charlie's on this frequency, we want to confuse him and make sure he's not giving us bogus input or commands. As you might guess, certain tactical terms are encoded. Now, I need you to stay alert, work hard, and run, not amble. Hit the ground at the first sound or flash from our perimeter. Don't talk to anyone outside the command bunkers. You have the same status as an officer as far as I'm concerned, and if someone tries to detain you for any reason, you have my permission to take their head off with your rifle butt. Don't fire unless fired on or unless you believe your life depends on it. Are you with me, McCl—Andy?"

"Yessir."

"I have as much faith in you as Matthews or Shifrin or any enlisted guy I got. I need you."

"All right, sir."

"Good. Announce yourself to Colonel Gallagher and Sergeant Major Foust. I know they know who you are, but it'll likely be nearly pitch black in their bunker. Besides, you have to tell them personally you're our guy. Tell 'em 'Fantastic is on scarlet. Observing code black. Cowboys are near position for maximum welcome in ten.' Means damn near what it says: We're on red alert, no lights, and we've got nearly everyone on line and being supplied with extra ammunition. Maximum field of fire assured within ten minutes. Okay?" He squeezed my shoulder. It struck me that Karch, who had recently extended, was hoping that I—among others—might extend, too.

"Yessir."

I left the command bunker and ran the half mile to battalions, alone, in an otherworldly universe. Starting with our own company, nothing looked the same. The signal unit next door was dark and seemingly empty. I had to strain to see the endless line of men to my right, lying prone on our front. I ran quickly but quietly behind them, ticking off the hulking landmarks in my mind: the basketball court, then Delta Company of the 96th, Charlie Company, Bravo, Alpha, and finally Headquarters Company and the battalion command bunker. Finally, I stood—I hoped—before Colonel Gallagher in the black interior of his command post. I could barely see outlines of human forms.

Condor One?" I asked.

"Yeah, whatcha got?"

"Colonel Gallagher, it's me, McClain, from the two-oh-ninth. I'm the runner." I delivered my message.

"Good boy, McClain. I'm gonna cut the code crap out between us. Tell Karch that unless something provokes it sooner, that around zero two hundred, I'm going to order a totally coordinated thirty-second burst with you guys, all of us, and even some of the other units beyond you. That'll include the signal company and transportation battalion to the north. If Charlie's out there, we'll let him know right quick what the fuck a field of fire is, what two thousand men within a one-mile line putting out sixty to eighty rounds each in a half a minute is like. Inform him he'd better be damn serious about the hereafter if he wants to fuck with us. Plus, these rear-echelon soldiers need to know how formidable they are. Not to mention we need to find out whose weapon works and whose doesn't." He nodded.

"Yessir. Is that it, sir?"

"Basically. Now listen, McClain. You're an old-timer. I know we can depend on you. If it gets hairy, get off the perimeter road immediately and cut behind the bunkers and the barracks. Proceed station to station. Get cover and stay down, and don't you move if you come under heavy fire. Once it's passed, go like hell. Okay?"

"Yessir," I said, almost allowing myself to feel important, then catching myself, realizing that what we were doing was infinitely safer than what Brian had had to contend with every day.

"All right. Take care. And McClain?"

"Yessir?"

"I've seen you damn near every day for a year now, hauling Prather around. I want to thank for that year. I want you to know, as your battalion commander, that I've extended, hopefully to help get this thing done with. We'd be honored as a military unit if you extended, too. Think about it." He thumped my helmet.

"You're welcome, sir. And thank you for the compliment. I will think about it."

"Okay, son. Go do it."

I made two trips. At two o'clock, under the direction of Gallagher, we fired thousands of rounds across the deserted Highway One.

"No one out there could be very happy right now," Karch said.

An hour passed. The halo from the ammo dump had all but disappeared. The faint glint of dawn slowly pulled itself over the horizon. Our sense of relief was overwhelming because we knew—or thought we knew—that Charlie wouldn't attack after sunrise.

The next five nights brought similar routines, though without the orchestrated field-of-fire exercise or the ammo-dump catastrophe. We learned that the ammo dump had been set off not by direct hits with artillery or mortars but by satchel charges that had been planted, intelligence presumed, by day. The idea that the Viet Cong worked right beside us in the Long Binh complex by day, then turned foe by night was unnerving, but no one could offer any other explanations. Vietnamese workers at the ammo dump had planted the charges.

On the seventh night, we took several incoming 176 rockets to our motor pool, losing a Euclid dump truck, two five ton trucks, and a jeep. As the night passed we heard that the transport battalion just to the north of us was taking some small-arms fire, which they returned in addition to calling in several hundred artillery rounds of our own, which seemed to nix our foe for the time.

I had just delivered a message of suspected movement on our front due west, saying that we were sending up flares. I had no sooner gotten Colonel Gallagher's acknowledgment and begun my hard run back when someone on the firing line in front of Bravo Company yelled, "Gook in the wire!"

Bravo Company was on a steeper incline down to Highway One than the rest of the units. If someone wished to attempt the impossible task of crawling through the wire undetected by the soldiers lying in wait, I supposed that would have been the spot to try it. The cry was followed by the instantaneous roar of two hundred M-14s and six M-60 machine guns. Simultaneously, several flares shot up, illuminating everything. For a couple of seconds I was taken aback by the flares because I had never seen so many directly overhead. The light they broadcast was a surreal red, and as they lingered passively, descending ever so slowly, their tiny parachutes gave them a festive air—an odd juxtaposition to the hell below, as if they belonged in some huge backyard celebration.

I wanted to sprint down to my unit, but I was drawn somehow to join the 96th Bravo boys blazing away just to my left. I dived in, between two soldiers who were reloading. One shouted at me, "They're here, man! We can't let the fuckers swarm us!"

I looked through the wire and down the incline. All I could see was a dark lump quivering from the rounds that continued to hit it. Some of the rounds headed across the highway, where I was suddenly sure a Chinese-style human wave attack—such as we had heard about from Top—was about to begin. Though I couldn't see anyone, I had two magazines and the need to become a part of the field of fire on which we so prided ourselves. I fired off a magazine across the road that I had driven down hundreds of times, thinking that I was finally at war.

No human wave attack ensued. The firing went on for a good ninety seconds, and then we brought down 105 and 155 artillery rounds on our suspected foe, delivered from a fire base ten miles away. The sound of shells coming over us was infinitely louder than I'd expected, and their explosions, scarcely a football field away, were twice as ear shattering. We waited, then shot up a good thirty flares after that, but with our imagination back under control, we saw no more sign of the enemy—only the *one* in the wire.

At dawn I returned to the spot in front of Bravo Company. By then soldiers were taking pictures. To my horror I stared down at the gelatinous remains of a man under our concertina wire. He had been shot hundreds of times by the 7.62 mm rounds of our M-14s and M-60 machine guns, and what remained was a bloody pulp, clearly discernible by scent. With no perceivable features, he could have easily been a Caucasian. Already shiny green flies the size of bees swarmed around him, and by ten that morning they were like a dark cloud. What, I wondered, could have inspired that man to creep under forty yards of coiled barbed wire, right under the nose of at least one hundred-fifty men?

He was stoned out of his mind," everyone said.

The incident spawned a strange sense of mean-spirited confidence, which took the place of fear, at least to a degree. I welcomed it.

Karch reasoned that the south end of Long Binh, which we occupied, had some irresistible targets, so for days we expected an attack. On February 9 a new kid from asphalt was killed when a mortar landed almost on top of him as he took cover in a ditch. We were devastated and shocked. He was the first person killed in our company area during my year.

Then, almost as if it were an act of God, my day came to rotate back to the States.

I had not considered extending. I had to get out. Yet my sense of guilt in leaving behind my unit and Shifrin and Champion was intense. But they, too, wanted me gone.

"When your time's up, you go, mothafuck, and when it's our time we'll be right on your ass," Champion said.

It seemed so typical, to leave right in the midst of some major happening that would cause me further grief. Without pomp in the orderly room, Karch presented me with the Army Commendation Medal. "You were one of my best, kid. You gave it your all every day and had very few fuck-ups. Now you go home—hurt, maybe, but a man, a man who knows."

Joe, who sucked at driving a stick shift, ground gears the three miles up to the 90th Replacement Battalion. "Hell, Joe," I said, laughing, "they ever make you a driver, they better get a dozen transmissions requisitioned."

"Listen, Andy. You'll either love or hate yourself for the decisions you make now. I want your word of honor that you'll be enrolled in college next fall. That would be the greatest gift you could give me and yourself and your future wife and kids. Ten years from now will be too late. Do you promise me, Andrew?"

"Yeah, okay." I replied, surprised. "I promise."

"Three months ago I had two best friends. Now I have one." He seized my arm. "I know you went through a ton of shit, but you have to make something of your potential. You're too bright to be happy without an education. Do you understand me? I care too much about you not to get on your ass about this."

I felt like a kid. "I know you do. I promise. I'll be in school. Thanks, Joe. Thank you for being my…brother."

We embraced, then he walked back to the jeep.

"Give my love to Jill when you write," I said, my voice thick with tears.

He turned. "You know I will, Andy. Take care."

During the three days I spent in the 90th Replacement Battalion, the VC hit Bien Hoa Air Force Base, whence I was supposed to depart, and my flight got postponed three times.

I could not believe the attitude of the replacement troops coming in. It seemed far worse than ours had been a year before, when simple fear and confusion reigned. Much had happened in 1967 and early '68, and the war had taken on a much graver meaning in our age group. Now, in addition to the fear, I detected guilt. Few even spoke of returning in twelve months, which had been the only topic of conversation I could remember from my first days.

Upon arriving at long last at the air force base, we had to wait again for two hours. Suddenly, shockingly, I saw two MPs, maybe three hundred feet away, escorting Donny Hobson to a small army plane. I hadn't seen him since his lightning-quick trial, and even then only for a couple of hours when we testified. Despite testimonies that supported his insanity plea, he had been sentenced to life in the army prison at Fort Leavenworth, Kansas. Handcuffed, he did not look up.

I wanted to call out his name but thought better of it. "Dear Jesus, God," I whispered as they escorted him onto the plane. My friend disappeared, with no life ahead of him.

When our time finally came to board the shiny Eastern Airlines 727, I was relieved, of course, and many of those around me seemed gleeful. We had made it! We were to begin a twenty-two-hour trip that would take us to Manila, then Guam, Wake, Midway, Honolulu, and finally San Francisco. We would process in at Oakland Army Base, then be bused to San Francisco International Airport. It should have been the greatest day of my life.

Standing in line, appreciating the comeliness of the stewardess's smile and her demeanor, I reached into my pocket for my boarding pass. My fingers brushed Alice Ann O'Neal's picture, which I had noticed that morning in a stack of letters in my duffel bag. I wasn't sure why, but I'd stuck in my shirt pocket. I pulled it out, and once again, the magic of her face swept me away. But then, I reflected on Brian, and Hobson, and Prather, and the Vietnamese kid that Prather had shot, and Noonan. In a way, all were gone forever because of the picture.

Suddenly, the photograph seemed dirty, even evil. The eyes seemed taunting, remorseless. I never wanted to see it again and flipped it, as I had flipped baseball cards five years prior, to the roasting tarmac while we still remained in line. It landed facedown.

"Hey, Kentucky," a friendly homebound soldier I had met an hour ago asked. "Who's she, another broad that ain't gonna make the cut when you get back to Louisville?"

I smiled at how wide of the mark he was. "You guessed it," I said.

He took his shoe and smeared the photo into the pavement.

I began to think about the trip itself. I decided to wear my ribbons. It didn't seem right to sneak around San Francisco International and pretend to be something other than a Vietnam veteran. I felt I owed it to the many who had given their lives. I decided I'd convince the guys I would get to know on our long flight that we should, perhaps, stick together in that horrifying place. I prayed my journey through Chicago's O'Hare and Louisville's Standiford Field, which I would probably experience alone, might come without attack.

My thoughts returned to Brian and the fact that he'd never see this day. The bubbly stewardess must have noticed my bloodhound expression, because she squeezed my arm. "It's okay now, hon, you're going home, and everything will be great."

"Yeah," I managed. "I'm sure it will be...someday."